FOOL'S errand

A CARTWRIGHT
BROTHER ROMANCE

Lilliana
ANDERSON
INTERNATIONALLY BESTSELLING AUSTRALIAN AUTHOR

FOOL'S ERRAND

CARTWRIGHT BROTHERS, BOOK 4

LILLIANA ANDERSON

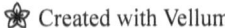

All the single ladies

FOREWORD

Yikes. Book four. You know what that mean, right? Only one to go. I'm both excited and sad for the end of this series, but boy, it's been fun getting here.

Sloane is probably my most relatable heroine to date. She's a little world weary, tells it like it is, and she loves a good game. That competitive streak is probably lifted straight from my own personality, but she was a great lady to write, possibly because she's closer to my own age than most of my heroines are.

Abbot is exactly as you expect if you've been following this series from the beginning. He's cheeky, he's a rule breaker, and he's loyal while also wanting to walk his own path. He's *sweet*. I love the things that come out of his mouth—even when they're dirty!

The family saga also continues in the following pages. If you're just jumping into the series now, all will be explained as Sloane learns the family's secrets. But if you've been here all along, you'll see things developing and setting up for our finale where we find out if the Cartwrights find their happiness as a group, or go their seperate ways. Only time will tell…

CHAPTER ONE
CARTWRIGHT PROPERTY
MANAGEMENT

GRIND. Grind. Grind.

Blow.

Holding the tiny brass key in front of me, I inspected the cuts and compared it to the original.

This was what my life had been reduced to. Copying keys and engraving pet collars to make ends meet. It was the twenty-first century, so why was it still difficult to make it in a male-dominated industry?

Things were so much easier when my grandfather was alive.

You know, I really hated making my business woes about gender, but what else explained it? As locksmiths, our business had thrived with Pop at the helm. Now that he was gone, I barely got a call out, and I didn't have a clue what I was doing wrong. I was good at my job. I could re-key a lock in minutes, break into your locked car when you lost your keys and even get a safe open that you couldn't remember the combination for. I had skills, *dammit*. I just needed some decent work.

Picking up another blank key, I inserted it into the vice and reset the grinder, ready to make a second copy. I hated that my phone—which rang all the time when Pop was alive—barely rang anymore. Was it so hard to believe that I was as capable as the man who trained me? It seriously did my head in. But I'd prove I could do this. A savvy advertising campaign would get things back on track… when I found some work to pay for one.

Just as I gripped the handle and started the grinder, the bell above the door jingled happily, contrasting my frustrated thoughts.

"Won't be a minute," I said, glancing up from my work before finding myself frozen in place, my mouth hanging open.

I may have started drooling. Hell, my eyes might have bugged out of my head and made that *hubba-hubba* sound like a cartoon character.

If I was a gif, I'd be Adam Sandler going 'So. Hot.'

Standing at the counter was this ridiculously sexy, all-of-my-erotic-dreams-come-true man. Dark hair, blue eyes, skin so golden brown it made my mouth water and my fingers tingle. Easily in his thirties, based on the laughter lines around his eyes, he was tall—crazy tall, which was awesome when I was over six foot myself—with broad shoulders and a slim waist. Bulges in all the right places, and just enough mischief in his expression to keep a girl on her toes. This man was grade-A eye candy. And he looked a little familiar.

As I mentally undressed the sun-kissed god at my counter, I also tried to place where I'd seen that face before. Being in a small country town, we didn't get a lot of models or TV personalities around here, so I didn't think that was it. I didn't go to school with him, there had never been anyone as drop-dead gorgeous as him at Rochester High, and he was too built to be someone I'd met via triathlons. The answer was tapping at my mind if I could just—my grip slipped in my distraction, the key jamming hard against the grinder. "Shit!" Sparks flew up in the air with an accompanying eeeee-owww sound. "Fuck!"

Not my finest moment.

The guy chuckled as I leapt back and shut the machine off, dusting my hands over the front of my work overalls to check for singes. *None. Thank God.*

"You know, I've heard of sparks flying when people meet, but I've never actually seen it before," he said with a shit-eating grin. *He's funny too.*

Based on the heat pumping out of my cheeks, it seemed my face was about as red as my hair. I was going to die from embarrassment.

"Yeah, well, now you have," I replied, trying to sound cool as I removed my safety glasses and ran my hand over the length of my long braid to make sure my hair wasn't on fire. "What can I do for you?"

His clear blue eyes gave me the once-over but showed little interest of a sexual nature, telling me his thoughts weren't anywhere near the gutter like mine were. It was the unfortunate curse of the tomboy. In my thirty-eight years on this earth, I'd never done cute or pretty. I dressed more for comfort than for display purposes. And on top of that, I had a very athletic build, helped along by the fact I competed in triathlons for fun. There were times when I was mistaken for a teenage boy—but I blamed the man bun fashion trend for that one.

"I'm looking for Trevor," Bronze god said when he'd finished mentally placing me in his friend zone.

"Trevor isn't available, but I can help you." Trevor was my grandad. Trev to those who knew him.

Squinting with one eye, he somehow managed to scrunch only half of his face up while still maintaining his good looks. "I really need Trev. When he gets in, can you tell him Jasmine stopped by? He'll know who you mean."

"Jasmine? You don't look like a Jasmine," I teased.

Bronze god grinned and took a step backwards. "She's an old friend of his. Family, really."

Old friend? Family? "Wait. Are you talking about Jasmine Cartwright?" *Oh my God.* That's how I knew him. "Are you one of her sons?" Growing up, I stayed at the Cartwright's house during the summer holidays. Pop had to work, and since my mum was incapable of being a parent, he would take me to Torquay for six weeks of sun, surf and fun. I'd loved it there. It was a big house with a pool and a tennis court, and a bunch of boys running around like crazy and getting into trouble that I was more than happy to take part in. It was the first time I ever felt like I fit in, and I'd pretty much been 'one of the boys' in every social situation since. Summer with the Cartwrights had been my favourite time of every year until I turned seventeen. After that, well, it *wasn't* fun anymore... I hadn't seen them since.

"Holy shit. I know you, don't I?" Without answering my question, he narrowed his eyes and took a second look at me as if he was trying to place me the way I'd been placing him.

"I'm *Sloane*. Trevor was my grandad?" I supplied. "You have, like four other brothers, right?" I wracked my brain for names I hadn't said out loud in over twenty years. "There was Toby, Nate, um…Sam…and twins—Kris and ah…Adam, Aaron? It's an A name…" I clicked my fingers as I tried to work it out.

"Abbot," he corrected before I could rattle off anymore.

I stopped clicking and pointed at him. "Abbot. That's right. I used to spend summer holidays with you guys until I finished school and started working here."

His eyes went wide as recognition dawned. "Holy shit. I remember. You broke Toby's tooth while we were playing footy one year. Blood everywhere."

That's what he remembers? Great.

"Yeah. I guess I elbowed a little too hard that day."

"I remember the hair. You were crazy."

The compliments were coming hard and fast.

"In a good way," he said to quickly recover. "We all thought you were cool."

Cool and crazy. That fact was now stuck in my head like a giant pin, deflating all the fantasies I'd had when he first walked through the door. *Cool and crazy.* So far removed from sexy and hot.

"What happened to you, anyway?" he asked when I didn't say anything else. "You were there every summer then you just…stopped."

The memory of humiliation and an argument between Pop and Jasmine surfaced, but I shook it off, pushing it back in the past where it belonged. "Got old enough to take care of myself," I explained, telling a half-truth. "So, which one are you, anyway?" I reached out and nudged him on the arm. He was so rock hard, it was like tapping against a wall.

"Abbot."

"Oh." The one whose name I couldn't remember. Excellent. "Sorry about forgetting your name."

He shrugged. "Sorry about forgetting your face." *Ouch.* OK, so I didn't have the most memorable face in existence, and he did say it as a joking response to what I said, but still, *ow. I'm forgettable. Cool, crazy and forgettable.* This was why I was thirty-eight and single.

"It's fine," I said, looking around at nothing really, but needing to focus my eyes elsewhere. "Um, listen, you obviously haven't heard—although I'm sure I notified your mum and she sent flowers—but Pop passed away a few months ago. Cancer. It's just me running things now."

"Oh shit, my condolences. I had no clue."

I waved his sympathies away because I didn't want to start getting emotional. "It's fine. It happened pretty fast. A few months from diagnosis to the end. I've kind of been reeling since then."

"Understandable," he said.

"And about your job, he left me the business, taught me everything he knew. So anything he could do, I can do too. Better even, because technology wasn't his strong point. So…" *Please give me the job so I don't have to report a negative quarter to my accountant on my first business statement as owner.*

"He taught you *everything* about his business?" He looked doubtful, which just got my feminist hackles up.

"Of course," I snapped. "You think just because I'm a girl I can't do what he could?"

He held up a hand, palm facing me. "This has nothing to do with you being a girl, or your ability. It has to do with what I heard."

"What did you hear?"

"That Trev was retiring the business, only doing jobs for friends."

I held up my hands and gestured around the shop. "Well, he obviously changed his mind."

He looked at me for a long moment, the muscle in the side of his stubbled jaw ticking slightly. His hair was a little on the long side, the tips of it hanging into his eyes and catching on his eyelashes when he blinked. "I need to make a call," he said, then he stepped outside, pressing his phone to his ear as the glass door swung shut behind him.

I couldn't hear anything he was saying from inside the shop, so I spent my time trying to piece together any information I had in my head about the Cartwrights. I was seventeen the last summer I spent with them, my memories were of touch football games, failed surfing lessons and petty theft. Yes, *theft*. Those boys had sticky fingers from a very young age. Pop had always said it was because they didn't have a positive male influence with their dad away in the big house. *Armed robbery gone wrong, I think.* Pop had always lectured me about staying out of their business and keeping my nose clean. I'd like to say I'd been a model citizen, but being 'one of the boys' had led to a lot of stupid decisions. It had been all fun and games until Nate had been caught stealing cars and went to juvie for a stint. He came out different, harder. Even when he was laughing, there was still a haunted look in his eyes. I was scared straight after that. I wondered if the Cartwright boys had gone straight as they'd grown as well.

The bell above the door jingled and the customer for the key cut walked back in, breaking into my walk down memory lane. When I finished serving her and cutting that second key I messed up, Abbot walked back into the shop.

"You're all done," I said to the woman. "Thanks for stopping by."

I watched in amusement as she turned then did a double take at the gorgeous man standing not far behind her. She said a breathy hello to Abbot then gave me an absentminded goodbye and left, sneaking glances back as she took her sweet time walking away. *I get it, lady. I totally get it.*

"OK," Abbot said, completely oblivious to the ogling as he slid his phone into the back pocket of his jeans. "You're in."

I grinned. *I'm in.* "Wait. In what, exactly?" Nerves burst to life in my stomach. *Does this mean they didn't go straight after all? What exactly am I agreeing to?*

Abbot laughed. "Very funny." He placed a business card on the counter. "You really think you're better than your grandad?"

"Depends on the job," I replied, reaching for the card and hoping for answers. While I wasn't *completely* opposed to breaking the law—I knew for a fact that Pop did the odd 'questionable' job over the years—I didn't want to do anything so risky I could get caught. *Orange is the New Black* was a great show and all, but I didn't want to be a cast member.

"One question," Abbot said, placing his index finger on top of the card so I couldn't take it.

"Dude. Are you giving it to me or not?"

He grinned. "Can you close up for the rest of the day?"

"I'm not exactly run off my feet here, so yeah."

"OK," he said, lifting his finger. "Let's see what you've got, Sloane."

Picking up the card, I read the front of it, 'Cartwright Property Management'. *Maybe this job was on the up and up?*

"What is this job, anyway?" I asked, turning the card over in my fingers. "You got a rental you need rekeyed or some—" I almost choked when I saw the handwritten figure on the back of it. "Holy…" *Shit.*

"That's your cut." *My cut? Of what?* "Be ready out front in half an hour and bring your safecracking kit. We've lost the code to ours." He winked like I was in on the conspiracy then turned and exited the shop.

The echo of the jingling bell reverberated in my ears as I stared at the card. That was a lot of zeros for what might only be a few hours worth of work. There was no way this was legit.

"Jesus, Pop," I whispered. "What the hell did you just get me into?"

CHAPTER TWO
ONE OF THE BOYS

THE FIRST THING I did when Abbot left was google for any robberies that had occurred over the last few days that involved a safe. Since I couldn't find any, I had to assume that a) the job was above board and they just *really* needed that safe open today and didn't trust anyone local to do it, or b) the robbery happened so recently that it hadn't been reported yet. I was hoping for option A because, besides the business, Pop hadn't left me any cash and I was struggling. I needed that money.

But, what if it was option B? Any sane person would put that business card through the shredder and run the other way. But I had history with these people, as did Pop. This wasn't just some rando walking into the shop and feeding me some bullshit about a 'found' safe. These were people Pop had trusted to look after me every summer holidays for nearly two decades of my life. He'd obviously worked for them over the years or they wouldn't have showed up looking for him today. The fact this opportunity showed up just when I needed it felt a lot like my grandfather giving me a helping hand from beyond the grave. Perhaps this was his way of pointing me in the right direction and showing me how to keep the business afloat. Maybe this was what he always wanted for me...*why* he trained me.

When Pop got sick, there were times when he'd said there were things he never told me, things he needed to explain. I kept telling him that he could tell me everything he needed to when he got better. Except he didn't get better, and we never got to have that talk. Maybe this was a way for me to discover everything I never knew.

With my heart pumping a steady rhythm against my ribcage, I pulled the door closed exactly half an hour later and locked up the shop. I added a note in the window that said 'Back Tomorrow' with my mobile number on the bottom in case there were any emergencies. I didn't expect many calls since there was a bigger locksmith in town that seemed to get all the business in our underpopulated locale.

As I leaned against the shop's façade, I began to realise how bonkers this really was. Some guy from twenty-odd years into my past turned up and now I'd agreed to go God only knew where with him. It felt loosely like the plot to every YA book and film in existence. I was the heroine, going about my life and feeling as though I didn't quite fit in until some handsome and mysterious bad boy came along and told me I was the chosen one. Either that, or I was Lara Croft in the latest Tomb Raider movie. Actually, that could be kind of cool. She was badarse in that.

Just as I was starting to feel a bit lame comparing my life to movies while standing on the footpath by myself, a dark grey Jaguar F-PACE pulled up to the curb. *A sexy man in a sexy car.* I may have started drooling again. That SUV was my answer to the 'if you could drive any car you wanted' question. I fucking loved Jags.

"Nice wheels," I said when he got out and walked towards me. He smiled because he knew that. Everybody who owned a Jag knew that.

"Got everything you need?" he asked with a frown, gesturing to the fact I wasn't holding a single thing.

"I do. If I take Lizzie." I pointed to my beat-up 1990s panel van in the space next to the shop. "All of my tools are in her, so it's easier than loading stuff in your car. I'm pretty much ready for any scenario with Lizzie by my side."

"Lizzie, huh?" He looked over my van with a slight smirk kicking up the corner of his biteable, tuggable lips. "Sure. We can take Lizzie."

"Great," I said. "Give me the address and I'll meet you there."

"I'll direct you." He took a step back and tapped on the passenger window. It slid down so smoothly it gave me a delighted shiver. I *really* wanted to sit in that car, lie in that car—no, *on* that car. It was so sleek and sexy.

"Jasmine," I said, snapping out of my car-lust as a dark-haired woman came into view. Despite the years, she looked almost exactly as I remembered her—slim and elegant.

"It's nice to see you again, Sloane. I was sorry to hear about Trevor. He was a good man."

I nodded in gratitude. "The best," I replied.

"I'm glad you're picking up where he left off. He always wanted you to. Ever since you were a little girl. He talked about your future a lot."

Did he? I found that strange since he was always on my back about walking the straight and narrow. *"Lookin' over your shoulder is no way to live, kid,"* he'd say. Still, I had to wonder if this was what he meant when he said he had things to tell me. Perhaps he just wanted me to live a 'normal life' until the time came for me to take over…who knew? It was hard to have these kinds of conversations about Pop when I was still mourning him. I regretted not letting him speak his peace when he'd wanted to.

Abbot took my silent contemplation as a cue to steer the conversation elsewhere. "Sloane wants to bring her van for the tools. I'll ride with her and meet you at the house?" *Wait. He's riding with me?*

Jasmine nodded. "Fair enough," she said, getting out of the Jag. I expected her to walk around to the driver's side, but instead she came towards me, giving me a firm hug. "Welcome back to the fold, Sloane. It's been too long." She smelled like a field of flowers on a sunny day. How did women do that? I was fairly sure I smelled like skin and metal shavings with a little grease thrown in for good measure. It didn't matter what I did, I could never smell like anything other than what I was. *Me.*

Welcome back to the fold.

As I hugged her back, emotion prickled my eyes because I wasn't expecting this kind of reaction when so many years had passed. "Thank you," I whispered as we parted. Then she held me at arm's length and studied me for a moment, her light eyes curious while her lips held a smile.

"You grew into a beautiful woman," she said, releasing me while also causing me to blush and look away. *Beautiful* and *woman* were definitely not words that were regularly combined when describing me. While I appreciated the kindness, I had a hard time believing they were true. "Well, we should get on the road. There's much to do." Turning gracefully, she walked back to the Jag and got into the driver's side, each movement so elegant and fluid that I felt as though I was watching royalty, not to mention a little jealous that such grace hadn't been bestowed on me. I had learned to be comfortable in my skin, but that didn't mean I didn't have moments where I wished for something more.

The engine started, the sound giving me a delighted chill as we waved her off. "I *really* like that car," I said more to myself than Abbot. But he responded with a chuckle anyway.

"We should go, too," he said. Then he held out his hand. "Keys."

"Oh no," I said, laughing at the absurd request. "No one drives Lizzie but me."

"Seriously?"

"Seriously. She needs tender loving care that not just anyone can give her."

"OK." He dragged the sound out as we walked over to her. "Why Lizzie, anyway?"

"She's named after that Ford in the Cars movies, because she's old and probably has a few screws loose too," I responded, opening her up.

With a laugh and a shake of his head, he headed for the passenger door.

"What? You've never named a vehicle before?"

"Never," he said, folding his big frame to fit inside.

I had to kick my door to get it to release, but once we were inside, I jiggled the key then started her up and she hummed just the way she was supposed to. "All cars should have a name."

"You think? What would you call my car?"

"Kitten," I said without a moment's hesitation. "She certainly purrs like one."

"Kitten. I kind of like that."

"Yeah? You gonna call her that now?"

"Not on your life," he said with a chuckle before he stretched out as much as he could in the small space. My eyes lingered a little longingly over his toned arms and the way his thighs pressed against the fabric of his jeans. The idea of spending extra time around eye-candy Abbot made me warm. So warm, I needed to turn the air on.

"Um, where are we headed?" I asked, needing to clear my throat as I took off the way the Jag had gone.

"Torquay," he said simply. "Just head for the motorway. I'll direct you to the house when we get closer."

"The same house I stayed at when we were kids?"

"That's the one."

"I think I remember the way."

He shrugged. "Give me a nudge if you get stuck."

"Why? What are you planning to do that will require nudging?" I asked as he wriggled in his seat.

"Nap," he responded, closing his eyes, his breath deepening almost immediately.

I had to laugh. The ability to pass out that quickly was quite the gift to have. He was obviously very comfortable with me if he could fall asleep that easily. *Just one of the boys, Sloane.* I sighed as I took advantage of the chance to study his features a little more closely.

You grew up good, Abbot. Real good.

After a long-term relationship that ended in nothing but

disappointment, I had all but given up on men. But that didn't mean I couldn't appreciate a fine specimen when it came into close contact. And it also didn't mean I had completely given up on sex...

Bad idea, Sloane. I gave myself a mental slap. In my experience, Cartwright brothers weren't interested in redheaded tomboys. A fact that brought the heat of embarrassment to my cheeks every time I remembered.

CHAPTER THREE
BUDS

ABBOT SLEPT for one of the three hours it took to get to Torquay, which left me to my own thoughts about the sanity of the situation I'd willingly put myself into.

The last time I saw the Cartwrights, Pop and Jasmine had fought. I remembered raised voices and knowing the argument was about me. When he'd finished yelling, Pop burst into the room and declared we were leaving. After that, I never went back to Torquay, and Pop never allowed me to work on any big jobs with him. I knew the two things were connected, but I'd never pushed the issue, my own awkwardness over that last summer making me relieved that I never had to return.

Still, there was obviously a heck of a lot more to Pop's work than I'd understood. And if I were going to take over his business properly, I'd need to know what it was. I hoped that taking this job would give me the opportunity to ask questions that would show me the path I'd been searching for since Pop's passing.

"You still surf?" Abbot asked as we neared Geelong.

Since he woke, we'd started reminiscing about times gone by and catching up on the in-between. He was easy to talk to. His voice had this calming quality that put me at ease even though my mind was whirling. It was nice to remember with someone who had history with Pop too.

"No surf in the country." I glanced at him with a slight smirk. "My lessons ended when my visits did."

"Bummer." He ran his hands through his hair and looked out the window. "What do you do for fun, then?"

I laughed. "There's more to life than surfing you know."

Turning to face me, he flashed a beautiful smile. "Are you sure about that?"

The smile was infectious, although his words had me shaking my head. "There's heaps. I run, I bike ride, and I swim. Hang out with friends. That's fun."

"Besides the friends part, that sounds a lot like hard work. What do you do, triathlons or something?"

"I happen to like triathlons. I like pushing myself to my limits."

With a sideways glance, he frowned. "OK."

"OK?" I scoffed. "Are you dissing my choice of recreational sport?"

With a chuckle, he shook his head. "Hey, your fun is your fun. You just wouldn't catch me going through all of that for the sake of a personal best."

My hands tightened on the wheel. "Let me guess, your idea of fun is catching giant waves and getting baked around a bonfire?"

He shrugged. "That *is* fun"

"That's clichéd."

"Clichés are clichés for a reason. Because that's what people like."

"Well, I've never really focused on what other people like. I'm fine just being me."

"And who are you, Sloane Slater—the girl with a name that sounds like a superhero's secret identity—what's your story?"

"Besides having a cool-sounding name?" It was my turn to shrug as I glanced at him briefly. He looked completely relaxed while I was conscious of every breath and sound. And it wasn't just because of this job and my grandfather. It was him too. I'd never been attracted to a guy years younger than me before. But here I was, nervous and clammy around a boy who became a man in what felt like the blink of an eye.

"What do you mean what's my story? Like what did I grow up to become?"

He stretched his arms above his head and laced his fingers behind his neck, his elbow not far away if I turned my head. "Sure. Let's go with that."

I released a chuckle then gestured to myself with one hand. "This is it. I didn't transform into a superhero— although, I went through a stage where I considered changing my name to something more basic. My life's been very simple: I went to school, hung with friends, and I worked with Pop. He died and I took over the business. You walked in and now I'm here. The end."

"That's it? No marriage, no kids?"

"Did *you* get married and have kids?" I shot back, a little defensive after years of that kind of question. It was like I hadn't fulfilled my destiny as a woman because I maintained my single status and didn't procreate. It didn't matter that I was fucked around for years by a guy who'd promised everything then gave me nothing. I *had* wanted those things once upon a time. But I had learned to let go. Learned to be happy as Sloane Slater, the girl who always lived outside the norm. Alone.

He laughed and shifted his position, leaning his elbow on the window ledge, hand running through his hair again. "No way. Marriage is not for me. So much fucking drama for a pussy when there are so many others out there. No thanks."

"Gee. Tell me how you really feel," I teased.

"Seriously though, in the last eighteen months, three of my brothers have gotten hitched. I have *never* known so much bloody drama."

"Three weddings in eighteen months? That's a lot. No wonder you're anti-marriage."

"It's not even the weddings that are the drama. It's the relationships." He sounded a little bitter. "We were all single, happily doing our thing, then suddenly all these women started moving in and they all lost their ever-loving minds. Nate fell first, then Sam. Now, Kris, my twin, is getting married in a couple of weeks. Nate is also expecting a rug rat. There's only me and Toby left now, but Toby is keen on settling down so I reckon he'll kidnap the next good lookin' sheila he sets his sights on."

I laughed at that. How absurd.

"Don't laugh, I'm serious," he said, although I felt sure he was still poking fun.

"*Toby* wants to settle down?" He'd always been the loner growing up. No girlfriends. No outward interest in anything romantic at all. *How things must have changed.*

"Desperately." *I never would have thought.*

"So, you're bummed about your brothers wanting to settle down because you wanted to maintain the bachelors until you all die kind of life?" I was beginning to think he would get along well with my ex. He had the same attitude all through his twenties, and even in his thirties while in a relationship with me, he was adamant that marriage was never for him.

"I don't know why it pisses me off. I mean, it's cool that they're all happy and shit, but things were simpler before. We did our thing, we had our fun, and everything was fine. Now there's chaos and anarchy and I hardly know my right arse cheek from my left nut anymore. I want it all to slow down and reverse a little. I miss what we were, you know?"

That was a lot to take in. But it sounded a lot like jealousy from where I was sitting.

"I guess things change as we get older. You're all in your thirties now, right?"

He nodded. "Toby is forty. Nate's thirty-seven. Sam is thirty-six and me and Kris turned thirty-three in March."

"Must be hard seeing your twin getting married. You're obviously close?" I glanced at him before flipping my indicator on to make a turn.

"We were."

The bitterness in his words caused me to press my lips together.

"Do you feel left behind?" I asked, empathising with his position.

"Nah. Not left behind. Just…pushed to the side." I knew that feeling all too well.

"I'm sorry. That really sucks." I reached over and gave his forearm a squeeze. *Fuck, his muscles are hard.*

He wiped a hand over his face and waved it off. "I'll get used to it."

We all do eventually. I pulled my hand back and placed it on the steering wheel, fingers tingling.

Falling quiet, he pointed out an exit then checked I knew where I'd be going from there.

"You know, Sloane. You're real easy to talk to," he said after a while, his hand rubbing against his thigh. "There's no pretence. I reckon we could be great buds."

"I get that a lot," I said, forcing a smile while thinking that was the story of my life. I was never anything more than a friend, even within my relationships.

Buds. Awesome.

PULLING up in front of a massive white rendered home, I cut the engine and told Lizzie not to leak oil all over their fancy driveway that could almost be classed as a small road.

"It looks bigger than I remember," I said, stepping out of my van.

Abbot shrugged. "It's always looked the same to me."

"You came here first," Jasmine called out, exiting the house with her handbag slung over her arm. "Good. They're all at the beach shack. No point in taking multiple cars. You can come with me." She indicated the black Chrysler sedan in front of her. *Wow, this family seems to have a whole host of fancy cars.* Either they really were in the real estate game, or their petty theft was anything but petty anymore.

"Didn't you want me to open something for you?" I asked, wanting to get the job done. Safes can take hours to crack, and I had a long drive back home when it was done.

"It can wait," Jasmine said, waving her hand breezily.

"Come and say hi to everyone first. I'm sure they'll get a kick out of seeing you again." *I doubted that.*

"Then I guess we're tagging along." Abbot's tone suggested he didn't see a point in arguing, so I shrugged and followed, sitting in the back seat of the Chrysler while Abbot and his mother got in front.

Jasmine spent the drive chatting about the plans for Kristian's wedding. "You'll love Veronica, Sloane. She was born to be one of us, a great fit for the Cartwright family."

"A great fit. Sounds like something out of Pride and Prejudice," I commented as Abbot turned in his seat to address me directly.

"Right? But, don't call her Veronica. Call her Ronnie. She *hates* Veronica, but Jazz insists on calling everyone by their full name."

I lifted my eyebrows. "Is that why you call her Jazz? To piss her off in return."

Jasmine chuckled, low and hollow. "You caught that, huh? I always liked her, Abbot, she catches on quick."

Abbot smiled and shook his head as he turned straight in his seat. "Don't get any ideas, Mother."

Jasmine shrugged, and Abbot looked out the window while I was left to make my own conclusions. It wasn't hard: Jasmine said she liked me and Abbot didn't want Jasmine thinking she could set us up. *Boom.* In the uncomfortable silence in the car, I took a breath and mentally threw my attraction towards Abbot out the car window. I already knew it wasn't reciprocated, and I didn't have room for hope and disappointment in my life anymore. I was simply too damn exhausted with life to deal with it.

"How was the drive down here?" Jasmine asked after a

while, glancing at me through the rear-view mirror while I replayed Abbot's and my earlier conversation. *We could be buds...*

"It was fine," I said on a breath. "We just caught up a little, talked about summers at your place and whatnot. Abbot doesn't seem to remember a lot about it. I think his standout moment was when I broke Toby's tooth."

"Oh." Jasmine winced. "I remember that day. He's got a great set of teeth now, and you'd never know his front tooth broke away."

"Not my finest moment," I admitted. "But it's nice to be remembered for something, I guess. Better than not being remembered at all."

"I remember other stuff too," Abbot interjected, running his fingers through his hair again as he looked out the window. It seemed to be his go-to motion, for comfort or agitation, I wasn't sure yet. "I remember we all tried to teach her to surf, but it was the one thing she couldn't master. I remember climbing over the rocks near the beach, and parasailing on windy days. I remember swimming and tennis and playing hide and seek around the property. Sloane hid in a tree once and dropped right in front of Kris and me. Scared Kris so much he nearly peed." He was smiling, but then he looked at Jasmine directly and the curve left his mouth. "And I remember you and Trev having a massive blue. I remember wondering why she didn't come back, and never seeing her again until today." It was safe to say Abbot surprised us both with his excellent recall of events, especially based on the way Jasmine's eyes widened.

"I just remember getting up to mischief and having a lot of fun," I put in, trying to smooth over the last comment about Pop and Jasmine fighting. It was the year before I turned eighteen so when the next summer holidays rolled around, I was finished school and old enough to start working full time. Pop hadn't given me the option to return to Torquay, and I was happy to put the whole embarrassing situation behind me, convincing myself it had been time to move on. Now, I felt bad for not trying to stay in touch.

"I think we all had fun back then," Jasmine mused. "Simpler times and all."

"Yeah, back when we were all barefoot and had to walk two miles in the snow to get to school," Abbot said, breaking any tension that was left in the car with the randomness of his comment. I laughed and thought about Pop. That was the kind of thing he'd say, and only served to feed my guilt for coming here. He'd gone to so much trouble to keep me away, keep me on the right side of the law. Money and curiosity brought me back, but was my being here making him turn in his grave, or was this the plan all along? I didn't have much time to ponder my current direction in life before we pulled up to an understated blue house that was positioned directly on the beach.

"Are you serious? *This* is the beach shack? I imagined a literal shack. Like a bamboo shed, or something." I laughed and got out of the car, breathing in the salt heavy air. It cleansed my lungs and tasted a little bit like freedom. "You know, I would sell everything I owned to live in a place like this." Tipping my head up to the sky, I let the sun warm my skin even though the wind had a cold bite to it.

When I opened my eyes, Abbot was smiling at me.

"What?" I laughed and pushed him playfully on the arm. "You're looking at me like I'm weird."

"You are," he said, laughing with me—or most likely *at* me. "Trev would have left you a mint. You could live anywhere you want, drive anything you want. But you're holed up in the middle of nowhere, driving a car that still uses a key to start it."

"Don't let Lizzie hear you talk like that." I met his eyes and pressed my lips into a serene smile, trying to keep my thoughts to myself. *A mint.* There was no such mint. Pop's accounts were practically empty. I had a feeling much of his life savings had gone to my mother, or spent long ago, bailing her out from her various messes. It had been rare for her to show up, but when she did, she was always in crisis. A gypsy at heart, Pop would always say. She couldn't sit still for long.

"What are we all doing out here?" Jasmine asked, walking over to a group of three men and two women. There wasn't an identical-looking person who could be Kristian, so I assumed they were Toby, Nate and Sam. It was strange looking at them. They were familiar to my eyes, but I couldn't tell exactly who was who. Twenty-one years was a lifetime. Faces and bodies had changed, and the teenagers we'd been were memories now, mere tickles in the back of my mind.

"No mistaking you lot for family," I said to Abbot as we headed towards the group. He made an amused sound then placed his hand in the centre of my back and nudged me forward.

"Let's see if they remember you as well as I do."

I was a step ahead of him and turned back to scoff when I caught his eyes a lot lower than my face.

"Did you just push me ahead so you could check out my arse?"

He grinned but didn't deny it. I rolled my eyes and tried not to smile too much. "Tobes, I'll give you a hundred bucks if you can tell me who this is," he called out instead.

Being closer to the men, I began to reconcile my memories with the faces and bodies they now possessed. *Toby*. I had to admit that he was the last brother I wanted to see again. He was the oldest of us all and the shortest out of the brothers. Although, short was a terrible descriptor for him. Toby was six-two as opposed to the tallest brother who seemed to be closer to six-four.

"Sloane?" Toby's voice was laced with disbelief. I smiled, the memory of the last time I saw him flooding my brain. I hoped he'd forgotten, or at least forgiven. My actions that day had been out of character and out of line. I'd regretted them ever since.

"Know many other redheads who can rock a set of coveralls like me?" I asked, stopping before him.

He laughed and pulled me into a hug that turned my nerves into happy butterflies. *Maybe he doesn't hate me.* "Holy shit, how long has it been?" he asked, stepping back to look at me.

"Almost twenty-one years," I said. "We got old."

He grinned. "You look exactly the same to me," he said, his eyes shining happily. It amazed me how you could spend years hoping you never had to come face to face with someone again, then when it happened, it was nowhere near as awkward as you imagined. Toby had always been the calm and responsible one—except for the rare moments he'd allowed himself to be led astray. I should have known he'd treat me the same way.

When he released me, he turned his attention to Nate. "You remember Sloane, don't you?"

"Sure do." Nate leaned down and wrapped me in a bear hug, spinning me in a circle before setting me back down. "What the hell happened to you, red? You left us a man down for footy." Nate and I were the closest in age. I was about ten months older than him. I remembered skateboarding with him and Sam…and grazed knees. I had also taught him how to pick a lock, and always felt partly responsible for his time in juvie. Maybe if I hadn't taught him, he wouldn't have been so bold?

"Life happened," I replied with a shrug, beaming because this welcome was more than I expected; kind of like finding something you thought you'd lost. There were a lot of emotions spiralling through my chest. "But I missed you guys. It's been too long." Nate nodded and I turned to find the third brother standing and smiling down at me. "Sam." I grinned and rose up on my toes to hug him hello. He was *so* tall and broad. A huge leap from the scrawny teen I'd seen last time.

"You've barely changed," Sam said, hugging me back.

"You've changed completely," I replied. "You were a beanpole the last time we met. Now look at you."

He laughed and stepped back, slipping his arm around a slender brunette with big eyes and a cute smile. "This is my wife, Alesha. Peaches, this is Sloane. We all kind of grew up together."

"Until I turned eighteen and decided I was too cool for this lot," I said, glancing at Toby as I shook Alesha's hand. His expression gave me nothing.

"Everyone calls me, Leesh," Alesha said, smiling kindly.

"Except Jasmine who calls you by your full name and Sam who calls you Peaches, right?"

She laughed, but in an uneasy way. "Yes. You already know about us?" Her eyes narrowed slightly, suspiciously. *Oh dear. I've put my foot in it without meaning to.*

"Oh no," I corrected quickly. "I literally just learned that by listening." I pointed at Sam then pressed my lips closed because I was making it worse and probably sounded condescending. "Anyway." I shook my head and made a 'gah' noise, poking out my tongue out to try and diffuse the situation with a little crazy. Then I turned towards a blonde woman with a curvy figure and held out my hand. "I'm Sloane, you must be Nate's wife?" I asked, meeting her honey-coloured eyes.

"I'm Holland," she said as she slid her hand in mine. "Nate calls me Duchess, Jasmine calls me Holland, and some people call me Holl."

I grinned. She got where I was coming from. "Which do you prefer?"

"Oh any." She waved her hand in the air. "You could even call me 'hey you' and I'd answer."

"OK, hey you."

She rolled her eyes and laughed at my lame joke, so I decided I liked her best.

"Where's Kris?" Abbot asked, looking back to the house.

"Inside." Toby jerked his head towards the front door.

"They need a moment," Alesha said with a knowing look in her eye.

"For what?" Jasmine asked. "There are things to discuss and we're all out here twiddling our thumbs."

"They just need a minute," Holland said quickly when Jasmine went to walk into the house anyway. Jasmine paused and turned on her, giving her *the look* she was famous for whenever one of us crossed the line as kids. I literally felt transported back to the nineties when we'd lost track of time and shown up an hour late for dinner.

"They can have a minute when we're finished," Jasmine said, holding Holland's unwavering gaze. *She's tough too.*

"Jazz," Nate warned, and Jasmine flicked her gaze to her son then paused before she smiled and relaxed.

"One more minute then," she said with a shrug. *Anything for her boys.* She was always like that. Being around them all again was totally weirding me out.

It was at that moment the front door burst open and Kristian emerged with a massive grin on his face, pulling a tiny blonde woman behind him. She was Veronica, I assumed.

Stopping, he looked at us all for a moment then threw his head back to the sky. "We're going to have a baby," he yelled with wild abandon. Then he picked up the laughing girl and spun her around in a moment of pure joy.

I smiled and held my hands together upon witnessing the happy scene, stepping back while the rest of the family cheered and embraced the couple. *I'm not supposed to be a part of this moment.*

It was strange how bearing witness to another person's intimate joy could make you feel incredibly alone. But that's what their happiness did. It reminded me of everything I'd never have, everything I'd waited and hoped for but never received. I had to look away and take a deep a breath. They'd greeted me with happiness and made me feel like a long-lost family member. But the fact remained, I wasn't one of the boys, and I didn't have much family of my own to speak of. Years had changed us all, separated our lives, and more than ever I was reminded that I existed on the outside, alone. I was, and always will be *just* Sloane.

I'd never felt more out of place in my life.

"THIS CALLS FOR A CELEBRATION," Jasmine said, clapping her hands together. "Book a table somewhere, I'm taking you all to dinner. *Two* new Cartwrights on the way." Her eyes glittered with excitement.

I hung back further from the family, leaning against her car while they all chatted excitedly. Apparently Holland was pregnant too, and Sam and Alesha were booked in for IVF. There was about to be a baby explosion within the Cartwright family. I could see why Abbot was feeling on the outer, as I was overwhelmed just listening to them.

"I honestly thought we'd never see you again," Toby said as he joined me against the car. Out of all the Cartwright men, he seemed the most put together: dress pants, button-up shirt with the sleeves rolled up, styled hair. He smelled nice too. Like he belonged in the city and not here. I remembered conversations near a bonfire, and dreams of being anywhere but here. I wondered if he still felt that way or if it was just the pressures of a teenage boy forced to grow up too soon that made him want to run.

"Well, I honestly never thought you gangly guys would all grow up to become so ridiculously good-looking. But here we are. You all look like you belong on the front cover of *Men's Health*, and I'm the gangly one back in Torquay."

"For how long?" he asked with a smile, his big arms folding across his middle. *Was this the part where he reminded me I didn't belong here?*

I squinted a little in the sun as I looked at him, those nerves coming back. "Just until I get this safe open. I reckon I'll be heading back later tonight if all goes well. I'd actually like to get started if you don't mind. As lovely as this all is, I have a long drive back home when I'm done."

Toby chuckled and wiped a hand across his clean-shaven jaw.

"What's so funny?"

"Just you. You're exactly the same."

"I'm really not."

"Whatever you say." The corners of his mouth kicked up. "Did Abbot tell you much about the safe?"

"Beyond the lack of a combination—which I assume means you guys stole it—no, he didn't tell me anything."

"OK. Well, it's old."

"Old can be easy."

"Moseler old."

"Four combo?"

He nodded.

"That's OK. I can handle that."

"No doubt. But the problem isn't the dial. It's what's around the dial."

I furrowed my brow. "What's around the dial, Toby?"

Pressing his lips together, he met my eyes for a moment before he answered. "It has an anti-theft device embedded in it."

"Bullshit," I gasped, my eyes going wide as I got a little excited. Back in the twenties, safe owners deterred thieves from forcing their way into safes by installing these anti-theft devices that contained a glass vial filled with Chloropicrin, more commonly known as tear gas. If the would-be thief tried to crowbar or beat their way through the safe door, the vial would crack and they'd get a very nasty surprise. The devices were completely illegal these days, but there were rare occasions when an old safe was still fitted with one. It was a safecrackers worst nightmare and wet dream all rolled into one.

Toby nodded. "That's why we sent for Trev. We need him to finesse the door open without disturbing the tear gas."

"Pop is dead, Toby. Bone cancer. Took him a few months ago, I was sure Jasmine knew but..." I shrugged. "I'll finesse the safe open." That was a lie. I had no clue how to finesse a safe open like Pop did. He could open a safe by 'feeling' the subtle changes in the weight of the wheels through the dial. In minutes, he could line the gates up with the drop hammer and be inside. Growing up, I'd begged and begged but he never taught me. When I opened safes, I did it invasively. With a drill. And that wouldn't work in this instance. *Shit.*

Toby's eyes dropped to look at his hands. "I'm really sorry, Sloane. I didn't know."

I shrugged. "It's possible I didn't tell you."

"Why didn't you?" Lifting his gaze, he met my eyes.

"I sent notices to so many people. I thought you were

included, I even thought Jasmine had sent flowers, but I don't know… There was a lot going on at the time."

He reached across and took my hand in his, giving it a squeeze before letting me go. "I understand. And I'm sorry for your loss."

I lifted my eyes to meet his, wishing I'd never messed up our friendship. "Thank you, Toby."

"Hey, let's go," Abbot called out, cutting into our conversation as he made his way over. "You're coming to dinner with us, and Leesh is gonna lend you some clothes."

"It's fine." I shook my head. "I'll just go home and come back tomorrow."

Abbot laughed and looked at Toby. "She's hilarious."

Toby raised his eyebrows and stood. "I'll leave you to it. See you at dinner, Sloane."

"What? No. I'm not going to dinner."

Abbot grinned and slid his arm around my neck, pulling me so I had no choice but to walk alongside him. "Yes, you are. Jasmine insists."

I opened my mouth to argue, but saw little point. The decision had been made for me, and honestly, being taken to dinner sounded like it could be OK. As out of place as I felt, I wouldn't mind spending a little more time with this family from my past. It was fun reminiscing good times, and maybe I'd gain a little catharsis over the not-so-good times. As someone far wiser than I'd ever be once said, 'time heals all wounds'. And we were adults now. Teenage angst and drama didn't need to matter anymore.

Abbot stopped abruptly in front of his twin and the newly pregnant Veronica, grabbing my arm so I stopped with him. "Ronnie, this is Sloane. Sloane, Ronnie." He gestured between us with his hand. "Kris, you remember Sloane, right?" Kristian looked lost for a moment. Then Abbot added, "She's the redhead who terrorised us when we were kids. She broke Toby's teeth."

"Tooth," I said. "Just one. And I didn't terrorise you."

Kristian's eyes lit like a switch was flipped on. "She used to jump out of trees yelling 'drop bear' right? Scared the living shit out of us."

"I wasn't *that* bad," I said, laughing at the resurfaced memory. Toby and Nate had been in on the whole drop bear fiasco too. It was funny to send the younger kids screaming.

The twins looked at each other then spoke in unison, "You were."

I rolled my eyes and smiled at Ronnie. "Congratulations on the baby," I said.

"Thank you," she replied, placing her hand on her stomach. "As long as it isn't twins, I think we'll be fine."

"Oh, I wouldn't worry about that," I said with a wave of my hand. "Identical twins aren't hereditary. Only fraternal twins are. And even if they were it would be completely dependent on you because you're the one who ovulates. Actually, it's really interesting." I watched her eyes go wide then glaze over as I started explaining how random an embryo splitting really was and the chances of it occurring. I was totally nerding out on her but couldn't seem to stop, even though I knew I should.

When I got to the end of my detailed explanation, I placed my hand on my head, registering the dazed expressions of my audience as I chuckled. "I obviously read too many articles."

"Well, you've put my mind at ease," Ronnie said with a strained laugh before she made some excuse to leave.

Abbot turned to me. "Wow. I reckon she thinks you're really cool now," he teased, causing me to roll my eyes.

"Very funny, douchebag." I'd probably already alienated two of the three Cartwright wives. I was doing well.

"I like how we've settled right back into name-calling."

I shrugged. "You said it yourself: no pretence."

"That's true," he said, slinging his arm over my shoulder again and leading me away. "Now let's go and get you prettied up. The restaurant isn't going to let you in wearing khaki overalls. Doesn't matter how good your arse looks in them."

I shoved him in the side and laughed. "I *knew* you were checking it out, creep. You got a thing for older women or just arses?" *What is this? Was he playing with me?*

"You're only five years older than me, Slater. And I looked because I'm a perv and can't help myself."

"So it's got nothing to do with *me* and everything to do with the fact I have a vagina."

"I have a bedpost that I like adding notches to."

"Always on the hunt, huh?"

"It's hard to switch off."

"I'll keep that in mind," I said as we reached the car, liking his honesty. "Hey Abbot." I turned to face him when he opened the door.

"Yes, Sloane?" He lowered his voice in this sexy way that made me want to giggle.

"Why didn't you tell me about me about the tear gas?"

Leaning on the top of the door, he grinned. "Because you said you were better than Trev."

"No one's better than him," I admitted. "And I, well, I pale in comparison."

His jaw twitched as he took a breath and glanced back to his family. "OK. But I reckon we keep that between you and me for now."

CHAPTER SIX
POP A MINT

DINNER WAS…INTERESTING but fun. It was loud and it was gregarious, with a constant flow of food and wine and conversation. I couldn't have worked afterwards even if I'd wanted to, and driving home was out of the question, so I stayed in the guest room at Jasmine's instead, wearing borrowed pyjamas, the clothes I'd borrowed from Alesha hanging over a high-backed chair. It felt strange to be in a room where nothing but my underwear belonged to me.

A creature of my own comforts, I struggled to sleep more than a few hours despite the exhaustive effects of the wine. I woke to darkness, showered in the en-suite bathroom, then dressed in the clothes I wore last night.

Running my fingers through my flame-red hair, I looked at myself in the mirror, my wide brown eyes appeared glassy and tired. The freckles across my nose stood out against my pale skin.

I rarely drank wine because it went to my head. Beer tended to be my drink of choice, but the Cartwrights had a lot to celebrate and the fancy restaurant didn't really feel like a beer establishment.

I have a headache.

Checking the cupboards, I found a packet of Ibuprofen and downed two with a glass of water. Then I headed out to the kitchen in search of coffee, texting the guys I normally train with to let them know I wouldn't be there.

Sick? A message separate from the group chat popped up from Mark, my ex. Like the good *buddy* I was, we'd remained friends after the split. I'd even acted happy for him when he announced his engagement six months after we broke up. Even went to his stupid wedding.

Did I already mention I was a glutton for punishment?

Me: out of town for a job.

Mark: when will you be back?

Me: probably tonight.

Mark: see you tomorrow then?

Me: sure

I put my phone down with a sigh, wishing I had the strength of character to let that guy go. It hurt to have contact and to pretend we were still friends, to smile when he spoke about his wife and their new baby.

That was supposed to be me.

I'd spent eight years of my life telling him I understood that he wasn't ready for marriage or kids. And it was my choice to end our relationship because *I did* want those things. Imagine my surprise when it turned out he wanted those things after all. He just hadn't wanted them with me.

I should have told him to go fuck himself two years ago.

But to cut ties with him meant I'd have to cut ties with everyone. All of our friends were the same big group we'd been part of since high school. For a long time, I was the only girl—big shock there—but as time went by, the ratio shifted and was almost even now that they were all married. The only singles remaining were this guy called Steve, who didn't wear enough deodorant and still lived with his mother, and me. I'd awkwardly refused any suggestions that we should date. It was like we were their charity cases and they wouldn't rest until we were paired off like them, tied off in a neat little bow. *Fuck that.*

Why am I friends with these people again? That's right. Because it wasn't easy to start over again in a small town. I had to grin and bear it or be completely alone. No one wanted that.

When the fancy coffee machine finished going through the steps, I had a hot latte in my hands as I slid onto one of the stools set up on the outside of the dark marble bench-top. Sipping slowly, I picked up my phone again and googled how old a woman could be before she was no longer fertile, switching my search term to 'how to remove old tear gas devices from safes' when I learned my chances of conception had dropped to five per cent from twenty. *Yikes.* My time was quickly running out.

The tear gas search served as the perfect distraction from my declining fertility. There were nightmare stories about HAZMAT teams getting called in when tubes were accidentally cracked upon removal. It was strongly recom-mended that an expert be called in, but then that's what I was supposed to be, right? I had no idea why I told Toby I could finesse the lock open like Pop could. They'd all find out I lied the moment I went in there and hours went by without an open safe.

Unless…

Sliding off the stool, I crept up the stairs and stood in front of the door to Abbot's room. He already knew I was in over my head. So, if I could get him to take me to the safe early, then maybe I could get the device removed and the safe opened before the rest of them even knew we were gone. I'd be a hero. It was worth a shot.

Lifting my hand to knock, I hesitated when I realised that would make too much noise and wake more than just Abbot. Instead, I quietly turned the handle and pushed inside. Bad idea. *Terrible idea.* Abbot was asleep on his stomach, the dim light of early-morning creating a blue hue against his golden skin. The sheet was pulled over his body. Just. I could see a nice round arse cheek peeking out the side of it.

Abbot slept naked.

And now I was being creepy by *watching* him sleep naked.

Maybe I should leave.

I kept staring.

God, he has a beautiful behind.

He looked good in clothes, but without them, he was even more drool worthy.

My fingertips tingled from wanting to touch him and my teeth ached from wanting to—

"What are you doing?"

Staring at your arse. "I want you to take me to this safe." I managed not to choke on my words as I hid my surprise over being caught ogling.

He lifted his head and squinted at me. "What time is it?" He reached for his phone and lifted it. "Five? What the hell is wrong with you? Don't you sleep?"

I held my breath as he flipped over and sat, using a

hand to pull his sheet across his lap, hiding is morning boner from my view.

Disappointing.

"I'm normally up training at this time. Plus, I can't sleep if I'm not home, so—"

"So you want to work instead?"

"Please."

With a sigh, he looked around. "Chuck me my jeans," he said, pointing to the rumpled pile at the foot of his bed.

I did as he asked then he twisted to the side, slipping his legs into his jeans, pausing before he pulled them all the way up. "Wanna turn around for this part?" he said when I blatantly watched his movements.

"Oh shit. Of course," I said, turning while he stood and pulled his jeans over his delectable arse, tugging a rather impressive hard-on inside the denim. I knew all of this because I was facing a mirror that gave me an unfettered view of his movements.

"Give me a minute to pee and we can go," he said, turning and meeting my eyes in the mirror. A grin spread across his face as he shook his head. "Seems you're a bigger perv than I am."

"You obviously work hard on that body of yours," I said, nodding towards his ripped abs and the V that pointed so temptingly to the inside of his jeans. "The least I can do is appreciate it."

He laughed as he grabbed a random shirt and sniffed it before pulling it over his head. "Appreciate all you want." *If you didn't put a shirt on, I could have.* I wasn't exactly hard up for eye candy if I was honest. I trained five times a week with guys who took looking after their bodies seriously. *But,* they were all married, we had history, *and* I knew their wives. Ogling wasn't on the agenda with them. Abbot, on the other hand, didn't mind the ogling, and well, he was hot, his body filled out in ways a triathlete's never was. They were lean, built for distance and speed. Abbot was…well, *built.* All over. In every way. I might only get a day around him, so I was storing up his deliciousness ready for when I went back home. Who wouldn't? Even girls needed a spank-bank.

When he disappeared into the bathroom, I took a moment to peruse his room while he did his thing.

Like the rest of the house, there were grey carpets with cream walls. A large wooden framed bed dominated most of the space with a bookcase, a dressing table drawer combo and a desk taking up the rest of it. On the walls were some surf-related posters, but my favourite piece was a framed print above the bed of five boys silhouetted against the setting sun.

"Is that all of you?" I asked as he exited the bathroom. He glanced up, and nodded as he found a pair of socks and picked up his shoes.

"Yeah. I think me and Kris were like four then."

"Who took the photo, Jasmine?"

"Nah. Some family friend." He laughed a little as he pulled his socks on. "You know, it even could have been you. It was taken in the summer."

"Maybe. We took a lot of photos back in the day," I said, thinking it would be kind of cool if that were true. It meant I would've been here all along in spirit. Why that mattered to me, I didn't really know. Maybe I was just getting sentimental in my mature years.

"Back in the day." He chuckled, tightening his laces. "You make it sound like we're old."

"I *am* pushing forty," I pointed out.

He looked at me like I was crazy. "Eighty is old. Forty is still young. Thirty-eight, younger still. There's still a lot of fun to be had, my friend. Don't quit living when there's still so much life ahead of you." *Who knew Abbot was so deep?*

Finishing with his shoes, he grabbed a jacket and led the way outside where we hopped into Lizzie and drove to Geelong where a storage facility loomed like a dark shadow against a colourful sky.

"Safe's inside. Grab your gear."

As I stood at the back of the van grabbing my kit, I wondered what would happen if it turned out I couldn't get this safe open for them. Would they send me on my way and find someone more capable? *Ugh.* I hated that thought. I *really* wanted that cash they offered.

"Got everything?" Abbot slid a cigarette between his lips and lit up.

"Besides gas masks in case I fuck up? Yeah, I'm good."

He sucked back on his cigarette thoughtfully, letting the smoke out of his lungs before he spoke. "You think we're gonna need them?"

"We should be OK."

"You're not exactly filling me with confidence here, Slater."

"Well, I'm not Pop, OK? There was shit he refused to teach me, so I don't know how long this is gonna take. I guess he didn't trust me to keep my nose clean if I knew everything."

"How'd that work out for you anyway?"

"Keeping my nose clean?"

He nodded.

"Less exciting. A hell of a lot less scary." Getting up to no good with the Cartwright boys had been fun when we were kids. But I was comfortable leaving that behind me when the reality of being caught became all too possible.

"Hmm, sounds boring."

I shrugged. "It was OK."

"And you think Trev would be cool with you coming back here and getting down and dirty after all this time?"

"Down and dirty." I laughed. "That's so not the right term for what this is."

He smiled, his cigarette between his lips as he took my toolkit from my hands. "It could be."

"Shut up." I rolled my eyes and scoffed, pushing against his shoulder.

When he laughed, smoke came out of his nose. "Listen, I'm sure you're gonna do fine in there. As long as you get this safe open, I honestly don't give a shit how fast or slow you do it." His words brought me great relief. All I had was an idea on how to finesse a safe open. It was something I'd never actually tried.

"What about the rest of your family? Will they give a shit if I don't open it right away?"

"I'll tell them whatever they need to hear," he told me with a wink, causing something funny to bloom in the base of my belly. "I've got your back, Sloane Slater."

"I appreciate that, Abbot Cartwright," I said with a small smile tugging at my mouth.

"Hmm, my name just doesn't have the same ring to it."

"It doesn't, does it?" I laughed, waiting as he finished his smoke then stubbed it out on the ground, pocketing the stub.

"Worried about DNA?" I asked.

"Always careful, Sloane. Trev should have taught you that."

"He didn't."

"Then allow me to give you a crash course: always act like someone's watching; keep your mouth shut about anything and everything you bear witness to; don't ask questions about shit that doesn't concern you; keep your money clean—no big purchases until after you've run your cut through the shop. You got that?"

"Yeah, I got that."

"Then let's get to work."

As we walked into the storage facility, my mind picked apart how naïve I must have come across. I was aware that Pop wasn't always on the up and up. Hell, I'd participated in some small-time shit while staying with the Cartwrights for six weeks every year. So, I wasn't completely clueless. I understood that this stuff happened. I just didn't know how or to what extent.

"Abbot," I said as he unlocked the door to a unit on the inside. He lifted his brow to let me know he was listening while he punched the code into an electronic padlock. "How?"

He lifted his head. "How what?"

"How do I clean it? Um…exactly?"

"Jesus, Slater." He shook his head, chuckling with amusement. "Do me a favour, will you? Don't ask any of these questions around the others."

"Will they take me off the job?"

He laughed a little harder, but I had no idea what was so funny. "Yeah, Sloane. They'd take you off the job," he said, opening the door to let me in a room about the size of a single-car garage. In the centre of the room was the safe, painted in camo-green that had scratched away a little at some point, showing the red underneath. The paint job was probably damaged while it was in transit from wherever they stole it from, but... *don't ask questions about shit that doesn't concern you...* Did the origin of this safe concern me? Probably not. I squashed the question as I walked around the solid-looking object.

"Why did that sound like sarcasm?" I asked instead.

"Because it *was* sarcasm. How the hell did you get to thirty-eight and have no clue how to cook the books? You worked with Trev this whole time. Are you saying he taught you nothing?"

I stopped, placing my hand on the top of the safe, the cool metal pressing against the warmth of my hand. It smelled like dirt in here. Dirt and cigarette ash. "He taught me how to be a locksmith." I squatted in front of the door and inspected the dial, turning it from side to side. "He always told me to keep my nose clean. Lost his shit when he found the stash of jewellery and crap that I'd collected when we used to go tourist trapping."

"I haven't been tourist trapping in years." He moved closer, his arms folded across his chest.

"It'd be weird if you did now, don't you think? It worked well when we were kids and got invited back to the caravans and holiday houses, but now..."

"I can get invited into caravans and holiday houses no problem."

The scoff came without me giving it permission. "As long as it's some hot young thing."

"Even guys. They wanna learn to surf, or they like having a beer with a local. It's easier than you think to get inside people's houses and steal their shit. The problem with tourist trapping was doing it on our home turf. Too many people learn your face and that's dangerous. You never shit where you eat, and you never keep the shit you take. Ever think that's why Trev lost his shit about finding that stuff?"

"So many uses for the word shit in only a couple of sentences." I smirked.

"I'm serious. When *we* say keep your nose clean, we aren't talking about walking the straight and narrow. We're talking about covering your arse and making sure no one can link you to the job once you've cleared out. Maybe he cracked it with you because you had a fucking stash of evidence. Everything gets liquidated, then you clean the cash by adding a little extra to your books each day. For you, maybe you add a few fake jobs like rekeying a door that doesn't exist. Or, when you do an actual job, you charge the customer one price and put another price in your books. That way, all the dirty money becomes legitimate and *your nose is clean.* Get it?"

I'd never thought about it like that before. "But why didn't he teach me how to finesse a safe when I asked him?" And was that why the business was struggling? Because I wasn't running fake jobs through the books?

Abbot shrugged. "I don't know, Sloane. Maybe he thought you were a dumbarse since he found you hoarding fucking evidence?" He pulled out another cigarette and lit up, stepping back so he wasn't blowing any of his exhale in my direction.

I sat back on my heels and thought for a moment. It made sense, but at the same time it didn't make sense at all. Pop had had years to teach me how to do the books and who his unsavoury clients were so I could keep things running when he was gone. But he had chosen not to, and I had no way of knowing if he was going to tell me everything before he died. *Ugh.* This was so messed up. I felt like I'd been doing everything wrong since Pop died.

Lookin' over your shoulder is no way to live, kid.

It was like I could hear his voice in my mind. He'd said that so often that I had to believe he *didn't* want me involved. Just like he kept me away from the Cartwrights for a reason, too. Abbot was wrong.

Standing up, I spun the dial with a dramatic flick. "I think you should get someone else to do this, Abbot. Pop didn't think I was a dumbarse. He was protecting me."

"From what exactly? Getting rich?"

"From prison. From people like you."

He ran his hand through his hair, shooting smoke from his nose in exasperation. "Now I'm insulted."

"That just makes it easier to say goodbye." I wiped my hands on the side of my pants and headed for the door.

"Whoa, whoa, Sloane Slater." Abbot caught me by the elbow, cigarette in the side of his mouth, the smoke curling up and causing him to squint one eye. "Not so fast."

"I made a mistake coming here, Abbot."

"No. You didn't."

"I'm disrespecting Pop. It doesn't sit right with me."

"What's so wrong about this? You're going to sit your cute little butt down in front of a safe and open the door. No one will find out, and you'll be two hundred and fifty thousand dollars richer at the end of it."

My mouth fell open. "That's more than double what you originally offered."

He pulled the cigarette from his mouth and rubbed at

the back of his head with his other hand. "Well, you were kinda supposed to haggle with me on that. Trev would have demanded more, so I start low and work my way up to the actual number. Negotiation one oh one."

"I see." A quarter of a million dollars to open a safe that hasn't been reported missing to the press. I pressed the toe of my worn-out sneaker into the concrete floor. I could do a lot with that amount of money. Make changes to the shop, advertise, fix up Lizzy, buy new sneakers…

"Please, Sloane. We don't have another safecracker we trust. Don't make me go back there and tell them I lost the only one we have."

Something about the pleading look in his eyes softened my resolve. *Two hundred and fifty thousand dollars.* The promise of a hefty chunk of cash melted it into a puddle on the floor.

"One job," I said, closing my eyes as I allowed the words to burst from my mouth. "I open that safe and then I leave and go about my life like a regular person, and you find someone else to do this shit for you in the future."

"I can make that happen," he said, his voice soft and his pillowy lips fighting a self-satisfied smile. I rolled my eyes as I reached up and pulled the cigarette from between his lips.

"Pop a mint, buddy. Your cigarette breath is killing me, and I'm not working with this stench filling up my nose. We're in an enclosed space."

He took the cigarette back and dropped it on the floor, squashing it beneath his foot. "Your wish is my command. Anything else I can do for your royal highness?"

I knew he was being sarcastic, but I answered anyway. "You can get coffee. I take mine white, with no sugar."

With a chuckle and a shake of his head, he placed his hand on the door. "Get to work, woman."

I saluted him before turning towards the safe. Two seconds later, I heard the lock tumble in the door. So much for trust.

"UM...I think you should come and look at this," I said, my voice shaking slightly as Abbot returned with two coffees and a bag of food. I'd removed the outer panel to the safe door while he was gone and was struggling with the sight in front of me.

Abbot placed his offerings on the top of a bank of filing cabinets against the wall and walked over to me. "What's up?"

"This isn't an old-fashioned anti-theft device. This is new."

He crouched down beside me, minty air blowing out of his lungs as he took in the sight before us. "What the fuck?"

"Most of these devices are about the size of my hand and only contain small vials of Chloropicrin. They were invented before drilling to open a safe was an option. Burglars would use a sledgehammer to knock the spindle off, or a crowbar to jimmy the door. That kind of forced entry would disrupt and crack the tubes, releasing the gas and sending the thief running." I spoke like I knew what I was saying, but I'd literally learned most of this information over my coffee this morning.

"But this is something else?" He indicated the flat glass casing that covered the entire midsection of the door. It was filled with the same noxious liquid, but it wasn't an old device leftover from the '20s.

"This is custom-built," I said. "Made specifically to prevent modern safecracking techniques. I'm surprised it didn't crack when you moved it. Wasn't it bolted down?"

"Yeah, but we used those crank levers that popped the bolts out of the floor. Super quiet and it saves us from breaking our backs. Plus, we saw the warning label, so we were super careful." He pointed to the sticker that said 'Caution. This safe is fitted with an anti-theft device.'

Closing my eyes, I spun the dial back and forth in my fingers, trying to see if I could feel any changes in the weight of the wheels. "The only way we're getting in is to figure out the code," I said. "I was hoping I could remove the vial and drill, but I can't without cracking the glass."

"You reckon you can figure the code?"

I opened my eyes and met his. "Eventually."

"What if we like, drain the chloro-stuff out of those vials?"

"How? The slightest bit of air will turn it into gas, and that shit doesn't just make you cry."

"OK. So what do we do?"

"I channel my inner Pop and do it by touch."

"How long is that going to take?"

"I don't know," I tell him honestly. "I've never done it before."

BY THE END of the day, I thought I had the first number range based on the gentle tap I was feeling between fifty-two and fifty-five. But there was no way to be sure until I could work out the other three wheels and try the sequence together.

Despite the way this looked in the movies, safe-cracking was not an easy thing. Only a handful of people could do it in less than an hour. Most took several, others took days. But when you understood the mechanics, it could be done. In time.

"Don't you two look picture-perfect together? You're just the right heights," Jasmine said when we returned to her place, her smile falling when she noticed our sullen expressions. "What's the problem?"

I opened my mouth to explain that I couldn't drill, and wasn't the finessing wizard Pop was when Abbot spoke for me.

"It's booby-trapped. A massive vial of tear gas. The dial locks up after every wrong turn, so it's going to take time for her to find the combination." He told a boldfaced lie so casually that even I almost believed it.

"Is there any way to disable it?" Jasmine looked at me for the answer and I shook my head truthfully.

"It's embedded in concrete. If we try to get it out, it'll crack the glass, then we won't be able to go near the thing without a professional cleaning crew, and that's gonna raise some flags." I read that a small vial would make a building uninhabitable for a week, so one that size could take a month to dissipate.

"Motherfuckers," she said, shaking her head as she stalked into the kitchen.

"Hey Abs. What's up?" a biker-looking dude said from behind the bench. He had dark hair and a big beard, and was in black denim and a white shirt with tattoos covering every available piece of skin on his arms and hands. I'd have found his presence alarming if it hadn't been for one thing: he was holding a palette knife in one hand while he turned a cake stand in the other, smoothing chocolate ganache over a twenty-centimetre tall cake. "Who's your friend?" the baking biker asked when he looked up and spotted me.

"This is Sloane. She's staying with us while we work out how to get that safe open without gassing ourselves."

"Hey Sloane," he said, placing his palette knife down as he stepped towards me. "I'm Breaker. Jasmine's fella."

"Nice to meet you." I smiled and shook his hand, a firm grip that pinched a little due to the fact he had some chunky silver rings adorning his fingers. "That cake looks great," I said of the creation he'd been icing.

"You think? I'm testin' out some flavour profiles for the weddin'. It's chocolate genoise soaked in raspberry sauce with a mousse fillin'. I love anythin' choc berry myself, but I wanna see what Ronnie and Kris reckon over it."

"Sounds amazing." I drooled at the thought.

"Kris'll eat anything," Abbot told him before grabbing my arm. "Come upstairs a minute."

Leaving Jasmine and Breaker to the cake, I followed Abbot up the stairs until we got into his room.

"What was that about?" I asked as soon as the door closed. "Why did you lie for me?"

He ran his hands through his hair and slumped into his chair. "I told you I'd tell them what they needed to hear. Jazz isn't always as cool as she seems. She doesn't always react well to bad news, so I thought it better if she was pissed at the safe owners and not at you."

"Who were the safe owners?" I tried, not really expecting an answer.

He shrugged. "That information is on a need-to-know basis."

Just as I thought. *Shit that didn't concern me.*

"Listen, I need to go back home. If this is going to take a while, I need some clothes, and I need to get someone to cover the shop." I had one employee who worked weekends so I wasn't on seven days a week. I had to hope he could cover completely until this job was done. I'd work something out.

"Sure," he said, his voice flat and his expression warring. "I'll take you out there tomorrow."

"I can go tonight."

He frowned. "Whatever. Fine." He stood up suddenly then swiped his keys from the bedside drawers. "Let's go then. We can stop and eat on the way." He stepped to push past me, but I blocked him with my hand to his chest.

"Are you pissed at me?"

"I'm tired."

"Then we can go tomorrow. I can wait."

Closing his eyes, he pressed his forefinger and thumb against the bridge of his nose. "No. Let's just go now. Get it out of the way."

"Are you sure?"

"Yes. Just...why did you want this job, Sloane? You

knew you weren't the same calibre as Trev but you acted like you were."

"Do you wish I wasn't here?"

"It's not that, it's just, the longer you're here, the closer you get to the family, the harder it is for you to leave." *Ouch.*

And here I was thinking they'd been *happy* to see me again. Guess I was wrong.

"I promise you that the moment this job is done, I'm out of here in a puff of smoke. I won't overstay."

"It's not even about that, it's just... Don't listen to Jasmine. She gets these fucked-up ideas in her head, and—" *Oh.*

"Is this about the picture-perfect comment?"

The softening of his expression was enough to confirm I was right.

"Worried I'll fall in love with you and refuse to go?" I scoffed, offended. "Don't flatter yourself. You and I are friends at best."

His eyes flashed. "You perv on all your friends?"

"If they look like you, hell yeah. But you can relax, I'm not planning to touch the merchandise. I know my place."

"Fine. Whatever." He let out his breath and raked at his hair again. "Let's just go and get your shit."

"Two-minute noodles OK?" I asked after rummaging through my barely stocked pantry for food since we drove straight through. His Jag was so smooth on the road that I was the one who fell asleep this time. Now I was starving.

"It's either that, or a tin of pea and ham soup with an ambiguous use-by date." I turned with the items in my hands and leaned against the counter, finding Abbot poking around my tiny flat, looking at the pictures on the walls.

"You're really into this triathlon thing, huh?"

I placed the soup and noodles on the bench and moved to stand beside him.

"That was at the Shepparton Challenge about five years ago," I said of the picture he was focused on. "We never win anything, but the participation medals are fun to pose with when you finish."

"Who's the dude?"

I turned away. "Which one? There are several in the picture."

"The one holding on to you like you belong to him."

"That's Mark. We were best friends in school."

"Were?"

I shrugged. "Things got complicated as we got older."

"Because you slept with him?"

"Something like that." I went back to the kitchen and started rummaging for a saucepan.

"Friendship between men and women never works out," he stated, following me in.

"I don't know." Filling the saucepan with water, I set it on the stove to heat. "Most of my friends are guys. Always have been."

"And how many of them did you end up sleeping with at some point?"

I picked up the noodles and looked at the pack like I needed the instructions. "A few. But that's not the point. Sex hasn't changed things. We're all still friends."

"Even Mark?"

I met his eyes. "I went to his wedding."

"And where did you sit? Up close to the bridal party, or somewhere in the back."

Closing my eyes for a second, I played with the pack between my fingers. "At the single's table." I'd been miserable and left early. When he called to ask where I was, I pretended that the champagne had given me a headache.

He released a burst of air from his nose. "In no mans land." He reached out and took the pack from my hands, opening it before dumping the noodle cake into the boiling water. Repeating it with the whole pack of five while he continue talking. "Despite what anyone says, men and women can't be friends without sex coming into it. It's basic biology. And once you do have sex, the friendship isn't the same anymore. You become something other than what you were."

"You sound like you're talking from experience." Picking up the flavour sachets, I shook them between my fingers before opening all five at once with a pair of scissors.

He made an 'eh' sound and bounced a shoulder while he focused on me tipping the powder over the noodles. "Every girl I try to be friends with, I end up fucking. Then, because I've never wanted a girlfriend, the whole thing gets messed up."

Scrunching the empty foil in my palm, I looked up to meet his eyes. "Then let me be the first girl you're actual friends with."

A smile crept across his face as he studied me. "With

the way you look at me? Nah, I'll end up fucking you too. Give it time."

He probably meant that as a joke, but it felt like an insult. Like he didn't want to have sex with me right now, but he'd probably cave after I wore him down. *Arsehole*.

"Don't do me any favours, Abbot," I snapped, collecting all the rubbish and dropping it into the bin. "I think my life will be just fine without a pity fuck from you."

I walked out of the kitchen and into my bedroom, grabbing my duffle and throwing random things into it—angry packing.

"What just happened in there?" Abbot asked, his huge frame filling my doorway.

I opened a drawer and grabbed a handful of underwear. "I shot you down, Abbot. That's what happened in there."

He held up his hands in surrender. "OK. Then why do I feel like you're pissed and I'm about to cop a face full of underwear?"

I looked at my hand and the collection of colourful knickers held in a ball, then threw them into my bag with a growl. "I'm *not* pissed."

Abbot laughed. "You're super pissed."

Opening the next drawer, I scooped up a pile of shirts and threw them in my bag too. "You know, I don't even want you to sleep with me. I am literally fine with being your friend. But you"—I shook my head and threw more shirts into my bag—"*you* act like I'm going to throw myself at you in desperation and you'll just fuck me, because why? It's rude to say no? You aren't God's gift to women, Abbot." I dumped the entire contents of the next drawer into my bag. "I can resist you."

When I looked up at him with fire in my eyes, there was nothing but mirth in his.

"Challenge accepted," he said.

I blinked. "Excuse me?"

"You heard me."

"You think you're going to tempt me into sleeping with you?"

"Not sleeping. Fucking."

"That's *not* going to happen."

He threw his head back and laughed. Then he walked out of the room, leaving me with an open mouth and an overflowing bag. *What the hell just happened?*

CHAPTER EIGHT
BATTLE OF WILLS

I ATE AVOIDING EYE CONTACT. Then I cleaned up our bowls with my head down. The entire time, I could feel him watching me with a smile fixed on his face.

"Want to make it even more interesting?" he asked as he took the bowls from the strainer and dried them.

"You know, I'm really not interested. How about you just put me back in the friend zone where I belong?"

"Who said you belong in the friend zone? With that arse?" He shook his head, blatantly staring at it. "You're top shelf."

I sighed. "Abbot, this is stupid. We're too old for silly games, and this is a conflict of interest. Never mix business with pleasure."

"So you admit that fucking me would bring you pleasure?"

I almost laughed. Of course fucking him would bring me pleasure. I was wet just having this conversation, but there was no doubt in my mind that sleeping with him would be a terrible idea. He was a criminal, for fuck's sake. I had history with his family and I was *trying* to maintain some sort of dignity around them. If they found out I was fucking Abbot it would look...I don't know...*desperate*? *Sad*? Like I couldn't get a brother closer to my age so I went after a younger one. *Ugh*. This screamed complicated, and turned on or not, it wasn't happening.

"Abbot." I said his name like a sigh. "I just want to do my job and get paid so I can get back to my life. I don't want to complicate it."

"I thought you said that men and women can be friends and have sex without complications."

"You're twisting my words."

He leaned closer. "I'm seducing you with logic."

A laugh burst from my chest, and I pushed him back. "No."

"Come on," he said. "We'll make a bet to make it fun. Just two friends trying to get into each other's pants."

"Uh, I won't be trying to get into your pants."

"Liar."

"You're so confident." I laughed. "Why don't you tell me how this bet would work? I'll see if I'm tempted."

"Well, you like competition, right? Consider this a challenge like one of your triathlons, except it's an exercise in willpower. You have to resist me, but I can't just take you—not that I'd do that, anyway. You'll have to give yourself to me willingly."

"You think you're that good?" I folded my arms, grinning because this was crazy. "OK. What are the terms? Besides sex, of course."

He thought for a moment, leaning back and folding his arms across his chest. "Timeline: I have until you open the safe to get you to open your legs." I rolled my eyes.

"And what happens if you don't succeed in tempting my knees apart?"

He grinned as I matched his level of crassness. "Then I double your money."

"You're going to pay me double *not* to have sex with you? Five hundred thousand?" I laughed, disbelieving.

"Absolutely."

"There is no way I'm fucking you now."

"Sloane, come on. I'm irresistible."

With a scoff, I shifted my hands to my hips. "Whatever, dude. What happens if your allure is too much for me and I cave?"

"Then you work for free."

My mouth fell open. There was no way I was giving up that money for a fuck. But if he was willing to pay me double to give him blue balls, then I was all for that. "You're on," I said, holding out my hand to shake his.

"I'm gonna be unrelenting, Slater."

"Do your worst, Cartwright. I can take it."

He grinned until the lone dimple popped in his right cheek. "You're so gonna lose," he said as he wrapped his large hand around my own, the warmth of his touch sending a heated jolt to the depth of my stomach.

"I don't think you understand quite how competitive I am, Abbot. Losing isn't an option."

"You've got a shelf covered in participation medals out there that says otherwise."

A laugh burst past my lips. I could pay that comment, but it didn't mean he was going to win. That shelf was a testament to my staying power. Quitters didn't get medals at all.

Gorgeous or not, Abbot Cartwright was *not* getting into my pants. He just gave me half a million reasons to buy a really complicated belt.

"HOW LONG DO you think opening this safe will take?" Abbot asked the next day when we were back in the warehouse at Geelong. We'd spent the night at my place and the morning getting all of my affairs in order before hitting the road. Not once did Abbot touch me, or even make a lewd remark after our conversation the night before. That was strange considering he was so adamant it was game on before we went to bed. But maybe after sleeping on it, he'd changed his mind and was going to call it off? Bummer. I already missed the five hundred thousand.

Glancing up from the notepad in my hand, I slid the pencil behind my ear and gave Abbot my full attention. "I watched a guy on YouTube who worked on this same model. He probably had the same level of experience as me, and it took him almost a month. So anywhere from a few days to a few weeks, I guess."

"A month." He nodded slowly, his lips pursed in thought. "OK, I can work with that. But, I think we should set some extra ground rules."

Ground rules. "About the safe?" My heart picked up as my mouth went a little dry. Maybe he wasn't calling the bet off after all.

"Quit being so facetious. You know I'm talking about our deal. Unless of course you want to back out."

"I'm not backing out," I said quickly, pulling the pencil from behind my ear. "What kind of ground rules are you thinking?" I scribbled some notes onto a pad of paper, hiding the waver in my voice with my concentration.

"Let's see... None of this touches my family. I don't want Jasmine getting it in her head that we're a thing." He was so bloody panicked over his mother. *Such a commit-ment-phobe.* It was like having a conversation with Mark all over again.

"That's not going to be a problem for me since I'm not the one chasing you. But I get it. No flirting around your family—especially your mother since she's got the wedding bug and wants all of her sons married and producing babies," I said, leaning closer to the dial as I wriggled it back and forth, trying to find the point where the hammer stopped dragging along the second wheel.

"Exactly. And I'm not about that life, so we keep this low-key."

"Gotcha. Secret flirting. What else?"

"No flirting with anyone else either. If Jazz thinks you aren't into me, she's probably gonna try set you up with Toby. That can't happen. I need your attention on me."

"But, what if Toby is my soulmate?" I asked distract-edly, teasing him as my twists of the dial got smaller and smaller and I strained my senses. I was so close to finding that number range, I just needed—

"Abbot," I shrieked as I was lifted off my low seat and planted on the top of the safe like seventy kilos of human was nothing to him. His arms caged around me either side as he leaned in, his chest brushing against mine, my legs spread either side of him. "This does not count as me opening my legs for you."

"You are *not* into Toby," he insisted, his light eyes boring into mine as our bodies pressed closer than they ever had before. My skin hummed from the pleasure of our mingled heat, my pulse quickening. "Right?"

His breath washed over me, and my body screamed, "Kiss me!" but I just swallowed and shook my head. *Not since he flat out rejected me.*

"Say it, Sloane."

"I'm not into Toby." *Anymore.* My words came out high-pitched, defensive. Nothing had ever happened between any of the Cartwright brothers and me. But that didn't mean I hadn't *wanted* something to happen. We were teenagers with raging hormones and I may have developed a crush on the quiet and controlled Toby. The feelings were never reciprocated and mine had long since faded. But still, it happened.

"No flirting with any of my brothers." He added that addendum to the rule then stepped back and turned away, running his hands through his hair as he blew out his breath.

"OK." I slid off the top of the safe, also running my hands through my hair. That was…hot, scary, *intense,* hot. Now the air was sexually charged, and I was shaking.

"You might want to lay off those kind of sudden movements in future," I said as I sat back in front of the safe, clenching my fists to calm the rush of hormones. "We don't want to risk cracking the vials."

He didn't respond for a few seconds, but when he did, it was with something I wasn't expecting. "No masturbating."

My fingers slipped and the dial spun so much it reset. "Excuse me?"

"No relieving yourself in any way unless it's with me."

I stared at him, wide eyes. "Fine. But you don't get to jack off either. Or mess around with anyone else until after I go home."

"OK. You *have* to spend time with me."

"Like on dates?"

"Kind of. I have to be given the opportunity to woo you. Time alone without that safe as a distraction."

"OK. But for this challenge to be won, there has to be actual naked sex. If we start messing around and I come to my senses, it doesn't count."

"If you orgasm while we're messing around, it counts."

"I can control myself," I whispered.

With dark, sexy eyes, he released a loaded breath. "You know what I think, Sloane?" I swallowed as I waited for him to fill me in. "I reckon you're so wet just thinking about me touching you that your clit is throbbing."

My eyes lowered, catching the impressive bulge pushing against his jeans. *Two years is too long to go without sex.* I had visions of him putting me on the safe again and fucking me so hard I screamed. *Pulse, pulse, pulse.* That no masturbating rule was going to be harder than I thought.

"Well"—I let out my breath before turning my attention back to the safe—"too bad you're never gonna find out."

Abbot chuckled then pulled his cigarettes from his pocket and shook one out. "Never is a strong word, Ms Slater."

"Maybe. But those things you keep puffing on make it easier for me to maintain my resolve."

"I've been chewing gum."

"Doesn't get the smell out of your clothes."

Leaning back against the wall casually, he slid the cigarette back into the pack and crushed it in his hand. "Thanks for the tip."

It wasn't a tip. A man going through nicotine withdrawals was distracted. If anything, it was a strategy. "You think you can quit just like that?"

"I can do *anything* I set my mind to." Of that, I had no doubt.

This game was going to be an erotic battle of wills. And after two years of little to no male attention, it was also going to be a hell of a lot of fun for me to be chased by a delectable specimen of manhood like Abbot Cartwright. I was actually looking forward to watching him squirm. *How fucking exciting.*

CHAPTER NINE
THINK OF THE MONEY

OPENING my eyes to the darkened room, I let out a sigh. I was really going to have to get over my inability to sleep anywhere but in my own bed. Exhaustion was not going to open that safe.

"You know, I have something that will help you sleep."

The fuck?

"What are you doing in here?" I yelped, pushing up on my elbows to find Abbot sitting on chair in the corner of the room, the bag I'd rested on it now sitting open on the floor. *How long has he been there?*

"Thought I heard moaning. Needed to make sure you were holding up your end of the bargain."

"Clearly, I am. What about you?"

"I have left several hard-ons unanswered during the course of the night. I'm doing fine."

"Hmmm. So now you're just watching me sleep?"

"That was sleeping?"

"Not really. I don't sleep much when I'm not home."

"Could that be because you were dreaming about me?"

I laughed. "Who knows? I can't remember."

"You know, sex can help with sleep."

The corner of my mouth quirked as I sat up higher, my forearms resting on my knees. "Can it now?"

"Yeah. One good orgasm and you could be out like a light."

"And let me guess, you want to be the guy to help me get there?"

He held his hands to the side in a magnanimous gesture. "I wouldn't say no."

Shaking my head, I laughed it off. "Nice try, Romeo. But you can go back to your own room now," I said, lying back and rolling to the side.

"I just put the idea of orgasming your way to a good night's rest in your head. I'm not leaving. I'm policing your pussy." *Policing my pussy?*

The man definitely had a way with words.

I rolled my eyes. "I promise not to twiddle my nub, hand over my heart," I assured him. "But I do need to sleep, otherwise I won't be able to work tomorrow."

"That actually works in my favour by giving me an extra day."

"Abbot," I whined, sounding like a little girl. "Go. *Away.*"

He chuckled and stood. "I'll listen at the door then."

"Oh my God." I picked up a pillow and threw it at him while he laughed some more.

Then he was gone, and I was alone, my eyes straying to the door and wondering if he was actually there. "Abbot?" I whispered. *Nothing.* Hmm. Now all I could think about was sex. Which I needed to quit doing if I was going to win this bet and a nice chunk of money. But waking up to a god-like creature watching me sleep and offering his services…it was tempting to say the least. It had been too long since I'd had a man's hands on my body, and something told me that being with Abbot would be unlike any sexual experience I'd had before. He oozed sexual confidence. He knew how to make a woman scream.

Rolling onto my back, I moaned out of frustration and desire as I covered my face with my hands and tried to ignore the heat pooling between my legs.

My door burst open, scaring me into a sitting position. "What the fuck, Abbot?" I clutched my chest.

"You moaned."

"I *groaned.*"

He moved his head from side to side, his expression contemplative, tense. "That's it. I'm sleeping in here tonight."

I opened my mouth to object, but when he reached behind his head and pulled his shirt from his body, I was at a loss for words. Then he dropped the shirt and hooked his thumbs in the waist of his track pants and I found my voice.

"Stop right there, mister!" I held my hand out, blocking my view from his waist down.

He paused and met my eyes, a mischievous glint in his. "It's nothing you haven't seen already, Slater. You already know I sleep naked."

"Not in my bed you don't. Especially when I didn't even invite you."

"New rule: we share a bed." *What*?

"You can't just add rules whenever you feel like it."

"Sure, I can. We're playing with *my* money."

Five hundred thousand.

"Fine then," I said, collecting the extra pillows to make a wall that would sit between us. Two could play at this game.

"Seriously?"

"Yep." I tucked the blankets around it so he couldn't slide underneath it. "And you keep your clothes on. I don't want to see a scrap of skin."

"Does this bother you?" He grinned as he made his pecs dance. I struggled not to smile.

"Not at all. I'm just wondering what Jasmine would think if she found you in my bed completely naked. I mean, it'll be hard enough explaining it if you're fully clothed. But naked..." I shook my head. "If you want to risk her jumping to conclusions then getting carried away, go right ahead and strip." I shrugged, trying to act nonchalant in an effort to get him to cover up. My hormones *could not* take lying beside him naked. I was likely to sleep-fuck the man.

"I see your point." *Thank God.* The commitment phobia was strong in this one.

He moved towards his shirt near the door. "So, that's your only objection? If there was no risk of Jazz walking in here, I could sleep naked? You'd have no problem with it?"

With a heavy gulp, I nodded. "I'm just trying to follow the rules you set out. You know, keep it low-key."

He narrowed his eyes just a touch as he nodded. "Yeah. Yeah, I totally get that."

"So you'll put your shirt back on and we can explain it away. Like, we fell asleep watching a movie or something."

"That could work. Or…" He reached a hand behind his back and flicked the lock on the door. "Now we won't get any unexpected visitors." *Oh shit.*

As he stalked towards the bed, his thumbs at his waist-band like a stripper in *Magic Mike,* I tried to make my eyes look away, but they wouldn't comply. I had to see this. With a dramatic whoosh, his pants were on the floor and he was standing stark naked beside the bed, his hands on his hips and a pleased-as-punch grin on his face.

"Nice cock." I gulped. It was *huge.* Way bigger than it seemed when I'd watched him dress the other day. Way bigger than any other I'd seen before. *Dear God, give me the strength to resist this man.*

He made a show of looking at his third arm like he'd never really thought about it before. "Thanks." Then he flopped onto the bed beside me, his dick bouncing with the impact. He practically destroyed my pillow wall.

I pursed my lips and fixed it up again, trying to keep my eyes anywhere but on him. He was getting comfortable and had barely covered his package with the blanket.

Pulse, pulse, pulse went my clit.

"Goodnight, Sloane," he said, the smile evident in his voice. He was obviously incredibly pleased with himself.

"Night, Abbot." *I wonder what a cock that size would feel like inside me…* I cleared my throat, trying to ignore the buzzing beneath my skin. Then I rolled away and pulled the blankets up to my neck. "Sweet dreams."

"Oh, I plan to dream all right." He let out a contented sigh, his breathing evening out within thirty seconds. *How the hell is he sleeping right now?*

I was seriously shocked at his ability to pass out when-ever he wanted to. I, on the other hand, felt like I was never going to sleep again. *I need to get laid so bad right now.*

Think of the money, Sloane. Think of the money.

I closed my eyes and tried to will myself to sleep.

Pulse, pulse, pulse.

CHAPTER TEN
THE DEVIL'S DOORBELL

THERE WAS OBVIOUSLY a point where my body gave in to exhaustion and let me sleep because the next time I opened my eyes, it was seven o'clock and Abbot wasn't next to me anymore. *Where the hell did he go?*

Sitting up, I rubbed my hands over my face and tried to tell myself that the feeling in the pit of my stomach wasn't disappointment. Did I really expect him to be here in the morning? And what would happened if he was? Cuddling? No. Even if something *had* happened between us, he didn't seem the cuddling type. I was just sexually frustrated and craving human connection. It was dangerous playing this kind of game after an extended dry spell. But, there was five hundred thousand reasons *not* to lose.

As always, I turned to exercise to ease my frustration. A long run would burn off the excess energy Abbot helped create.

Digging through my bag, I pulled on a sports crop bra, a racer-backed singlet, and a pair of three-quarter leggings.

Then I grabbed a zip-front jacket before pulling my hair into a ponytail and adding socks and shoes.

The room I was using was just off the rumpus room that opened out onto the in-ground pool via two big sliding doors. Beyond the rumpus was a kitchen and what I recalled was an office or some sort of study with a hallway beside that leading to the stairs and the formal lounge and dining areas.

I headed for the kitchen first, needing some water and a snack before I set off. The soft glow of the light above the stove guided my way, but it was the figure standing at the island bench that caught my attention. Abbot. Shirtless. With wet hair. *Ow. My ovaries.*

"You smell like the sea," I said, catching a whiff of him as I moved past and opened the fridge.

He moved so quietly that I didn't realise he was behind me until he spoke. "And you smell like"—he dipped his head so his nose was in my neck then inhaled, sending shivers of unfulfilled longing through me until he lifted his head—"peanut butter." My hormones ground to a screeching halt.

"What?" I placed my hand against his face and pushed him away. "You are *terrible* at this."

He laughed, leaning back against the bench and grabbing an apple from the fruit bowl. "I happen to love peanut butter."

I grabbed a water and wrinkled my nose. "Doesn't mean I want to smell like it. Yuck."

"You're adorable when you make that face."

I rolled my eyes. "Put a shirt on."

"Take yours off." He made his pecs dance again.

I laughed. I couldn't help it. The guy was annoyingly adorable.

"I'm going for a run."

"That's a shame. I was going to ask if you wanted to join me for a shower."

"Does this actually work for you? The teasing. The lewd suggestions and the stripping. It's like you're in high school."

He grinned and took a bite out of his apple. "And you keep blushing like a school girl."

"I do not," I objected, feeling the heat in my cheeks even as I said it. I wasn't fooling anybody. Everything about him did things to my body.

With a chuckle, he walked away. "Enjoy your run, Sloane."

I let out my breath. I was going to run until I was too exhausted to even contemplate sex.

MY LEGS TOOK me all the way to the beach, along the shoreline, farther still until I saw a familiar blue house with a few familiar figures heading towards it with surf-boards under their arms.

"Hey," I said, a touch out of breath as I stopped near them.

"Oh, hey Sloane," Ronnie said, smiling my way. "Where's Abbot?"

I shrugged. "Back at the house, I guess."

"I'm surprised they let you out without an escort," Alesha said. Then Sam nudged her with his elbow and they exchanged looks that held enough meaning that they didn't need words.

"Why would I need an escort?" I asked, curious. *Had they been talking about me behind my back?*

"You don't," Kristian said. "Leesh is just worried you won't know your way back to the house."

"Oh, I've been here enough times to remember. But thanks, mate," I said, nudging her on the arm. "Sweet of you to be concerned."

She gave me a smile and a chin lift.

"How's the job going?" Sam asked. "I heard there's a problem."

"Yeah. A big one. But we're getting there. Abbot is bored out of his mind babysitting me. It isn't really a spectator sport." *Such lies.*

"You know," Ronnie started, tucking her blonde curls behind her ear. "If you're still around this weekend, we're having a sort of combined bachelor-bachelorette slash rehearsal dinner thingy. You should come."

I touched my head nervously. "Ah, I don't know. I don't want to intrude."

"You won't be. It'll be fun. Just food and drinks and a run-through of the ceremony. Mainly food and drinks, though."

"Um… OK. Well, if I'm still here, sure."

Ronnie beamed. "Great. You wanna come in for coffee or something? Are you done with your run?"

I looked between all their faces, completely open and willing to have me along. It was lovely to be invited, but still, I felt out of place. Twenty-one years had been too long, and I didn't fit in with the group anymore. Just like back home, everyone had grown and partnered off while I just stayed the same, single Sloane.

"I've still got a way to go. It was nice seeing you though," I said before saying goodbye and jogging off. I wasn't sure if they thought I was rude for not wanting to join them, but it just didn't feel right. Especially without Abbot there. Even discounting our bet, I was more comfortable around him than I was with the others. He was like an old pair of shoes that still fit. Everyone else was... different. It would take a while for me to feel welcome around them again.

Slowing to a walk as I hit the driveway of the Cartwright house, I found Jasmine sitting with Breaker and Toby as I went through the gate to enter by the pool. Toby lifted a hand and smiled.

"Morning," I said brightly, my body feeling well worn and heavy after exercise.

"Abbot's not with you?" Jasmine asked with a smile that didn't touch her eyes.

"He came surfing with me this morning," Toby said.

"Is he missing, or do I need a guard?" I asked as I picked up the water bottle I'd left behind and took a sip. It was weird that everyone kept asking after Abbot. Was I no longer trusted to walk around on my own?

"Abbot's inside," Toby said without answering my question. *Is he dismissing me?* Wouldn't be the first time.

"You remember the rules, don't you, Sloane," Jasmine enquired, her eyes dropping down then lifting up to take me in in my entirety. "They haven't changed much in the time you've been gone."

"Of course." No talking about what goes on in the house. No inviting anyone back without permission. There were more, but it basically equated to 'keep your fucking mouth shut, or else'.

"Then we shouldn't have any problems that require an escort."

"None that I can think of." I gave her a tight smile, memories of that final summer becoming more present in my mind. "If it's fine with you, I'll go grab a shower before we head out to the warehouse." I was also hoping I could wash off the creeping feeling that was climbing up my spine. I'd forgotten how filled with secrets this house was.

"Don't let me keep you," she said with a wave of her hand—like a queen dismissing her subject. *I could see where Toby got it from.*

It was so strange, as I walked away from her obediently, I felt just like a teenager again. My mind conflicted as I recalled snippets of conversations, instructions from Pop, grooming from Jasmine. She'd wanted to teach me how to be like them, train me the way she'd trained her boys. Pop had always refused. He'd trusted me not to get involved but I'd gotten involved anyway. *What did he expect?* He left me here each year, knowing the kind of people the Cartwrights were. From what I understood, he and Jasmine ran together back in the day, before Jasmine's husband was arrested over a job gone wrong. They'd disbanded and gone to ground after he was caught, changed the way they did things but always stayed in touch. They had trust. But even that seemed to waiver when it came to me and my future in the 'family business'. I often questioned myself over that stash he'd found. It was stuff I'd never want for myself. Girly things like jewellery and perfume. It made no sense that I kept it. I *knew* I wasn't supposed to have it, and I didn't even hide it well. Maybe I'd wanted him to catch me. Maybe, the guilt over Nate going to juvie made *me* want to get caught. Because I had deserved to get caught, too. I was the one who taught him to pick locks, after all. If I hadn't done that, he wouldn't have been able to steal that car. *Ugh.* Who knew what I was thinking. Teenage motives didn't always make sense to adult minds, and I was incredibly confused at that time of my life. I was angry all the time and lashed out at the people around me, often doing things that were out of character and I later regretted. Things like throwing myself at Toby. I stopped for a moment and shook my head; I didn't even want to deal with that memory.

Pushing the past out of my mind, I headed for the linen cupboard in search of a towel. When I returned, voices from the three outside filtered through the open back door, clear as a bell.

"You know we'll need her on this next job too," Breaker said. "We won't get that transport emptied without someone like her on board."

"She needs to get the safe open first," Jasmine said, sounding unimpressed. *Jesus. I'm doing my best.*

"Give her a chance," Toby responded. "It's her first job for us, and it's a bloody hard one." *First and only job.* Abbot obviously hadn't relayed that information yet.

"Trev didn't train her well enough."

"Are you surprised?"

I wondered if they knew I could hear while I took quiet steps towards my room, turning the handle without sound and slipping inside. I hated hearing people talk about me.

As far as I was concerned their opinions of me weren't any of my business.

"Are you sneaking in so I don't find out you're home?"

Holy fuck!

Abbot. I spun around so fast that our noses collided and we both reeled backwards, clutching our faces and groaning.

"What are you trying to do to me?" he groused, dropping to sit on the edge of the bed.

"Me? What are *you* doing? You shouldn't be in here when they're all outside. You are being the *opposite* of low-key?"

"Oh, I totally fixed that."

"How."

"Told Jasmine you're not into dudes."

I stopped blinking. "You told your mother I was gay?"

He shrugged. "She had that matchmaking look in her eye. I had to do something."

"So you told her I was a lesbian." I rolled my eyes and dropped the towel on the chair Abbot had been sitting in the night before.

"Do you have something against lesbians?" he asked slowly, narrowing his eyes.

"What? No! Love is love. I just—hang on, why the hell am I justifying myself to you? You *lied* to your mother. Again."

Giving me that boyish laugh of his that took me back to happier times in this house, he reached out and grabbed my hand, pulling until I was sitting beside him.

"Don't be mad, Sloane. I promise I only did it for your protection."

"How has being gay ever protected a single person in this world?"

"Where my family is concerned it's for the best."

I pressed my lips together, unimpressed. "Explain to me why."

"I can't. So you just need to trust me when I tell you I had good intentions."

He kept his eyes on mine, the contact so strong and sincere that I had no choice but to believe him. He made me melt.

"OK. I trust you. But I still won't be sleeping with you," I said, standing up, wickedness entering my mind. "Especially since I'm into girls now. Such a shame, really." I pouted as I unzipped my jacket and started peeling off my tank so I was just in my sports bra and leggings. "We could have had so much fun." I slung my clothes over my shoulder and stood with my hand on my hip.

"Sloane." His voice thickened as he stared at my midriff. "You have *abs*."

"I know," I said breezily, twisting from side to side because I was damn proud of them. "Must be a *lesbian* thing." I gave him a wink then walked into the bathroom and locked the door, a massive grin on my face.

"No ringing the devil's doorbell, Slater," he called out before I flicked the shower on.

Devil's doorbell? I laughed to myself as I stripped down to nothing, catching sight of my naked body in the bathroom mirror. *Since when did I ever flaunt this?* I'd always thought myself so boyish—wide shoulders, long arms and legs, a chest that was barely there. And because I trained so hard, my muscles were defined and strong. I had *never* felt sultry in any way, especially given I'd always been one of the guys. But just now, watching Abbot bite his lip and resist touching? I'd felt...attractive. *Sexy.*

I placed my hands over my face to muffle my laugh. This thing between us might just be a game that wasn't leading anywhere, but *my God* it was *fun*. I hadn't felt desired in a very long time, and Abbot's reaction to my body felt pretty fucking good. *I* felt pretty fucking good, and I was really thankful for that.

CHAPTER ELEVEN
WRONG BROTHER

"COME ON. We need to take a break," Abbot said, taking me by the shoulders and pulling me away from the safe. It was already Friday. I'd been at this safecracking thing for almost a week now, and I was fairly sure I had the number ranges narrowed enough that I could start trying combinations soon. Thank God, because turning a dial back and forth all day was starting to send me cross-eyed crazy, even though I was so close I could taste it.

"I'm close, Abbot. Please."

"I have been desperate to hear those words come out of your mouth, but that's *not* how I imagined them."

I turned around to face him, a smile on my face. "You just don't quit, do you?" I'd managed to keep my hands to myself even though he continued to sleep beside me, naked as the day he was born. I was getting good at closing my eyes or looking away just as he dropped his pants to keep the temptation to a minimum. But it was hard. *So hard.*

Especially in the mornings.

He lifted a hand and brushed a few wayward strands of hair away from my face. "You should probably just give in. Put us both out of our misery."

I had to fight closing my eyes, because his touch felt ridiculously nice, and I wanted to lean into him. He'd been in my space all week with his teasing and innuendos. It was childish and relentless, yet oh so welcome. I loved his hands on my skin, his eyes on my body and his words in my ears. It would have been so easy to lift up on my toes and plant a kiss on that gorgeous mouth of his, fuck him against the wall or on the dusty floor of the storage unit. I'd thought and dreamt about it enough times that it was seriously tempting. But so was half a million dollars.

I didn't care how hot the guy was, no cock was worth losing out on that amount of coin. *I'll go bankrupt without it.*

"You've never had to work this hard for a girl in your life, have you?" I asked, placing my hand against his chest as a barrier of sorts. "I'll bet they usually throw themselves at you, big breasts and big lips, desperate to turn the rich boy's head."

"I like all kinds of breasts. It's the nipples that are the fun part." His eyes lowered to the area where my breasts should be, so small that even I forgot I had them some-times. "And from the way yours like to bud up and press through your shirt, I reckon they're real sensitive. I'll bet that if I placed my hand right here"—he held his hand about a centimetre away from my chest without touching—"and rolled them between my fingers, you'd whimper and squirm and beg me to pull them with my teeth."

Please tell me I didn't just gasp. It was getting harder not to react as he got bolder. He knew I was turned on. But

I was stronger than that. Stronger than my impulses. *I hope.*

"You know, I think a bit of sunshine will do us good," I said as I took in a breath, forcing my voice to be chirpy instead of deep and breathy.

Abbot grinned and slid a piece of nicotine gum into his mouth, chewing as he kept his eyes locked on mine. He was really taking this no smoking thing seriously. I gave him props for that. *He even had a sexy chew.*

"Then let's go. I'll buy you lunch."

We bought sandwiches from a little cafe then headed to Geelong Botanic Gardens to eat and stretch our legs on my request since I'd been sitting hunched over for too many hours to count.

It was pretty there, the sun offering a gentle warmth on an autumn day, heating my skin and making the world seem more alive and colourful.

"My neck is killing me," I complained as I dropped my empty packaging in a nearby bin then pressed my fingers into the tight muscle to relieve it. "I think I'll be glad not to see another safe again once I'm finished with this one."

Abbot dropped his rubbish in the bin along with mine then gestured for me to move closer to him. "Come here. I'll fix it for you."

He led me to a bench seat then stood behind me, picking up my long hair and sweeping it to one side. "Why do I feel like I'm about to get a dick pressed into me?" I joked as the breeze drifted over my skin, tickling.

"Relax. This is *not* a seduction attempt." Then he pressed his fingers into my trapezius and I just about howled in pain. "Breathe," he said with a calm voice.

"Oxygen helps, tensing up and holding your breath doesn't."

"Can't I just stretch?" I grunted as his fingers found every knot across my shoulders and up my neck then proceeded to press directly into them. I'd had massages before, but they'd been relaxing. This was torture.

"Stop being a baby. Surely you've done some sort of sports therapy where they do this."

"Nope. I've never had an injury."

"You're lucky then," he said, just as I felt the knot he was working on click and release, a warmth spreading all across my shoulders and causing a slight moan to fall from my lips.

"OK. You know what you're doing," I said as I relaxed into his hands and felt all the tightness in my muscles drift away.

"I'm glad you noticed." His fingers lightened their touch then he moved my hair to the opposite side and worked on my other shoulder. I was grunting in pain again.

"Where'd you learn to do that?" I asked when he was done and took a seat beside me.

"Remedial massage. I did a course when I was, like, twenty-three, I think. Thought I might get out of the family business, do things my own way for a bit. But that didn't go down so well, so I dropped out and I'm still here. Lucky you, huh?" He stretched his arms out across the back of the bench as he relaxed into his position.

"That really sucks. Do you regret dropping out?"

He bounced a shoulder. "I dunno. I mean, I thought it would be a good job at the time. But I like the flash cars and the easy life I have now. This life gets in your blood, you know?"

I nodded, making a thoughtful sound because even after all the years of walking the straight and narrow, I'd slipped easily back into life around the Cartwrights. It was like a song I hadn't heard for years but still remembered the lyrics to. Bad notes and all.

"I want to tell you something," I said after a while of watching birds pick for bugs in the grass. My mind was filled with memories of the past becoming clearer each day. It made my actions feel more current, and I knew I was going to have to deal with them by talking to Toby. But, I needed to talk to Abbot first. This thing between us was fun, and it worked because we were being honest with each other. I didn't feel right continuing this without coming clean.

"I'm listening." He turned so he was giving me his full attention.

A tightness crept up my throat and I cleared it away so I could speak. "Do you remember my last summer with you?"

"I remember all the summers." The fondness in his gaze made my stomach flicker.

"God, you're sweet when you want to be," I said under my breath. I was glad he'd made it clear he didn't want anything long-term because I'd struggle not to fall for him otherwise.

He grinned. "What about this last summer?"

I took a deep breath for courage because this was something in our shared history that I'd been keeping to myself. "I was kind of fucked up that year. You guys were pulling that credit card scam."

"The one where we copied them with a strip reader."

"Yeah. I was scared of getting caught, so I refused to be a part of it."

"You were *scared*? I thought you were just trying to get with Toby since you kept getting him to take you to a movie while the rest of us covered for you." I sat up a little straighter. Wait. *Did he know?*

"Um…" I touched my forehead, slightly rattled by his perception of things. "I was scared of going to juvie. Felt guilty over teaching Nate how to pick locks and, I don't know, there was a lot of shit going on back home with my mum and..." I frowned then looked at him, distracted by the plainness of his statement. "You really thought I was trying to get with Toby?" *I wasn't, well, at first…*

He shrugged. "We all did. You kept going off with him and whispering together. It was obvious something was going on."

"And that doesn't make you feel weird pursuing me now?"

"Why would it? It's not like anything happened between you two."

Oh my God. He knew. *Fucking Toby.*

"What makes you so sure?" I said each word carefully.

He ran a hand through his hair. "Because Tobes is a monk. Always has been. He warned us all away from you the moment we hit puberty. And there was no way he was going against his own rule. He's rigid as fuck about honour and stuff like that. Well, unless your name is Holland."

"What?"

"Point is, Toby *never* mixes business with pleasure, and any relationship he's ever had has been in secret. I didn't even know if he liked girls until he kissed Holland and he and Nate had a massive blue over it."

"He *kissed* Holland."

"Yeah. It's like the *one* time Toby showed feelings for anything other than his dog."

I narrowed my eyes. "So, he never told you anything about me?"

He mirrored my expression. "No. Why? Are you saying something *happened* between you two?"

"No." I practically shouted the word. "Absolutely nothing happened."

"Then why all the questions? Did you *want* something to happen? Wait. Do you *still* want something with him now?"

"No." I grabbed his hand. "Absolutely not. But...I did kind of embarrass myself in front of him."

"Does this embarrassment have anything to do with why you left and never came back?"

I nodded, rubbing at my forehead because I really didn't like reliving this memory. But I needed to get it off my chest after holding on to it for so long. "I should give you some context first."

"I'm listening."

"So, when I arrived in Torquay that year, I'd been fighting with my mum, and I was in shit with Pop over finding that stash. The idea of getting caught felt all too real for me, and I couldn't deal with that stress on top of everything else. So, I told Toby I wanted out the first night I was there, and he said he understood, that he hated the life too and offered to help me so Jasmine wouldn't get the shits over me not pulling my weight. While you guys covered for us, we kicked back and had a lot of conversations that summer. We grew close and I ended up confiding in him about what happened with my mum." I paused and shook my head, hating how pitiful this made me sound, but it was important to explain my state of mind. "I hated her so much at the time. You see, I had never had a boyfriend before because I was always the friend and never the girl-friend. But when she showed up that year, I was getting serious with my first one. She made a big deal about it and we talked, like, I don't know, how best girlfriends would talk, you know? Giggling and shit, sharing details." I closed my eyes, feeling sick as the words hit the tip of my tongue. "She fucked him."

"She *what*?"

I pressed the pads of my fingers together. "My mother had sex with my eighteen-year-old boyfriend."

"Fucking hell." He breathed out the words as he leaned back against the seat. "Did you catch them?"

I nodded, refusing to cry over something from so long ago, but it still hurt. Even after I'd forgiven them. "I was messed up when I got here, and I mistook Toby's under-standing and friendship for something else. It wasn't even that I was super into him, I just wanted a guy to choose me for a change. So…I threw myself at him and Pop basically saw everything." I said the last part really quickly because it was the most embarrassing.

"That's what he and Jazz were fighting about?"

I nodded, feeling shitty. "Toby told me he couldn't see me in that way because I was more of a sister, and I lost my shit, crying and carrying on. I ran out of his room and Pop caught me, thought something else had happened and lost *his shit* at Jasmine. I came clean with him after we got back to Rochester, which I guess is why he still worked for you guys on occasion, but I was always too embarrassed to come back, and Pop never offered. I think he was relieved that I was happy being the straight-laced one in the family."

"I had no clue, Sloane, I..." He let out his breath. "Your mum sounds like a piece of work."

I leaned back so we were shoulder to shoulder. "She's...interesting. I hated her for a long time, but I've learned to accept her now. Just like I learned to accept that I was just a little out of my mind that summer and that it didn't have to mean anything."

"But you still didn't come back."

"Well, I didn't really have my catharsis until a couple of years ago when my relationship with Mark blew up and I was forced to do a lot of soul searching. Then Pop died, and I kind of expected to see you guys at the funeral."

"I'd have been there if I'd known."

"I know. But do you know what's weird?" He shook his head. "Jasmine sent flowers. I thought that maybe I'd skipped notifying her, but when we went to my place to get my things, I checked the condolence cards and hers was there. She knew."

He placed his hands on his thighs as he quietly absorbed that information.

I nudged him with my shoulder when the silence stretched too far. "Seems we're all pretty fucked up, huh?"

He lifted his brow. "Well, our parents certainly are. Jury's still out on the rest of us."

A smile crossed my lips as a burst of air left my nose. "You know, Abbot, I've missed you all these years."

"Me, or Toby?"

I nudged him again. "All of you. Are you jealous now?"

"That you threw yourself at Toby? Fuck, yeah." Was he serious?

"It was a mistake," I said, still feeling regret over my brazen actions. I'd gone to his room in nothing but a robe and dropped it to the floor dramatically. He turned away and told me to cover up. He didn't want me like that. My seventeen-year-old self-esteem shrivelled up and died then and there.

"A huge mistake. You picked the wrong brother. If you'd come to my room, there's no way I'd have turned you away."

"You were *twelve*."

"Yeah, well, I would have done my best to make you feel like a woman." He was so ridiculous.

"You *are* fucked in the head. The jury just came back on that one."

"Were you a virgin at the time?"

"No," I responded, laughing and shaking my head at the same time.

"OK. I don't feel so slighted now."

"You are so weird."

He shrugged. "I prefer honest, but sure."

"If it makes you feel better, if I was going to throw myself at any brother now, you'd be my first choice."

A huge grin spread across his face and he wiggled his brow. "Then my plan is working."

"I take back the comment I made about you being sweet."

"You can't. It's already been said and I'm keeping it." He stood and held out his hand. "Come with me."

"Why?"

"Because I'm taking you out as per our agreement."

"You don't want to back out now that you know Toby saw me naked?"

"*He saw you naked?*" His eyes bugged open and he dropped his hand to his side with a slap.

"For, like, a second. Then he looked away."

"Is that all? Fuck, *I've* seen you naked for longer than that."

"*When?*"

That cheeky grin of his reappeared along with the suggestive eyebrows. "Wouldn't you like to know?"

"Yes, actually." I jumped up and pushed him in the chest playfully.

"Besides recently in my dreams, over twenty years ago. I'm not quite as pervy now as I was as a kid."

"You are unbelievable."

"And yet, you're smiling." He winked then grabbed my hand, lacing our fingers together. "Let's go."

A grin stretched across my face. "Where and why?"

"You'll see. We're going to do something fun."

"Like what?"

"Woman, can you quit questioning me for five minutes and trust me?"

"I'm trying to ascertain whether this is some kind of trap."

With a laugh, he pulled me closer to him. "You'll have to come with me to find out." He leaned down slightly, his mouth so close to mine I could feel the heat of his skin. But he pulled away, taking my breath with him. *Damn.*

"Fine," I said, falling into step beside him, our hands still joined. "I *guess* I can trust you."

"Good. Because I trust you too, Sloane Slater," he said,

lifting our joined hands and pressing a kiss against my fingers.

My heart leapt in my chest.

Careful, Sloane.

It's just a game.

CHAPTER TWELVE
CAT AND MOUSE

"MINI GOLF?" I asked with a laugh when we pulled up in front of a fenced-off property on Bellarine Highway.

"Not mini golf." He turned down the private road that took us inside the parking lot.

"Then what?" I asked, looking around until I saw some more signage. "Oh. A maze."

He pulled into a parking spot and cut the engine. "We're going to play a game."

"What kind of game?" I sensed a hint of tomfoolery in his plan.

"The kind of game kids play. But I assure you, it'll be a hell of a lot more fun when we do it."

Getting out of the Jag, I looked over at the giant wooden maze. "Why am I suddenly afraid?"

"Don't be. It's totally innocent." He pushed his door shut. "Ish," he added.

"Innocent-ish. I'm gonna need more information than that, buddy."

"All in good time, my dear. All in good time."

After going inside the main building and paying our entry fee, Abbot and I stood at the mouth of the maze.

"Rules," Abbot stated.

"I don't even know the object of this game yet."

"First one to the end of the maze, obviously," he said with an expression on his face that read, 'duh'.

I rolled my eyes. "That's it?" With a shrug, I turned to enter the maze, but he caught my arm.

"Not quite. There's a catch."

I relaxed my shoulders. "Of course there is."

"I'm going to give you a five-minute head start."

"That's a big head start. I'm fast, you know. Sure you want to handicap yourself like that?"

"Absolutely, little mouse."

"Little mouse? Oh, I see. The kid's game. We're playing cat and mouse."

He grinned like he'd already become the cat who got the cream...or the mouse. "I haven't told you the catch yet."

"OK, lay it on me."

"If I catch you, you kiss me."

"Not cat and mouse, catch and kiss." I took a deep breath as I considered his idea. Kissing wasn't sex. And if I could figure out the maze first, he wouldn't even get the chance to put his lips near mine. I could do this. "You're on."

A slow grin spread across his face as he lifted his arm and pressed a button on his watch. "Run, little mouse. *Run*."

Fighting a grin, I took off into the maze, trying to remember the map I'd studied while inside. I'd already plotted a course through, knowing that it would take a zigzag pattern that doubled backwards before an almost circle took me to the exit.

I was going to defeat this thing.

At the five-minute mark, I heard him call out, "Coo-ee."

Grinning, I returned the call then quickened my pace. There was no way he could catch up. One more right and three lefts before I was…*shit*. I'd taken a wrong turn somewhere.

Shit. Fuck. Shit.

Looking up, I tried to find some sort of landmark to gauge my position. But the walls were ten feet of white painted wood, and there wasn't even a tree to help guide me.

"Excellent," I muttered, before catching sight of what looked like a cubby house on stilts with an orange flag on top.

The centre of the maze.

If I can get to there, I might be able to figure my way out.

With renewed determination, I headed for the flag, twisting this way and that, honestly feeling a little dizzy but also glad that I hadn't heard any footfalls closing in. He still hadn't caught me. I was in with a chance.

As I got closer to the centre, I realised that I hadn't bargained for anything if I made it to the exit first. I could have asked for a ceasefire on all flirting for twenty-four hours or I could've asked for the keys to his Jag so I could go for a joyride. There were possibilities I hadn't even thought to explore. And now either he won or I didn't.

But was being caught and kissed really such a bad thing? I didn't know if I could consider that losing. I'd been thinking about those lips of his since he walked into the shop, and maybe a taste would help take the edge off…

Reaching the centre, I went straight for the cubby and climbed the side, hoping there'd be a map or at least enough height to plot a new course.

"I thought you were never going to get here," Abbot quipped from his position on the floor, legs stretched out in front of him. He seemed to always be waiting to pounce. *How the hell did he get here so fast?*

"You were supposed to catch me," I said, taking a seat on the ground next to him. "This looks a lot like waiting."

"I've been chasing you for days. Thought it might help to change things up a bit."

I smiled, suddenly nervous as I took a deep breath and looked at his mouth, waiting.

Instead of moving closer, he spoke. "Did you ever kiss Toby?"

I frowned before shaking my head. "Never." I hoped my admission wasn't going to become a problem for us. In a way, it would work in my favour if it did. But then it wouldn't be as fun. And I was having *so much* fun hanging out with Abbot.

"Did you ever kiss *any* of my brothers?"

"No." They'd either heeded Toby's warning or had never considered me in that way. While I was glad for that now, I hadn't been so happy about it in my youth. There were only so many bonfires you could attend where everyone hooked up but you. The cute girls got the guys, and I got to wait around or walk home by myself. In the end I quit attending.

"I know Kris and I were the annoying little kids growing up, but I've gotta tell you, I had a serious crush on this redhead chick for years. I thought she was so badarse and fearless. I always wanted her to think I was badarse and fearless too."

His hand closed around mine, lacing our fingers together. I closed my eyes at the intimacy of the simple touch. "Is that what this is, Abbot?" I looked up and searched his eyes. "Are you just living out your adolescent crush?"

"Maybe," he whispered, moving closer.

I appreciated his honesty. He wasn't calling this any more than it was. I was a conquest. A notch that never was.

Lifting my hand, I placed it against his face, blocking his mouth before it could reach mine. *This is just a game*, I reminded myself. One that I agreed to. I needed to keep that in the forefront of my mind so I could guard my heart and keep my emotions in check. *A game about sex and money.*

"You didn't catch me," I said, taking some power back as I got to my feet. "I found *you*. The kiss doesn't happen."

Nodding slowly, he watched me the way a tiger would watch a lamb. "Then I suggest you run, Sloane Slater. Because I won't give you a head start this time."

"OK. But if I win. I get to drive the Jag back to Torquay."

He moved, about to stand. "Deal," he said. Then I turned, jumped off the cubby, then sprinted away as fast as my legs could carry me.

I got five turns before I hit a dead end and needed to double back, my heart thumping in my ears as I tried to stay in the lead.

Two more turns, a straight shot then a choice of left or

right. I chose right, took two steps then hit a giant wall of man.

"Caught," Abbot said, his hands gripping my waist before wrapping around me as he claimed his prize.

My mouth.

Ohhh.

Never had I been kissed with such dominance and strength. *This* was why a girl was referred to as a flower, because I literally bloomed beneath his skilled mouth, craning my neck as though he was the sun and I needed his mouth to exist.

His fingers went into my hair and pulled just enough, telling me he wanted more and was struggling not to take it. When we landed against the wall, I knew I was in trouble. Kissing Abbot was too much and too little. It was intense, glorious. And oh God, I wanted more. *I've made a terrible mistake.*

As his mouth dominated mine, I finally understood why he thought he was irresistible. Because he actually was. All I wanted to do was tear the clothes from both of our bodies and let him do whatever he wanted with me. I was losing control.

Stop.

"Stop," I gasped. "Stop, Stop, stop." I didn't want to, and when he responded immediately by dropping his forehead against mine, I felt disappointment in my chest.

"Stop," I said again, placing my hands against his chest. The word was more for me than him. "Stop."

He moved away, and I was suddenly very cold.

How the hell did he learn to kiss like that? This player definitely had game. I didn't even trust myself to stand after that, leaning against the wall to remain upright.

"OK," I said, my voice a little breathy. "I guess, um, we should find the exit and get back to work."

"Work?" Abbot shook his head, a laugh that didn't sound amused coming out of his chest. "That's your first thought?" My first thought was, *I wonder what else he can do with that tongue,* but that wouldn't make me half a mill while work would. Work was a distraction. A necessary one.

"It's why I'm here, Abbot."

He lifted a hand like he wanted me to wait then walked a few paces away from me, hands on his hips as he took a moment.

Is he pissed at me for ending the kiss?

I straightened up and placed my hands on my hips, annoyed that he was reacting like a child who didn't get everything he wanted for Christmas. "You can't honestly think I'm going to fuck you in the middle of a maze, Abbot. The prize was a kiss. That's what you got. Deal with it."

Turning around, he looked at me like I had two heads. I was obviously missing something, because his reaction made no sense. Running his hand back and forth over his hair, he let out a huff of air. "Let's just go, OK?"

"Are we cool?"

"Of course we are, Slater. We're ice cool." I had no idea what that even meant. But I wasn't going to stand still while thinking about it. My entire body was still on fire after that kiss. I was likely to throw myself at him and beg him to do everything I just told him I wouldn't do. I needed to keep moving, treat this like a triathlon. It was the only way I'd win.

MAYBE ABBOT WAS RIGHT ALL ALONG. Anything physical between friends did change things. A simple kiss —no, not simple, a crazy passionate, all-consuming kiss— had turned our playfulness awkward. I already missed what we were.

"This isn't the warehouse," I said when he pulled up outside a mall.

"You need to buy something to wear for the rehearsal dinner. Jasmine's orders."

"Jasmine's orders?" Why did that fill me with dread?

"Her exact words were: no overalls and no ill-fitting jeans or shirts."

"She's dictating my clothing choices? No offence, but she's not my mother. *My* mother doesn't give a fuck about my clothing choices just so long as I'm nowhere near her when I'm making them," I snapped, getting out of the car and slamming the door. *Fuck these people.* I was acting like a petulant teenager all of a sudden, a slave to my raging hormones while lamenting my lot in life. *Screw them for taking me back to this feeling.*

"Sloane." Abbot's deep voice boomed behind me as I entered the air-conditioned mall.

"I'm not ashamed of who I am, or how I look, Abbot," I said, stepping into the first store there was and riffling through the clothes. "I know how people see me. I'm not stupid enough to think I fit in. But if you, for one second think you can change me, maybe like me better if I dressed up and put on some make-up, then you're sorely mistaken. This is me. It's who I am and who I've always been, and I'm not changing a fucking thing for—"

I didn't finish my sentence—*couldn't*—because Abbot's mouth collided with mine and swallowed my words while dousing my anger, rendering me powerless against that skilful mouth of his. *Wow*.

With his hands on either side of my face, I whimpered while his tongue very kindly forced me to shut up.

"I don't want you to change," he whispered when he was through, and I was basically jelly in his hands. "I was relaying a message, and I did it in a really shitty way."

"You can tell your mother to stick that message up her arse."

He laughed, still holding my head to his. "OK." His fingers played in the back of my hair, like he wanted to pull me closer. "Did you know you were looking at kid's clothes?"

"What?" I turned my head and looked around, noting the bright red branding of Cotton On Kids. "Oh."

He chuckled as I pulled out of his grip and left the store, staying a step ahead of him in an effort to get my head to clear after the latest bout of lust and anger.

"I'm not going to that dinner, by the way," I said over my shoulder, slowing down so he could catch up.

"She won't let you stay at the house alone. You have to come."

"Am I untrustworthy all of a sudden?"

"Don't take offence. Jasmine doesn't trust anyone outside the family."

Outside the family.

That really hit the nail on the head.

"Fine, I'll go. But I'm wearing a suit."

"A suit?" The dimple teased the side of his face.

"No overalls or ill-fitting jeans. I think a suit will fit that bill, don't you?"

He grinned. "Let's go get you a suit."

WITH ORDER RESTORED BETWEEN US, we left the mall eating ice creams with matching suits, shirts and shoes in bags slung over our shoulders. Getting two of everything had been the most fun I'd ever had shopping. I'd never gotten into the whole retail therapy thing, but the looks on the sales people's faces had been fantastic. They'd obviously never matched up a couple quite like us before. Not that we were a couple. Just that we were two people and two was a couple. The kiss—kiss*es*—hadn't changed anything. We remained friends *only*.

Or, so I kept telling myself.

"Why do you still live with Jasmine?" I asked once we were clicked into the Jag and heading back to Torquay.

"I don't. I'm just staying there at the moment because it's weird living with Kris."

"Oh. You were sharing a house?"

"Up until recently."

"Were you kicked out when Ronnie moved in?"

"Nah. I left 'cause I didn't wanna hear them fucking all the time."

"I can see how that would become a problem."

"Don't get me wrong. Ronnie is cool, and she makes him happy."

"But you were happier when it was just you and Kristian?"

He scrunched up his nose. "Does that make me a cunt if I say yes?"

I shook my head. "No. I mean, you guys shared a womb. You're as close as siblings can get. It makes sense that you're missing him when you've always been a part of him. In a non-gay way, of course," I teased.

He laughed. "Not that there's anything wrong with that."

I sighed. "Seinfeld was the best. Why is it that everything you grow to love, to count on, ends up going away?"

"Loss is a part of life."

We fell silent for a moment, jumbled thoughts tumbling through my mind and most likely his too. Life was pretty messed up.

"Listen," he said as he tightened his grip on the steering wheel. "I shouldn't have told Jasmine you were gay."

I brushed his comment off with a wave of my hand. "Forget it. It's not like it's the first time people have thought that about me. I'm not very feminine and I've never been married. They assume."

"You *are* feminine."

I rolled my eyes then smiled. "You're sweet." Not that I believed it. The only feminine thing about me was my sex.

"Don't tell anyone." He glanced at me before turning his attention back to the road.

"So"—I turned a little in my seat so I was facing him —"were you actually serious when you said you did that to protect me?"

"Yeah," he said straight away. "My family…" He took a deep breath and released it with a heavy sigh. "Your grandad was right to steer you away. You really shouldn't get close to us."

"And yet you brought me here and you're making sport out of getting me into bed."

"Never said I was a nice guy, Sloane. I'm a selfish cunt who never apologises."

I looked out the window. "You and every man I've ever dated."

"What's the deal with you and that Mark guy, anyway? I've seen you text him a few times this week. What is he doing? Keeping you strung along for a side bit in case he feels like it?" *Ha! Fat chance if that's what he wanted.* There was no way I'd be the woman he cheated on his wife with.

"It's not like that. We're friends. He doesn't know how not to have me in his life." Which was where I was stuck too.

"How's that working for you?"

I shrugged. "It's OK. I mean, we were together for years. And we were friends before that. Our lives are completely blended, so if one of us walks away, they'd have to start all over." Mark and I met in high school and had been best friends right up to our twenties when we became something more. Twenty-five years of friendship was difficult to say goodbye to, even if we didn't work out as a couple.

"Would that be so bad?"

"Starting over?" I took a deep breath, trying to picture having a life anywhere but back home. It was my baseline, where I guess I belonged. "I don't think so. I'm comfortable in my life."

"Bullshit."

"Excuse me?" I would have laughed except it wasn't funny.

"If your life was so awesome, you wouldn't have been so quick to drive out here with me."

"Now you're my saviour?" I shot back.

"I think getaway driver would be more fitting."

"Jesus. You think you know me so well, don't you?" When it came down to it, he barely knew me at all. Even if he'd known everything about me in the past, twenty-one years changed a person. I wasn't an angsty teenage girl anymore.

"Am I wrong?"

He wasn't. But I wasn't anywhere close to admitting that to myself. "Maybe I'm just here for the money, Abbot."

He scoffed. "Bullshit."

"You keep saying that. But it's true. There's no *mint*. I don't know what Pop did with it. Maybe he left it to my mother. I have no clue. I just know that his accounts were dry."

"What about his workshop?"

"There's no money at the shop."

"Not the shop, Sloane. The *workshop*."

"What are you talking about?"

"The workshop. There's like, a hundred different safes there that he'd use to keep his skills up. We dropped more than a few off to him ourselves."

Why don't I know anything about this place?

"Do you remember where this place is?"

"Shit. You seriously don't know what I'm talking about, do you?"

"I have no fucking clue. I've never seen it."

"Then…as much as I enjoy this thing you and I have going on, then I agree this should be the only job you do with us, Sloane. If you don't know about the workshop, there's no way Trev wanted you doing this stuff once he died." He *definitely* didn't want me doing this. But, I did have to wonder if this workshop was part of what Pop had wanted to tell me. There was obviously a lot about his life I didn't know.

"I overheard Jasmine, Breaker, and Toby talking the other day. They mentioned some other job they need me for after this. Do you know what that is?"

"I'm not sure. Breaker has some big job he needs us to do after Kris's wedding. It's probably that, but I don't know exactly what it is."

"They said something about a transport."

He glanced at me quickly, his brow knitted. "A *transport*? Are you sure that's what they said?"

I nodded. "They said they were going to need someone like me or they wouldn't be able to unload the transport fast enough."

He looked ahead for a long moment then shook his head. "That son of a bitch."

"Do you know what they're talking about?"

He nodded, still frowning. "Yeah, I think I fucking do."

I STOOD outside throwing a stick for the little Boston terrier who lived at the Cartwright house and never seemed to tire of a game of fetch. They'd been inside arguing for the good part of an hour, and Rogue was still wagging his tail excitedly each time I lifted my arm to throw.

The moment we'd returned to the house, Abbot told me to wait outside while he went and spoke to his mother. He'd been tense ever since I told him about the transport job I'd overheard. And now I seemed to be responsible for a family altercation, which hadn't been my intention. I needed to remember whom I was speaking to in future. The Cartwrights weren't normal people.

As I waited obediently, all I could hear was random bouts of yelling. One of which was Abbot saying, "Hitting that drug transport is insanity and you know it." I had to agree with him on that one. Getting involved with drugs was never a good idea. Everyone knew that.

"Hey." Toby appeared in the doorway, voices growing louder then quiet as he opened and closed the sliding door. He moved towards me, hands in his pockets. *Rip the Band-Aid off, Sloane.* When I opened my mouth, it wasn't quite as easy to talk as it had been with Abbot. There was history here.

"Do you ever dress down?" I asked instead. He had on a blue button-up shirt and grey tailored pants.

"I wear a wetsuit surfing," he responded with a smile.

"Well, that's something, I guess."

"Do you ever dress up?"

"Nope." I threw the stick and watched Rogue's little legs lift his black and white body off the ground while he ran for it. "I'm more about comfort than class."

"This is comfortable," Toby said, leaning against the glass-topped outdoor table.

"Sure it is." I laughed. This back and forth wasn't getting us anywhere.

I turned to face him and pressed my lips together, ready to begin just as, "*Tell him no,*" was yelled from inside.

"Abbot sounds pissed," I stated, chickening out again.

Toby looked past me and squinted from the glare bouncing off the pool surface. "Yeah, well, they're all going to be pissed."

"Why?"

His eyes met mine. "They have to do a job they thought they wouldn't have to."

"Hitting a drug transport?"

"I can't say exactly."

"Well, for what it's worth, I'm with Abbot. I think it's crazy."

"We don't really have a choice in this one. We owe a favour."

"To the bikers?"

"You seem to have a lot of information." He folded his arms across his chest.

"I have these nifty things called ears and a brain that puts things together. I heard you saying you needed me for the job. You people aren't nearly as discreet as you think you are."

"I suppose we're used to talking freely within these walls."

"I don't suppose I have much of a choice in whether I do this job or not."

"With Trev gone, you're our smithy now. It has to be someone we know and trust." It was a compliment and an order rolled into one. I understood how this all worked, that Jasmine was in charge and what she said went. But it didn't mean I had to like it. Or accept it. I wasn't a kid anymore.

"You know I don't want this life, Toby. Pop never wanted me following in his footsteps either."

"You were born into this life like the rest of us, Sloane. We don't always get what we want. You should know that by now." *I did know that. All too well.*

"Is that why you're still here? Because you don't feel like you have a choice?"

A sad smile curved his mouth as he looked at the tip of his shoe. "Family commitments trump personal dreams or ambitions. Pop understood that. He knew this was inevitable."

"He'd be rolling in his grave if he knew I was here."

He met my eyes. "He *trained* you, didn't he?"

"Yes, But—"

"But, nothing. He kept you away from this life as long as he could. I give him a lot of credit for that. But you need to face reality: inheriting his business means inheriting us too. We're all family, bound by the secrets we keep. You understand that, right?"

We're all family.

I'm outside the family.

Which one was it?

These people seemed to speak in riddles, pulling you close with one hand and pushing you away with the other.

"Of course I understand that. And I won't tell anyone else about this drug job if that's what you're getting at."

"Breaker doesn't want any of it to get out before the wedding. He's like a father to Ronnie, he wants her to have the fairy-tale day with as little stress as possible. No business talk."

"He's the boss now?"

"He's whatever Jazz wants him to be."

"Of course. And it's cool. I can keep a secret."

"Can I be sure of that?" he asked, his handsome expression assessing me. "Abbot wouldn't be in there losing his shit if you hadn't relayed what you overheard."

"Are you seriously questioning me? Do you even remember the summer I was fourteen?" Rogue sat at my feet with the stick in his mouth, looking up at me hopefully. I took the stick and threw it as far as I possibly could, hearing it brush against the leaves in the treeline. "You would have been sixteen. It was the year before Nate got caught."

"It was a long time ago." I didn't know if he was being intentionally vague or had just glossed over the memory.

"Well, you and I—being the eldest of the bunch—decided that it would be cool to get into Jasmine's vodka stash."

He nodded. "I remember."

"Then you remember feeling drunk and brave and showing me Jasmine's *other* stash."

He closed his eyes, the memory obviously reminding him of our stupidity at the time.

I continued. "We rode dirt bikes into the bush and set

up empty cans like they do in the movies. Then we took out the two handguns we stole from her stash and proceeded to try and shoot them down—not as easy as it looked in the movies. The kick on those things was bigger than we expected. And the bullets, well, those were *real*." I lifted the leg of my army-green overalls to reveal a long scar on the side of my left calf. "To this day, I've never told a soul that you accidentally shot me. I've always said I got it falling on a rock." Rogue returned, and I knelt down this time, scratching the old dog behind the ears, taking the stick from his mouth before turning to Toby. "I have a lot of memories that I haven't shared, Toby." I handed him the stick.

Holding it in both his hands, he turned the stick around. "I appreciate that."

"However," I started, folding my arms across my middle as I forced myself calm. It had been hard enough discussing this with Abbot, let alone Toby. "In the essence of full disclosure, I did tell Abbot what happened before I left."

His jaw went tight before he lifted his arm and threw the stick for his dog. "I was kind of hoping you'd forgotten about that."

"How could I? It was my most humiliating moment."

"I thought what you did was incredibly brave. Albeit misplaced." He met my eyes, his gaze soft and kind. *I really hope that's not pity.*

"I know." I touched my forehead as my stomach twisted from embarrassment. "I know. And I guess what I'm trying to do here is say what I should have twenty-one years ago. I'm sorry, Toby. I was messed up that year and I don't know what I was thinking. We were friends, and I messed up."

"It's OK, Sloane, really. There's nothing to be sorry for. I understood at the time. It was just a line I wouldn't cross, and I hope that *you* understand that."

"I do. Really. And I respect that. And I promise there's not going to be a repeat performance. You're safe around me."

"Because you're gay?"

I opened my mouth to reply, uncomfortable in the lie while nurturing a growing desire to punch Abbot in the arm.

"Yeah. I didn't believe it when he said it, and I don't think Jasmine did either. But, I do believe that there's something going on with you and Abbot, and Abbot is trying to keep it hidden."

"There's nothing going on," I said, my voice getting a little breathy as my memory slammed me with images of Abbot's masterful mouth. *My God, I want to kiss him again.*

"I caught him coming out of your room Wednesday morning."

"We're not sleeping together."

He held up a hand. "Abbot knows you're off limits. Jasmine has rules about relationships around the family that he obviously doesn't give a fuck about."

"I assure you there is *no* relationship. He's playful and teasing. Nothing else. I swear to you." Up until this moment, I'd been finding Abbot's concerns about his family a little over the top. Now, I wasn't so sure.

"I believe you. Just…whatever the fuck is going on, keep it out of the house and far away from Jasmine. I don't want you getting hurt over this. Or dragged in any further than you are."

"*Nothing* is going on." I moved back, wanting to walk away.

"Sloane." He caught me by the arm. "We grew up together, OK? Despite the years, I still care about you like family, and I don't want to see you hurt. You deserve better and whatever game he's playing isn't going to end well."

Did I really deserve better? I kept being reminded that this was my birthright. So what the hell did it matter how deep I got? It didn't seem like I was getting out regardless of my own desires, or Abbot's assurances. I was their new 'smithy'. Toby just said so himself. So, if I was to be at their beck and call regardless, what the fuck did any of it matter?

I inhaled a frustrated breath and met his gaze again, light blue eyes full of kindness and chagrin. Using my free hand, I patted his as it remained wrapped around my upper arm. "I appreciate your concern, Toby. I really do. But, I'm OK. I'm a big girl now. I can handle myself, and I can handle Abbot too."

"It's not Abbot I'm concerned with. It's the consequences of you two sneaking around and getting caught."

"Why? What the hell are the consequences?"

His jaw clenched as he released his hold on my arm and shook his head slightly. "Just promise me you'll be careful. There are a lot of things you don't know."

"I'm gathering that." I stepped away, needing to walk off some frustration since this was obviously as far as this conversation was going. "Maybe I'll see you around, Toby."

"Sloane?"

"Yeah?"

"Are we OK?" The sincerity in his voice made my aggravation drop a notch, so I stopped moving away,

"Of course, Toby, always." Despite the awkwardness, I'd always found my friendship with Toby special. He'd always been good to me.

"I'm glad." He smiled, so handsome, but so...*lost* inside. I could see that boy who wanted to escape, hiding behind that well put together façade of his. *Which reminds me...*

"You know, I never told anyone we planned to run away that summer. All the important secrets, I'll take to my grave."

He looked at me for a long moment before responding. "I appreciate that."

"I know. You're a good man at heart, Toby."

"I'm really not." His arms tightened around his middle again.

"Yes, you are. You're just stuck in the wrong world."

"Aren't we all?" He held my gaze with his.

"I'm not stuck." I held my hands out to the side and walked backwards away from him. "See? I'm walking away right now."

He grinned. "Oh yeah? And where are you gonna go?"

"Wherever my feet take me. Home. Queensland— that's where we planned to go, right?"

"You know they'd only send me to bring you back?"

"What if I didn't want to come back?"

He leaned forward, his eyes darkening a little. "I'd force you, Sloane," he stated, his voice harsh and frankly a little jolting.

I stopped dead in my tracks. "You're serious."

"As a heart attack. I did not grow into a good man. I grew into a man who is loyal and gets shit done."

My entire body grew heavy as I studied the man who wasn't a nineteen-year-old boy with hopes and dreams anymore. Time changed so much and had taken that away. "That makes me really sad, Toby."

He ran a hand through his hair, messing up the neat styling. "You and me both." Then he flipped the chair closest to him around and pointed at it. "Why don't you sit down and I'll get us a drink? As far as I know, you were asked to wait here, not take off on your own."

"Am I being detained?"

"You know something, Sloane, I have no fucking idea. I just do as I'm told. So should you." He pointed at the chair again before he slipped inside and headed to the kitchen for those drinks.

For a moment, I stood rooted to the ground, contemplating whether I wanted to comply or run the other way. Running would be stupid. I knew that. I wasn't naïve enough to underestimate what the Cartwrights were capable of, just like I was never so naïve as to believe that Pop wasn't in on it all. But I'd become incredibly adept at turning a blind eye. Now, in the thick of it, it was something I couldn't do anymore. I needed to accept that I *wasn't* an outsider anymore. Family or not, I had stakes in whatever was going on too. It was naïve to think otherwise, and naïve to think I could walk away.

I took that seat.

"Sorry, Pop," I whispered, just as the little dog whined at my feet over the stick. Leaning closer, I looked into his big brown eyes and panting face. ""I made a huge mistake coming back here, didn't I?"

Toby had always been serious, but I'd never seen that darkness in his expression years ago. Fierce. Protective. Strong. Yes.

I did not grow into a good man. I grew into a man who is loyal and gets shit done.

My heart broke a little seeing just how true that was. Perhaps he'd named his dog after himself. Rogue—a dishonest or unprincipled man. I hoped there was more to Toby than that. The softness in his heart couldn't be all gone.

I sighed. Rogue looked at the stick then back at me, so I threw it and watched him run, feeling like I was sitting in the centre of a deep hole I'd dug for myself.

Just think of the money, Sloane.

I could see that becoming my new mantra.

CHAPTER FOURTEEN
NO GIRLY FRIENDS SHIT

A TAP SOUNDED on the door. "Ready?"

I looked in the mirror, nervous. "Yeah. But do you think this is a dumb idea?"

Abbot opened the door to the en-suite bathroom of my room and grinned when he saw me. "You look great. I think this is a fucking fantastic idea," he said, casually slinging his arm over my shoulders as we took in our combined appearance.

It was time for the rehearsal dinner and we were standing there dressed in exactly the same outfit. It felt like rebellion at the time of purchase, but now it felt childish and silly. But, that's what Abbot was, I supposed—a big kid. It was also what I liked about him if I was truthful. He made life fun again, which I'd loved until my conversation with Toby the day before. Now, I worried how this was going to come across to the rest of the family, and whether they'd read something more into it. I still had no idea what these *consequences* were, but to be safe, I'd locked Abbot out of my bedroom last night then took a sleeping tablet so

I could rest. Fat lot of good it did, though. When I woke this morning he was right there, stark naked and snoring softly with his arm draped across my waist. Cheeky bastard.

It felt so good though...

"I really don't know," I said. "Maybe I should call Alesha and ask to borrow something again. She's my size."

"She'll already be at the restaurant. And don't worry, they're gonna think this is hilarious. I promise."

With a swallow, I straightened up my tie. "Let's go then."

The last ones to leave, we headed out the front of the house where the Jag was parked next to Lizzie. My poor girl had been neglected since I hadn't needed anything more from her for the safe and I'd been indulging in Abbot's Jag. But I quietly promised her that we'd be back together soon. I was determined to figure out that combination before next weekend since I didn't want to be here for the wedding as well. It felt strange enough going to this dinner when I wasn't even invited in the first place.

And it's not like I expected them to invite me anywhere. Hell, I hadn't been a part of their lives for so long that I was surprised any of them had remembered me, so there was no way I'd have expected a wedding invite. But, I didn't want to attend Kris and Ronnie's wedding as an obligation either. It felt shitty being a last-minute add-on.

"I feel like the Danny DeVito to your Arnold Schwarzenegger in this," I said as we pulled up outside the restaurant and stood beside the car.

Abbot loosened my tie a little and popped the top

button of my shirt. "You're much cuter than DeVito. Don't sweat it."

"I also feel like this is akin to walking in there with my middle fingers in the air. Don't you?"

"Mm-hmm. That's precisely what this is."

"Don't you think that's a shitty thing to do to your brother?"

"Which one?"

"Kristian. The one getting married."

"He'll think it's funny. And Jasmine will spend the night fighting off an aneurysm. It'll be great. Relax and go with it, Sloane Slater. You've got this." Did I? I didn't feel confident that I *had* anything anymore. My life seemed to have exited my control.

The moment we walked inside felt more like revealing my naked body than entering in a three-piece suit. I had no idea how those gathered would react and was sweating bullets as a result. Abbot had made sure we were the last to arrive, so there was a full room of people when he pushed open the door and held his hands above his head.

"Ladies and Gentlemen, may I have your attention?" *Oh no. This is worse than I expected!*

"What are you doing?" I asked between my teeth. Although, he didn't answer. He just flashed me one of his mischievous smiles then winked before continuing.

"I'd like to introduce you all to my replacement twin, Sloane Slater. She can't surf and we're yet to test out her wingman skills, but she looks mighty fine in a suit and has a wicked sense of humour."

"I am going to kill you," I whispered in the beat where the room didn't quite know what to do. Then Kristian burst out laughing and clapped his hands together, the sound puncturing the air until the rest of the room joined in. *Sheep*. Although when I caught a glance of Jasmine, she had a mixture of mirth and annoyance in her eyes as Breaker said something in her ear before pressing a kiss against her bare shoulder.

"Just take a bow," Abbot told me. "They all know you're one of us now." Was this another move for my protection?

Folding at the waist dramatically, I flicked my hair back then added a curtsy for good measure. That got me a few laughs and a praise-filled smile from Abbot.

"Come on, I'll introduce you to everyone."

We walked across the room, stopping to say hi to friends of the Cartwrights—some also knew Pop and offered condolences—as well as some bikers and their women. No one was introduced as Ronnie's family, though. Did that mean her situation was a little like mine? Or, were the bikers her family?

"You know, I never would have told you two apart if it wasn't pointed out," Holland joked as we made it to the table with all the brothers and their significant others.

"I know, right?" I responded with a smile. "Put Kristian next to us and we'd look like triplets."

She gestured for me to take a seat, which I did. Then Abbot placed a beer in front of me while he stood talking with his brothers. Alesha sat with us.

"Hey, Sloane. Glad you're still here," she said with a smile. "You and Abbot seem to be getting along well."

"We're not together," I said. "Just friends."

"Oh, I know." Then she touched me on the knee. "I heard."

"Yeah, so did I," Holland said leaning on her hands.

She pursed her lips and studied me. "But I don't know if I'm buying it. You"—she wiggled her shoulders like the action would help her conjure the right words—"you light up around him."

"I light up around him. OK." I widened my eyes like I thought she was crazy then took a swig of my beer and looked away.

Was I that obvious? Ugh. Abbot had been teasing and taunting so much that the sexual frustration was probably rolling off me in waves. And the kissing, my God, I still hadn't caught my breath.

Damn Abbot's no-masturbation rule.

"You know, she totally does light up," Alesha agreed. "Huh. What does that mean, Sloane?"

"It means that I'm so incredibly lonely in my life that Abbot's goofing around is actually funny to me." *That should put a stop to their questioning.*

"Sure," Holland said with a smile. "Just watch how you look at him around Jasmine. She won't let you leave if she decides you're a good match." Another warning.

"I seriously feel like I'm sitting in the middle of a period drama with you people sometimes. Who talks like that?" With a quick shake of my head, I stood up and touched Abbot on the arm to get his attention, telling him I needed some fresh air.

He followed me outside.

"Want a hit?" he asked, pulling out an e-cigarette and holding it out to me.

"What is that? Weed?"

He wiggled it at my eye level with a cheeky glint in his eye. "You tell me."

Taking the vaping device, I held it to my mouth and

inhaled, smoke flowing over my tongue and tasting like…
"Apple?" I blew the smoke out and frowned. "What
the hell?"

He took the device back and leaned against the
building as he inhaled. "Some homeopathic shit. Supposed
to give you focus but it tastes like—"

"Toffee apples."

He nodded. "Those things are fucking delicious."

Resting my back against the bricks beside him, I took
the device when he handed it back and had some more. It
was like lollies without calories. Clever.

"You know, my mum used to buy me these," I said,
passing it back. "When I was a kid."

"Vaping devices?" I could tell he was poking fun by
the glint in his eye.

"Funny. Toffee apples. Whenever she showed up,
she'd go straight into 'funnest mum ever' mode and take
me out, feed me junk and ignore my bedtime. I thought she
was so cool, and I always begged her to stay so it could be
like that all the time. But she never would. I'd literally turn
around and one second she'd be there and the next she'd
be gone. *Poof.* Not to be seen until she was in trouble
again and needed Pop's help." Pop had loved his daughter,
but the disappointment I saw in his eyes more than once
had propelled me to be better to him than she was. His
flighty, gypsy daughter had no clue how to take care of
herself, let alone anyone else. So, I'd made it my life's
purpose to be reliable. I often wondered if in doing so, I'd
become such a doormat that no man would ever find me
attractive. *Men like to be challenged.* And they'd never
had to chase me, I was just…there. Too reliable.

"Was this before or after she fucked your boyfriend?"

Somehow, I managed to laugh at that. "Before. I was, like…ten."

"You still see her?"

"She came for the funeral. Asked me about money during the service then left while I was in the shower that night."

"She sounds amazing."

I chuckled, smiling softly. "She has her moments. And she is who she is. The trick is not expecting anything. That way, there's no disappointment."

He offered me a vape again and I shook my head.

"Want to go back in?" he asked, shifting so he was now standing in front of me, blocking the diminishing sun with his size.

"You think they'd notice if we left completely?"

"You having that much fun?"

"Holland and Alesha think I light up when I look at you."

He laughed. "Well, I am pretty awesome."

"Maybe I'm just constantly on my guard, watching for your next move."

Placing a hand on the wall next to my head, he took a quick look around then dipped his head. "I'm not going to surprise fuck you, Sloane."

I inhaled a shaky breath. "I never know *what* you're going to do."

"But you're having fun, right?" His mouth pulled up at the corner.

I nodded. "You make me feel like a kid again."

"Is that a compliment, Sloane Slater?"

Reaching up, I took a hold of his tie and ran my fingers

down the silk. "Yeah, Abbot Cartwright, that's a compliment."

He grinned then pressed his mouth to mine, kissing me deeper than was appropriate in a public place, even though we were hidden around the side of the building. It felt far too good, too distracting, too tempting. I couldn't keep letting him take liberties or I'd go broke.

"Abbot." I turned my head away, breaking our connection first.

"I caught you, Sloane. Kissing you is my prize."

"You already took your prize. Plus a bonus one at the mall after."

"Ah, ah, ah," he tutted. "The deal was if I caught you, I get to kiss you. There was no cap on the number of times." *Cheeky arse.*

"That's a loophole you're inserting right now, and you know it."

"But am I wrong?"

Grinning, I pulled my bottom lip with my teeth. "Technically, no," I admitted, kind of pleased about it because I *wanted* to keep kissing him. My problem lay in my own ability to keep it that way.

"You're gonna have to be better at this game to beat me, Slater."

"You think?"

He leaned down and sucked gently on the lip I was biting. "I will win you."

I shook my head, my grin uncontrollable. "How about you save the games for elsewhere? Anyone could walk out here."

He stepped back. "I know, I've been listening for footsteps. We're cool."

"Give me another puff of that apple thing."

With a grin he handed it over. "Addictive, right? And it's all stuff that's good for you."

Once back inside, it was assumed we'd gone for a cigarette since I was the only one who knew Abbot had quit smoking. We bounced around a little, talking and larking about with the brothers before Breaker clamped his hand on Abbot's shoulder.

"Seems you forgot to greet your mother," he said, squeezing so that Abbot winced a little.

"Well, *Dad*, I noticed you were busy sucking on her neck, so I thought I might leave you to it."

"Don't call me Dad," Breaker said, looking unimpressed. "She tried to catch up with you for a smoke outside but didn't find you. Where'd you go?"

Abbot shook his head. "We were there. Must have missed her."

Fuck. Did she see us? I didn't like the way the family kept making thinly veiled threats about not being allowed to leave if Abbot and I were thought to be a thing. It was unsettling.

"Listen," Breaker said, leaning closer to Abbot's ear. "I get that you're pissed with me over that job right now, but don't let that get in the way of your love for your brother."

"Their precious wedding is safe. Relax."

Breaker's gaze drifted from Abbot to me, down the length of my suit then back to Abbot again. "Looks that way."

"Sloane is my date for the wedding. We're having some fun."

I am?

"Well, you might want to talk to the bride and groom about that. RSVP date passed and all that."

"Kris is cool with it. He likes Mini-me." Abbot slung his arm over my shoulders as he was wont to do.

"Don't think you'll be finished your job by next weekend?" Breaker directed at me.

"Well," I started. "I've noted the possible ranges for each of the four wheels. Now it's just a matter of testing the different combinations to get that damn gate to drop without doing anything to disturb the vial."

"I know you were just speaking English, but fucked if I understood any of it." Breaker looked at me, bewildered.

"Oh, you see, the lock consists of four wheels called a wheel pack." I held up my fingers to try and explain visibly. "Each of them rotate on a single rigid post—"

Breaker placed his hand over both of mine, stopping me mid sentence. "That's a really cool story, Sloane. But it needs less words." He gave me a wink then walked away.

"Are lock mechanics really that boring?" I asked Abbot, who laughed.

"Fuck yeah," he said, just as Kristian came over and clapped his twin on the back.

"We're doing the ceremony rehearsal in five, then we're eating and getting the fuck out of here. After party at the shack. You cool with that?"

"Are you kidding me?" Abbot said. "Party is my middle name."

Kristian laughed then looked at me. "How about you, Kris the second? Up for something a little less stuffy when this is done?"

"I will literally do anything to take off this tie at this point," I said.

He grinned and clapped me on the arm. "That a girl."

With most of the room seated, the bridal party was called to the front of the room and talked through their positions for the ceremony. It was being held on the beach, but since you needed a permit for that, the practice run was done indoors.

"Wait, we're unbalanced," Jasmine said, stopping the proceedings as she looked from side to side.

"Jazz," Kristian warned, his eyebrows raised as he stood before the celebrant holding Ronnie's hands.

Jasmine moved from her spot as a bridesmaid—a strange place for the mother of the groom—and held her hand against her chin. "There are too many groomsmen compared to bridesmaids," she said, pointing to the four brothers on Kris's side, while Ronnie had Holland, Alesha and Jasmine on hers.

"There isn't anyone I can ask," Ronnie whispered, looking a little embarrassed as her eyes begged Jasmine just to get back in place. *Poor girl. This must be mortifying.*

"Nonsense," Jasmine countered. "Sloane can do it. Why, she's practically family, right?" With a broad grin, Jasmine's eyes landed on me before she gestured for me to get up and join them.

I shook my head and opened my mouth to object, trying to get a clue from Abbot as to how I was supposed to play this. He looked almost...bored.

Is that how he really feels about all this? Bored?

"Come on," Jasmine insisted, waving at me still.

"You'd be helping me out," Ronnie said, helping to plead Jasmine's case. "The Cartwrights are my only real family. I've never done the girly friends shit so I'm short a bridesmaid. Will you join in?"

"Do I have to wear a dress?"

She laughed. "Culottes?"

I stood up. "Deal." Ronnie seemed like my kind of girl. *No girly friends shit.* I definitely identified with that.

As I walked up to the front of the room, I noticed Abbot's mouth twitch in amusement. *I guess he's not bored, after all.*

CHAPTER FIFTEEN
ACE OF FUCKING SPADES

"CULOTTES, HUH?" Abbot said later when we were sitting around a bonfire, beer in hand and a salty wind whipping our hair. "Do you ever agree to anything without cutting a deal first?"

I shrugged. "What can I say, I'm a competitive person."

"I've noticed. It's what I like about you."

"Sport in the hunt."

"Huh?"

"You enjoy the chase."

He grinned. "I honestly do."

"What do you think would happen if I actually gave in to you? Think you'd loose interest right away then go back to chasing surf bunny tail again?"

His chest bounced with laughter. "Surf bunny tail? I've never heard that one."

"Probably because I just made it up."

Shaking his head, he downed at least a quarter of his beer bottle as he focused on a couple of girls jumping around on the sand in a dance that made their tits bounce hypnotically. "See those girls over there?"

"They're your usual, right?"

"Yeah. They're easy. Just wanna party. They go home the next morning, and maybe we hook up again, maybe we don't. No biggie. But there's no sport in it, you're right about that. I enjoy this game we have going on."

"I like how confident you are of winning."

"I like how confident *you* are of winning."

"I give in and I become one of those girls over there."

"You would never be one of those girls, Sloane."

"Let me guess, because I'm *different* to other girls? That's such a cliché." And generally the first excuse guys used when they told me they weren't interested.

"No." He laughed then finished his beer. "It's because you would have fucked me already if you were like those girls. Which, by definition *does* make you different."

I grinned and shook my head. He had me there.

"How about we up the stakes a little?" he suggested after a while.

"In what way?"

"Well, I've already won kissing. How about we play a game where heavy petting is on the table?"

"Heavy petting?" I cleared my throat as my insides formed a cheer squad that screamed a resounding yes. "That's a bit of a jump, don't you think? How about second base?" My voice cracked a little on the second last word.

He considered my words. "Are we talking over clothes or under?"

"Um, under?" Damn throat kept getting thick.

"OK. You wanna choose the game?"

I looked around the party, trying to see if anyone was watching us and would notice if we left. Jasmine and Breaker had gone home after the dinner, and Toby had left after the first hour, saying something about a boat.

The other Cartwrights were quite caught up in their significant others, and the remaining guests were simply hangers-on.

"If you have a pack of cards and somewhere private, I definitely have an idea," I said.

Abbot sprang to his feet. "I need a deck of cards," he yelled.

"I WANT SOMETHING THIS TIME," I said, kneeling on the opposite side of a coffee table while shuffling a deck of cards. He'd brought me to an apartment building about ten minutes walk from Kristian and Ronnie's place that had all the mod-cons and looked out over the beach. It was a family owned property that none of them had ever lived in, but had all used from time to time since it was in the centre of town.

"And what exactly do you want, Sloane Slater?" Abbot had removed his jacket and tie and was sitting in his vest and white shirt, sleeves rolled up, the top two buttons undone. There was just enough of a pectoral bump showing to make my heart rate kick up. *I can have fun with him without having sex. I can have fun with him without having sex.* It was my new mantra to build confidence for when thinking about the money wasn't quite working.

"Like, if I win, you take me to the workshop you told me about."

"Done," he said without any hesitation.

"I feel like that was too easy, and I should have asked for more." I narrowed my eyes as I placed the cards in the centre of the coffee table.

Abbot sat with his back against a grey couch, his long legs angled so one bent to the side and the other worked as his armrest, his forearm resting on his knee.

"Too late now, the terms have been set. But for the record, I would have taken you to that workshop for free."

"You are an arse."

He grinned. "And you love it." No. But I did love *his* arse.

I shook my head. "OK, so we're playing 'high card, low card'. We both cut the deck and the high card wins. Best three out of five."

"That's all?" he asked, lifting a stack of cards off the deck and flipping it up to show the Jack of clubs.

"That's all," I confirmed, doing the same. "King of spades. I win that one."

"Serious? Where's the skill in that?"

"That's the point really. There is no skill. It's completely random so the fates get to decide." I pushed the cards towards him. "You shuffle this time."

"You really believe in that stuff?" he asked, his big hands obscuring the cards. "Fate."

"Of course. I mean, the world is so far out of our control that there has to be some defining reason as to what happens to us. Otherwise, what's the point?"

"To go down laughing."

"Maybe that's your fate?"

He placed the cards on the table. "Maybe. Pick."

"Four. Diamonds."

"Nine. Also diamonds."

"One all," I said, collecting the deck.

He rubbed his hands together. "Start unbuttoning that shirt, Slater, I've got incredible luck."

"You're so confident. Where does this come from?" I shuffled the deck as he got to his feet and went to the kitchen in the open-plan living area.

"In this line of work, confidence is everything. I hesitate at the wrong moment and the people I love are in danger." He took two glasses out of the cupboard and grabbed a bottle of vodka out of the freezer.

"Danger of being arrested, or are there other forces at play here?"

He grinned as he set the glasses and vodka on the coffee table, but it was more of a sad grin than happy one. "Devil's in the details, Sloane." He sat back on the floor and poured drinks, two fingers of straight vodka each.

"What would happen if you told me exactly where that safe came from and how you got it?"

He pushed the vodka towards me. "It's not worth the risk. How about you cut the deck?"

"So pushy. OK." I placed the cards back on the table then took the very first off the pile. A six.

"I've got a good chance here." He smiled, wriggling his fingers in the air before he took a stack of about twenty cards and held it up. "Seven. Ha ha. Told you I was lucky."

"Very lucky." I undid one button of my shirt, eyes on his as he watched my fingers work.

"One more win and that shirt is toast."

I smiled and lifted my glass to my lips. "Don't keep a

girl waiting," I said, downing the contents in one gulp. My eyes went wide. "Holy mother of God," I gasped and coughed. "What the fuck was that?" My eyes watered and my throat burned. *So much for playing the seductress.*

"Cinnamon vodka," he said with a laugh. "You all right there? Need some water?"

"Why didn't you tell me?" I hacked, nose running, eyes watering as he jumped up and got me some water and tissues.

"I thought you would've read the label."

"I was too busy looking at your bedroom eyes," I admitted when I got myself cleaned up and under control.

He released a great belly laugh. "Bedroom eyes," he repeated, calming down. "I don't think I've ever known a woman like you, Sloane."

"And what kind of woman am I?"

"Straightforward. Honest. I don't have to guess what you're thinking because you just say it, and the only games you play are the ones we're both in on."

I thought on his words for a moment, twisting my empty vodka glass around on the table. It wasn't the first time someone had said those things to me, but it was the first time it sounded like a compliment.

"You're not like other guys either," I said.

"You sure about that?" he asked, sipping his vodka the way I should have.

"Yeah. Most guys will string a girl like me along for years. But not you. I know exactly where I stand and where this leads. I'm under no grand illusions, and that's…refreshing."

"Where exactly do you think we stand?" He picked up the cards and shuffled.

"Friends," I said simply before smiling then adding. "With potential benefits."

He grinned. "Friends with potential benefits."

"Do you disagree on the term?"

"Not at all. But I do wonder if—*when*—it becomes 'friends with benefits' whether those benefits will be something we enjoy each time we see each other, or if this is a one-job-only deal."

"You really want to risk that with your family watching us like hawks?"

"Deny, deny, deny. They can suppose all they want as long as we never confirm."

"Hmm. You make it sound so easy."

"It could be."

I grinned and reached for the stack of cards. "I guess we'll just have to see if the benefits are worth a repeat performance." I cut the deck and showed a jack of hearts.

"Oh, they'll be worth it," he said with confidence. "I'll have you know I get excellent feedback." He cut the deck but held his card face down so I couldn't see.

"You survey all your conquests?"

"They keep coming back with no promise of commitment. Do you think I need to survey them? Or do you think the writhing and screaming of my name and calling me a god might do?"

"Such a bragger." I had to laugh. "Show me this card, King of the Clits. Let's see if I undo another button, or whether I do this one back up."

He lifted his card. "A two," he said with a laugh.

I sucked the air through my teeth. "Oh, too bad for you." My fingers twisted the open button back to closed.

"So cruel."

"So fun."

"You enjoy torturing me, don't you?"

"Only as much as you enjoy torturing me," I replied.

"I fucking *love* torturing you."

"Glad we're on the same page."

We continued cutting cards and drinking vodka, managing to get to an equal score of four all. My buttons, going up and down until we got to the final draw.

"This is the one, Slater. I can feel it in my boner."

"OK." I laughed, feeling a little lightheaded. "Why don't you pick first, then?"

"No way. It's your turn to go first. Can't have you cheating your way out of this somehow."

"I never cheat," I said, cutting the cards and holding mine up. "Queen of hearts." *How fitting.*

He sucked in a breath then held his hand over the deck, closing his eyes as he whispered, "Come on, King."

My heart beat like crazy, desperately wanting him to find that king too. Making out with him shirtless would be the perfect end to an incredibly fun Saturday night. *I can say no to more. I can stop whenever I want.*

With a quick movement, he selected his card and held it up, eyes closed, squinting, before he looked at what he held. "Ace of fucking spades." *Shit.* He dropped the cards with a sigh. "Sorry, buddy," he said to his crotch.

"Wait," I said, standing while working my buttons open with shaky hands. "Aces beat kings."

His eyes darkened, and he licked his lips as I moved towards him. "I thought we were playing high and low, not poker."

The shirt fell open at my sides, revealing the skin of my belly and the centre of my bra. The little bow was the girliest thing about my outfit. "Which rules would you prefer, Cartwright? High and low or poker?"

Sucking in his breath, he lifted his arm and placed a hand on the line between my abs, his fingertips teasing at the base of my bra. "Poker," he said. "Definitely poker."

Then he took a hold of my hips and I lowered myself so I was straddling his lap, our mouths connecting as he pushed the white shirt from my shoulders and worked the clasp of my bra free.

My fingers couldn't get his shirt open fast enough, and he tugged the damn thing off as I dropped my bra on the floor. Then we sat back and just looked at each other—his bronze skin, my freckles. His gloriously toned pecs, my tiny breasts and pert nipples. I ran my fingers over his skin, watching his expression change while I felt the heat and hard length of his dick pushing beneath me. I was glad he was turned on, firm and pulsing with want. It gave me a confidence in my own sexuality that I didn't know I had. This stunning man wanted me. Seemingly as much as I wanted him, and he was willing to win each item of my clothing, taking great delight in doing it.

I was under no illusions that this was anything more than physical. But sometimes, that was all a girl was happy with.

"Kiss me, goddammit," he practically growled as he grabbed the back of my head and brought my mouth to his. Our bodies pressed closer, skin to skin, our naked torsos feeling so good I caught myself wishing that the rest of us was naked too. *Fun without sex. Money.*

"You're an amazing kisser," I gasped as his mouth moved down my neck and his hands wandered over my skin.

"So are you." His words were almost lost in a mumble, his lips and tongue tasting and teasing, searing a line towards my—

"Oh my God."

His mouth clamped down on my nipple and sent a zap of erotic energy straight to my clit.

I dropped my head back, my hands gripping his broad shoulders as he treated my breasts to the pleasure of his mouth.

"I could suck on your nipples all day," he said, taking a moment to let his fingers do the tweaking while his tongue slid along my collarbone. "Preferably, all night."

"Oh yes." I rolled my body against him, hands in his hair, his cock pressing between my thighs. It felt so good that I didn't know if I could stop.

"Sloane." Grabbing hold of my arse, he stood and shoved my legs so I wrapped them around him.

"What are you doing?" I asked on a pant, wishing for the friction of his cock and his mouth on my nipples to return.

"Taking you to the bedroom so you can't keep grinding on my cock like that." He buried his face in my neck and sucked.

"That's a terrible idea." My voice was an unconvincing whisper. "How is that going to slow this down?"

"I'm not trying to slow this down. I'm trying to get more comfortable." He dropped me on the bed and leaned over me, his tongue running along the waistband of my pants as his hand covered my breast.

"Second base only," I gasped. "We should be making out like a couple of fumbling teenagers."

"I was super handsy as a teenager," he countered,

pulling a nipple into his mouth. *Oh my God.* "I also didn't stop at second base."

"This isn't the time to tell me about your past experience." I was going to come from nipple play alone. I was going to come, and I was going to lose half a million dollars because I couldn't contain myself when his mouth was doing what it was doing. *Oh God.* I had to stop this, had to do something to take my mind off that tongue. *Wait.* "How old were you when you lost your virginity?" His tongue swirled and tugged, my hands ran across his massive shoulders as I hissed between my teeth.

"Ah, ah, ah. I know what you're doing, and it's not going to work." He moved to my other nipple and flicked at it with his tongue.

I don't want to stop. This feels so good.

"But I want to know."

"Not telling." His mouth closed over the tight little bud and my back lifted off the bed. *Holy shit.*

"I lost mine on my seventeenth birthday," I forced out, fighting my desire to keep going. *Money. You need that money.*

He lifted his head, my nipple releasing from his mouth with a *pop.* "To the guy your mum..."

I nodded. Then he sat back on his knees and blew charged air out of his mouth. "That's fucked up."

"It is what it is," I said, disappointed that he stopped while relieved that my tactic worked. I wasn't sure that I could actually bring myself to make him stop. I wanted to come so bad. *Throb, throb, throb.*

Grabbing the blanket from the end of the bed, he pulled it up so I was covered to my neck then lay down beside me, releasing another breath slowly. "I lost mine at fifteen. Wendy from Ballarat."

"That was her full name?" I tried a joke, rolling onto my side so I was facing him.

He just gave me a sideways glance. "She was here with her family during the September school holidays. It was a bit of a catastrophe."

"Why was it a catastrophe?"

"She was a virgin too. Neither of us realised she'd bleed, and turned out she had this thing about the sight of blood. She passed out when she saw the sheets and I thought I'd killed her. Called an ambulance and everything."

"Oh my God. How traumatising."

He lifted his brow and grunted in the affirmative then a grin spread across my face.

"You thought you fucked her to death?" The giggle erupted up and came out my nose as a snort when I tried to stifle it.

"Yeah, laugh it up, funny girl. The ambos pissed themselves laughing at us too."

"You've gotta admit, it's pretty funny." The laughter just kept coming as I imagined him horrified because this girl had passed out. I felt mean, but I couldn't stop. "You thought you killed her. With your dick!" I threw my head back into the pillow, cackling uncontrollably, tears coming out of my eyes. "How did you ever trust yourself to fuck again?"

Glancing at me, he folded his arms across his chest, obviously perturbed. "I never fucked another virgin again, that's for sure."

Slowly, the bubble of laughter reduced itself to a smile

and I wiped the tears from my eyes. "I thought you said you would have taken mine."

We locked eyes and my heart jolted inside my chest. "Yeah, well, you're different. If we'd been closer in age back then things would have been different too."

"You think?" I returned to my side and let my gaze wander over his delicious body. He had a knack for saying exactly the right thing. Then I let my fingers follow, wandering up his ribs then over his pecs.

"Yeah," he said, watching my hand move against his skin, stark white on bronze.

"What makes you so sure?"

"Because then it would have been me you confided in instead of Toby. Me you came to."

"Does it really bother you that I went to him with those things?"

"Nah, I get it. But I still wish I'd been older so it was me." It still amazed me that he'd felt that way all those years ago. It made me feel good about myself, that someone had actually wanted me then...and maybe a little now.

I pressed a kiss to the point where his shoulder muscle joined with his bicep. "I wish it was too."

He let out a slow breath. "That was a dirty trick you played just now, bringing up your mum."

"You brought her up, actually."

"Yeah, but you had to know I'd make the connection."

I ran my fingers down his abs and watched him shiver under my touch. "All's fair in love and war, Abbot."

"Hmm, I'll remember you said that."

"Think about it while you kiss me." He lifted his

brows, hope and excitement lighting his eyes. "Just kissing. I'm the one who gets to do the touching this time."

"OK. But the pillow fort comes down tonight." He leaned over so his arms caged me beneath him.

"Only if you wear underwear." I slid my hands up his delectable sides to his strong back.

"I never wear underwear." He teased his lips against mine.

"Then the pillow fort stays."

"Fine. I'll wear underwear. But you can't put your shirt back on."

"Deal," I whispered, arching my body up so our chests touched, the blanket providing my loophole barrier.

He sucked gently on my bottom lip. "This feels a lot like winning, Sloane Slater."

"I know," I gasped, my fingers pressing into his bare skin. I was in control again, and the money would be mine. "I know."

"WHERE DO you think you're going?" Abbot asked the next morning when he found me getting dressed. We'd fallen asleep for a few hours after exhausting ourselves kissing and touching. There were no orgasms. We were both careful not to push the other too close to the edge—a beautiful drawn-out torture at the time—but as it hadn't helped with my travel insomnia, I was up and getting ready to work.

"I'm going to work on the safe," I said, tucking my shirt into my trousers. "Well, after I shower and get some clean clothes. You're obviously coming with me." *I wish.*

Maybe after the safe is open…

"It's Sunday, Sloane. No work on Sundays. Even crooks need a day off."

"I wasn't aware of that, seeing I've only been a crook for the last week."

"You've been a crook all your life. You've just been on sabbatical. Now, get your shirt off and get back into bed."

I looked at him, the mess of hair, the shirtless chest, the beckoning eyes and kiss-sore mouth, and all I wanted was to remove every stitch from my body and beg him to fuck me—just like he wanted. But then I'd lose and this trip, getting mixed up with his family again, would have been for nothing. So, I shook my head and stepped backwards. That bed was a dangerous place. Those hands, that mouth, they were weapons against my ability to refuse him. "I want to run. Maybe swim."

"Got a little pent-up energy, Slater?" He grinned, his eyes wicked as he pulled the blankets back and revealed the giant tent happening in his pants.

I'm drooling.

I'm staring.

Look away!

"I haven't trained properly for days." I turned and moved to the door. "You can join me if you like."

"Running?"

"Or swimming."

"How about I take you to the gym? You can do all that there, even use the bikes so you can get the full triathlon experience."

"Your gym has a pool?"

"It's a health club. It has everything. Come on."

He got out of bed and pulled his own shirt on. I felt a bloom of disappointment as the buttons went up and his chest went away. Then we grabbed the rest of our clothing from the living area as we exited the apartment.

"Why do you stay at Jasmine's when you have access to this place?" I asked, my thumb pointing over my shoulder as we headed downstairs.

"That's a very good question." It actually seemed like he hadn't thought of it prior to this moment. "I guess I just packed up my shit from the beach shack and dumped it at Jazz's without thinking much about it."

"Too busy pouting over being the odd twin out?" I teased, pouting my lips as we pushed out onto the footpath.

"Something like that." He slipped two pieces of nicotine gum in his mouth then inhaled deeply. "Fuck, I could do with a smoke this morning. Last night was…" He let his words fall away as he did this combination of shaking and nodding his head. It looked like confusion.

"Frustrating?" I offered.

He shook his head and inhaled through his nose, moving his arms towards his chest like he was trying to conjure the word he wanted. "Interesting, intense. *Fun*. It was fun."

"Getting blue-balled is fun? OK." I laughed, and also took a deep breath. There was something healing about it. It relieved the sexual tension we continued to build upon, but just a touch, and just for a moment. It was right back there when I looked at him again.

He grabbed his crotch and adjusted it with a grin. "Yes, Sloane. Not fucking you right away is *fun*. Now, get in the damn car. I need a cold shower, and about three hours working this off at the gym."

"I thought you said the gym isn't fun."

"It isn't. It's necessary."

ONCE BACK AT the big Cartwright house, I made a beeline

for my bedroom and the shower. It wasn't normal to shower *before* going to the gym. But, after last night, it was required. I smelled like Abbot and Abbot smelled like me.

Abbot.

He was boisterous, cheeky, persistent but in a good way. He made me laugh so much that my cheeks hurt. And I wanted him, badly. It would be so easy to relieve some of that longing between my legs with a few well-aimed passes of the shower's handheld spray. But I resisted. Rules were rules. And I wanted to play fair.

Besides, Abbot was right. This slow teasing was a hell of a lot of fun. I think that when the time came—*if* the time came—for us to take this all the way, the build-up would make the moment explosive. No real technique required. I imagined that the simple connection would be enough to tip us both over the edge. *Wham bam pow!* I laughed to myself at the thought.

Once out of the shower, I towelled myself off and pulled my gym clothes on, packing my swimsuit in a back-pack so I could take full advantage of the club's facilities.

With my hair combed and pulled into a ponytail, I paused with my hand on the door handle when I heard voices.

"When did you two get back last night?" The voice sounded like it came from Breaker. He'd obviously caught up with Abbot in the kitchen.

"I got back this morning," Abbot replied. "Not sure about Sloane." I could tell he was trying to sound purpose-fully disinterested to cover his lie. At least that's what I hoped I was hearing.

"She spent the night here?" Breaker wasn't convinced.

"You tell me."

Their silence stretched a little longer than seemed comfortable, so I took that as my cue to intervene. "Hey guys," I said, a big fake smile on my face as I wandered over and gave them both a friendly tap on the arm. "How's it hangin'?"

Breaker frowned. I didn't think he liked me much. "A little to the left," he responded. "How about you?"

"Neatly tucked between my legs like all good vaginas should be, thank you very much. Any coffee on?"

Abbot moved his hand across his mouth, obscuring a grin before he gestured to the coffee pot. "Help yourself. Sleep well?"

"Oh, I don't really sleep much at all," I said, pouring a mug of black gold.

"You two get separated last night?" Breaker asked casually. Abbot opened his eyes like he was trying to send me telepathic messages.

"Not really," I said, blowing on my coffee as I lifted it to my mouth. Abbot slapped his hand against his face and it was my turn to hide a smile. "I just came back early. Read a book on my phone. Abbot was busy with some bimbo, so I didn't want to stick around like a third wheel."

"A good wingman always knows when it's time to go home," Abbot added and I pointed at him while winking because it seemed the right thing to do in the moment.

"Didn't hear you come in," Breaker said, still looking a little doubtful.

I shrugged. "I don't tend to make a lot of noise if I think someone is asleep."

Breaker looked between us. I felt like I was being interviewed by a fed.

"Morning," Jasmine said as she stepped out of the stairwell wearing a long white silk robe with large pink flowers printed on it. "We're all up early." I was so thankful for the timing of her entrance because I didn't think Breaker believed a single word Abbot and I were saying, which would obviously lead him to question why we were lying. I honestly wasn't completely sure why myself, but it seemed important to head the warnings and not let Jasmine learn about Abbot's and my...attraction? Game? I wasn't really sure what to call it, which further added to the need to keep whatever it was to ourselves.

"I was going to the gym to get some training in," I said, offering her coffee. She smiled gratefully.

"Are you going with her, Abbot?" she asked, seeming super chipper, as if her question was innocent as opposed to being an order. It was a little strange, because she'd been very short with me during the week. Perhaps Breaker rocked her world last night and she was revelling in her post-orgasm glow this morning?

"I was gonna surf, but sure, I can take her. There's a gym at the aquatic centre if you want to go there?" he asked as if we hadn't already made these exact plans.

"Sounds great." I smiled, picking up my bag and heading for the door, my coffee forgotten. "I'll meet you in the car."

He followed me out about ten minutes later, and I wasn't sure if I was pissed or just confused. That whole interaction just felt wrong and uncomfortable.

"Thanks for that," he said once we got in his Jag.

"Don't thank me, Abbot. Every time I interact with your family I feel like shit."

"I don't know what to tell you besides they can't know anything is going on between us." He started the car and backed out of his spot.

"Because there are rules I don't know about and you're petrified your mother will start planning your wedding too. I get it, Abbot. I do. And I'm not getting too attached. I'll get out of here the moment the job is through. But that doesn't mean I enjoy lying about you fucking some other woman when I was the one in your bed last night." Memories of my last relationship fuelled my disappointment in this conversation, the commitment phobia, and the way Mark had always downplayed our relationship around others. It felt like that all over again. It wasn't even that I'd started to like Abbot as more than a friend—because I understood exactly what this was—it was that he seemed so fucking freaked out that anyone could possibly want him in a relationship with me...*of all people*. He was going to great lengths to keep them guessing, when it was obvious that he'd never hidden one of those beach bimbos from them. *Why is having a fling with me so different?*

"Sloane—"

"Leave it, Abbot. I'm fine."

"I'm not trying to rush you out of here."

"That's only because you want more time to play this game of ours. What if I said I don't want to play anymore?"

"Then we stop," he said simply, and for some reason that felt more offensive than lying to his family about our friendship and my sexuality. I hated that he seemed so blasé.

"Fine. Then I think we should stop."

"You want to stop?" *No. Fuck no. I want to keep going, I want—*

"It's for the best," I said, folding my arms over my middle as I looked out the window. "It's obviously too complicated for you. I don't want to be in the way."

With a sudden swerve of the wheel, he pulled the car off the road then grabbed my hand. "You aren't in the way, Sloane. That has never been what this shit with my family is about. It's…it's just complicated. But you, *you* aren't the complication."

"I still think we should cool it," I said, looking at our joined hands. I didn't want to cool it. Lord knew I wanted to do a hell of a lot more than make it to second base with this man, but it was a stupid game. One that could cost me dearly. Financially, obviously, but also my heart if I wasn't careful. *And I'd had enough of that in my life already.*

"OK." He released my hand, seeming absolutely fine with my decision as he pulled back into traffic.

One small taste, and he was done. Fuck. Me. I'm that easy to pass over?

Story of my life.

"Back to just friends then?"

"Yep." He twisted his hand on the steering wheel as we stopped at a set of lights. "But, ah, if you change your mind, I'm cool with that too." Glancing at me, his eyes did a quick sweep of my body and he licked his lips. "I'd be *very* cool with that."

Wait. Why do I feel like this is another game?

With a short laugh, I reached out and hit him in the arm. He was such a dick. But in a funny way. He easily diffused any sort of tension between us with a little humour. Nothing seemed to faze him. And as we drove to the aquatic centre, everything seemed fine between us. *Normal.* We were back to being just friends. Just like that.

No more sex games…which was for the best. Obviously.

Really, it was.

It was…

"HOW MANY SIT-UPS do you reckon you can do?" Abbot asked when he found me on the gym floor, peddling the stationary bike.

"I don't know," I said, puffed, sweaty, pumping my legs while trying not to focus on his ripped and glistening chest. He was making me ridiculously thirsty and regretful. I already missed our game. "I've never tried to the point of failure."

He placed his hand in the centre of the handlebars. "You know, if we were still doing this thing, I'd challenge you for third base."

"Third base, huh? You only just got second. Plus, we're not doing that anymore." I pushed my legs harder, faster, trying to distract myself from thinking about what that would be like. *Why, oh why, did I tell him I wanted out?*

"What if we were still playing? What would you have said?"

I stopped peddling and grabbed my towel, mopping the

sweat from my face, neck and chest. "I'd say that you needed to pick something smaller than third base."

"How about I pick to restart our game?"

"We only just called it off."

"I miss it already." I'd missed it straight away.

"From the beginning, or where we left off?"

"Where we left off, but with one major change. I move you out of the main house. We can stay at the apartment and forget about the shit with my family."

"Don't you think they'll be even more suspicious if we shack up together?" It would be so much harder to say no to him without having to worry about getting caught. *Is he trying to kill me?* No. Just fuck me.

"I'll tell Jasmine her and Breaker fuck too loud for me, and since I'm your designated keeper, it makes sense that you'd stay there with me." *Designated keeper?* So much for that trust they went on about.

I got off the bike. "I don't know, Abbot. It sounds too convoluted to me."

He ran his hand through his hair. "It's perfect really. We get our privacy and we won't have to worry about my family. Tell me last night wasn't awesome for you and I'll back right off."

"Well, I'd be lying if I said that," I replied, blushing slightly from the memory.

He grinned and placed his hands on my hips, pulling me closer to him. "Play with me again, Sloane."

I rolled my eyes. "You still won't win," I whispered, fighting a smile.

With a chuckle, he hooked a finger beneath my chin and tilted my head up, his lips brushing against mine as he spoke. "Maybe. But I'll have a fantastic time trying."

■ ■ ■

"Fuck! OK, you win," I groaned, dropping back on the mat, my abs screaming in pain. Almost a thousand sit-ups later, Abbot sat up and pumped his fist in the air triumphantly.

"Oh, it is on, Slater. On like Donkey Kong."

"Nerd." I laughed and it hurt like a bitch. "Ow."

"Donkey Kong isn't nerdy, so you deserved that. It's a classic."

"Do you still have those little handhelds we used to play as kids?"

"Sure do. They're in my wardrobe at Jasmine's."

"Tucked away with your comics and porn mags?" I teased.

"I never brought porn magazines. My charm let me learn about women firsthand."

I chuckled. "Such a Casanova. Help me up."

He got to his feet and held out a hand, helping me slowly stand up. I stretched my arms above my head and leaned back to lengthen my tight abs. He stood there watching.

"How are you acting like your abs aren't burning?" I asked, twisting from side to side.

"Because they aren't. I do a couple thousand sit-ups every day."

"Guess that explains the ripped abs. And why you chose this competition to get your way. Touché, Mr Cartwright. Touché."

"I'm not just a pretty face," he said, handing me some water. I drank thirstily. "Ready to head back?"

I shook my head. "I need to swim first. It'll help with the pain in my abs."

"Tell you what," he said, checking his watch. "You go swimming and I'll come back in about an hour."

"Where are you going?"

"To get our shit from Jasmine's. We're moving out."

"Wow. You move fast."

"No point in wasting time claiming my prize. Especially when I don't know how long I have with you."

I laughed. "Not long. A few more days and I'll have that puppy open."

"You're coming to the wedding next weekend, so technically, I have at least a week. Which, mind you, is way less than the month you originally quoted me."

"Hey, I'm better than I thought. But I can go home and come back for the wedding," I pointed out. And since our little competition would be over by that point, we could finally bump uglies in glorious fashion. I'd have my money then come back for my reward. It was a perfect plan. I could hold out just a little longer.

Abbot narrowed his eyes slightly. "I can see we need to discuss our deadline again."

"No discussion needed. When the safe is open, the game is over, I go home half a mill richer, and *you* can go back to your regular beach bimbo-fucking schedule." I tapped him on the chest. "I'll see you in an hour, Abs." It was the first time I'd called him by his nickname, but it seemed fitting after what I just witnessed.

■ ■ ■

"OK. So, I'll be taking this room over here and you get the main bedroom since technically this is your place," I said, walking across the living area to the farthest door. My body snapped to a halt when Abbot took a hold of my arm.

"I don't think so, S. Same rules as before. Just without

the pillows down the middle of the bed." He pulled me towards the main room. *He's persistent. I'll give him that.*

Planting my feet, I extracted myself from his grip and smiled sweetly up at him. "We weren't sharing at Jasmine's, hot stuff. I had my own room and you were *sneaking* into my bed each night."

He grinned and slid his hands around my waist, fingers finding their way under the fabric of my T-shirt, brushing at my skin. My breathing grew heavier, completely undermining any protest I put up. "You're just afraid you can't trust yourself around me twenty-four-seven."

"I doubt I'll be here for a full seven days."

He grunted unhappily, having already made it clear how put out he was to only have a few more days to win the next two bases, the final one needing to be given willingly—begged for, even. I was pretty sure he was starting to doubt his prowess, which must have been hard for a man who was used to getting what he wanted. I loved watching him squirm.

"All the more reason to share a room." I rolled my eyes then he tipped my chin up until I looked back at him. "Come on, Slater. I'm gonna be in your bed, anyway. What difference does it make if we share a bathroom and a chest of drawers too?" It made a huge difference. The times when I showered and changed were the moments where I gave myself my daily pep talks. I needed that reprieve to stay strong. Still, it was tempting...

"Play me for it," I suggested as a compromise while twisting the button at the centre of his chest. He'd come back from Jasmine's wearing a short-sleeved button-up shirt with a pair of jeans. He looked so good in everything he put on his body. *Better when it was off, though.*

"It's the first Sunday of the month. I have to go back to Jasmine's for a family meeting and don't have time for a game." At least he sounded disappointed.

"Then flip a coin. Heads I take that room and sleep alone."

"*No way.*" His eyes grew big at the prospect of losing the most intimate part of our relationship.

"Tails." A cheeky grin curved my mouth as I pointed to the second bedroom. "And I share with you, always shirtless, underwear on, no barriers."

A grin curved his mouth too, and I was pretty sure his dick just got hard.

"So, skin to skin? All night long?" He narrowed his eyes as he waited for clarification.

"Skin to skin. All night long." I pressed my body against his, confirming he was definitely hard. *Pulse, pulse, pulse.*

"OK. I can get behind those odds," he said, releasing me then pulling a fifty-cent piece from his pocket.

"Wait. I want to check it."

"Sloane, I don't carry double-sided coins in my pocket." He flipped it back and forth so I could clearly see the Queen's silhouette and the Australian coat of arms. "Not that you'd ever know it if I did." He closed his hand around the coin in his palm then turned his fist from side to side and opened it again, the coin now gone.

I gasped like a little kid. Magic was cool at any age. "I have zero faith in your coin toss being fair now."

He reproduced the coin. "I'll be fair." With a wink, he showed me it was the same coin then balanced it on his thumb and forefinger, preparing to toss.

"Don't catch it," I said. "Let it fall to the floor."

He laughed. "The floor it is." Then he flicked his thumb, sending the coin spinning in the air, catching the light on the silver surface before it landed with a soft thud on the carpet. The Australian coat of arms face up, an emu and a kangaroo depicted either side of a shield. Tails. I lost.

Is it bad that I'm happy about this?

"Yes!" He pumped his fist in the air before picking me up and throwing me over his shoulder, carrying me into the room caveman style.

I laughed as he flipped me onto the bed and I landed with my head against the pillows.

"Congratulations," I said as he climbed over the top of me, holding himself so our legs were entwined and I was caged beneath him.

"I'm not even gonna pretend that I wouldn't have been pissed if I'd lost that one."

"Seems you just keep winning, Mr Cartwright."

"Funny that. It's almost like you want me to but don't want to give in too easily."

I grinned and placed my hands against his ribs, loving how broad and firm he was. "You don't think you've been winning fair and square?"

He brushed his lips over mine. "I know I haven't." Then he took my mouth in a toe-curling kiss that had my fingers searching for his buttons and twisting them open.

He groaned unhappily, his mouth still moving with mine as his hand slid beneath my shirt to cup my breast. He groaned again.

"What are you doing?" I giggled after he made yet another unhappy sound.

"I have to go, and I don't want to stop." He stuck his

head beneath my shirt, licking his way up the centre of my stomach, making me glad I'd showered at the aquatic centre.

"You're stretching my shirt." I laughed, pressing against his shoulders. He came back out, his hair all mussed as he rested his chin on my stomach and gave me puppy-dog eyes. "I'll still be here when you get back," I said, running my fingers through his hair.

He closed his eyes and hummed with pleasure. "Don't move from this bed."

"Not even to pee?"

He laughed. "You are a bigger kid than me."

"I guess that's why we're buds."

He jumped off the bed and straightened his shirt. "With potential benefits," he added, turning to face the mirror to finger-comb his hair. "I'll be back in a few hours. There's a remote on the dresser. Netflix on the TV. If you want food, you'll need to order in or go out. Just keep your phone with you."

I touch my head in salute. "Yes, captain, my captain. I promise to be good."

He held a finger out to me, a stern look on his face. "No masturbating. I'm trusting you here."

I traced my finger over my heart in a crossing motion, grinning. "I give you my word." Although, it was seriously tempting to gain a little relief, but I wasn't a cheat and my knees would stay together. "But if you're that worried, why aren't you just taking me with you?"

"Taking a girl to a family meeting would mean something we don't want it to mean. It's best you stay here." There were those unspoken consequences again.

"It is for the best," I said, sitting up and pulling my

shirt over my head before lying back on the pillows with a sigh. "None of them believe the whole gay thing anyway."

He licked his lips, his Adam's apple bobbing as his gaze travelled over me. "They said that to you?"

"Yep." I placed my fingers against my chest near my collarbone then ran them down, feather-light until I reached my waistband. "Toby, Holland and Alesha all said they didn't buy it." I walked my middle and index fingers down the centre seam of my leggings and sighed before resting my hand flat on my thigh. "I think it's wise of you to leave me here all alone." When I met his eyes, they were clouded with desire, his jaw ticking as his hands clenched by his sides. "See you later, Cartwright. You don't want to be late." I grabbed the side of the doona beneath me and wrapped it around my body, completely hiding from his view.

Biting my lip to stop my giggle, I listened, wondering whether he was going to blow off the meeting or change his mind and take me with him so I couldn't touch myself. But he did neither, instead letting out a disgruntled moan before tearing himself from the bedroom and muttering about 'sitting through a fucking meeting with a hard-on' then slamming the front door.

Uncurling myself from the doona, I let that giggle loose before stretching out on the bed with a giant smile. Minus the weird family shit, it was a shame that the job was almost over because it meant that this would be over too, the flirting, the teasing. *Will he still want me if I open the safe without giving in?* Hmm, he *had* suggested that if I were to return, do more jobs with the family, then we could hook up again... What were his exact words?

I do wonder if—when—it becomes 'friends with bene-

fits' whether those benefits will be something we enjoy each time we see each other...

Could I be that girl with him? The kind who comes and goes with no expectations or commitments? I'd lived without commitment with Mark for eight years and that had really sucked. But then, I'd had expectations back then, expectations I wouldn't have if I were to embark on a casual thing with Abbot Cartwright. With Abbot, I'd always know exactly where I stood. And it didn't mean that I couldn't keep an eye out in case Mr Right came along. It would just ensure I was thoroughly pleasured in the interim. Something I could definitely see myself returning for. And since it seemed I wouldn't have much choice in continuing to work with the Cartwrights, I couldn't see why I shouldn't have my cake and eat it too. I was a twenty-first-century woman, after all. I didn't need commitment to take my pleasure.

Folding my arms behind my head, I let out a contented sigh and gave myself a mental nod. I could do this. I could win this game then have sex with Abbot without letting my emotions get in the way.

Yes!

That was my path. No love, no feelings, no commitment, just fucking. I'd go home and then—

I'll go home and you can go back to fucking your beach bimbos.

Oh shit. Could I handle sharing?

Fuck.

I don't think I can do this after all.

"WHEN ARE YOU COMING BACK?" Mark asked over the phone when his text bearing the same question had gone unanswered. I was up the street picking up some groceries and getting something for my dinner and didn't hear the alert go off. Plus, I was kinda ignoring him.

"Couple of days?" I said, picking meat off a chicken bone and sucking it into my mouth as I spoke to him on speaker.

"Are you asking me or telling me?"

I laughed. "I'm telling—guesstimating. There's a lot going on down here. The job is complicated, and they're old friends of Pop's. It's just…it's taking time."

"What does that even mean?"

I released a sigh. It was difficult feeding someone you cared about a story with very few facts. I had no idea how Pop did it for all those years. Although, people didn't tend to ask this many questions of guys, did they? "It means I'll be back sometime between Wednesday and the following Monday. How's Terry?"

I didn't hate Teresa…*his wife*. Despite the fact that she had exactly what I'd waited eight years for, I didn't dislike her one bit. She was lovely, she was beautiful, and she was good. I couldn't hate her, but I was jealous of her. Mark's and my relationship had stalled, and I'd been the one to end it. We wanted different things, I'd said. I could live without marriage, but I wanted kids before I was too old to have them. He said he didn't. So, I left. I left and entered singledom again, and it was amicable between us. We'd stayed friends. We convinced all of our other friends that our split was a mutual agreement, that we still cared for each other…but not in *that* way anymore. I was even OK when he started dating again. I honestly thought it would be the same thing—no marriage, no kids. Imagine my shock when he took me aside and told me differently. "We're getting married," he'd said. "I really want you there. You're my best friend." As the knife twisted in my gut, I'd smiled and congratulated him. Bought them a ridiculously expensive gift and went out of my way to welcome Teresa into our friendship group. I even let his kid call me Aunty Sloane.

I didn't hate Teresa. I didn't even hate Mark. But I did hate the way their relationship made me feel, the way his persistent need to remain in my life forced me to be part of *theirs*. This break away from seeing him daily had given me a lot of clarity. Our relationship wasn't healthy.

"Why are we doing this, Mark?" I asked, interrupting him as he told me about how hard pregnancy was on Terry with a toddler in tow. *I don't want to hear it.*

He paused. "Doing what, Sloane?"

"Pretending to be friends."

"You don't think we're friends?"

"I think we do a great job at pretending to be."

He sighed. "Sloane…"

"Mark…" I mimicked, childishly.

"What's going on with you?"

"I just…I think…I *know* that we need to call this. I need a fresh start, and I don't think it's fair to Teresa."

"What do you mean? We haven't done anything wrong." *Calling me your best friend when you're married to another woman is doing something wrong. To her. To me.* It hurt. It had been hurting me for a long time, and he'd never had a clue. Or didn't care to notice.

"Then it's not fair to me."

"Sloane."

"Saying my name isn't changing anything, Mark. This hurts me. Your happiness hurts me." It felt so good to be saying it. Finally.

"You can't be serious, Sloane."

"I am. You couldn't give me what I wanted, and I understand that I wasn't the right girl for you. And I'm over you. I'm over what we were. But I just can't keep watching and cheering you on while you live out the life *I* wanted with someone else. I deserve better than that, Mark."

"Sloane," he said again, more stern as if that would make a difference.

"Goodbye, Mark." I disconnected the call with a gentle tap of my finger…*and it was over*. Twenty-three years…*gone*.

And I felt lighter.

Looking around the apartment, I took a deep breath as I flipped my phone to silent and placed it face down. It was so quiet yet peaceful. I could see the roiling surf through the floor-to-ceiling glass door that led to a balcony. The hum of the ocean's power made me feel at peace when I was a little shaky, a little messy on the inside.

Grabbing a bottle of ginger beer from the fridge, I went out onto the balcony and sat with my feet up on the outdoor modular, watching beach goers have their fun.

Deciding to start over and leave behind the life I'd built back home wasn't an easy decision. But it was the right one. I knew that much. Staying put had made my life stagnated. I was no different to the girl I had been when I lived with Mark, the girl I was when I'd finished school. I was almost forty, for fuck's sake. If I didn't make changes now, I might never live my ideal life.

But what *was* my ideal life? Was it being the locksmith to a bunch of criminals who would slowly crawl out of the woodwork as time went by? Or was it something entirely different? I could quite literally make any choice I wanted at the end of this job. Two hundred and fifty grand for opening a safe. The same again for resisting Abbot—that was the difficult part. And if I sold my apartment along with the shop, I could get another five hundred again. I could be a millionaire and do anything, *anything* I wanted once that money was cleaned. I could even live by the beach.

Hmm. That would be nice.

I could learn how to surf again, run along the beaches instead of potholed country roads. Maybe I could take up those iron man competitions. I could work part-time to keep myself busy. Then maybe I could find someone...

Someone who makes me laugh like Abbot does.

Makes me feel sexy like Abbot does.

Someone like Abbot.

Just not Abbot himself. He wasn't made for relationships. He'd made that part very clear with his crazy cover stories.

I touched my fingers to my lips and laughed at myself for going along with this game of his in the first place. It was childish, and it didn't even have a real point. But it was fun, and I wasn't going to apologise for enjoying myself when I'd been a straight line for so long.

After cutting ties with Mark, I knew I could never be a *sometimes* girl with Abbot. I could play this game, maybe have sex with him at the end of it. But then I needed to cut ties with him too. I knew my heart too well, and I couldn't repeat this thing we were doing. I'd only want more. More than he was willing to give.

"This doesn't look like the bed where I left you," Abbot said from the doorway, closing the screen as he stepped out and took a seat next to me, a beer already in his hand.

"It's too nice out here," I said with a smile, liking the way he shifted close and slid his arm around the back of the lounge suite, inviting me in. *One more week.*

"That it is." He held up his beer and I tapped mine against his, clinking glass then drinking in silence. "I tried calling you on my way back."

"My phone is on silent inside."

He drank from his bottle, just a sip. "I saw that." He placed his bottle on the frosted glass coffee table then leaned back, relaxing next to me. "I also noticed there are a lot of missed calls. Is that Mark guy harassing you?"

I sighed, leaning forward to put my smaller brown bottle next to his tall clear one. I stayed forward though, my elbows on my knees. "I told him I can't be friends with him anymore."

He didn't respond straight away so I glanced over my shoulder to catch his expression. Bewildered, perhaps just curious. I wasn't sure.

"Not because of you," I said quickly. "So don't freak out. I did it because you were right. I wasn't comfortable being his friend and having his happiness rubbed in my face. It was this constant, *why her and not me*? And it wasn't healthy."

"OK," he said, his voice soft. "What's the plan now?"

I shrugged. "Sell up, I guess. Find myself some new roots. I like the sea. I'd like to get myself a shack of my own somewhere." I took a deep breath and closed my eyes, before remembering who I was talking to. "Not here with you, so you can relax. There are a lot of coastal towns out there. I'll find one I like."

"I wouldn't hate it if you moved here." He cleared his throat and picked up his beer again. "It wouldn't suck having you around."

Smiling, I leaned into him with a sigh. "You're sweet. You might not think so, but you really are."

He played with a strand of my hair, winding it around his finger as he chuckled. "I'm really not. My motives are entirely selfish." He reached over and hooked a finger in my top, pulling it far enough forward that he could look down.

"What night would I be?"

He released me then frowned. "What *night*?"

"Monday? Tuesday? Saturday? Would there be a roster?"

"Um. I don't know, Sloane. I like having you around and I'm playing this by ear."

"I'm sorry." Reaching out, I placed my hand on his. "I'm tense after my conversation with Mark, and I'm taking it out on you when you've been nothing but straight with me."

"It's cool."

"It's not, but thank you for being you." I nudged my shoulder against his. "*Sweet* you."

"You're making me blush, Slater." He reached forward and picked up his beer, drinking a good mouthful this time.

I sat back against the seat and sighed, thinking about what I would do once I packed up my life. "You know, I think I need to find my own place in this world. If I came here, you and me would fall into the same sort of thing I had going with Mark. And there's no future in fucking for fun."

"I'm starting to feel rejected here."

I laughed. "I'm not rejecting you. Our game is still happening. I just want to make changes to my life when it's over. I'm not getting any younger and if I'm honest with myself, I do want the whole marriage and kids thing. If not marriage, then at the very least, kids. I'm kind of on the clock for that one."

"I respect that."

"Am I freaking you out?"

"Only because my window is getting smaller and smaller. I need to up my game. I have to win the next two bases before you're off the market for good."

"I doubt it'll happen that quickly, but I feel your urgency." I grinned and took a mouthful of my drink.

"Feeling it too, huh?" He chuckled. "You are so gonna

beg. Once we're at third base, you're not gonna wanna stop."

Not likely, Abbot. I need that money to start my new life. Losing was never an option, but with my new plan, it was even less so.

Keeping my lips sealed, I rested my head on his shoulder, drinking sideways. It worked at first, then a trickle escaped down my chin.

"Ah shit," I said, sitting up and trying to catch the drip with my hand.

"Here, let me clean that up," Abbot said, tilting my chin up and licking my spill with his tongue. It was weird and hot at the same time. Then his mouth met mine and all the weirdness fell away. There was only kissing and gorgeous man; moans and fingers searching for skin.

"My shirt is making me itchy, Cartwright," I whispered against his mouth.

He smiled. "Then let me help you out."

Within moments, we were shirtless on his bed. *God, I love making out with this guy.*

"FUCK." The hissed expletive and sudden movement beside me shocked me out of my sleep.

Abbot jumped out of bed and made a dash for the bathroom. Holding his dick through his boxer briefs.

It took a moment for my sleep-addled mind to realise what happened, but when I did, I started giggling.

"Did I just win by default?" I asked with a huge grin when he came back looking slightly embarrassed.

"Coming in my sleep doesn't count, Sloane."

"You said no coming unless it was with each other." I got up on my knees, not caring that I had no shirt on and only bottoms. He'd seen me like this plenty, and I wasn't shy.

His mouth quirked at the corner as he leaned against the doorframe. "That was definitely *with* you."

"Default! Default!" I chanted, bouncing on the bed.

He laughed, his eyes dropping to my chest as he made his way back to the bed and knelt on the end of it. "I do *not* accept your victory," he said, crawling towards me. "But I do have a way to make it even."

I stopped bouncing, the predatory look in his eyes sending a jolt of awareness right to my clit. *Pulse, pulse, pulse.* "How?"

"Well," he said, grabbing my thighs and pulling so I flipped back on the bed. *Oh God. I'm going to come. He's going to make me come and I won't lose the money. Oh. Yes.* "We could have a momentary stay. Pause our competition long enough for you to"—he leaned over me, running his tongue between my breasts before kissing the gentle curve underneath the left one—"climax."

"How exactly would I climax…exactly?" I knew I said the same word twice. But I was struggling to make a coherent sentence, so I was to be forgiven.

"Well," he whispered, licking and sucking his way down my body until his face was positioned right where I wanted him. *Throb, throb, throb.* "You could do it yourself. Or…we could play for third base and I could do it for you." He pushed my thighs open and I let them fall willingly, watching him kiss over the thin cotton of my underwear.

"Over clothes or under?" I could only whisper.

"Over." He ran his nose up my centre and I moaned at the contact, the building ache so ready for touch after days of teasing without satisfaction.

He inhaled. "I can smell you, Sloane." His fingers trailed lightly down then back up, pressing against my opening and my clit. "I can feel you through your panties. Wet. Were you dreaming of me too?"

Yes. "Maybe."

He chuckled. "You were." Then he leaned down and

placed his mouth right over all my best bits, licking over the fabric, the pressure of his tongue causing me to arch my back and lose my mind.

"Oh God."

"Mmm. I can taste you." He shifted a little and touched his fingers to my inner thigh, right where the cotton met my skin. "I bet that if I slipped my fingers just under here"—he teased the edge of the elastic—"you'd feel like silk and your pussy would be so greedy that I could slide my fingers right in." *Do it.* He moved his fingers to my centre, staying on top of the fabric as he pressed against my seam. *I want him to fuck me. So bad. I don't even care anymore.*

He inhaled again. "Your scent is making me so hard, Sloane. So wet and ready for me. Just like you were in my dream. I slid inside you and it was so tight. I lost my mind. I'm losing my mind now. I want you so bad." He clamped his mouth over my pussy again, my underwear so drenched they were barely an issue. *Fuck me, fuck me, fuck me.*

"Abbot." I grabbed his hair, my hips rocking as his mouth worked, applying just the right amount of pressure and friction to have me… "Oh God. I'm coming. I'm coming." My hips lifted off the bed as I writhed beneath him, howling like a mad woman until he slowed his stroking tongue and brought me back down, panting, out of breath. "Holy fuck that was fast." *Too fast.* I wished it had lasted longer, but I was too on edge, too ready for him. *I've been ready since he walked into my store.*

"If you were a guy, that would be very bad." Abbot chuckled, kissing his way back up my body. I smiled and kept my fingers in his hair.

"But since I'm a girl, it adds to your prowess."

"I am the god of your clit right now," he said with a triumphant smile as he held himself above me. I could feel his new erection against my thigh.

I get it, Abbot. I want to do that again too.

"You are so full of yourself," I teased, my hands moving down to his shoulders, chest and ribs. He released a delighted shudder then kissed me, long, slow, his skilled tongue drawing a whimper from my chest. Being with him, just in this small way, had felt as amazing as I'd imagined. I already missed being able to touch him after I was gone.

"I would much prefer it if you were full of me," he whispered, nibbling my ear and pressing himself against me. And I considered it. For a moment. A wonderful tempting moment. But then I remembered the money and I pulled my lip with my teeth and shook my head.

"The stay is over. We both came. And don't think I didn't notice that you never played me for third."

"I played *with* you for third."

"Doesn't count."

"I can't go back to not touching that heat between your legs, Sloane." His words were a strangled gasp as he pressed his pulsing cock against my thigh. I shuddered out my breath.

"Then pick a game." Having him touch me like that without coming again was going to be absolute torture.

He pulled back and kissed the tip of my nose. "Yahtzee."

A laugh burst out of me. "*Yahtzee*?"

"Yep. And I'm awesome at it, so be warned." He pushed back onto his knees and held out a hand. "But first, let's go get cleaned up. I'll even let you take the first cold shower."

"Such a gentleman," I said as I walked ahead of him to the en-suite.

He slapped me on the arse before I could make it through the door. I yelped then laughed.

"And don't you forget it, Slater."

CHAPTER TWENTY
LEVEL THE PLAYING FIELD

I AM A YAHTZEE CHAMPION. And it sucks. With my time in Torquay coming to an end, I'd actually been looking forward to some rubbing and teasing down south. The kind of frantic making out you did with your first serious boyfriend before you were ready to have sex. I wanted to get close to coming then push Abbot away with a breathless, "*Stop!*"

Winning *really* sucked.

Still, there was plenty of enjoyment to be had. Kissing and naked chests, massages and tongues on salty skin, fingers teasing waistbands. The restraint was tantalising all on its own, and I loved every moment with him. But I was ready for more. Something I was never going to get if Abbot kept losing games while also making it hard for me to work.

It was now Wednesday and I hadn't seen the safe since Friday. Which I guess would be fine if I wasn't getting so desperate for release. One orgasm was not enough. In fact, it had made it worse, and I was getting seriously crabby.

On Monday, I'd been sent to a tailor to have the brides-maid's dress turned into a playsuit. It should have only taken a couple of hours, but Abbot said he had business in town and dragged me all over the place until he decided dinner was more important. Then we played blackjack for third base. I won, the pants stayed on.

On Tuesday, he had lawns to mow. That's right, *lawns*. Seemed that Abbot's regular job was running a land-scaping business with Kristian. I was left at the apartment all day to twiddle my thumbs even though Toby offered to babysit my safecracking efforts. Abbot had refused and childishly taken the battery cables out of Lizzie so I wouldn't be tempted to go out there by myself. I was pissed and bored. I went for a long run then ruined it all with Netflix and junk food. By the time he got home from his work, I wasn't in the mood for any games. So he ordered pizza and joined me on the couch. We made out a little then fell asleep in each other's arms. Found out I was wrong about Abbot; he was the cuddling type.

And I was sleeping. Despite feeling hornier than ever, I was actually getting some rest. Maybe it was the orgasm; maybe it was the fact I was getting used to sleeping next to Abbot. Either way, the fact I was sleeping well in a bed other than my own was a bonus. I was going to seriously miss everything about him when I was gone.

"Take me to the safe," I demanded, straddling his waist, my hands either side of his head on the pillow.

He opened one eye, barely awake, a slow grin spreading. "Sitting on me half-naked isn't gonna convince me to get out of this bed."

"I'm serious, Abbot. Take me to the safe. Keeping me away isn't getting you any closer to your goal." I wriggled my hips so my arse rubbed against his morning wood. He groaned.

"That feels like it is."

"Have you ever considered that I want the safe open so I can get paid *and* be free to—"I rolled my hips again —"beg you to fuck me?"

His cock pulsed between my thighs and I moaned from want.

"You can fuck me right now, blue. No begging required."

I slid from his waist and he groaned in disappointment. "You haven't even won third base yet. Besides, I need to get paid."

"You really need money *that* bad?"

"*Yes*, you dumbarse," I yelled, picking up my pillow and hitting him in the chest. "How many times do I have to tell you that Pop didn't leave me any?"

He caught the pillow and tucked it behind his head, looking at me with a thoughtful frown. "Are you saying you're broke?"

"If you hadn't walked back into my life dangling a cash incentive, I'd be bankrupt before the year was out."

"Shit. I didn't realise it was that bad."

I got out of bed and pulled on a shirt. "Don't go throwing the game now that you know. I want to win this fair and square. And I don't take handouts."

"I have no intention of giving you a handout, Slater. A bet's a bet. You knew the terms and your situation going in. *But,* I think I can help level the playing field."

"How?" I pulled on a pair of loose-fitting black pants.

"Give me ten minutes and I'll take you."

"To work?"

"No. To your granddad's workshop. If he left money and we find it, we're fucking on it."

Hell yes.

I mean, no. "Hell no. If we find money, I'll give you third base."

"Over clothes or under?"

I squirmed a little where I stood. If we found money, I could afford to push this a little further. "Under."

"Oh, Sloane." He grabbed his cock in his left hand, the white sheet doing little to hide just how hard and large it was. "You've got yourself a fucking deal." *Indeed.*

CHAPTER TWENTY-ONE
HIGHLY INAPPROPRIATE

"SO, um, I sent you a text before we left today," Abbot said, hand on the wheel as he guided Lizzie along the highway on our way to Bendigo. It was about half an hour from home and two and a half hours from Torquay. And the only reason I was allowing him to drive my girl was because he knew where Pop's workshop was and I didn't.

"I haven't really been checking my phone much lately." Mark continued to call or text, so I kept it on silent most of the time. "What did it say?"

"You'll have to open it and find out." There was a teasing note to his voice that made my insides wake up excitedly.

"Now you've got me intrigued." I reached over the back of the seat to grab my pack, rooting around inside for my phone. "Let's see what Abbot sent that was so—" My cheeks immediately heated and I pressed my phone, screen down against my chest. *Holy shit.*

"Just a hint at what you're gonna get after I win third base today." Glancing my way, he wore a shameless grin.

I lifted my phone again, the screen lighting the full screen image he'd sent through. *Throb, throb, throb.* It was a photo of him in the bathroom mirror. Naked. Holding his enormous cock. *Holy fucking hell.*

He wasn't shy.

"You're that confident there's money here, huh?" I placed two fingers on the screen and zoomed in. *Wow.*

"I am—*hey*! Are you zooming in on my cock?" Surprise and amusement coloured his laughter.

I tilted my head to the side. "What else did you expect me to do? This thing is massive. I have to work out whether it'll fit."

He chuckled. "See, that's what I expected you to do— think about having me inside you. I want to plague your thoughts, red."

I shut off the screen and rested my phone face down against my thigh. "You already do." The words came out as I released my breath.

"Need me to pull over so we can scratch that itch?" Glancing at me, he wiggled his eyebrows and I laughed, pushing him against the shoulder.

"You are *relentless.*" I blew out another sigh. *I'd love to scratch that itch.* More than once. More than twice. *Until I couldn't possibly come anymore.*

I had a feeling he was going to ruin me.

"Let's just get to the workshop and see if you get your prize, first." A smile teased the edge of my lips, funny I was actually considering myself a prize when I'd never felt that way before. This game was doing wonders for my self-esteem.

He clicked on the indicator. "And what a prize it will be."

Steering Lizzie through the industrial part of town, Abbot pulled up in front of a yellow building that housed four brown roller doors, each belonging to a different business. As we got out of the van, we assessed the security risk before preparing to break into door three.

"I'd say Trev had this alarmed," Abbot said, pointing at the cameras mounted either side of the door.

"That would make sense," I said, crouching down and pressing my finger against the locked slide bolt. "He's used BiLocks too."

"They're supposed to be unpickable, aren't they?"

"That was the original claim. Of course that caused the picking community to prove them wrong. There are even YouTube videos explaining how these days."

"Can *you* pick it?"

"I can." A humourless laugh bounced out of my chest. I'd gotten caught up in the craze too, spending hours working the tiny gates. But, I'd gotten there in the end, lock picking was always a skill I took pride in. "It'll take a while, but once it's open we'll be in."

"The benefits of knowing a locksmith."

"You can still pick locks, right?" I asked as we walked back over to my van and gathered what I needed. I got my picking kit along with my cracking kit for the safes Abbot said were inside.

"Simple ones." He leaned against the open door, arms folded as the sun beat down overhead. "But, we steal keys whenever we can."

"Sounds risky."

He shrugged. "Making noise forcing entry is riskier. Getting keys is all sleight of hand. We had to be excellent pickpockets before we were given anything bigger."

"I always thought of you like the boys in Oliver Twist," I said, closing Lizzie's doors.

"But with better food." He chuckled, holding his hand out to carry my stuff.

"What happens when you can't get keys?"

"There are other ways to get inside places besides the front door if you look like a tradie. But for cars we have special tools, and anything beyond that was when we called Trev."

"But now you call me." I crouched back down in front of the lock and inserted the tension tool into the keyhole, angling it as I wriggled my pick inside.

"If that's what you want."

"I really don't know," I said, tapping my pick against a pin to test for false gates. "I haven't decided yet. Toby acted like there was no choice, though."

"When did you talk to Toby?"

"When you and Jasmine were busy yelling at each other over that transport job." I moved my pick to the next pin. "He questioned me about what I knew."

"And what did you tell him?"

I paused my movements and flicked my gaze to meet his. "What he needed to hear."

He went quiet for a moment, picking up one of my other picks and twisting it in his fingers. "He obviously trusts you then."

"What makes you think that?" I asked, clicking the next pin in place.

With a shrug, he dropped the pick into my kit. "The family meeting would have gone very differently if he didn't."

"And that's all you can say on that subject?" I looked

at him with a small but understanding smile.

"That's all I can say."

"Well then, I suggest you shut that sweet mouth of yours up so I can concentrate."

He chuckled. "Yes, ma'am."

It took a good fifteen minutes to get both locks open, but when I did, I stood up and stretched with my arms above my head, cracking my back. "Will you do the honours?"

Abbot stepped forward and lifted the roller door with a dramatic tug of his arms. It flew up and hit the end of the track with a clang that reverberated through the unit. The *empty* unit.

"What the fuck?" Abbot murmured.

"Where are all the safes?" Panic gripped my heart. "You told me this place was full of safes." A lead weight landed in my stomach as a little sparrow swooped down from the rafters and flew out the open door, taking my hopes with it. *Where the fuck is the money?*

"Maybe that guy took everything," Abbot suggested, squinting up at the sky as the little bird flew away. It was a shitty joke. But I laughed anyway. It was either that or cry.

"Who could have done this?" I asked, stepping inside and turning around. There was a spot on the wall where an alarm panel was. But even that was disconnected. Someone had come and shut everything down.

"Could have been anyone, really. Hearing of his death, some thieves wouldn't be able to resist the easy take." He spotted the disconnected alarm system. "Or he could have had a failsafe set up. Someone he trusted to shut this down in the event of his death."

Someone he trusted. *Someone who wasn't me.*

"Is that a normal thing to do?" Spotting a door in the back corner, I wondered if it was a bathroom or an office and headed towards it.

"It is when you have others to protect."

I wasn't the person he'd trusted. I'd been the person Pop had protected.

"I wonder who he'd trust to do all that." Could Jasmine have done this? Someone else? A contact I didn't know about? I pushed open the door to uncover an office, empty save for an old crappy desk. I walked over and went through each drawer. Empty. Empty. *Empty*.

Sighing, I leaned against it. *I might just fucking cry over this.*

"I'm sorry, Sloane." Abbot placed a hand on my shoulder and pressed lightly with his fingers.

"What are you apologising for? You didn't do this."

"I'm not apologising. I'm offering condolences, which is a very different thing. I got your hopes up."

"You did. Fucking on a pile of money might have been a joke, but it would have been pretty bloody epic."

He chuckled and moved a little closer. I wanted him to hug me, comfort me. But that wasn't what we were.

"Now there's no third base and absolutely no way you're winning this bet—not that you ever had a chance."

He grinned and tucked my hair behind my ear. "I love that *you're* pissed over missing third base. Especially since I reckon you won't be able to say stop when I've got my fingers sliding along your slit, teasing you so close. *So close.*"

Throb, throb, throb.

Fuck me. Fuck me. *Fuck me.*

"Calling it a slit is so crass." I forced my breathing steady as I met his eyes.

"What would you prefer I call it?" Taking a hold of my thighs, he lifted so I was sitting back on the desk and he was standing between them. Groin to groin. "Your *flower*?"

I laughed. "Not that."

"Sex, hole, box?"

"They're worse than slit."

"Your cunt?"

I shivered. "Why does the worst of all the words sound so heated coming from your mouth?"

"Hmm. Cunt it is." Fuck me. *Fuck. Me.*

"Or pussy. I don't mind pussy."

"Noted." He pushed his hard length against me, leaning lower, lower to claim my mouth. *I'm too turned on for this.*

"And, um, Cynthia."

He pulled back suddenly, curiosity replacing the heat that had been taken over his eyes. "*Cynthia*?"

I lifted one shoulder. "That's what I call it." I literally *just* made that up to stall him so I could calm down.

"Cynthia the cunt?"

It was even funnier when he said it. "Yeah."

A grin tipped his lips then laughter bubbled from his chest. "You are something else, Sloane Slater."

"What? Other girls don't name their twats?"

"Twats." He laughed harder, shaking his head.

"You are such a child," I said, laughing as well.

"I'm not the one who named my privates *Cynthia*."

"You don't like it?"

"I am never going to call it that."

"Well, at this rate. You'll never get to call it anything. No third base and a safe sitting uncracked. We may never get to that home run."

"Hmm." He slid his hands around my waist and pulled me to standing. "I've got a feeling you'll be worth the wait."

"I'll regrow my hymen if we wait much longer."

Chuckling, he pulled me against his chest. "Ready to wave the white panties and surrender, Slater?"

"*No*. I'm ready to open that safe and win my money."

Wrapping his arms around me, he held me closer. "You are so adorable when you're horny."

I shook my head and wrapped my arms around his torso, speaking against his chest. "I'm cranky when I'm horny."

"You're beautiful when you're cranky."

What? I looked up at him, those words the last thing I expected him to respond with. *I'm beautiful?*

"You're also beautiful when you're sleeping, when you're concentrating, and when you're disappointed over an empty workshop."

He thinks I'm beautiful.

"Is this a new tactic to get me to give in?"

He shook his head. "Just the truth."

"Careful, Abbot. I'll start telling people how sweet you can be. Those beach bimbos won't go home when they find out." *Beach bimbos.* An endless line of willing women that I couldn't forget. They were waiting for him and his attention to return, I was sure.

Something flickered behind his eyes before he released me and stepped back. "I can be a dick towards you if you prefer."

"No." I caught his hand before he could get too far, pulling to urge him back. I liked him against me. "I like you exactly as you are."

He slid a hand into the side of my hair and tilted my head to his. "I kinda like you too, Slater."

My heart picked up speed as he lowered his lips to mine, the sexual charge between us so thick in the air it was practically crushing us. *I should stop this.* I wasn't at my strongest mentally, too many days going unsatisfied had turned me into an edgy mess. I didn't know if I could stop once we started.

Fuck me. Please.

Movement in the doorway caught my eye *just* as his lips touched mine. I jerked my head back. "*Mum?*"

"That isn't typically what a girl says when I try to kiss her, but if that's your kink."

"No, dummy," I said, smacking him against the chest. "My *mum* is here." I pointed to the doorway where she stood, giving Abbot a little finger wave when he turned around.

"Oh," he said, holding out his hand. "I'm Abbot—"

"Cartwright," she finished for him, her eyes travelling up and down his beautiful body, her words like a purr. "I know who you are. I'm Emma—"

"Slater," he finished for her, grinning his dimple-popping, panty-dropping grin. She blushed. *Oh my God.*

I'm going to throw up.

What the fuck is she doing here?

And why the fuck is he giving her that *smile?*

I was not going through this again.

"How did you know we were here, Mum?" I asked, folding my arms and swallowing my reaction down.

Surely Abbot wasn't falling for her overtly sexual countenance. Not after all I'd told him. He wasn't like that.

But he was a man.

It was to be expected when faced with a woman like my mum. Free-spirited, oozing sexuality and feminine charm, she looked far younger than her fifty-nine years, and had never met a man she couldn't lure into her bed.

Without even trying, she looked a thousand times better than me. While I was in black pants and a knit jumper with my hair in a braid and no makeup on my face, she was wearing a pair of fashionably ripped jeans that looked painted on her long legs and a striped low-cut top that showed off her medically enhanced breasts perfectly. She had full painted red lips and her red hair was in a messy bun. It looked so effortless to the untrained eye. However, I knew that her hair was really a mousy brown that she dyed to match mine because of the compliments I received as a child. She'd later reported that she'd never had an easier job pulling men who wanted to know if the curtains matched the drapes. Apparently they did because she dyed downstairs too. I was nine when she told me that. Highly inappropriate.

"Nice to see you too, sweetheart." She smiled and tore her eye-fucking gaze away from Abbot. "I saw you two breaking in on the security feed. Thought I'd come and say hi."

"Why are you even here?"

"That sounds like you aren't happy to see me, baby." She tilted her head like she was a puppy dog who meant no harm. "I'm happy to see you." *Gawd. How, after all these years was she still able to do that guilt thing?*

"I'm happy to see you, Mum. I just wasn't expecting you."

She leaned in and smiled. "I wasn't expecting you either."

For a second I wasn't sure if she was talking about today or the fact I was a surprise pregnancy.

"Do you know what happened to Pop's workshop?" I asked, deciding to get straight down to business since my mum and I weren't great at the whole small talk thing.

"Exactly what he wanted to happen." *She* was his fail-safe? "Why don't we get out of here?" she suggested.

Abbot and I followed her out, at least a metre of space between us the whole time. *And so it begins...*

CHAPTER TWENTY-TWO
A FUCKING MESS

MUM'S HOUSE WAS QUAINT. A raised cottage with white timber cladding and a verandah out the front where she had a bunch of plants and a porch swing set up.

"How long have you lived here?" I asked when she ushered us inside and I noticed the knickknacks and clutter everywhere. For a person who never put down roots, this place certainly looked very cosy.

"Oh, a while," she said with a dismissive hand as she filled the kettle at the sink of the galley kitchen. *A while…*

We stood on the other side of the bench as she asked how we took our tea, something a mother should have known about her daughter but didn't.

"Sit, sit," she said, bringing over a tray with the tea and some chocolate biscuits. "How long have you two been together?" She looked between Abbot and me.

"It's complicated," I stated, while Abbot said, "We're not."

Mum's brow lifted. "Therein lies the complication."

It's only a game, Sloane. It was only ever a game.

I swallowed my reaction to Abbot's dismissal to focus on the matter at hand, why we were there in the first place.

"How about you just explain the empty workshop?" I asked.

"Trevor Slater *loved* to party in his youth. Did you know that?" She smiled, resting her chin in her hand as she looked off into the distance. *That is so not the answer to the question I asked.* But I waited for the point nonetheless. "He wasn't always the reliable old locksmith living in a country town to provide the best life for his poor abandoned granddaughter. No. Trev was one of the finest cat burglars this country had ever seen." She whispered the last words like they were a chant for a spell —reverently.

"A cat burglar?"

She nodded. "Never caught. Only questioned once over the job your father went down for." She directed the last part to Abbot. "He appreciated that your dad didn't talk. It's why he worked for you for so long after retiring from the game. Felt he owed a debt." She placed her hand over Abbot's and gave it a squeeze.

Don't touch him.

My possessive thought didn't surprise me, but I didn't like having it when Abbot wasn't mine to be possessive over.

I looked away.

Abbot didn't move his hand. "I was too young to remember Dad before he went away. But the others said he was a mean bastard. I guess it's good he did something decent for someone."

She nodded with understanding. "Our lifestyles harden us."

"Us?" I asked, turning back to her.

"Of course," Mum said, looking like she thought I might be dense. "Skills passed from generation to generation. Dad taught me everything I know, same as he did you. You just didn't have the stomach for it, so we never fully brought you in."

"I don't understand. Why was he always giving you money?" My brain was starting to hurt.

"To launder. Part of my cover is working a food stall at festivals. All cash." She winked.

"I thought he was laundering through the shop."

"He was. But sometimes there was too much. I took care of that."

"Why didn't I know *any* of this?"

"Because you didn't want to know. After you had your breakdown, Pop and I both agreed that your life should stay as normal as possible." *My breakdown?* That's what she was calling it?

"I didn't have a *breakdown*, Mother. You slept with my boyfriend."

"And I apologised. But you can call it what you want. We just felt you were too emotional for this life."

Too emotional. I wasn't too emotional. I simply needed someone to love me enough that they wouldn't stab me in the back. I needed some grounding, some direction. Everything around me kept moving and changing, and I'd just wanted to be still, find something to hold on to. Something that was mine.

Not that it got me anywhere.

"If I'm too emotional, why did he leave me the shop?"

"Because you're a good locksmith. He thought you

could make a go of it." So, I was a failure of my own making. Excellent.

"The shop is a bust, Mum."

"Of course it is. There's not enough work in that town for anyone. Is that why you're here with a Cartwright looking for money? You're broke?"

"Heading that way."

"We hired her for a job," Abbot put in, unsolicited and unnecessary. "She'll be fine."

I shot him a look that said, "Why tell her that?"

Mum's botoxed brow twitched a little. "Chip off the ole block after all, huh?" Her eyes shifted between us. "I get it now. Like mother, like daughter. Do a job, make some money, have some fun on the side, then get the hell out of there. I love it." She smiled as she reached across the table to me. "You know, I have fucked so many men in my time that I still can't work out who your father was. I *think* he was a stockbroker I slept with to get access to his employee codes. But, I've never been sure. Could have been the concert violinist with the Stradivarius. Oh, it was worth *millions* that thing." She physically shivered over the memory.

"Sounds like you've had an interesting life," Abbot said, taking a mouthful of tea.

"Well, I'm excellent in the sack, very flexible." She whispered the last part then winked.

No. No. Nope.

I stood up, my jaw so tight my inner ear hurt.

"Where are you going, honey?" Mum asked, sweet as the endearment she gave me. "We're just talking."

Taking a calming breath, I sat back down. *None of this*

matters. He's not yours to lose. Focus on the money. "What happened to Pop's cash, Mum?"

"I have it. When Dad died, the lawyer contacted me and gave me an envelope with instructions. I followed them to the letter and his money is in a safe place. Away from sticky fingers." She glanced at Abbot again.

"So, I got a failing business and you got the money that was keeping it afloat."

She smiled. "I'm simply doing my part taking care of it. There's actually a substantial amount of money for you —all clean and legit—waiting in a term deposit once you hit a certain milestone."

"You're being vague, Mother."

"Well, I don't want to embarrass you in front of your friend." She kissed the air in his direction. I was going to shake her until her false eyelashes fell off.

"Oh, I think you're managing that just fine."

"What?" She feigned confusion.

Pressing my fingers to my forehead, I fought off a tension headache. "Just tell me what the milestone is."

"You'll get it on the eve of your wedding." She produced a magnanimous smile and looked Abbot dead in the eye. He cleared his throat and ran his hand through his hair, looking away toot sweet.

"That's ridiculous," I said.

"It was his money. He can set any rules he wants."

"Surely that's not legally binding. Can't you just release the money to me since you're in charge of it? It would mean a lot to me, Mum. And after all we've been through, don't you think it would be the right thing to do?"

"Hmm. No. Rules are rules, my dear girl. There is honour among thieves, and this was important to him. He wanted to see you happy and living your life." She looked at Abbot. "Like her enough to marry for money?"

"I have plenty of my own." His response was so fast that it brought tears to my eyes. Stupidly.

You know where you stand. It's a game.

"Well, maybe one of your brothers," Mum said as if she could pimp me out that easily. Pay someone to marry me? How pitiful did she think I was?

I turned away, swallowing the lump in my throat as I tried to breath through my emotions. Abbot was telling her that most of his brothers were married now, and all I could here was the whoosh, whoosh of angry blood in my ears.

Calm down. None of this matters.

"Tell Jasmine I said 'hi' when you get back home. We need to make some time to catch up."

"I'll do that," Abbot said.

"Good. Jazz and I go way back." She reached out, finding a pack of cigarettes beneath a magazine before lighting up. "Do you smoke?"

I turned back in time to see Abbot inhale longingly. Suddenly, I needed to get the hell out.

"Fuck the money," I spat, standing up and walking straight out the door to my van. Abbot followed so fast that he jumped in at the same time I did.

"You OK?" he asked as I started the ignition and took a deep breath.

I nodded then shook my head instead. "I don't know. I just…" *Hated watching her flirt with you. Hated watching you smile back. Hated how fast you refused to marry me…* It was stupid, and I had no real right to feel the way I was feeling. I guess my mother just brought the worst out in me —jealousy, distrust… "She isn't an easy woman to have as a mother." Putting Lizzie into gear, I planted my foot to put as much distance between my mother and me as possible.

"Makes sense that you are the way you are," he said after a while.

"Meaning?"

"You're so dead against becoming her that you're the exact opposite."

His words hit home a little too hard, and I didn't have a thing to say. Out loud. Internally, I was in turmoil of not feeling wanted, not feeling trusted and above all, not feeling loved. *Loveable. Desired. I'm the exact opposite of my mum, he says.* In a word…less. And the way Mum and Pop had made my decisions, conspired without my knowledge…it was just wrong. *Have I always been in their way?*

"What are you gonna do about the shop and the money?" he asked, not saying a thing about the fact we were heading to Rochester instead of Torquay.

"I'm going to open that safe and make my own damn money. That's what I'm going to do."

"You know—"

"Don't, Abbot." I held up my hand. "Whatever it is, I don't want to hear it. For one night, I want to go home and ignore the fuck out of all this stuff."

He stayed quiet until we were about two steps inside my flat. "Sloane."

"I'm going for a shower." I threw my backpack on the couch and headed straight for the bathroom.

"Will you stop and talk to me a second?"

"About what, Abbot? My mother flirting with you? Or asking you to marry me for money? Oh wait, wanna talk about how when you said no, she asked if you could spare a brother for her desperate daughter? That was a *fun* moment."

"Sloane."

"Just leave me alone, Abbot." I slammed the door of the bathroom, the dark brown of the wood making the small cream bathroom seem more crowded than usual. I pulled my jumper over my head and threw it on the tiled floor, pulling out my hair tie and loosening my braid with a heavy sigh. *I hate feeling like this.* Out of control. Unwanted.

"We need to talk, Sloane." Abbot tapped on then opened the bathroom door, taking away my small amount of privacy when all I wanted was a moment to find my fucking calm.

"What the fuck is wrong with you?" I yelled, turning on him. "I'm not in here fucking masturbating if that's what you're worried about. I'm in here dealing with the train-fucking-wreck that is my life. So, please, *please* give me a goddamn fucking minute."

"If you would listen, I'm trying to help you."

"Help me by going away." I turned back to the mirror. "Better yet, leave. And take your fucking game with you. I'm done."

"Sloane."

"I forfeit, Abbot," I yelled. "You should be happy."

"Will you just talk to me?" He held his hands out, pleading.

"This is bullshit. I said I'm out."

He didn't move, just turned his head to the side and looked at me with those beautiful blue eyes that were breaking my fucking heart...because I wanted something I knew I couldn't have. I wanted him. Not just this game.

Every time I thought about him moving on to another woman, I felt crazy. I couldn't do this and be OK walking away anymore. I needed to end it before I fell too far.

"Go, Abbot. I'm out. I don't care about the money anymore."

"Sloane." His voice was even softer now. I wanted to punch him in that handsome face. *Why won't he leave?*

"Don't believe me?" With fingers shaking with frustration, I unbuttoned my pants and pushed them to the floor.

"*Sloane.*" This time my name was a warning.

"I forfeit. You win." With my eyes locked on his, I shoved my hand inside my panties, plunging my fingers inside my ridiculously wet pussy, my mouth falling open with a gasp because I'd been craving penetration since we started fooling around. I leaned back on the vanity, my fingers working in and out, in and out. "You win."

With his mouth set in a stern line, he shook his head from side to side, eyes dark as he twisted the fly of his jeans. "You seriously wanna play like this?"

I moved my fingers defiantly.

"Fine." He pulled his cock out, holding it in his hand. "You wanna do this? Let's do this. First person to come." *He's making a competition out of masturbation?*

"Fine," I ground out through my teeth, pausing long enough to push my panties to the floor and get more comfortable on the vanity, angling my hand so I could push deeper before I slid my fingers out and teased my clit. So angry yet so turned on. "Oh God."

Abbot's breath came out in grunts as he leaned against the doorframe, his strong arm moving his hand up and down his shaft as his eyes stayed fixed on my fingers going in and out of my pussy. Watching him watch me was turning me on even more. We were out of control, out of our minds and playing games we couldn't handle. "I'm close, Sloane," he warned.

No.

I didn't actually know what was at stake when one of us came. Did we lose the money? This argument? The forfeit? I had no real clue what happened, but I knew I needed to come first or my point wouldn't be made and—

Abbot groaned then shuddered, white fluid shooting out of the tip of his cock in spurts. *Holy fuck.* In my frenzy, it was enough to send me over the edge, my hips bucking as my clit pulsed against my finger, my free hand hit against the wall. "*Ohhh.*"

The reality of our madness hit embarrassingly hard and fast. I froze, my fingers still pressing against my thrumming clit, my eyes downcast. I couldn't look at him. He couldn't look at me either. And with our chests heaving, we slowly released ourselves and stared at the semen in the centre of the tiled floor.

"I win," he announced, his voice flat.

"This is so stupid," I whispered, my eyes burning as I picked up my pants and pulled them on, needing to cover myself even though I didn't have a scrap of dignity left. "What the fuck are we even doing?"

Abbot tucked himself back inside his pants and blew a heavy blast of air from his lungs. "We *need* to talk."

"Not now, Abbot, I just need you to go. *Please.*" My eyes pleaded, my emotions too raw to deal with *anything* right now.

He looked at the cum on the floor then back at me, unmoving.

"*Go.*"

Reluctantly, he backed out of the bathroom. I was quick to close the door and lean against it, the tension in my chest so tight that I wanted to scream it loose. Instead, I put my face in my hands and sobbed. It was possible that I had no money, no future, and no friends. Not bad for two weeks worth of work.

What a fucking mess.

And I wasn't talking about the cum on my floor.

CHAPTER TWENTY-THREE
MUMMY ISSUES

"YOU'RE NOT HEARING what I'm saying, mate. She deserves better. So fuck right off and let her live her life. If I find out you're sniffing around her again, I'll remove the teeth from your mouth one by one."

The front door slammed just as I burst out of my bedroom, barely awake after falling asleep in an emotional heap.

"Who the hell was that?" I demanded, pulling a hoodie over the singlet and leggings I'd changed into after my shower the night before. I'd exited the bathroom to find my flat empty. And while I'd told him to leave, finding Abbot gone had hurt far more than I cared to admit. Instead of facing why I felt that way, I dragged some clothes on my dejected body and curled into a ball, willing myself to sleep off my emotions. When I woke during the night, I found him right beside me, the big spoon to my little.

He came back.
I don't know why...

"Who do you think?" He stood with his hands on his hips, his eyes tired. We'd really messed things up between us last night. "He saw your van and couldn't help himself. Fucking weasel."

I looked at the floor. "Mark isn't a weasel. He's a doctor."

"Big whoop."

I shook my head, moving past him to go out the door. If I was fast, I'd catch up to Mark and explain...I don't know, exactly. But I needed to say something to him, even if it was just to get him to stop calling me.

Abbot caught me by the arm. "If you chase after him, he's got you, Sloane. He wins."

I pulled my arm free. "Not everything in this world is a competition, Abbot."

He grunted as I breezed past him then ran down the stairs, hitting the street just as Mark was getting into his Lexus.

"Hey," he said, standing with his arms on the top of door, the morning breeze blowing lightly against his dark blond hair. "You've been avoiding my calls."

"I have." There was no point denying it. "I told you I was done."

"And now you have a guard dog to keep it that way."

"Well, if you took the hint instead of chasing me down..." I let the rest of the sentence go unsaid as I looked up to my unit where I could see Abbot watching us with a coffee and a disapproving glare. "I don't really know what he is to me, if I'm honest." He was the man I shared my bed with. The reason I smiled and laughed more in the last week and a half than I had in years. He was the reason I was opening my eyes to the world around me, and why I finally felt strong enough to let the ties of my past go. He was important to me.

"Don't think he likes me much," Mark said, following my gaze.

"That's because he thinks you're being dishonest and stringing me along."

"I get it. He's willing to give you everything you want as long as you cut all your old ties and run away with him? There's a name for those kind of men, Sloane."

"I have my own mind, Mark." How dare he.

"Tell me I'm wrong."

"You're wrong. He doesn't even want me like that." And that was the clincher.

You like her enough to marry for money?

I have enough of my own.

That moment with my mother was a moment of clarity.

It wasn't like I was expecting a proposal, but the blatant dismissal of anything going on between us had hurt. It opened my eyes. Wide open. I'd been convincing myself that I could play this game for fun without feeling. In truth, I was secretly falling for every smile, every wink, and every soft-spoken word. He was stealing my heart with his passionate kisses, chipping away at my soul with his tender touch. And I was letting him. Lying to myself and falling, tumbling. Blundering.

"He doesn't want you, but he's chasing your friends away? Yeah, there's a name for that too—narcissist."

"Don't do that, Mark. He's honest. Something *you* should have been from the start." Abbot had *always* been straight with me. I gave him a huge amount of credit for that. I'd known where I stood from day one, but still...

Falling, tumbling. Blundering.

"He's obviously protective of you, whatever he is." Mark pressed his lips together and studied my face, his head tilting a little to the side. "You seem different."

"Maybe I've always been this way. Maybe you just didn't notice."

"You're throwing our friendship away, Sloane."

"That's because I don't need it anymore."

"Because of him?" He pointed up to Abbot. "What about me? Who am I without you?"

"You're Terry's husband. Kate's father. A well-respected trauma surgeon. A triathlete. A friend to more than just me."

He blew air out of his nose, a laugh, but not quite a laugh. "See. You know me so well. I'm struggling to believe that you really want to throw over twenty years away because some oaf told you to."

"He's not an oaf," I said, looking back up to Abbot who was still watching over us like a gargoyle. "He's… fearless and badarse. Everything I think I forgot how to be."

"Why do you want to be fearless and badarse? You're fine as you are—independent and capable. Come and have coffee with me. Talk this through."

I shook my head, still looking up. "No. I won't be changing my mind because it's time for me to move on, start a life that's all my own. I feel like I've been living in the remnants of everyone else's, and I need to be selfish for once. Think of myself."

He looked at me for a long moment, seeming to want to say something but changing his mind. A common occurrence with Mark. He never had a lot of fight in him when it came down to the actual confrontation. Not like Abbot who was nothing but fight. *Fearless. Badarse.*

Abbot.

"Well, call if you need me. I'm always here."

"Thank you. I appreciate that."

Then he nodded and got back into his car, leaving me to wonder why he even came. He didn't really want *me*. Seemed he was just comfortable in that habit of *us*. Something I had been guilty of too. But it was time for change.

"So that's it? You two buddies again now?" Abbot pounced on me the minute I returned upstairs.

"Not that it's any of your business, but no. I meant what I said about selling up and starting again. I won't have as much capital to start fresh now, but it'll be OK. I'll just downsize, make it work."

He looked at me like I was speaking Dutch. "I won the forfeit, Sloane. The five hundred K is yours once the safe is open. You should be happy." That last sentence sounded a little condescending to my ears.

I narrowed my eyes. "*No.* I quit first."

"I *came* first." *Excuse me?*

My head drew back, confused, frustrated as I studied his stern expression glaring back at me.

We were competing to be the one to throw in the towel? I didn't know how to feel about that. Was this his pity? He was being charitable? Quitting on his own terms? Fuck that. Obviously he thought he had to pay to get rid of me, and quickly.

"You won the forfeit?" I checked, saying each word carefully.

"And now you have your fucking money so you can go away and live your dream life." He didn't look away, or flinch when he said it. He *was actually* paying to be rid of me.

It made sense. He'd found out I was completely broke, and knowing I needed a husband to collect the money from Pop would make any commitment phobe run a mile. Forfeiting that money was his way of making sure I didn't need to return to Torquay for the sake of a job.

You can go away and live your dream life.

I folded my arms across my chest. "Then I guess all that's left is to get that safe open so we can be done with this," I said, grabbing my bag from where I'd dumped it the night before. "And each other."

He followed me without a word. I wanted to cry.

WITH MY HEADPHONES in and old-school RHCP blasting in my ears, I worked through the shrinking list of combinations. One after another, I crossed each failed one off and moved to the next. *The faster I'm done, the faster I'm home.*

In my periphery, Abbot was pacing back and forth, bouncing a tennis ball against the wall and generally being distracting. I really wanted him to go wait outside or something so I could work in peace. Especially since after almost three hours cooped up in the van with him, we could barely speak to each other without getting snappy.

Despite what anyone says, men and women can't be friends without sex coming into it. It's basic biology. And once you do have sex, the friendship isn't the same anymore. You become something other than what you were.

Abbot and I didn't even have to have sex for things to get messed up. I wished we could rewind the last twenty-four hours and go back to playing for third base. Better still, go back to the day in my flat and never agree to the bet in the first place. But nothing could erase what had passed between us, the nightmare of my mother, and the embarrassment of my reaction last night. I just needed to be done.

Bounce, bounce, ba-bounce.

I tugged an earbud from my ear, the lyrics from *Higher Ground* spilling into the room. "Would you quit it?" I bit. "Go and pace in the hall or *something* if you can't sit still."

Catching the ball in one hand, he looked at me and stilled.

"Thank you," I said, sliding the earbud back in and spinning the dial to reset, starting again. 52. *159. 33. 445.* I tried the handle. No go.

Cross that combination off the list.

Just as I struck my pencil across the numbers, my earbud fell from my ear, tugged out by a pissed-looking Abbot. "This is fucking ridiculous."

With a sigh, I put the bud back in my ear.

He tugged it out again. "Would you just *talk to me a second*?"

"What's to talk about?" I started dialling again. *56 right...*

"The fact you cracked it after your mum's, had a masturbation fight with me and have barely spoken to me since."

"There's nothing to discuss and I'm busy." *160 left...*

"You can dial and talk, Sloane. The game is over now, so this is just us. What the fuck is going on with you? Are you pissed about the money? Are you pissed at your mother? Or are you pissed at me?"

"Why would I be pissed at you, Abbot?" My voice came out flat as I dialled the next two numbers.

"You *are* pissed at me." He narrowed his eyes, like he could see what my problem was if he studied my expression close enough.

Rolling my eyes, I gripped the handle. "Drop it, buddy. I'm a big girl who will get over it."

"Buddy," he repeated. "You're being passive-aggressive, Sloane. Speak your mind like the big girl you claim to be."

Releasing the handle, I turned in my seat so I was facing him properly. "I'm embarrassed. Over the way I reacted after seeing my mother and what we did in my bathroom afterwards. I'm *pissed* that after everything I told you about her, you just sat there and let her touch you, *flirt* with you, right in front of me. Like, if I wasn't there you'd be fucking her against the wall."

He opened his mouth to speak, but I jumped in before he had a chance. "Don't, Abbot. I don't want reasons or excuses. This has all happened before. She swoops in, fucks up my life, fucks my boyfriend, then leaves. It's really fun. I'm sorry we couldn't stay longer so you could get the full experience," I shouted, irrationally, angrily… pathetically. I could hear myself going on, and I wanted to stop it, but it all came spilling out. "You should have told her you were with me, Abbot. You didn't have to profess your undying love or anything like that, but at least"— frowning, I shook my head and grabbed the handle—"at least pretend you're more interested in me than you are in her. Just once, I need someone to do that. That's what a real friend would do." I turned the handle, expecting a solid reaction like every other time, but instead, it shifted with a click.

I did it.

Holy fuck.

"I did it," I whispered. "I fucking did it."

Pulling the door open, I gasped at the sight of the stacks of money inside. I had no idea how much was there, but it had to be millions. Millions. *Where did they even get this?*

I looked up at Abbot who didn't seem anywhere near as excited as he should. And I understood that my jealous-girlfriend tirade had completely freaked him out. OK. Great. Honestly, it had freaked me out too. I didn't want to be this girl.

And now I can go home.

"How about we just ignore everything that happened and call it a day?" I said, trying to salvage some dignity. "You can pay me the original two-fifty and we'll forget all about the game and my mother and whatever we were supposed to be to each other." I smiled and touched my hand to my head, trying not to cry. "I obviously got a little too involved here and...I think it's best if I just go and we don't see each other again. I mean, if it's urgent and you haven't found a new locksmith, I'll help. But we can't...I can't...*friends with benefits* really won't work because—"

"Shut up, Sloane."

"—I feel too much towards you, Abbot and I know you don't feel anything for—"

"Shut the fuck up and let me speak," he boomed, shoving the safe door shut with a loud bang.

My eyes stung with tears as I jumped in my seat.

"My God, you just keep banging on and spouting shit and you haven't *once* given me the chance to speak or explain my side." He blinked rapidly. "Did *you ever* consider how *I* feel?" A tear slid from his eye and he frowned. *Oh God. Abbot's emotional?*

I felt awful for reducing this strong man to tears and stood, my hands up in apology. "Abbot—"

"I wasn't flirting with her. She touched *me*, and I gave *zero* response. And if you had let me fucking speak to you without fighting me at *any* point in the last twenty-four hours, I would have told you what I wanted…" He paused and frowned, lifting his hand to touch his cheek. "Why am I fucking crying?"

"Because I hurt you." I sniffed and wiped my eyes, shaking my head because I regretted being such a moody bitch to him when at the crux of it, he'd been nothing but good to me. "I'm sorry, Abbot. I—"

Looking at his hands, his expression fell before he met my eyes. "Tear gas. Holy shit, Sloane. The *tear gas*."

"What?" I looked at the safe, my eyes going wide as a hairline fracture crept along the glass and the liquid started to react and hiss. "Tear gas," I yelled.

"Run!" Abbot grabbed me and pushed me towards the door, hitting the fire alarm before he closed and locked the unit then ran with me through the hall, our eyes and noses pouring disgusting fluids and making it hard to see.

"It burns so bad," I cried, hands out because I could barely see. Light flashed just ahead and Abbot shoved me into the parking lot, gasping for fresh air.

"Oh my God," he grunted. Grabbing his shirt and wiping at his face. "Fuck, that makes it worse. It's on our clothes." He tore his shirt off. "Get your clothes off. We need cold water. There's a hose around the side." He pointed and I followed him, stripping to my underwear and hobbling along on the gravel barefoot.

I stepped around the side of the warehouse and was immediately blasted with a spray of cold water. I shrieked and held my hands out in a futile effort to protect myself. "Oh God." I rubbed my hands over my face, wiping the water and snot away. "Stop. I'm OK." I coughed and hacked, my nose and eyes pouring from irritation.

He gave me a break and sprayed himself. Rubbing at his skin as the cold water ran over his body. He leaned over and shot the spray into his face, making disgusting grunting noises to get all the mucus out.

Totally grossed out, freaked out, and freezing, I hugged my arms around myself and shivered. He seemed just fine, which made sense since those beach showers were always freezing cold. "Here." He handed me the turned-down hose. "Swish water around your mouth and splash it in your eyes and up your nose. You need to clean as much of it out of your sinuses as possible."

Taking the hose, I did as I was told, complaining and spluttering the whole time. "This is the *worst.*"

"I know," he said, hand on my back. "I fucked up."

"What are we going to do?" I gasped, leaning against the warehouse in the sun. "The fire brigade is going to come, right? What do we tell them?"

Abbot spat on the ground, water dripping from his body as he shook his head. "The alarm doesn't alert them." My eyes travelled over the length of him, lingering on the wet boxer briefs that hugged his manly shape. I closed my eyes and pushed all my thoughts of that away. I couldn't do any of that with him anymore.

I coughed instead. "Who does it alert?"

"My family." His red-rimmed eyes moved over my body, and the black underwear that clung wet to my body. "You cold?"

"Freezing." My teeth chattered as he pulled me against him, rubbing his hands over my skin to warm me up. *Oh God, I'm going to miss this.*

"Lizzie got anything inside her we can use to dry off?"

"M-m-maybe," I forced out.

Picking our way across the gravel to Lizzie's side, I realised I was missing one very important thing.

"Keys," I said.

"And a locksmith is no good without a picking kit."

I nodded, pulling on the handle even though I knew she was locked. "Can anyone see us from the road?" I asked, hearing the distant hum of traffic.

"No. We chose this place because it's private. Stand back." He placed one hand on my shoulder, moving me to the side as his other hand hurled a rock through the driver's window.

"*No!*" I yelled, watching Lizzie's window shatter and crumble before he reached inside and opened her up.

"You'll thank me when you're dry," he stated, leaning inside and rummaging around until he came out with a crusty-looking towel that I'd probably used after a swimming session months ago and forgot about. "Use that."

"Thanks," I said, wiping the stiff fabric against my skin. It was scratchy, but it softened up as it absorbed the excess water.

"You've got a jumper in here too," he said, tossing it my way. I threw him the towel then pulled the jumper over my head. I felt instantly better.

"What are you doing now?" I asked as he came out with a plastic bag.

"Getting our clothes." He found a stick and walked across the gravel, picking up our discarded clothing and dropping it in the plastic bag.

After that, he walked around to where we'd rinsed off with the hose. And I let out a sigh.

We had really fucked this thing up. I'd let my unresolved mummy issues get the better of me, and he…well, he didn't want the same things I did. I wanted a life. I wanted a house, a husband, kids, a dog… All things a commitment phobe like Abbot couldn't give me.

"You are so fucking lame, Slater," I said to myself. It was so stupid of me to think I could ever have sex for fun. I'd always believed that men and women could be friends despite having sex, while Abbot believed all male and female relationships ended over sex. Ended. I was beginning to think he was right.

A black sedan pulled into the parking lot, breaking into my analysis. The cavalry had arrived, Toby behind the wheel and Sam in the front seat. I gave them a small wave and waited by Lizzie for them to park.

"What happened?" Sam asked, jumping out of the car and looking at the warehouse, possibly for an actual fire.

"Tear gas happened," Toby observed, his voice calm as he stepped out and lowered his sunglasses. I swear he looked like he was about to laugh. "Look at her face."

I smiled and dramatically wiggled my fingers at my face. "It's a new look I'm trialling."

"Holy fuck. You look like you have that rabbit disease," Sam said.

"That's what I was going for," I said. "So, it's working. Excellent."

Toby looked at the ground and hid his smile. "Where's Abbot?"

"Around there." I pointed to the side of the building. "Rinsing the gas out of our clothes, I think."

"Uh, I don't think he's rinsing them," Sam said, pointing to a small column of smoke rising up.

"What? He's burning them? No. I loved that hoodie."

"Sucks to be you." Sam clapped me on the arm then jogged towards where Abbot was having his own private bonfire.

"I suppose he's burning my shoes too." I pouted, wriggling my toes against the small stones that felt more like knives at this point.

"I'd say so," Toby said, glancing at Lizzie, reacting to her smashed window with a raised brow then pulling the back passenger door open of his car. "Why don't you sit?"

"My underwear is wet from Abbot hosing me. I'll mess up your upholstery."

"I don't give a fuck about my upholstery, Sloane. Besides, it's leather. It'll dry."

"OK." I took a seat with my feet perched on the edge of the car and the door still open while Toby stood not far from me.

"Wanna tell me how you got gassed?"

"Would you believe that it erupted all on its own?"

"No."

"I see. Well, I pissed off your brother and opened the safe at the same time."

"What'd he do? Slam it shut again?"

I nodded. "We didn't even notice it cracked at first.

Too busy yelling."

He took a deep breath and nodded, hands in his pockets as he looked over the building. "We're going to need to find someone to scrub the place clean, decontaminate and such."

"You know someone who can do that?"

Toby turned back to me. "I can make some calls. But you're going to need to stick around until it's safe to get back in there."

"I gathered that," I said, pressing my lips together. "Not only is the money in there, but my shit is in there too. I need it."

"Plus, I hear you're in the wedding party now."

"Oh yeah, the wedding. I'd conveniently forgotten about that." A wedding in the bridal party with Abbot. *Well, that won't be awkward at all.* "Do you think," I said slowly, "that I could stay at the house instead of with Abbot?"

"Did he do something?" Toby's concern seemed real.

"No." I lifted a hand. "We just…we aren't getting along. I need a little distance." And to not feel ashamed over our masturbate-off the night before *and* my skitz out over my mother's flirting. Not to mention the whole money-marriage thing. Space was the least of what I needed. I'd also lost my pride, my dignity and my self-confidence. I needed to learn how to be me again. I needed to be alone.

"Are you sure, Sloane?" Toby asked, studying my expression.

"I'm positive. Help me run away from my problems? Please. For old time's sake."

He nodded once. "I'll get it sorted."

CHAPTER TWENTY-FOUR
STICK AROUND

HOW AWKWARD TO BE A BRIDESMAID TO a person you barely knew. I'd had my hair and makeup done, smiled awkwardly for photos, ridden on the back of some biker's Harley, and tried to be both useful and unobtrusive. All while avoiding Abbott's gaze.

He was the best man. *Of course, he's Kristian's twin.* I was the bridesmaid tacked on the end of the row to balance numbers. With my red hair and height, I'd always felt like I stuck out like a sore thumb, but today, I felt even more out of place. *Part of the family...* albeit unwanted.

Every movement Abbot made alerted my senses, and like vinegar on a paper cut, it stung to be near him. It had been three days since the tear gas incident. I'd returned to the spare room at Jasmine's, thankfully without the need of an explanation (Toby was a man of his word) and had since kept myself within the Cartwright group, too busy with last-minute wedding prep to notice the false emotion behind my smiles. They were a protective shield because I knew Abbot wouldn't dare discuss our *almost* fuck around his family. I was safe. At least on the outside.

Inwardly, I was torturing myself analysing every word we said in our frustration, especially the part when the tear gas started leaking and I'd actually thought Abbot was crying because he had feelings for me. Out of everything that had happened between us, it was that moment that caused the most embarrassment. I wanted to kick my own arse for being such a sap. I knew—*knew*—my feelings towards him were one-sided.

Daily, I'd asked Toby when the warehouse would be open so I could get my money and my things, hoping I could get out of town before the wedding. But his answer was always 'soon'. If 'soon' didn't happen *really soon,* I was getting a hazmat suit and going in there myself.

I wanted to go home. I wanted to lick my wounds. I wanted to pretend none of this ever happened.

Two weeks with the Cartwrights had been enough time to get my heart tangled in their world enough for it to crack—just a little. It wasn't broken by far, but I felt sure that would be inevitable, if I stayed.

"Pair Sloane and Abbot for the photos," Jasmine instructed as we stood on the windy beach waiting for the photographer to get the post-wedding shots. Dresses were whipping up in the breeze, but I was sitting pretty because my dress had been converted to a playsuit. Pants were everything.

Abbot is everything.

My heart skittered about in my chest as he moved closer to me then slid has big hand around my waist, fingers brushing against my skin because these outfits had a ridiculously low back.

I inhaled. *God, he smells good.*

"Cold?" he asked when I shivered. And I nodded because it was true. Whoever thought spaghetti straps on a beach at the end of autumn was a good idea clearly forgot how cold this part of the country could get.

"My nipples could cut glass."

"I'll give you my jacket when we're through."

"It's OK. I'll be fine."

"Sloane."

"Leave me be, Abbot. *Please*." I was going to cry if he pushed any harder or acted any kinder. I needed this…*everything* between us to be finished.

"Everyone say 'dolphin dicks'," the photographer said, causing us to laugh so we smiled for the photo. I went along and smiled when prompted then quickly moved away from Abbot the moment I was able.

"You're doing great," Jasmine said when we were almost finished. "Thanks for doing this. It means a lot, and I'm so happy to have you back with us."

I smiled. Again. "I'm happy to help."

She touched my arm. "You're cold."

"I'm fine, really."

"Abbot. Give Sloane your jacket."

"I already offered and she doesn't want it," he responded.

"Nonsense," Jasmine scoffed. "Just give it to her."

Pressing his lips together, he walked over and slipped the jacket from his massive shoulders then draped it over mine. "There." He patted the top of my arm, jostling me. "That better, buddy?"

I forced out yet another smile, the tension between us

stretched so fine it could snap at any moment. "Just perfect. Thanks, buddy."

"My pleasure. Anything else? You want my shoes? My pants?"

"I didn't even want your jacket." I spoke between my teeth.

"Jesus Christ," Jasmine said, looking between us. "Why don't you two just fuck already and put us all out of our misery?"

My eyes went wide. Abbot's face went red. Not from embarrassment, but from annoyance. I was surprised he wasn't growling.

"I don't know what you think you've been doing," she added. "But, you haven't been fooling anyone."

"That bullshit about Sloane being gay," Alesha put in with a giggle.

"And the matching suits," Holland said with a cackling laugh.

"And the fact you had your tongues down each other's throats at the rehearsal dinner," Breaker put in. *Oh, so someone did see that. Excellent.*

"Plus, they left early together," Sam said. "I kind of thought they were going to fuck then. But, based on Abbot's expression, I'm thinking no."

I took a breath, my mouth opened, and my mind searched for words. There were consequences to having a relationship around this family. I'd been warned countless times. What the fuck was about to happen? "Um…"

Abbot pursed his lips and shook his head. Then he started clapping. "All right. Great work, everybody, you're all fucking Sherlock Holmes. But you're wrong about one thing. There's nothing going on. No tongues, no fucking, *nothing.* I mean, we barely made it past second base. Right, buddy?" He locked eyes with me, the cool indifference in his making me feel a little sick.

"Right. It turned out that I wasn't down to fuck." I set my jaw.

"Then why all this tension?" Toby asked. "Is he acting like a baby because you *wouldn't* fuck him?"

I cannot believe I'm having this conversation right now.

Pressing my lips together, I folded my arms across my chest and looked at the ground, toeing the sand. "It's complicated."

Kristian moved in and slung his arm over his twin's shoulders. "Would you just tell 'er, bro," he said, his voice soft and cajoling.

I snapped my head back up, suddenly interested in what Abbot's twin knew that I didn't. "Tell me what?"

Abbot knitted his brow for a split second then shook his head. "Nothing. It doesn't matter anymore. Let's just enjoy the wedding, guys. Today is about Kris and Ronnie. Can we focus on them, please?"

A slight murmur sounded throughout the family as they muttered things like, fine, and 'we were just trying to help.'

We finished the photo shoot then headed back up the beach, Abbot and I keeping our distance. "I'm real sorry about back there," I said to Ronnie the moment we had the chance to speak. "I never wanted to take anything away from your day."

She smiled and touched my shoulder. "Nothing could take away from today, Sloane. I just married the man of my dreams and became a legal member of the kind of family I've always wished for. If it turns out that includes you, then all the better. I want nothing more than to see Abbot as happy as his twin." She laughed then hugged me and I went a little stiff. "This all has a way of working itself out in the end. You'll see." She rushed to catch up with Kristian who caught her around the waist and kissed her like they existed only for each other. I felt…jealous. *I wanted that.*

"He looks at you just like that you know," Holland said, falling into step beside me. "It's the real reason why we didn't believe any of his weird reasons to spend time with you. He looks at you like you're his world."

I smiled but I doubted that. Abbot Cartwright had no interest in making any woman his world. He was only interested in women as a revolving door and a new notch on the post of his bed. *Single until I die.*

"I hope you're talking about Abbot," I replied, deflecting and turning her comment into a joke. "Because it would be super weird if you were talking about Kristian. I mean, he just got married to Ronnie, so if I was *his* world…."

Holland laughed and looped her arm with mine. "Stick around, Sloane. You'll see what I'm saying is true. These Cartwright men wear their hearts on their sleeves for all to see. Well, everyone but them."

Stick around.

I didn't know what Holland thought she was seeing on Abbot's sleeve, but she couldn't have any idea about what had really gone down between us. At one point I thought I'd made a friend in Abbot, and even though I hated that nothing would ever come of *us*, I realised it was his friend-ship I'd miss the most. He truly got me. Pushed me. His friendship had been as relentless as his pursuit, and I would miss that.

Stick around? To experience more of his indifference and friendlessness? There was no way I was sticking around for any more of that. I was getting out of town the moment I got my stuff back. Then I was going to start somewhere new. *Somewhere nobody knows me.*

CHAPTER TWENTY-FIVE
A LITTLE TOO MUCH

WEDDING RECEPTIONS MEANT AN OPEN BAR. Wine, beer, spirits and champagne. I drank them all, finding I cared less about how much I missed Abbot with each mouthful—I admitted how much I cared to myself after my third...no, *fifth* drink—and more about beating myself up for every shitty thing I'd ever done wrong in my life.

"And I haven't been perfect," I said to a woman with glittery eyeshadow and bleach-burned hair. "I've done my fair share of arseholey things when it comes to love. When I was nineteen, I kissed a boy when I was dating someone else, simply because he gave me a lift to a party and I felt I owed him something. *Stupid.* It all came out and I looked like a tart, which was *never* what I wanted. I wanted to be loved. I wanted to be seen for the woman that I am." I blinked rapidly, squinting one eye before pulling off the fake eyelashes that had come loose. "I never wanted any of this."

"You might want to take the other one off too. You look a little unbalanced, love."

"Well, I feel unhinged." I fumbled and tugged at the lashes on my other eye. "Ow."

The woman gave me a sympathetic pat on my knee and took the opportunity to bail.

"Story of my fucking life," I said, dropping my fake eyelashes into my empty glass before blowing a raspberry. Weddings sucked.

A bottle of water was placed in front of me.

"Drink," Abbot commanded, taking the seat to my left.

I looked at him over my shoulder, imagining it to be a coquettish move that in reality probably looked like I was about to pass out. I took a drink. He brushed my hair behind my ear.

"I like you too much," I blurted, the alcohol loosening my lips more than normal.

"I know." He spoke softly, his fingers brushing lightly over the skin of my arm.

"I can't be your friend." The words came out in a loud whisper.

"I know," he whispered back, lowering his head to press his lips to my shoulder.

I closed my eyes as his lips did warm tingly things to my alcohol-numbed body. "You can't do that. I'm not playing anymore."

"Neither am I," he said, holding out his hand. "Dance with me."

"I'm too unco to dance."

"Then lean against me and sway. Please, Sloane. Say goodbye to me."

That sobered me. "Goodbye?"

"The warehouse is clear. You'll have your money and your backpack by morning."

"So soon?"

"Isn't it what you wanted?"

Tears pricked my eyes, but I nodded. "I just didn't expect…" Instead of finishing, I cleared my throat and smiled. "Yes, I'll dance with you."

Slipping my hand into his, I followed him onto the dance floor where he pulled me close and swayed like he'd promised. It was hard being this near to him again. I wanted to lean in and sink against his skin, peel his shirt away and run my hands over his chest like I'd done so many times before. I wanted to take him to bed and sleep beside him, one more time.

"You look beautiful tonight," he said, his eyes taking in my made-up features.

"I feel like a painted clown."

He shook his head. "Far from it. I also like this dressy pants number."

"It's a playsuit. Every time I pee I need to completely undress."

"I like it even more now." He grinned, eyes twinkling as mine rolled back in my head. *How can he tease when this is our end?*

"Yeah, well, I'm looking forward to getting back into a pair of leggings and a big T-shirt."

"And socks. Don't forget your socks."

I smiled. "I do get cold feet."

"I know. Just like I know that you don't like the wine you've been drinking half the night. And you'd rather wear my tux than that playsuit. That you watch happy couples with longing in your eyes and will do anything to be a good friend even though you want so much more. I know that you like to sleep on the right side of the bed, facing your left side, that you roll your eyes when you're emotional, and you ramble when you're excited or confused about something."

"You seem to have learned a lot in a couple of weeks."

"That's because I like you too. A little too much."

I rolled my eyes. "Abbot."

"Don't fight it, blue. Just put your head on my chest and let me hold you. I haven't worked out what I'm doing with you yet."

You and me both. With a sigh, I placed my hands and my head on his chest, curling into him and listening to the beating of his heart and the intake of his breath as we swayed. We swayed to the slow songs. We swayed to the fast songs, and when the DJ called last dance, we stopped swaying and stood still, my hands curling into fists that contained the fabric of his shirt.

"I'm not ready for you, Sloane Slater," he said, swallowing hard. Tears burned my eyes, but I nodded, understanding. We didn't want the same things. It was as simple as that.

I uncurled my hands, flattening my palms on his chest, ready to push away. Then his arms tightened and he kissed my forehead for the longest time.

"I need to go, Abbot," I whispered.

He released me.

One last look.

I drank him in from head to toe, taking a final breath of the air around him. Then I smiled. I walked away.

And we were over.

Ending before we started. Before we could get too deep.

Our reasons were simple: I wanted more than he could give, and he liked me too much to string me along. There would be no compromise. That wouldn't be fair to either of us. There would just be two people, walking separate paths, forever changed by a game that had no winner.

He's not ready for me.

CHAPTER TWENTY-SIX
A TWENTY-FIRST CENTURY WOMAN

MINIMALISM. It sounded like a cool idea at first—get rid of my worldly possessions, my apartment, the shopfront, Lizzie...then live with the barest of necessities. Perhaps what I could fit into a backpack.

When I began, it was cathartic throwing away the clutter I'd collected over the years. Participation trophies, shoes I would never wear again, books I'd bought to look smart but never read. I felt weight lifting from my shoulders with each unnecessary possession I discarded or gave away. But then I was finished going through my entire apartment and stripping out the store and I looked around, realising I still had a lot of crap left over. I didn't want to live a life without a comfy couch, or a bed without great back support. I liked having more than one pair of runners as well as three different kinds of bikes. And Netflix was my spirit animal in the off-season, so a large-screened TV was key. Also, I couldn't bring myself to say goodbye to Lizzie. She had been a reliable vehicle for so long that I couldn't stand to list her for sale. So I made a different decision. Move near the sea and become a mobile lock-smith. I was thinking of calling it 'Chicks with Picks'. Get it? Because I'm a girl who can pick a lock. But then, it rhymed a little too closely to 'chicks with dicks' and would probably just make people think I was a lock-picking transvestite. So, maybe that name sucked. But it was a work in progress that would be a very easy way to clean the money I made on the safe job— the *original* two-fifty, because Toby took care of giving me the cash. He paid me, and I left without saying goodbye to everybody else the way an injured possum ran the moment you looked away.

"Will they hate me for disappearing like this?" I'd asked when Toby had handed me my things the morning after the wedding.

"What kind of a question is that?" he'd asked with kindness in his eyes. "We could never hate you. But, are you sure you don't want to stick around? At least find out what your next job is?"

I shook my head. "You can tell me when the time comes. But, Toby, if you find someone else who you trust, don't tell me at all."

He nodded once, understanding. Then he gave me a hug. "In that case, stay away, Sloane. For another twenty years at least."

That made tears spring to my eyes. *Leave and never see them again?* I admit to crying a little (a lot) as I drove away. It was hard to leave the Cartwrights. Harder to walk away from the feelings I'd developed for Abbot. But I knew it was for the best. The Cartwrights were better left as a memory of fun times and fondness. Those misfit brothers occupied a special place in my heart that could never be replaced, but I wasn't right for their world. I'd struggled with it twenty-one years ago, and time hadn't changed that. Fearless and badarse might have been my descriptors once, but I didn't feel like that anymore. It was as if being with Abbot had brought out those characteristics, and although it had been me, I felt...*less* now we were apart. And what Mark had called me—independent and capable—wasn't really a true fit either. I'd thought myself independent, but it was only now that I was stepping away from what was *comfortable* that I would be acting independently. I *was* capable. I had proved myself an excellent locksmith and could be proud of that. Now it was time to discover *who* I was. I would prove to myself that I was self-sufficient and self-contained. I'd figure it out. Eventually.

Sighing, I sat in my decluttered unit, sparkling clean because I'd just had an open house. I'd put my place on the market the moment I got home, and now I was reading an email from the agent, telling me I already had two offers. It was time to decide where I was moving.

Scrolling through recommendations for family friendly coastal towns, I took a sip of milky tea and imagined doing this very activity with the sea breeze brushing against my skin. It had been a month since I'd felt it, and I missed it. Almost as much as I missed a certain brother. *Abbot.*

Just as the mental picture of his teasing smirk took hold, there was a knock on my door to strip it away.

"What happened to all your stuff?" my mother said, walking inside without an invitation.

"I don't recall giving you a key, Mother," I said, turning in my chair.

She shrugged. "I don't need keys, baby." Dropping her

weight onto my couch, she let her head sink back and sighed out of comfort, closing her eyes.

"Um…are you going to tell me why you're here, or just take a nap?"

"A nap would be great, but I do have a reason for stopping by." She sat up and leaned forwards, her elbows on her jean-clad thighs, long silky scarf hanging from her neck, hair and make-up done to perfection.

"I'm dying in anticipation," I deadpanned.

She grinned. "Oh, honey. It doesn't seem like you're happy to see me."

"Am I ever truly happy to see you?"

"Understood. I'm a shitty mum. I get that."

"You're a woeful mum. In fact, you were never a mum at all. Just some woman who breezed in and out of my life once or twice a year and fucked things up when she felt like it."

She swung her feet around so she was lying across the length of the couch. "That's not true. We had some great times."

"When I was a kid and you fed me so much junk food I threw up? Yeah. Those times were awesome."

"Come on, Sloane. It wasn't *all* bad." She folded her arms behind her head and got a little more comfortable.

"You're right. It wasn't," I admitted. "But…I had needed you." No outings, no late-night giggling and being silly, no flashy gifts or breaking of curfews would ever make up for all the time she missed. Fact is, I grew up and she missed it. She missed it all. "I needed you and you were never there for me."

"What happened with the Cartwright boy?" she asked,

changing the subject before I could get too deep into what her absenteeism had meant for me. *Typical.*

I sighed out of exasperation and shook my head. "Nothing happened. I finished the job and left."

"I really thought he'd marry you."

"Why? Because you offered to pay him."

"Well, he *is* a Cartwright."

"He's not interested in marriage, Mum. I don't think anyone could pay him enough to want the whole kids and wife experience."

"Meh. It was worth a shot," she said, shifting so she could reach into her back pocket. She then leaned forward and flicked a folded piece of white paper across the room to me. It spun like a Frisbee and landed on the carpet two feet away from me.

"What's this?" I asked, leaning to collect it between two fingers.

"Your inheritance."

"I thought I couldn't have this until I got married?"

She shrugged. "You could have it whenever I felt like giving it to you."

"Wait. That caveat was bullshit?"

"As if your grandfather gave a shit if you were married or not. Open it. You'll be happy."

I pressed the paper between my palms and looked my mother in the eye. "Why the hell did you say I had to get *married*?"

Sitting up, she held her hands out to either side. "Because I thought he'd go for it. You two were obviously into each other. Jasmine and I thought you'd make cute babies together."

"You and *Jasmine thought...?* What the fuck, Mum!"

"Hey, I thought I was doing you a favour. Get him to think marrying you is his idea and we all get what we want."

"We? What do *we* want, Mother?"

"Babies. You want kids. I want grandkids. Jasmine wants grandkids."

"Jasmine has two grandkids on the way. Maybe more if all goes well for the others."

"Two grandkids to replace *five* sons?" She shook her head. "That's not enough. She wants to retire, Sloane. *I* want to retire. If there's no one to take over, everything we've worked for will go away."

I pressed my fingers into my forehead and tried to make sense of what she was saying against the throbbing in my head. Just being in the same room as my mother gave me a headache on a normal day. This was some migraine-level shit. "What *exactly* are you saying?"

"I'm saying that it was no coincidence Abbot was the brother who hired you for that job."

"Explain."

"Mind if I smoke?" she asked while she lit up, giving me little choice.

"*Explain* yourself, mother."

She blew cigarette smoke into the air, contaminating the orange blossom scent from the candles I'd burned earlier. "After Dad passed, Jasmine got in touch and we talked about the future. Our future. Your future. She and I have been doing this for a long time, kid. And it's not something you want to be doing til the day you die. We want to live a little too, you know? Reap the rewards of our labour. So, she asked if you'd be open to taking on some extra work and whether you were still single."

"Single so she could set me up with Abbot?"

She grinned, blowing smoke out the side of her mouth while she pointed at me with long red nails. "You're catching on. Abbot had some mega crush on you as a kid, so she thought you might be the one to break through that Peter Pan syndrome of his. The job was the meet cute and the carrot in your hand was the incentive." She indicated the paper I was holding. "But, he was a tougher nut to crack than we expected, so..." She sighed in a way that dismissed everything as no big deal. "No point in holding out anymore."

My jaw hurt from clenching so hard. My chest hurt from not screaming *enough*. My stomach hurt from swallowing bullshit. My head just plain hurt. How could she? How *dare she?*

She'd colluded behind my back and tried to manipulate my life. Once again, she'd made a fucking mess.

"Get. Out," I growled through my teeth.

"Sloane." Her voice was soft, pleading. I couldn't even look at her.

"Get out." I stood. "Get out. Get out. *Get out!*"

Getting to her feet, she put her cigarette out in the soil of my pot plant. "I don't know why you're being like this."

"Get out," I yelled.

She raised her hands. "I'm going. I'm going."

I followed her to the door, ready to deadbolt and chain it after her. Nail it shut if necessary. Anything to make sure she didn't come back in.

"For the record, Sloane, I was only doing what any mother would do when her only daughter is childless and pushing forty. Your eggs won't keep forever, you know."

A scream erupted out of my chest as I tore up the piece

of paper in my hands. "Get out of my fucking life and take your fucking money with you. I want *nothing* from you, do you hear? *Nothing.* All you do is meddle and make a mess. I just want to be *alone*."

"You don't mean that, sweetheart."

I slammed the door and flipped the locks, sliding the security chain in place as my chest heaved and my eyes burned.

Was I seriously *that* pitiful? So wretched that everyone else felt the need to make my decisions for me? First Pop and my mother, and now *Jasmine*?

No wonder I was unhappy. None of my decisions were ever mine. They were all guided by older generations thinking they knew better and had the right to make my choices for me. Well, it was the twenty-first century and I was a twenty-first century woman. I could do all of this on my own.

Pacing back and forth in my living room, I blew out huffs of air, trying to calm the swirling storm in my mind. I was so done with this life. Thank God I had offers on my apartment, because I was out of here.

After I gave that other meddler a piece of my mind.

With my mind made up, I picked up my keys and stormed out the door. Jasmine had lied and manipulated me. She needed to stay the fuck away from me too. I was done. So fucking done.

CHAPTER TWENTY-SEVEN
CONSEQUENCES

"JASMINE!" I bashed against the front door. "Get the hell out here. I have a bone to pick with you, you meddling piece of shit."

The front door opened with a dramatic pull. "Whoa, whoa," Toby said, catching me by the elbows before I could rush past him. "What's going on?"

"Your mother is a meddling piece of shit is what's going on. Jasmine!" I yelled past him.

"She's not here."

I stopped pushing and met his eyes. "Her car is out front."

"She's off somewhere with Breaker. I don't know when she's coming back."

I forced my arms straight at my sides, relaxing my hands and I tried to figure out what came next. "Well...when is she back?"

"I just said I don't know."

"Yeah, but like, is it overnight or just today? How long am I waiting here?"

He folded his arms across his T-shirt clad chest. *T-shirt? On Toby?* "If it's to hurl abuse at her, I suggest you wait forever. She doesn't take kindly to being called a— how did you put it? A meddling piece of shit?"

"I honestly don't give a fuck what she thinks, Toby. She's been messing with my life and I need her to back the hell off."

"Why?"

"Excuse me?"

"Why do you need her to back off?"

"Because I don't need her and my mother colluding to marry me off."

"OK. But, in the last month what has she done to you?"

I opened my mouth, ready to argue but there was nothing to say. I hadn't even heard from Jasmine since I left.

"Exactly," he stated. "I told you I'd take care of it, and I did. So, unless you want to get dragged back into all the shit Abbot and I fought to get you out of, I suggest you jump back in that old van of yours and go back home. *Now*, Sloane."

"But..."

"I'm not kidding. You can't be here."

With all the teeth pulled out of my fight, I stumbled back. Did he know I was being set up with Abbot? He didn't seem shocked in the slightest. *What the hell is wrong with this family?*

"Oh excellent," he muttered, lifting a hand as the rumble of a Harley motor came our way. I turned to find Breaker riding up the long driveway with Jasmine on the back.

"What do I do?" I asked, suddenly in a panic. Did I leave or did I stay? Did I face Jasmine or keep my mouth shut? What was the play?

"Say hi. Tell her you were passing through and realised you forgot something."

"Forgot what?"

He disappeared for a second then came back holding onto an old jumper that he shoved into my hands. It was then I realised he was not only wearing a T-shirt but track pants as well. *The man did relax after all.*

"Sloane," Jasmine said when Breaker pulled up and cut the engine. Her voice was light and airy as she pulled off her helmet and ran her fingers through her hair. "What a nice surprise."

"Hi. I was just passing through and realised I forgot this, ah…" I held the jumper up and read the printing on the front. "Torquay High jumper."

I glanced at Toby who looked like he wanted to slap himself in the face while Jasmine came closer. "Class of '95. That was your year, wasn't it, Toby?"

"That was the wrong jumper," he said, snatching the jumper back, trying to salvage the situation.

"Save it," Jasmine quipped, obviously not buying it. "Why don't you come inside, Sloane. Tell me why you're really here."

"I…"

Breaker clapped a hand on my shoulder and pressed his fingers in a little too firmly. "Think it's best if you do as you're told, missy." He frogmarched me towards the door in Jasmine's wake.

Oh fuck. This can't be good.

"Jasmine," Toby said in warning.

"We're just talking, Toby. Relax." She gestured for me to be taken into the formal living room while she asked for Breaker to 'be a dear' and get us something to drink.

We sat in silence while he brought us tea and cookies that he'd 'baked this morning' then stood in the archway like a sentry, the leather cut he was wearing displaying his Grim Order membership. Intimidating.

"Am I in trouble here?" I asked, feeling uneasy and a little foolish. I'd always been told there were consequences for getting too close to this family, but this was the first time I'd ever felt like there could be any real danger in associating with them. *Stupid.* How could I be that naïve when I knew what they did for a living?

Jasmine sipped her tea and crossed her legs. "I was under the impression that you no longer wanted anything to do with our *business*. We appreciated the work you did for us, and as a favour to Trevor—God rest his soul—we released you from any further commitment. For the second time in your life, mind you. Care to explain what you're doing here now?"

"Uh…" I looked around for Toby, wanting his guidance, but he wasn't in my line of sight. I was on my own here. Did I go with the truth, or did I make something up?

"Mum told me about your plan." I went with the truth.

"Oh, she did? Not the brightest thing she's ever done. Doesn't she know you're the quintessential redhead, full of fire and fury?"

"I'm afraid my mother doesn't really know me at all."

"Or did she *want* you to come back here?"

I pressed my fingers against my forehead. "Why don't you tell me?" I had no fucking clue anymore.

"As far as I was concerned, we were done." Jasmine sipped her tea and nibbled the edge of a cookie.

"I'm here to make sure we really are."

"You seem so confused, Sloane. I always told your grandfather that you needed a more stable female role model in your life. Someone to guide you and help you find your true path."

"Funny, he used to say your boys needed a stable male role model of their own."

Her eyes flashed. "My boys got *everything* they needed from me. I turned them into *men.*"

"Men, or *soldiers* in your games?"

Her smile fell. "I don't expect you to understand, Sloane. Trevor kept you sheltered for a long time, and I'm sure you preferred that. But you don't get to come in here with your cloistered opinions and judge my choices or the way I run this family. My rule is what keeps us all safe. It's what keeps us going, wealthy, powerful, and strong. I built us up from nothing and I will make sure that this family continues in that manner long after I'm gone. Whether it's with you, or without you."

"So you're orchestrating a breeding program? Do you understand how insane that is?"

She laughed. "Don't be ridiculous. I'm simply choosing women who are the best fit for this family and my sons. Who better to choose a wife for them than me— the person who moulded them? You should be flattered I considered you worthy." *Flattered?*

"You have lost your mind."

She sighed, seeming bored. "You're being dramatic. I'm an even better matchmaker than Breaker is a baker.

Have you tried these cookies?" She took a bite and spoke around the crumbs. "They're to die for."

"Thank you, baby," Breaker said from his post.

"You are so talented," she said, kissing the air in his direction before turning back to me. They were so weird. "Anyway, you've seen with your own eyes how happy my married sons are. Did I choose wrong for them? Was I wrong about you and Abbot, too? Tell me you feel nothing for him and maybe I'll consider your opinion."

I opened my mouth, but there was no way I was going to deny the feelings I had for Abbot. They'd only deepened in the time we were apart and were as true and as strong as my heartbeat. "It's still wrong," I whispered.

"Go and tell Abbot you're in love with him." It was a challenge, not a suggestion.

"He doesn't want me."

She narrowed her eyes, assessing me. "Are you sure about that?"

While she studied my expression, the unmistakeable roar of Abbot's Jag came up the drive. *He's here?* That was some epic-level timing.

"Here's your knight in shinin' armour," Breaker said, looking out the front window. I ran my hand over my hair and pressed my palms together.

Jasmine smiled and folded her hands in her lap. "Five... Four..." *Why is she counting?* "Three... Two..."

"What the fuck is going on?" Abbot yelled, bursting through the front door.

"One," Jasmine said at the same time. Sipping her tea and chuckling as Abbot continued.

"*Sloane?*"

"I'm in here," I called out, relieved he was here. I felt instantly better with his presence.

He appeared in the archway next to Breaker, his chest heaving, his expression stricken. *He's so damn beautiful. I've missed him so much.*

"Toby's been up to his usual tricks," Jasmine stated, her face serene as both sons entered the room.

"This does concern him too," Toby said, taking the seat farthest away from his mother. Abbot sat beside me, and despite the intensity of the situation, my heart did a little happy dance inside my chest.

"Why are you here, Slater?" he asked softly, his eyes searching mine.

My heart quit dancing. *Way to make a girl feel unwelcome.*

"She's come to help with the transport job. Haven't you, Sloane?" I wasn't sure if Jasmine was lying to cover up the real reason, or if she was giving me a command.

"Uh, I don't know about that. I actually came to find answers," I said, turning back to Abbot. "Like, why our mothers were trying to bribe us into marrying each other."

Abbot leapt back so fast, I thought he might hit the end of the couch and topple onto the floor. *A commitment phobe to the very last breath.* "Fucking *what*?"

"Oh my God," Jasmine said with a dramatic eye-roll. "You're both acting like I held a gun to your head. I orchestrated a meeting. Emma gave you a little push. Neither of which worked out, so we let it go. Get over yourselves. It was a set-up, not a marry or die situation."

Abbot glared at her. "Don't even think about it."

"Don't worry, sweetheart. I know how you feel about such things. I gave you the choice. You chose wrong, by the way. You let her go and you've been a nightmare ever since." *He has?*

"I…" Abbot shook his head, looking between his mother and me. "You're a manipulative bitch, Jasmine." *Whoa.*

"Call me a name I haven't heard before," she stated without even flinching. "But she's back now, so either man up or quit storming in here to save her from my evil ways. It's getting old, and despite what everyone else thinks, I think Sloane belongs here. With us. I helped shape her. She's one of us." *Is this woman serious?*

"She deserves to choose her own path and be happy, Mother," Abbot ground out.

"We tried that. Twice. And her path led her here. Twice. That's kismet if ever I saw it."

I don't like where this is going.

"Do not force a wedding, Mother," Abbot said, his voice like the stomping of a foot.

Ow. I knew how against this he was already, but *ow.*

"I'm not asking you to. But, there *are* consequences." She turned her attention elsewhere.

"Don't you dare look at me," Toby put in, and I thought I might scream for the second time that day. Instead, I jumped to my feet.

"I don't want to marry *any* of you," I yelled, storming towards the door while muttering to myself about the insanity of these people and the fact they actually had the gall to think they could decide *my* life for me.

"Maybe you should sit back down," Breaker said, catching me by the arm with a firm grip.

"I don't want to sit back down. I want to go home. Coming back here was nothing but a fool's errand."

"No," Jasmine said. "You made the perfect choice coming here. We have a job coming up that requires your lock-picking skills. Stay, teach my sons what you know, and we'll compensate you handsomely. I don't need you to marry into the family to utilise your skills. But what I do need is your understanding that you operate as a consultant from this point on. When I require your efforts, I will contact you directly, give you a price, and the rest of the job will come out of your own pocket. You will liaise with Toby or me, and depending on the work, you may have contact with the others. However, since you aren't joining the family, you won't be socialising with us anymore. There are to be no public connections or meetups, nor joint celebrations or parties—*nothing* from this point on. You get in, you do the job, and you get out. You'll remove our information from your phone and contact us only via an unlocked Blackberry that will be changed out regularly. You never come back to the house. We are no longer friends. Do you understand?" *Wow.*

I was suddenly a business associate, no longer welcome in their home. In their lives. And it stung. Only a moment ago she'd berated Abbot for letting me go, but now she was forcefully pushing me out of her family once and for all. I didn't know what was beating in that woman's chest, but it couldn't possibly be a heart.

"Do I even have choice?"

"Not anymore, no," she stated simply, getting out of her chair and walking towards me. "Now, we'll get you set up with what you need. Toby?" She swung her eyes in his direction momentarily, returning her attention my way before continuing. "There's a lovely resort in town. I suggest you make use of their serviced apartments and facilities to keep yourself close but out of the way while we're in training for this job. A month or two should do it, but Toby will fill you in on the particulars when you're settled."

"Ah." It was a small sound of exasperation while I stood at the mouth of the room and wondered how the fuck coming here to yell at her turned into a job I wasn't allowed to say no to.

"Fine. I'll marry her," Abbot said suddenly, his eyes closed and his brow creased like he was defeated.

Defeated.

Jasmine grinned.

Fine. I'll marry her.

What the actual fuck?

"Stick it up your arse, Abbot," I returned, scrunching my face up in utter offence. *How dare he?* "Stick it so far up that you choke on it. I don't want you. Not like this. Not at all. Fuck this. Fuck all of you."

Why even suggest that? So I wasn't cut off from the family? It didn't make any sense, and I was above taking scraps. I had *some* pride.

When I turned this time, Breaker let me go. Not that I got far; the front door was locked. "Can someone let me the fuck out of this house?" My voice sounded hoarse with emotion.

Toby came up behind me with a set of keys and unlocked the door, holding out an old Blackberry phone and a Post-it Note with a number written on top of an address. "Don't call us on anything but the Blackberry. This is what the job's worth and where you need to be on Monday at nine in the morning. Take the weekend at home, pack your stuff, and remember—if you try to run, I can find you. Wherever you are. I will bring you back."

I snatched the items from his hand, feeling sick to my stomach. "I get it. Show up for work. Keep my mouth shut and do as I'm told."

"That a girl," he said.

"Fuck you, Toby."

"For what it's worth, Sloane. I tried, OK?"

"Tried to leave or tried to keep me out of it?"

He smiled softly as he opened the front door to let me go without an answer.

With a tight ball of emotion in my chest, I turned the phone over in my hand, a black piece of ancient-looking technology that I wasn't even sure how to use. *I tried...*

Seemed none of us could fully get out.

TAKING a detour to Bendigo on the way home, I stopped in to visit my mother, needing to talk to *someone* who knew Jasmine. I didn't care that I'd screamed at her earlier in the day, the woman was the kind of person who could stab you in the thigh then say, "Oh my God, that was so five minutes ago," while you were howling in pain. So, I had no problem showing up unannounced demanding answers and clarity.

"Sloane," she said with a smile when she answered her door, still wearing that silk scarf even though she was home. "This is unexpected. Come inside."

Leading me towards the lounge room, she opened a cabinet that was full of liquor bottles. "It's after five, so

I'm offering a drink instead of tea. Unless of course you want Long Island."

"I have to drive."

"So, whisky neat?"

"One finger," I replied, taking a seat on her floral couch.

"Here to shoot the breeze or talk about this job Jasmine has you doing?" She handed me a glass and sat across from me.

"My God, she's already told you?"

"Of course. We've always talked where you're concerned."

Sipping my whiskey, I leaned back in the chair. "Why is everyone messing around with my life?"

She shrugged. "Have you considered it's because we care?"

"Wouldn't caring mean you support me in following my own path?"

"People care in their own ways, baby. It doesn't always fit our expectations."

"You think that's what my problem is? I expect too much?"

"I don't know, Sloane. I honestly don't know why you'd expect anything after your upbringing. I was raised by the same man, and I certainly don't. Trevor always cared, but he wasn't the most loving man."

I sighed. My mother had a convoluted way of looking at things. I knew she left me with Pop because she 'wasn't the mothering kind'. But if she thought he'd fucked *her* up with his stoic ways, why put that on me too? Ugh. No wonder I was fucked in the head.

"So, what do I do about this job offer of Jasmine's?"

"It's not a job offer, sweetheart. It just *is*. Do what they ask, get paid and keep your nose clean."

"Keep my nose clean. Pop always said that too."

"He said it to me as well. Or did he say 'keep your money clean'? I can't remember which one."

"Think you can help me with that?"

"Cleaning your money?"

I emptied my glass. "Yeah." I didn't like the woman in front of me, and I had no remorse feeling like that. But on the drive there I'd made a decision: this was business. I'd been forced into a job I didn't want, to work with people I needed to keep at arm's length. *There are to be no public connections or meetups, no joint celebrations or parties... You get in, you do the job, and you get out... You never come back to the house.* I'd covered myself with an armour of detachment and come here. This wouldn't be a bonding session but a necessary schooling of skills I'd never been shown. It was my life now, and I would—*could* —embrace it.

"My pleasure." She smiled and stretched her arm along the back of the couch. "It's all about finding a business that accepts cash payments..."

CHAPTER TWENTY-EIGHT
THE LAST WORD

AFTER A LIFETIME of being at loggerheads with my mother, we had finally found some common ground with my re-rebirth into the criminal world. We spent much of the weekend together, going over the details of how I could operate as a consultant for the Cartwrights while keeping undetected by the law. Something she had managed to do her entire life—among the other various illegal activities she'd taken part in.

Besides fucking, breaking and entering seemed to be her field of expertise. "It's in our blood," she'd explained over Chinese takeaway, adding that she'd always been so disappointed that I'd let my fear of being caught keep me away from that calling. "I'm glad you've come to your senses now though."

"I really haven't," I'd assured her. "I just don't have a choice anymore."

She'd waved her hand in the air and replied, "Potato Potarto." Obviously not caring *how* I came to be following in her footsteps, and only concerned with the fact she was finally able to share her knowledge. I'd never seen her more excited.

With the offers in on my flat and the shopfront, I packed my bags and left her in charge of putting everything else in storage before settlement happened in three month's time. I was putting a lot of trust in a woman who had always seemed like a flake while I was growing up, but this past couple of days had shown me she was a shrewd businesswoman who would never let emotion get in the way of a job. I couldn't say I liked her more than when I'd arrived on her doorstep a few days before, but her business acumen and success spoke for itself, and I was wiser because of it. I had no doubt she could handle transporting my stuff to the empty workshop that was once Pop's.

"Do the Slater name proud, OK?" she said once I'd loaded my bags into Lizzie. I gave her a hug, grateful that she was finally doing something *for me*. "And if you get a chance, *try* to have sex with Abbot. It'll do you good."

"Oh God, Mum. That ship has sailed. I told you Jasmine forbade me to have contact with them outside the job."

"*Pish*. Jasmine can't dictate what you do in your free time. There's always ways around the rules, baby. Believe me, I made a career out of breaking them." She'd winked and I'd laughed at her audaciousness while getting into my van. Despite our tattered history, I'd never not loved my mum. You could love somebody and struggle to be in the same room as them at the same time.

"I'll contact you soon to check on things here. Call if you need me." That was probably the first time I'd ever said that to her and meant it.

"Just think about the sex part," she called out as I drove away.

Again, I laughed, glancing at her in the rear-view mirror as my old life shrank away. No more Rochester, I'd said goodbye to old friends, old life. When this job was finished, I would find somewhere new to set down roots. Somewhere I could find my own happiness without any meddling.

Just think about it.

Fine. I'll marry her.

Angry didn't even touch the surface of how I was feeling towards Abbot right now. The defeated way he'd said those words. No self-respecting woman would ever accept that kind of proposal. What the hell was wrong with him?

Despite being angry, I did still think about 'the sex part'. Lord, it was all I did some nights awake in bed—that photo he'd sent me a favourite in the spank bank—unable to sleep because I'd become so used to having him beside me that *my* bed wasn't the most restful place for me anymore. *It was inside his arms.*

I suppose I had to delete that photo now, too.

I hated that idea. Besides the significance of that image, deleting the Cartwrights from my contacts and ending any sort of social communication with them hurt my heart. I understood it was about breaking ties and maintaining secrecy surrounding jobs, but I didn't want to ignore the fact these men had been a large part of my life. That Abbot had a huge chunk of my heart.

That part *really* sucked. I guess I still had my memories.

Driving back, I spent a lot of that time going over

every detail of every moment I could remember about Torquay. I tried to keep my thoughts to the PG childhood memories, but they quickly turned MA (sometimes R) rated with the yearning I still felt towards Abbot. He'd gotten under my skin and it wasn't so easy to shake him—delete him, like Jasmine had said. *How am I supposed to work with this family, with him, when I feel this way?*

I guess it was finally time to stop running away from my problems, something I'd become terribly good at in my thirty-eight years.

With my final Rochester to Torquay trip behind me by mid-afternoon, I parked Lizzie inside the Wyndham Resort. After getting a great deal on a little apartment since it was the off-season. It had two bedrooms and a living area with its own kitchen so I could cook my own meals and make myself more at home than I could in a regular hotel room. I was ready to do this job—whatever 'teaching them what I knew' was. All that was left to do was twiddle my thumbs until nine the next morning. *That's a lot of hours to fill.*

I looked around the apartment, pursued the pamphlets spruiking the resort's facilities, flicked through the channels on the TV, and stared at the ceiling.

This is really boring.

I needed to *do* something.

With the resort only five minutes away from Bells Beach, I figured a long run along the shoreline would be a great way to work out the kinks of travel and wind down for the night before showing up ready for work the next day.

For anyone unfamiliar with Torquay, it was a surfer's paradise—as long as you could handle the cooler temperatures. There were numerous beaches with different types of waves that varied depending on the weather. But you could be guaranteed to find a decent swell at one of the main beaches to suit your style.

I didn't surf. My lack of grace wasn't made for balancing on planks without biting a sandbank. But, I could definitely appreciate a good swell when I saw one.

As I touched down on the beach, the wind whipped stray granules of sand at my face and my flicked hair around. I pulled it back into a ponytail while I looked out to water and noted the messy whitecaps and tall waves. Locals were either preparing to tackle the waves or catching their breath after surviving the swell. Even more were in the water, performing aerial stunts that never ceased to amaze me.

The cool air felt good in my lungs as I ran along the firm sand where the water receded. I loved the sea, loved the way the water roared and the wind howled. Such power. Such life. I felt so at home here and wondered how I'd ever survived living inland for so long.

When I was done with my run, my limbs heavy and burning from use, I slowed to a stop then lumbered up the sand, shaking out my thighs as I climbed the wooden stairs to the street level. There were still people dotted every-where, as dedicated surfers didn't miss a great set of waves. I caught snippets of conversation in the car park, bragging about one-eighties and tube heights. Then I heard a giggle and turned towards it—a flirtatious sound amid the chest thumping—and that's when I wished I'd stayed indoors.

"Shit," I whispered to myself, also regretting that I hadn't worn a cap. I could have pulled it down over my face and ran in the opposite direction. Anything to avoid witnessing this…

Abbot was standing against his Jag, grinning his sexy grin while talking to a blonde girl who had one of those round arses that are in fashion these days. I knew this because she was wearing a set of bikini bottoms in fluorescent pink that sucked right against her arse crack like it was painted on her skin, barely covering her butt cheeks. On the top, she had one of those hoodies on that showed off her slender midriff. There was no real point in wearing it, really. She couldn't have been warm. I could see her goosebumped skin from metres away.

But mostly, she was young. Really young. Like, no older than twenty young. Way younger than me…and tiny. The perfect size for someone like Abbot, who would undoubtedly prefer the small and cute rather than the tall and boyish.

Forget him.

When she touched Abbot's arm and spoke, I wanted to touch *her* arm and push. Perhaps with a closed fist.

When he tucked her hair behind her ear, I remembered him doing the same to me, and I looked away. Perhaps there were tears in my eyes.

Stupid, stupid, *stupid.*

What had I expected him to do? Sit and pine for me the way I had been for him? Try to convince me that I really was his one—that he'd *actually meant* that proposal? He hadn't even tried to call me, obviously deleting my number like his mother had commanded. *I'm such a fool.*

Stupid. *Stupid. Stupid.*

He was what he was. And he'd never hidden the fact he was a player. I knew that. I was just…

I was hopeless.

Hopelessly devoted like sad Sandy in *Grease*. The difference was that I wasn't Olivia Newton John and he wasn't John Travolta, and this wasn't a fucking musical that finished with a happily ever after. Abbot was the man he always told me he was. He used women for fun and he was never their friend, romantically or otherwise. I knew that. Just like I knew he'd said he'd marry me because he felt Jasmine was forcing his hand.

"Fuck this."

Delete him, Sloane. No more pining.

Turning in the opposite direction, I took a calming breath then walked casually away, pulling my red hair over my shoulder and holding it in my hand as an attempt at hiding it from sight. I intended to circle the car park and come out at the road, completely avoiding Abbot and his latest conquest. *No socialising. Only the job. Delete, delete, delete.*

Let go.

"Sloane?"

Crap. I walked a little faster.

"Sloane!"

I broke into a jog.

"Wait up." Within a couple of strides, he appeared beside me.

"Abbot." I feigned surprise while my foot caught on a small stone. He caught my arm to steady me and I wanted to throw myself at him.

Love me.

I didn't.

"Why didn't you stop? I was calling you."

"Because we don't know each other any more." I

pulled the arm he was holding from his grip and flicked my hand to add a little disconnect from my reaction to being close to him again. "No socialising."

"That's a bullshit rule and you know it." I didn't really know about that. Being this close to him felt impossible. Jasmine may actually know what she's talking about.

"Who was your friend?" I asked, changing the subject, not even caring that it made me sound jealous. I was.

"My friend?"

"The girl you were talking to back there. She your latest FWB?"

"FWB?"

"Friend with benefits."

"What?" He shook his head. "No. I haven't... She's just a girl, Sloane."

I scoffed. "Aren't they all?" Then I pointed to the resort across the street, needing to get away from him. *I don't think I can do this.* "This is me." Without giving him the chance to say another word, I jogged across the street.

"Sloane!"

He kept yelling after me, but I just picked up my pace and didn't stop until I was back inside my apartment. "Shit, crap," I gasped, locking the door and leaning against it. "I can't do this." I couldn't be near him, couldn't pretend I felt nothing whenever he was around. With tears threatening, I rushed straight for the shower and stripped, standing under the stream, hoping the noise of the water would somehow drown out the noise in my mind.

It didn't. Everything about the way I reacted towards Abbot was too raw. It had only taken two weeks to fall for him, but it felt as though it would take a lifetime to recover. Getting out of the shower, I wrapped myself in a towel and headed to the living area where the Blackberry was on charge. I needed to call Toby and tell him that I'd work with him only. I could teach him whatever he needed and he could show the others. I'd happily take a cut in pay.

"You need to quit throwing tantrums and running when things aren't going your way." Abbot sat on the couch in the dimly lit room, curtains drawn over the large glass sliding door.

"What the hell are you doing in here?" I gasped, clutching the towel at my chest as I almost fell against the kitchen bench.

He stood and moved towards me. "You know what, Sloane, I don't fucking know. I can't seem to walk away from you."

"Maybe you should."

His head moved side to side as he drew closer, stalking, cat-like. "It'd probably be best, right? Lord knows you make me fucking insane with your—"

"So go. I don't want you here anyway."

He stopped in front of me and closed his eyes, teeth clenching. "—inability to let me get a *fucking word out*," he said, his voice low and deep as he placed his hands on the side of the bench and caged me in. "Why won't you *ever* let me speak?" That part was a whisper as his face lined up with mine.

"Maybe I'm afraid of what I'll hear." It was probably the most honest I'd ever been with him.

"Sloane." His warm breath washed over my face as his eyes flashed and dropped to my lips. Without warning, his mouth collided with mine, intense and hungry, the force of his tongue demanding as his hand went into my wet hair and the other one grabbed my arse.

Set aflame, I whimpered against his lips, hands grabbing at his shirt and pushing at the fabric, desperate for the feel of his skin. He broke contact, his eyes dark and hungry as the took me in for the split second before his pulled his shirt over his head and dumped it on the floor.

"Abbot," I whispered when he reached for me again.

"Shut up, Sloane." His lips took control of mine as he grabbed my hips and hefted me onto the bench, shoving my towel out of the way so my nakedness pressed right against his warm chest. He moaned and wrapped his arms around my torso, practically crushing me against him as we devoured each other's mouths.

My fingers dug into his ribs, sliding to the waistband of his pants and pushing, my movements frantic and jarring, desperate. With one hand, he shoved at his pants and freed himself, the hot head of his dick lining up with my opening and pushing inside.

I gasped, the sound caught in his mouth as he grunted and sheathed himself with my body.

Oh God.

Oh God.

He felt even better inside me than I'd imagined, and I could barely respond to his kisses as his hips swivelled back and forth, pushing and stretching my insides so I was nothing more than an orgasm waiting to happen.

With no sounds except the gasping of our breath and the meeting of our bodies, we rocked together on the edge of that kitchen bench, weeks of restraint and fighting, culminating in this frantic bout of skin slapping and guttural moans. I felt set to explode.

"Abbot," I uttered, so close to my release. He caught my bottom lip in his teeth and sucked back, his hips picking up speed, filling me so deep, so completely, over and over until I dropped my head back and released a low howl, coming harder than I'd ever come in my life.

He lowered his head into the curve of my neck and slammed his hips into mine with a shudder, his cock twitching in my depths, spilling his release. *Holy fuck.*

Wrapping my arms around his head, I let out a whimper that was so filled with emotion I almost cried.

"I'm sorry," he whispered, the man who never apologised, hot breath against my neck. "I couldn't…"

I held him tighter. "It's OK." *Holy fucking hell.* "It's OK." I was sated, yet yearning. Our collision too sudden and too brief. "But, Abbot?"

"Yeah."

"I think we need to do that again."

He chuckled so his entire torso shook against mine, his cock still inside me hard and ready. "I think you're right."

I placed my hand on his cheek and pulled back a little so I could meet his eyes. "I need to tell you something first."

"No, you don't, Sloane," he said, straightening up and sliding his big hands along either side of my face, his light eyes looking deep into mine before he spoke. "I already know."

"You do?"

He nodded. "I love you too."

My heart just exploded.

Then he brought his lips to mine and kissed me so softly and tenderly that I was incapable of stopping my tears this time. "I love you," I mumbled through our moving mouths and my sobs. I had a desperate need to get those words out.

He smiled. "Couldn't let me have the last word, could you, Slater?" Brushing up with his lips, he ran the tip of his nose alongside mine, the fingers of his right hand trailing down my spine. I shivered.

"I can let you have the last word."

"I doubt that." Sucking against the skin along my jaw, he chuckled.

"I can. I'm letting you have the last word right now."

"Uh-huh." He nibbled at my ear.

"Technically that isn't a word—"

"Sloane."

"Yes, Abbot?"

"Shut the hell up so I can fuck you again."

"OK."

CHAPTER TWENTY-NINE
SOMETHING WORTH MAKING IT BACK FOR

"WE NEED TO TALK ABOUT THIS," I whispered as we lay in the king-sized bed of my serviced apartment. The sheets, once crisp and white, now twisted between our tangled limbs.

"*Now* you want to talk." Abbot slid a hand along my ribs then down to my arse, pulling me closer against him. "Every time we talk, we fight. I suggest we just keep fucking."

"I'm serious. There are consequences to this, aren't there? Or are you planning on loving me from afar?"

"No, Sloane, I plan on loving you right here. In fact..." He got out of bed, and I made a sound of disappointment the moment we weren't touching anymore.

"Where are you going?" I pushed up on my elbows to watch the muscles in his arse popping with every step he took. *That arse is mine. Finally.* And I knew it wasn't because of our mother's meddling. It was because we were made for each other.

He returned with his wallet in his hand. "I want to show you something."

"If it's condoms, I think it's a bit too late for that."

"Not condoms. But you know I'm clean, right? I've never not used one until today."

We'd come together frantically, so I was relieved to hear those words. Although they didn't surprise me, Abbot wasn't a careless man. And normally—when he hadn't been driven to distraction by a stubborn redhead—he showed a lot of restraint.

"I trust you would never do anything to harm me," I said as he slid back into the bed. "But I think we should use them going forward. At least until we're sure about what this is."

"You're not sure."

"I am. But you've never had a relationship. What if this doesn't work for you?"

"Slater. I'm sure."

"You're sure?"

"Yes." He laughed a little, like he couldn't believe I had any concerns about us. "And I can prove it to you"— he opened the brown leather wallet and rummaged through some cards and old receipts—"with this." A small square of folded paper.

"What is it?" I took it from between his fingers and opened it up, noting the red numbering on the top right that told me it was an invoice, as well as the name of a jeweller. "You bought some jewellery?" The handwriting was a bit scratchy, but I could make out the letters CT and the word 'gold'.

"It's the date I want you to see." He tapped the top of the paper with his finger.

"This is just after Kris and Ronnie's wedding. A few days after I went home."

He slid his finger into the coin section of his wallet and pulled out a ring—a small gold ring with diamonds all the way around it. "I bought this before we knew we were set up. Before you were designated to the hired help, you need to know that I'd chosen you before anything else. I was waiting though. I wanted to have something that was ours alone, no prying eyes, so I bought this in preparation. When I saw it in the window, I knew it was the right ring for you. You wouldn't like anything too flashy that could get in the way."

"I don't understand." I thought I did, but I didn't want to assume.

"I didn't say I would marry you because Jasmine forced my hand. It was what I wanted, but I was pissed at her for fucking up my plans and..." He shook his head and twisted the ring between his fingers.

"You made plans for us?"

He tapped his head with his index finger. "Attempted to."

I'd had so many people making plans and decisions about my life, but something about learning that Abbot had been making his own plans involving me was flattering more than it was frustrating. *It means he cared.*

"Tell me about these plans." I pressed up on my elbow, turned to face him.

"This job we're doing isn't safe, blue. I mean, no job is one hundred per cent safe, but this one...it's fucking insane-level dangerous. I don't like the direction the family business is headed. We used to pull pretty basic break and enter stuff on wealthy people who had big insurance policies. There was good money in that and the risk was low. But over the last eighteen months, the jobs have gotten bigger and increasingly riskier. There's a reason for it, but"—his tongue snuck out to wet his lips—"this isn't what we signed up for." He glanced up from the ring and met my eyes. "I want out. When this job is done. *If* we survive it, you and me, we're done with this life."

If?

"Let me guess, Jasmine won't let you walk so you'll have to run?"

Setting his lips in a solid line, he nodded then looked back at the ring. "I planned to run to you. Win you back, or even sling you over my shoulder caveman style. Then I'd find you that perfect beach shack you want and we'd get married and make some demon spawn of our own, spend our days raising kids and enjoying each other."

"That sounds pretty perfect to me." I kept my voice soft, lying close as I listened to him speak, my heart filling up a little more with each word.

"I need you to know that I was never rejecting you, blue. I was always protecting you, even when it was just a game."

"When did it stop being a game for you?"

"About the time I moved us into the Esplanade apartment. When you were talking about wanting to live by the sea and get married and have kids, I thought about what that would look like, and for the first time in my life the idea didn't freak me out."

"That's actually kinda sweet."

"That I didn't break out in a cold sweat at the thought of commitment?" He chuckled slightly. "I don't know about sweet, but it was definitely momentous. It got me thinking seriously about my life and how a wife and kids would fit in. And I think Trev got it right with you, keeping you away from all this bullshit and letting you live a normal life."

"Normal didn't really get me anywhere."

"But it kept you safe. You didn't grow up having to be careful who you were friends with or who you had a relationship with because you couldn't risk bringing anyone into your world. I don't want that life for my kids, blue. I want them to surf, and I want them to play footy, and date the girl who sits up the front in roll call, bring her to Sunday dinner, family barbecues and walk around in public holding her hand. I want them to have friends and fall in love without it being a life or death situation." He frowned as he let out his breath then met my eyes, his shining, beseeching. "Do you want that kind of life with me, Sloane Slater? One away from here, just the two of us?" He held up the ring, the diamonds catching the light and glittering before me. So tempting.

"It's beautiful, Abbot." Placing my hand over the top of his, I covered the ring with my palm and took a deep breath. "But I want you to ask me when the job is complete and I promise I'll say yes," I whispered, keeping my eyes locked with his and watching for his reaction. It wasn't that I didn't want that life with him. Lord knew it was everything I'd been hoping we could become, and everything I'd ever wanted. Marriage, kids, a home by the sea. It was my dream, and this beautiful big, *sweet* man wanted to give that to me. I just couldn't say yes, not yet, anyway. There'd been too many decisions made about my life that hadn't had my input, and this wouldn't be one of them.

"You want to wait?" he asked, his eyes searching mine.

I nodded. "Not because I don't want to marry you, but because that's when the time will be right." I now understood his reasons for waiting, his frustration when it felt like Jasmine was trying to force him into making a decision when I'd turned up the other day, and why he'd blurted out a crappy proposal in the most unconventional of ways. He was biding his time to protect me, and my temper kept making it hard for him to do that. "If this job is as dangerous as you say, then you'll need something worth making it back for. I expect you to return and run away with me, Abbot Cartwright. Can you do that?"

Leaning in, he pressed his lips to mine, inhaling deeply. "I can do that," he whispered, sliding the ring back into the coin slot of his wallet.

"Good." I rolled almost on top of him, leaning my arms across his chest as he relaxed back into the pillows. "Now, I want to know what we do about your family in the meantime."

He ran his fingers up and down my upper arms sending delicious shivers rippling under my skin. I loved having this man touch me, loved that he was mine. Loved *him*.

"There's a family dinner at the house tonight. Come as my date. They all know what that means."

"What does it mean?"

"That you're my girl and I intend on making you a Cartwright."

"Who says I'll be taking your name?"

He grinned, laughing a little from his nose as he brushed my hair behind my ear. "Always gotta find something to argue about. It doesn't matter what name you take, Slater. We won't be here for it to matter."

"And are you really willing to walk away from all this? Leave your brothers—your twin?"

He took a breath that seemed heavy when he released it. "Yes." One simple word. So much meaning.

"OK. So we go along with everything in the meantime letting everyone believe we're here for good?"

"Right. With you coming to dinner tonight, Jasmine will feel like she's won and won't be watching us as closely. Then we train for this job, and the moment it's done we get on the road and never look back."

My stomach burst to life with hundreds of butterflies, I didn't know if this would work. Toby had made a point of telling me he could find anyone and drag them back. But, maybe Abbot knew his brother's tricks well enough to outsmart him. Either way, it was worth a try.

"I like that plan. I'm nervous, but I'm with you." I'd follow him wherever he wanted me to go. The last month had been absolute shit without him, and I didn't intend to feel like that ever again.

Abbot popped his dimple as he studied my face with nothing but affection in his eyes. "I'm glad you're finally mine, Sloane Slater."

"I'm glad too." It might have taken twenty-one years for the timing to be right, but he was definitely worth the wait for me. I hoped I was worth this risk he was taking too. I understood his desire to get out, but I also understood the other side of that coin, the reason I was so easily pulled back. This life was in our blood. Could we ever really escape it?

CHAPTER THIRTY
FUCKED-UP SHIT

I ARRIVED at Jasmine's by seven, a cheesecake in hand and butterflies in my gut. There had been so many times that I'd walked through this door with no nerves at all, but I'd never been someone's girlfriend—*Is that what I should call myself?* Either way, it was different this time. Abbot and I were announcing our relationship as well as manipulating the situation to our own desires. Freedom.

Abbot had gone ahead of me to speak to Jasmine before I got there. Something told me he wanted to read her the riot act so she didn't give me a hard time. The woman was incredibly mercurial, so I appreciated that he'd do that for me.

"Sloane," Jasmine opened the front door with her breezy demeanour in place, her smile said welcome and her apron said relax. I didn't believe either though. Experience had taught me to always be on my guard around her.

"Am I late?" I asked as I handed over the dessert. Her house was filled with hustle and bustle, all hands on deck, preparing a feast that looked big enough for a kingdom.

Welcoming me like a lost daughter, she ushered me inside. "Not at all." She placed her free arm around my waist as she guided me to the kitchen where I waved hi to Alesha, Holland and Ronnie, all busy preparing food. "You're right on time. We're making spaghetti from scratch. You still like spaghetti?"

"I love spaghetti."

She grinned. "When you were little you used to say that my spaghetti was your favourite food in the whole world."

I sniffed the air and my stomach growled. Abbot and I had been too busy doing other things to worry about food all afternoon. "I've never been able to recreate it."

"She puts Vegemite in the mince," Alesha said from in front of a giant pot. "That's the secret."

"Good one. Now she won't need to come back for it." Jasmine stood with her hands on her hips. Alesha stuck her tongue out and chuckled. *Playful Jasmine? Interesting.*

I scrunched up my nose. "Vegemite?"

Jasmine nodded. "Strange but true. The boys are outside getting the patio heaters started if you want to say hi. I'm sure Abbot is eager to see you." She couldn't even hide her grin as she pushed me towards the sliding door as if refusing wasn't an option.

"Oh hey, Sloane," Kristian said from where he leaned over the side of the heater.

Abbot was crouched down beside him with the door where the gas cylinders lived open. "Hey, blue. We're trying to discover fire but we're struggling."

"Want me to take a look?" I asked with a smile, noticing that he seemed to be settling on calling me by my childhood nickname, an Aussie slang term for redheads—

blue. It was a silly ironic name that was only used by those closest to me. He'd called me a lot of different names since I'd come back here, I wondered if this one would stick or if he was trying it on for size like all the others.

"It's cool," Abbot said. "The igniter isn't clicking. I'm just checking the gas line to be safe."

Kristian lifted his chin. "I hear you're in on the insanity of the job my wife cooked up." He stood up straight and laughed with his hands on his hips. "My wife. It's been a month, and it's still fun saying that."

"I'll bet." I grinned, his smile infectious, although it didn't escape me that Ronnie seemed to be the mastermind behind whatever craziness we were gearing up for. "Married life seems to agree with you."

He nodded. "It really does. Looks like we get to send this guy to the altar next," he said, clapping Abbot on the shoulder.

Abbot kept his head down. "I have to get her to say yes first, mate," he said, causing me to smile as I thought about the ring tucked safely in his wallet.

"You'll say yes, won't you, Sloane?"

I smiled. "The wrong twin's asking me, right now."

"No time like the present, brother." Kris tapped Abbot on the butt with his shoe.

"Fuck off." Abbot slapped his twin's foot away, both of them laughing.

I cleared my throat. "So, what makes the job so insane?"

"Haven't you heard?" Sam came up behind me, handing Abbot a stick lighter for the heater.

"All I know is it's a transport of drugs."

"Yeah," Sam said. "A *government* transport. Top security. It's gonna be a magical shitstorm that we'll need unicorns to get us out of."

"Unicorns?" I laughed, uneasy. *A government transport? Holy fucking hell. No wonder Abbot is worried about this one.*

Kristian took over in plain English. "We need you to teach us how to pick those BiLocks. Abs said you've done it before."

"A few times. It's not the easiest thing in the world though." I tried not to react too harshly to the origin of the transport, partly so I didn't seem like a liability and mostly because I didn't want to put any more stress on Abbot. He needed me to be confident in the job.

"That's what we heard," Sam said. "Seems there's two armoured vans full of drugs locked in security cases. Those cases use the BiLocks, but we don't know how many we need to pick yet."

"How fast do you need them opened?" I asked with a frown.

"As fast as humanly possible," Abbot responded.

"That'll take practice. Do I have to get you into the armoured van too?" That would be dangerous.

"No," Abbot said, standing up now that the heater was working. As he hit his full height, my eyes went up and my heart fluttered. It was interesting that a man identical to him in looks was standing right beside him and had given me no reaction at all, but with Abbot, it was…at my centre. "The actual robbery has to be a smash and grab. Fast as possible. Lots of noise." He mimed explosives. *Crap.*

"You don't like noise," I said. He'd said they always

opted to do a job quietly so they didn't make a scene and raise the awareness of would-be witnesses.

He held his hands out to his sides. "Necessity outweighs preference."

Necessity.

"OK. So, you hit the armoured trucks, unload the cases, then you take them somewhere and we unlock them?" I asked, trying to piece together the extent of my involvement.

"You won't be unlocking them," Toby said, stepping through the sliding door with beers in hand. He passed them around as he continued. "You're the coach who'll teach all of us. We'll have maybe fifteen minutes to get the cases open and empty before the handover. Anywhere between twenty and forty locks, each case has anti theft tech, so we can't force entry without ruining the drugs."

"I see. How long do we have to train?"

"The court case associated with the product goes to trial in three months. After that, the drugs are being transported to a special facility for destruction, which is when we hit. That gives *minimum* of three months to learn how to pick those locks at world-record speed."

"And a maximum of?" I asked as I took my beer from his grip.

"Three months and one week," he said. "And since we're bringing you in, confidentiality is obviously a non-negotiable clause here."

"I swear by the scar on my leg," I told him.

He nodded with a secret smile.

"You'll be expert lock pickers when I'm done with you."

"That's what we expect," Toby said.

"Enough business talk," Jasmine said from the door. "Dinner is ready."

Moving to stand beside me, Abbot held out his hand and I clapped mine into his grip, our fingers entwining. "So far, so good," he said, kissing my knuckles. "Just remember that no matter what they say in there, we chose this."

"What the hell are they going to say?"

"A whole bunch of fucked up shit, blue. And I need you to ignore it."

"Do I nod and smile?"

He grinned, looking relieved. "It'd help."

"OK. Then that's what I'll do."

Guiding me by the hand, he took me head first down the rabbit hole. Fucked-up shit didn't even begin to explain it.

CHAPTER THIRTY-ONE
DROWNED IN SECRETS

"WHAT DID YOU THINK?" Abbot asked as he walked me to my van after dinner and more drugs heist discussion, among other things.

"Of the spaghetti? I don't know, it's kind of weird now that I know there's Vegemite in it."

He laughed. "You know I'm not talking about the food."

"Well…" Stopping when I reached Lizzie, I turned to face him, double-checking we were alone as I leaned against her. "I think you're right to be concerned, and I also think your entire family, wives and all, are insane." I kept my voice low so only he could hear me. Over dinner, I'd learned how deep Jasmine's matchmaking efforts had really run. Holland and Alesha had literally been kidnapped and threatened with their lives to marry Nate and Sam. And Ronnie had damaged Kris's car and been taken prisoner, but they'd fallen in love instead. They all swore it was the best thing that ever happened to them, but

I didn't know if it was the truth or the Stockholm syndrome talking.

"It's a lot to take in, I know. And I was against all if it from the start. But they really are happy together. Crazy but true." He leaned in and pressed his lips to my shoulder. "I'm glad this thing between us happened without any of the same bullshit."

I closed my eyes and revelled in the sensation. "They just played chess with us, didn't they?"

"You know, I don't even care how it seems. I know what I feel is real, that my choices were my own. No one made me fall in love with you."

"That was actually my master plan, and I'm kinda shocked it worked," I teased.

He grinned. "Wanna get out of here?"

"Come back to the resort with me?"

"Why don't you grab your stuff and come back to our place?"

"Our place?" I lifted my brow.

"Yeah. It didn't feel the same once you left."

"I will. Soon. But I've kind of paid for a whole month at the resort. And they have room service." Placing my hand against his chest, I toyed with the buttons on his shirt.

"I like your way of thinking."

"So how about you go and get your stuff and meet me there? Don't forget the condoms." I whispered the last part close to his ear.

"It's a date." He kissed me briefly then stepped away.

"And don't think I don't have at least a thousand questions for you over all that." I flicked my gaze toward the house.

"I'll be an open book."

"Really?" I expected some 'need to know' crap.

"Absolutely. You're in the circle of trust now. That's kind of why they unloaded on you in there."

"Like an initiation—drowned in secrets?"

"Something like that. I'll see you in about thirty minutes?"

"I'll be waiting."

He smiled then pulled me against him, kissing me goodbye.

"Give her the ring," one of the brothers yelled from inside the house. We broke our kiss just in time to see a scuffle at the window before the curtains dropped back in place.

"Looks like we're being watched," he whispered.

"And that they know about the ring."

"Kris does. He knows where I'm at. He won't say anything."

"He must be a really good brother."

Abbot turned his body towards the windows and held up a middle finger. "The best." Laughter erupted from inside the house. "We should go before they get Kris to impersonate me and propose to you himself."

"I'd never fall for that," I said. "I've always been able to tell you apart."

"Just another reason why I love you."

CHAPTER THIRTY-TWO
PERFECTION

I DID a running leap at Abbot as soon as he walked in the door. Thirty minutes felt too long at this early stage. He caught me with ease, a grin on his face as I wrapped myself around his torso like a koala on a tree. I had no intention of letting go.

"This is a better welcome than I was expecting. I thought you'd bombard me with questions first."

Sucking on his bottom lip, I pulled back and shook my head. "No family shit. Sex first."

He chuckled. "You're wearing too many clothes, blue."

"I could say the same about you, Cartwright. But, if you take me to the bedroom, I think we can fix that problem for both of us."

"I'm learning not to argue with the redhead," he said, heading for the bedroom still carrying me. "Boy, this place is big." He let out a grunt, making a dramatic show of stumbling and wheezing as he made it to the end of the bed.

I slapped him on the chest when he collapsed us both

onto the mattress and pretended to pass out with his face buried in my neck. "I am *not* that heavy." I laughed, rocking my body beneath him to get him to move. "Get up. I want. Ohhh, you *are* up." He groaned as I lifted my thigh, pressing into his hard length.

"Mmm." His lips brushed against my pulse, making their way along my jaw. Suddenly we weren't joking around anymore.

"Abbot," I whispered, loving his name on my lips as his fingers lifted my shirt and found my ribs, taking hold.

"Sloane." The soft rumble of his voice leaving his mouth just as his lips pressed to mine. *So good.*

I whimpered, my whole body coming alive as we moved together, the same way we had earlier but with less desperation. We had all night this time.

"Can I tell you something?" His fingers toyed with my nipples through my bra.

"Anything."

"I missed these tight buds so much. I jacked off daily thinking about them in my mouth." He tugged my shirt over my head, roughly pushing away the cups of my bra and ridding me of the thing. Then his mouth found my breast, showing me exactly what he'd missed.

"My God, I missed this too," I gasped, arching into him as his tongue flicked at my nipple before he shifted to my other breast. "And since we're being honest, I used that picture you sent me—"

"To ring your own doorbell?"

With a laugh, I nodded. "Yes."

"That's hot."

I ran my hands over his shoulders, his chest, needing to touch him, needing more of him. When my fingers found the hem of his shirt, he sat up and tugged it over his head in one fluid motion.

"You're hot," I murmured, running my hands over his golden muscles, so defined and glorious that my insides stuttered at the sight. This beautiful, stunning, model-like man was mine. *Mine.*

"And you are absolutely perfect," he said, his voice husky before he leaned in and nipped my lips.

"No, you are," I teased in a whisper.

His hands slid down, thumbs on my nipples, sending delicious ripples down to my core. "You are," he returned, grinning wickedly before he kissed me again then travelled down, his tongue running lazy circles along my throat until he was back to sucking my nipple into his hot mouth, teeth grazing, tongue teasing.

I hummed with pleasure as his fingers moved along my belly then he pushed my pants to the ground, his mouth now where his fingers had been.

"I love the way you taste right here," he said, running his tongue just below my navel. "It's sweet."

I propped myself on elbows as I released a chuckle. "That's because I keep Skittles in my belly button," I joked.

His shoulders bounced with laughter, as his mouth skimmed over my skin. "Skittles, huh?"

"What else is a belly button for?" I grinned, breathless as his mouth left a trail of fire everywhere he touched.

"Well, you can do this with it," he said, running the tip off his tongue around the edge of the tiny opening. "And this." He slipped the very tip of his tongue into the crevice and pressed down. A jolting tingle made its way between my legs.

"That's definitely more fun than using it for Skittles," I gasped, sliding my fingers into his hair.

He lifted his head and smiled up at me. "Nothing is better than Skittles, blue."

I laughed, then I made an *Ohh* sound as his mouth returned to my skin and one of his hands drifted lower, over my thighs, then back up again gently raking over the fabric of my underwear.

He inhaled, his fingers so light in their teasing. "I fucking love the smell of you."

I arched towards his touch, wanting more. "Abbot."

"You know," he said, resting on his elbow as he drew lazy circles over the cotton triangle, making me insane with want. "I still have a pair of these."

The corner of my mouth twitched. "They must be uncomfortable when you wear them."

He chuckled, his fingers sliding lower to where I was wet, dampness soaking through. "I didn't wear them, Sloane. I sniffed them like a fucking creep and pulled on my dick, imagining I was with you."

His admission made my breathing shallow as the memory of his strong hand curling around his massive cock took hold in my mind. It was an incredible turn-on to be that desired, even more so that he would admit it to me. I loved how open he was.

"You don't have to imagine anymore," I said. "You're with the real thing."

In response, he growled then tugged my underwear down my legs, and suddenly I was naked. He knelt on the bed and parted my thighs, taking a moment to let his eyes roam all over my body.

"Is being with me what you imagined?" I asked, feeling a little exposed as he continued his perusal.

"It's better than that," he said, sliding his fingertips between my folds before pushing inside. "Mmm. So much better."

I cried out, rocking my hips and meeting his strokes.

"Feel good?" he asked in a sexy, wicked voice that knew very well it felt good. His firm fingertips and the perfect speed of his movements a sweet, torturous heaven. "I could torture you like this forever."

"I thought you could suck on my nipples forever?" Each word came out as a gasp, which by the quirk of his lips gave him great delight.

He shifted over me, nipping at my bottom lip. "That was all night. This"—he pushed his fingers in deeper, curling them into my G-spot—"I could do this forever. I love watching you squirm."

"So cruel." I kissed his chin and raked my fingernails over his shoulders.

"So sexy."

I'd never felt sexy the way I did with him. He brought it out in me.

"So responsive." His lips returned to my mouth, tongue moving while his fingers moved in and out of my body, drawing circles around my clit before diving right back in.

"Please, Abbot."

"She's finally begging," he murmured right next to my ear before he ran his tongue along my lobe. "I like it." I shivered, my nipples aching as my insides screamed for release.

"*Please.*"

"Not yet, beautiful blue. I haven't finished playing with you."

Beautiful blue. It sounded like a rhyme and warmed my heart. I truly believed I was beautiful to him. He'd made me feel nothing but beautiful from the moment his interest became known to me.

Beautiful.

I'd never believed it before, but with his eyes on me, I could see that even tomboys were beautiful, and they didn't need a makeover to prove it. Just a man willing to see them for who they were.

Abbot slid down my body, hands pushing at my knees and spreading me open. Then he glanced up, meeting my eyes briefly before his face dropped and his tongue joined his fingers.

"Oh God," I cried out as he hummed while sucking my clit.

"You taste even better than you smell."

"No more talking," I forced out, placing my hand on the top of his head. "Only sucking."

He chuckled then dove back in, his mouth sucked while his tongue swirled and fingers curled. It was too much, and I clenched my fists, one in his hair, the other on the sheets. Then all at once I came apart, making a sound that could possibly be described as the mating call of a howler monkey.

"Holy fuck," I said as my internal spasms calmed and he kissed his way back up my body. At some point he must have shucked those unnecessary pants of his off because I could feel the damp, smooth tip of his cock, tapping along my leg.

"I need to be inside you so bad right now," he said,

sucking gently on my lips. Pulling on a condom, he positioned himself at my entrance and I lifted my head to take in the sight of his impressive man stick—or branch in Abbot's case.

I rocked my hips to take him in. "Please," I begged. "I want you inside me."

"Slowly." He pushed at my entrance and I felt myself stretching around him. "I want to make it last this time."

"Oh wow." He was so big. Some might say too big. To me, he was exactly the right size.

"You OK?" he asked once he was fully seated, and I nodded, mouth open, barely able to speak because I was so fucking full.

"You feel so good, Sloane." He moved in full strokes, massaging my insides with his thick length. "So good."

I gripped his forearms. His biceps. His shoulders.

Then I wrapped my legs right around him and urged him deeper.

He leaned forward, mouths together, noses side by side, my arms winding around his neck as he thrust and kissed and thrust and murmured.

Sex with Abbot was an experience like no other, and I felt like I was discovering what making love was *supposed* to be like. With Abbot inside me, I felt like everyone else had been doing it wrong.

So wrong.

Losing my mind to sensation, I existed on some other plane where all that mattered was desire and chasing orgasms. I was caught between wanting to stay connected like this forever and wanting that orgasm caught.

The orgasm won.

"Abbot," I howled as my body tightened then released, exploding around his length, coming undone.

"Fuck." He pushed deep and ground his hips against mine, giving my orgasm a little more life as he found his own release in gentle pulses. He dropped his weight, hot breath on my neck.

"Hey Sloane." He lifted his head then brought his mouth close to mine. "I love you," he said on his breath.

"Say it again," I whispered back, my arms wrapping around him.

He smiled. "I love you." He kissed me as I grinned like the goofball I was, this moment becoming my favourite moment of all. If everything turned to shit after this, it'd be the moment I held in my heart and called happiness…perfection.

"I love you," I said again. Perfection.

CHAPTER THIRTY-THREE
FOOL ME TWICE

"I REALLY SHOULD HAVE SPENT last night working on my picking skills," I said to Abbot as I dropped several padlocks into the shopping basket he was holding. They would be the practise locks we trained on.

"That hurts my heart, blue."

Beautiful blue.

I smiled at the memory and leaned into him, kissing his lips. "I said should, not that I wanted to. Last night was magical, much better than doing work, *or* dissecting the insanity of my life right now."

"Three months then we're free."

I liked that he was being positive about this. I, unfortunately, was imagining a future of conversations through Perspex barriers and conjugal visits. This three months might be the only months we had, and I wanted to make the most of them.

"I think we should make this three months as fun as possible," I said, running my hand over his chest. "Stay at the resort, spoil ourselves."

"Kind of like a reverse honeymoon?" His eyes lit up with interest.

"The rest of our lives will be the honeymoon, Cartwright, but yeah. We take time, relax and enjoy each other so you go into this job at the top of your game."

"Tell you what," he said, dropping a few random things into our basket so it wasn't just about the BiLock padlocks. "Let's *play* a game."

"We're back to the games now?"

"This one is a sex game."

I grinned. "Weren't they all sex games?"

"OK." He chuckled. "You got me there, but hear me out. We're gonna mix work and fun."

"Shoot."

"For every ten seconds we knock off the time it takes to pick these locks, I'll make you come."

"So, if I knock off a full minute that's six orgasms? You're on."

"Hmm, I'm gonna get a sore tongue." He kissed my nose then pulled back when his phone went off in his jeans pocket. "Bro?" He pressed the phone to his ear.

I turned to walk away and give him privacy, but he caught me by the back of my jeans and pulled me to him, our basket now on the floor.

"How long?" He listened then said. "Cool. See you soon."

"Soon?" I asked as he slipped the phone back into his pocket and retrieved the basket.

"That was Nate. There's a meeting."

"I thought we were starting lessons at nine?"

"We have new intel to go over."

"Oh, well just drop me back at the resort and I'll work on my speed." I pointed to the locks.

"You're coming too."

"I'm coming to a meeting? Again? Do they need my field of expertise or something?"

He grinned then gave me a peck on the lips. "Nah. You get to hang with the wives and play nice."

"But I don't play well with other women. I especially don't do well with crazy kidnapped women."

He laughed like I was the most adorable thing in the world. "They're not crazy. Just had crazy beginnings. Ask them about it, they'll tell you whatever you wanna know."

"You know I'll be doing exactly that, right?"

"I expect nothing less. Now, let's go. They're waiting."

The wives. Yikes. How would *that* go?

"WE NORMALLY DRINK through these things, but we're all pregnant or trying to get pregnant," Holland said, thumbing towards Alesha on the last part.

"I'm highly emotional and on hormone injections," Alesha said with a half-smile. Despite the make-up, she looked quite tired. "IVF."

"We can get you something though," Ronnie added.

My eyes were a little too wide, feeling strange that they all just basically spoke for each other. *It's like a cult.* A cult of kidnapped baby makers. *So fucking weird.*

"I can live without alcohol," I said, generally preferring a Bundaberg ginger beer to the alcoholic kind anyway. And besides, there was a tiny sliver of wonder if Abbot's and my unprotected moment had sparked a life of our own.

Would that indoctrinate me into this? Yikes. But it was something I'd have to talk to him about. I knew he was receptive because he'd already mentioned kids. But I needed to know how he'd feel if it happened right away.

"There's plenty of junk food though," Holland assured me. "Even though chocolate gives me killer heartburn."

"OK." I sat on the couch opposite Holland, glancing at her belly, then glancing at Ronnie who wasn't showing yet then to Alesha who seemed to have a lot on her mind. "Is there some baby-making clause in the Cartwright marriage contract or something?"

Ronnie laughed.

Alesha shrugged.

Holland muttered, "Jasmine would put it there if she could."

"I've heard," I said.

"Right?" Holland said, her eyes lighting as if she'd just found an ally. "She thinks these kids will continue running her empire, but my child will have *nothing* to do with it." She kept her voice low but dropped it even lower when she added, "Especially now the Grim Order is involved."

"They offer us protection," Ronnie pointed out, lifting her brow as she looked at Holland.

"As long as *our* men do the heavy lifting on this drug heist. But, who takes the fall if this goes south, Ronnie?"

"It won't go south," Alesha insisted. "They'll plan out every move, run every scenario. They're going to be fine."

"And then what?" Holland's eyes moved between Alesha and Ronnie, wanting answers I wasn't sure they had. "I have never been more frightened of a job than I am of this. We came back here to fix things and all we seem to do is get deeper and deeper."

"Well, we wouldn't be this deep if you and Nate hadn't run off in the first place," Alesha snapped. *They ran?* Seemed Abbot wasn't the only brother looking for an out.

"I know, OK? I know this is our fault. But surely there was some other way to end this. I mean, I watched Sons of Anarchy and you can't just do one job and walk away. Those MCs always drag you back."

Ronnie picked up a box of Favourites and offered it to Holland. "You watch too much Netflix, Holl."

Taking a Cherry Ripe, Holland pouted as she unwrapped the chocolate. "There's no such thing."

"Breaker promised it's just this one job. The Grim Order want to dominate distribution on the east coast, and this will help them do it," Ronnie explained, filling some gaps in for me too. "The boys will get in and get out. When they hand over the drugs that's the end of it."

"Freedom, hey?" Holland said. "I'll believe that when Nate and I go back to Portland and actually get to open our bookstore without another job popping up."

"You want to open a bookstore?" I asked, growing more intrigued by the second. "As a front?"

"No. A legitimate business," she explained with a sigh. "Australian author focused. A café. Moving ladder on the book wall."

"And Jasmine knows this? She's letting you out?"

Alesha started laughing, quickly followed by both Ronnie and Holland.

"I'm taking that as a no," I said.

"It's a nice dream to have," Holland sighed, taking another chocolate. "But Jasmine will never let any of us out. Not willingly, anyway."

"And you know Toby would just hunt you down,"

Ronnie put in. "That man has a sixth sense." *I'd force you back.* Toby might be a problem.

"I don't know," Holland said. "He helped us before."

"Before when?" I asked.

"When we left the first time," Holland explained. "He helped Nate fake his own death and we took on new identities. We overlooked a few things, which is why we're back here. But, he helped…" *Perhaps all was not lost.*

"You know," I said, my brow furrowed in confusion. "I'm getting a little lost here. Why don't you start at the beginning?"

Holland smiled and looked at Alesha. "Well, you know that saying, 'fool me twice'?"

"Of course."

"That's how it began with Nate and me. He tricked me, and he robbed me. Twice. And somehow, I fell in love with him."

CHAPTER THIRTY-FOUR
WHAT IF

"YOU'RE QUIET," Abbot pointed out on the way back to the resort. "Did something happen?"

I shook my head, frowning a little as I focused on nothing in particular and tried to let the gentle strains of Ben Howard's *Every Kingdom* calm me down. "I'm decompressing."

Holland told me how she and Alesha had tracked down the thieves that had robbed her. Instead of calling the cops, they'd snooped and gotten caught, which was when the whole kidnapping and forced marriage happened. Although, for Holland, there had already been a strong attraction between her and Nate. They'd fallen hard for each other and Holland had even learned to accept that her husband was a thief. What she couldn't accept, however, was any involvement in the drug trade. It had been her deal-breaker. When she found out Nate had been growing poppies to supply a local drug cartel, she'd booked it. Unable to live without her, Nate burned down the poppy field and faked his own death, thinking that would dissolve his Cartel connections, and then they ran away together. New names and everything.

"How much did they tell you?"

"Everything important, I think."

The Cartel, however, wasn't so forgiving and came after the family on the day of Nate's funeral. At that point, the only person who knew Nate was still alive was Toby since he'd helped him disappear. But he'd given up their location when he realised they needed Nate back to clean up the mess he'd made.

"So you know why we're in this mess with the Grim Order?"

"I think so. Nate pissed off the Cartel and you had to pull bigger jobs to pay them off."

Abbot tightened his grip on the steering wheel. "He got greedy, got in over his head."

"And now you're all paying for it?"

He lifted a shoulder, his expression weary. "We're family."

By the time Ronnie entered the picture, they were bleeding money. It was her connection with Breaker that brought the Grim Order onto the scene. He saw an opportunity to help out the women he cared about and his club at the same time. The Grim Order got the Cartel out of the picture, but now the Cartwrights were indebted to them. It was a fucking mess.

"Do you really think the Grim Order will honour the deal?" I asked, my confidence in escaping this world becoming shakier by the second.

"He gave his word that it was a favour for a favour. We have to believe that."

"Because there really is honour among thieves?"

"Something like that." He glanced at me then took my hand in his, lacing our fingers together. "Hey, not getting cold feet are you?"

I shook my head. "Ronnie says that Toby always drags everyone back, which he's threatened me with before, so I believe it. And if we've got the Grim Order looking for us too, where the hell are we gonna hide, Abbot? How are we gonna run, and live, and have a family? How are we gonna be free? What are we gonna do?" My breath came in short bursts as my chest tightened and my mind flashed danger signs.

Flicking on his indicator, Abbot pulled over to the side of the road and got out, rushing to my side of the car and opening the door. "Come on, blue," he soothed, unclipping my seatbelt and pulling me out with him, gathering me in his arms. "Just breathe. It's gonna be OK. I'll make it OK. I promise."

I fisted at his shirt with my hands, curling my body against him. "Nate and Holland tried—"

"And they failed because they asked goodie-two-shoes Toby for help. I'm not making that mistake."

"But Kristian knows."

"And he would *never* give us up."

I lifted my head and met his eyes. "Even to Ronnie?" In my experience, every person had one person they trusted. So you had to expect that every secret was told to at least two people.

"He won't tell a soul." He hooked a finger under my chin. "Besides, I won't be telling him where we're going. Only that we're leaving."

I closed my eyes and rested my head back against his chest, listening to his heart and his breathing the way I had when we'd danced at the wedding. Slowly, the panic I'd allowed to take hold eased from my body, finding strength in his arms.

"We're gonna be OK, blue" he said, swaying me gently in time to the music that played in the car, a song called *Bones* that seemed movie soundtrack-fitting to the moment.

As the crescendo wound down, I took a breath and looked up. "What if I'm already pregnant?"

"Then I have even more incentive to get this right."

"You can't get caught."

Taking hold of my face in his hands, he pressed his lips to my forehead. "I promise you, beautiful blue, I will do everything in my power to come back from this job and run so far away with you that no one ever tracks us down."

I nodded, taking a deep breath. That was all I could ask of him, really—a promise that we were going to be OK. There were so many variables and pieces at play that the odds felt insurmountable. I'd been overwhelmed with information and felt awful that I'd let my fear get the better of me. I wanted to be strong for him and show him that I was confident he'd return to me safe and sound. Two days in and I'd already doubted. I hoped that the coming weeks of training and preparations would put my worry to rest. But, how could it? They were robbing a government drug transport. The reality was that the three months together might be the only time Abbot and I had. I hated that possibility.

"YES!" I held up the open BiLock in triumph. I'd done it. After hours and hours of working on the fucking things I'd finally opened one in under thirty seconds. *Finally*.

I leaned back in my chair with a happy sigh and stretched my arms above my head to relive the kinks in my neck, the soft rhythm of Abbot's gentle snoring the only congratulatory cheer in response to my success. He'd fallen asleep on the couch hours before. He'd insisted on waiting up until I was ready to go to bed with him, but he didn't make it. *Poor baby.* But he needed his rest; he owed me a fuckload of orgasms since I'd dropped my picking speed from over ten minutes in just a few days.

Standing before twisting at the waist a few times, I smiled at his sleeping form, my chest swelling with the love I felt for this gentle giant.

There was no doubt in my mind that to the outside world this man was a formidable force to be reckoned with, highly intimidating to anyone who crossed him, but to me, he was just a big softy, a teddy bear, a lost boy…

While he belonged to a tight-knit family, I still saw him as a lost soul, happy only now because he'd found his mate.

I knew that, because that's how I felt too. Despite making my own life over the years, I'd never felt that I belonged as much as I did when around Abbot. He was my other half.

Grabbing a blanket from the laundry cupboard, I pulled it up his body then gently brushed my fingers through his messy hair. I'd seen photos of him with hair down to his shoulders on the wall at Jasmine's and wondered if he was growing it out again. The long hair suited him, added to his boyishness. But I loved his hair either way. I loved him. It was so surreal to have this man—the boy from my past—as the love in my life. It had happened so suddenly, yet so slowly. A clashing of hearts helped by the passing of time.

Kissing his forehead, I left the open padlock and the stopwatch on the table next to him then went into the bedroom to change. I was tired, but restless. And since the resort had a beautiful heated lagoon pool right outside the apartment, I thought a late-night swim might be exactly what I needed.

Putting on my black string bikini—purchased solely because I'd dreamed of coming back to taunt Abbot with a show of excess skin—I covered up with a robe then exited the apartment via the sliding door closest to Abbot, leaving the curtain open a touch so he'd know where I went if he woke before I returned.

I smiled to myself as I dipped my toe in the water, swirling it through the warmth and watching the steam rising into the warm air. At nearly three in the morning, I had the whole place to myself.

Dropping my robe on the nearest chair, I hunched against the cold and rushed for the warm water, feeling like I was walking into a giant glowing bath the deeper I got.

Diving beneath the surface, I frog swam until I was forced to surface for breath, releasing a tiny giggle as I pushed my wet hair out of my face and rolled onto my back, floating and looking up at the night sky.

This is happiness.

Stars scattered like a mess of breadcrumbs in the sky, reminding me of the vastness of creation and how small a single person really was. It was easy to feel as though I was at the centre of it all, but in truth, a single person was just a speck for a moment in time. For a person to mean something to this great big universe, they'd have to move mountains, travel through the stars, change things. But to each other, we were everything. And to one very special person, *we* were their universe.

I took in a clearing breath, laughing a little at how deep and wishy-washy my thoughts were going. I sounded like all those girls in high school I'd listened to and rolled my eyes at. *My, how things change.*

Rolling back over, I dove beneath the water and swam to the widest part of the lagoon, deciding a few laps back and forth were in order. The exercise helped to ease the stiffness in my shoulders and work off that extra energy I had buzzing below the surface of my skin. Well, I'd hoped that's what it would do. After several laps, my muscles were weary but my mind was wide awake. I felt as though I would never to sleep again, fuelled by the energy of life's new direction.

Stopping when I hit the far side of the lagoon, I rested

my elbows on the ledge and let my gaze land on the sliding door behind which Abbot was sleeping. Life was so crazy. Back when we were kids, I remembered thinking that Kris and Abbot were the most annoying little boys. They were always getting into trouble and making a mess of the games the rest of us came up with. Sometimes, we'd agree to play hide and seek with them and not bother to find them just to get them to leave us alone for ten minutes. It felt mean now, but at the time, we were just doing what kids did. And Abbot and Kris never seemed fazed by anything we did to deter them. Instead, they retaliated by playing pranks whenever they got a chance, their identical little heads thrown back in laughter with every success. Now, Abbot was a man. He was still annoying, but in the best possible way. I hadn't smiled so much in years…I also hadn't cried as much either. But that was love, I supposed, elation and fear, desire and worry. I had never *ever* felt this way about another person, never experienced so much angst in the times I was alone to the time he returned. It wasn't that I didn't think he'd come back from whatever drill they were running, it was that I didn't feel complete any more without him. It was strange for me to experience. Even in the years I was with Mark I valued my alone time. Now, I didn't want a second to pass where I couldn't shift my gaze and find him near. I needed him.

A smile crept across my features as the sliding door to our apartment opened fully and the man of my heart stepped out. I saw the moment he spotted me, the white of his teeth blinking in the night like a happy star. He made his way down the steps towards the water's edge while I dipped under the water and swam to him.

I saw him before I emerged, lying on the side of the

pool with his arms folded under his chin. He was smiling, happy to see me. *Happy, happy, happy.* I sounded like a broken record, but what else could I call it when that was what it was? Abbot and me together was happiness personified. I wasn't going to pretend otherwise.

Breaking the surface, I gasped for air and grinned right back, placing my hands on the edge just near his arms.

"Hey," he said, that gorgeous dimple of his making my stomach flip.

"Hey," I replied, water dripping down my face. I reached a hand up and slid the tip of my finger right into the curve of that dimple as I pulled myself up enough so our faces were level. "I fucking love this divot in your cheek."

He chuckled then wrapped his hand around the back of my neck and kissed me, soft at first, then long and hard. I loved kissing him, loved the way he dominated my mouth and took what he wanted. My soul—a little piece at a time. I was more than willing to feed it to him as I took his in return.

When he released me, I dropped below the surface of the water, blowing bubbles before coming back out to meet his mouth again.

He laughed against my lips, kissing me as I clung to him like a mermaid kissing a sailor and pulling him into the deep. Slowly, he slid forward until he dropped into the pool with me, both of us going under, wrapping ourselves together as we kissed and pretended that we didn't need air.

"You still have your clothes on," I said when we finally broke apart, my hand against the wet fabric of his T-shirt.

"I couldn't resist," he returned, between kissing me

and pulling that shirt off his head. "I had to be in here with you." He threw the shirt so it landed in a wet heap on the side of the pool.

I reached for the waist of his jeans. "I think you should take these off too," I whispered, nipping at the corner of his lips.

"Blue, we're in *public,*" he teased.

"Public?" I looked from left to right. "I don't see anyone around, do you?"

He grinned and wriggled out of his jeans, letting them drop to the bottom of the pool as he caught me around the waist and brought me close, our legs swirling beneath us to keep us afloat.

"You got the lock open," he whispered, teasing my lips with his. "Twenty-nine point five five seconds."

"Precisely." I slid my hands over his muscular back, loving every inch of his skin.

"Know what that means, right?"

I pulled at his bottom lip with my teeth. "Pool sex."

He grinned then sealed his mouth over mine as we dropped below the surface, kissing and touching, the strings of my bikini top floating loose as his hands roamed my skin. When we came up, he pressed me up against the side of the pool, my back to the wall.

"Hold on," he ordered, a glint in his eye as he positioned my hands either side of my head.

"Oh really?" Anytime you were told to hold on during sex was always a good omen.

"Really." He quirked an eyebrow then tugged at the strings either side of my bikini bottoms, whipping the fabric from between my legs, letting the water touch my bare skin.

"Now what?"

He placed both sections of my bikini on the side of the pool and ran his tongue up the side of my neck. "Now we see how long I can hold my breath for."

I giggled as he took a dramatic lungful of air and dropped below the surface, grabbing my thighs and planting his face right in the centre of them. Logistically, it was a difficult move to pull off, but my God, I wasn't giggling anymore. He covered my clit with his mouth and flicked it with his tongue, making me drop my head back so I could literally see stars.

"Oh," I gasped into the night, struggling to hold on to the edge of the pool when all I really wanted to do was grab him by the hair and fuck his face.

As my orgasm built, I closed my eyes, my mouth open, my body set to explode. A blinding light hit my eyes, and I scrunched them tighter, readying my body to let go.

"Ma'am."

"*Oh.*"

A throat cleared. "Ma'am."

I tipped over the edge, my hips convulsing, my mouth open and gasping, all at the same time as I opened my eyes and found a security guard with a torch shining on our escapades.

"Holy shit!" I let go and grabbed for my bikini, immediately dropping beneath the water and pushing Abbot from between my legs. We had a momentary exchange—the man had serious lung capacity—where we came face to face and he frowned and I pointed upwards while trying to get my bikini back around my body. A beam of light shone through the water between us and he looked up, wide eyes. I nearly died.

Abbot shot up to the surface, his body moving around me so he blocked me from the security guard's view. Not that it mattered, I was pretty sure the guy copped a good eyeful while I came right in front of him.

When I surfaced, my bikini somewhat covering my important bits, Abbot was thanking the guard for being understanding and assuring him it wouldn't happen again. I couldn't even look at the man.

"The rules are for everybody's safety, sir."

"Understood. We're getting out now."

The guard nodded and just stood there.

Abbot laughed. "You're going to watch us get out?"

"I'm just doing my job, sir."

"All right then," Abbot said with a sigh, placing his hands on the side of the pool then launching himself out of it with a push of his arms. If that wasn't impressive enough, when he stood to his full height—head and shoulders above the security guard—he also sported a gigantic erection that, despite the dim lighting, clearly showed off every ridge and vein while standing proudly against Abbot's body.

The guard almost choked and looked away, his eyes wide like the image was imprinted on his mind and he was still seeing it. I dropped under the water to hide my laughter, taking the opportunity to grab Abbot's jeans.

When I reappeared, the guard was walking away and Abbot was holding out my terry robe, a towel around his waist and a shit-eating grin on his face.

I mouthed, "Oh my God!" and took his hand as he helped me get out of the water.

"Busted," he said as he draped the robe over my shoulders and we both ran for the apartment, giggling like little kids the whole way.

"His face when you got out of the pool!" I squealed once we got through the door, clutching at my stomach as I cackled so hard I could barely breathe.

"You liked that, did you?" He laughed, shivering as he grabbed the blanket from the couch I'd covered him with earlier and wrapped it around his body.

"It was priceless," I said, opening my robe as I stepped into his space. "Especially since he shone the torch in my eyes just as I climaxed."

He opened the blanket, welcoming me in, our bodies pressing together, skin to skin. "That dirty bastard. I'm glad he copped an eyeful of cock."

I giggled, looking up at him, admiring absolutely everything about him. "I'm so happy with you," I whispered, resting my hands on his chest.

"Me too, blue." He lowered his head and I meet him on my toes, our mouths joining and moving in harmony. I pulled at the strings on my bikini and let the fabric drop to the floor, my naked body still wrapped in our robe and blanket dome.

"Let's get rid of this pesky towel." My fingers found the fold at his waist then tugged it loose. The fabric fell, freeing his cock, once again rock hard. "That's better." Leaning close, I cupped his arse, his skin cool against my hands.

He pushed my robe off my shoulders and let it fall to the floor. "This is unnecessary."

I smiled. "So is this." I pushed the blanket away, and then we were both naked, standing in the middle of a moonlit living room.

"You know, that security guard is probably watching us through the glass door."

I slid my hands over his shoulders and laced my fingers behind his neck. "Then I guess we'd better give him a good show."

Abbot grinned. "I was meaning that we should shut the curtain. But sure, I'm game." He picked me up and I squealed, wrapping myself around him until he pressed my naked back against the glass of the door.

"You are *bad*." I laughed as he hooked his arm underneath my thigh.

"Do you object?" His shaft pressed enticingly against my centre, pulsing with need.

What the hell? It was after three in the morning and that guard was probably back in his security office watching the grounds and questioning his sexuality. No one would see this.

"Do it. And fuck me so hard they see your balls slapping."

He burst out laughing then kissed me really hard. "God, I love you," he said, shifting his hips before pushing inside me.

I gasped at his intrusion, tightening my hold. "I love you too," I whispered in his ear, kissing his skin and losing myself to the sensation of this man filling up my body with his big dick and skilful strokes. "I love you so much."

WE WERE ASKED to leave the next morning. Something about indecency and a noise complaint—when Abbot got going, his thrusts really rattled that door. *Bang, bang, bang!* What a night.

I complained about the pervy security guard and ended up with a full refund over the partial they were offering and left the place with nothing but good memories. I even left them an excellent Yelp review.

Once we were packed up, we drove the short distance to the Esplanade apartment Abbot had referred to as *ours*. That man was insanely sweet when he wanted to be. He seriously made me all gooey inside. *Ours.* He'd already carved out a place in his life for me, even though I wasn't supposed to return to his apartment at all.

With only enough time to dump our bags, the next stop on the day's agenda was Jasmine's place where the others were just getting back from surfing.

"Here's the lovebirds," Toby said with a smile as he helped unload boards from the back of a people mover.

"Was starting to think we'd be learning these locks on our own," Sam teased but Alesha nudged him in the arm.

"They're at the start," she said in our defence.

Abbot beamed and hooked his arm around my shoulders, pulling me in close and kissing my head.

"As long as there's never an end, I'll be a happy man."

I elbowed him, blushing. It was one thing to be wishy-washy with each other. But in front of others, I didn't know. I'd always played my relationships low-key in public, but then, I'd never felt love in this way.

He kissed me again. "Deal with it, blue." I rolled my eyes and he laughed, then I slid my arms around his waist and hugged into him. *What the heck?* I could do PDA.

"Jasmine here today?" he asked Toby as we all headed in.

"A little later. She's off with Breaker somewhere."

"What's the deal with them?" I asked as I slipped onto a stool in the kitchen.

"They're together," Alesha stated.

"Yeah, but how serious are they?" I asked. "I mean, isn't she still married?"

"She is," Nate said. "But there's no relationship. Our father forbade contact after he was sentenced."

"Jasmine will be a Cartwright till she dies. But she and Breaker are as together as the rest of us," Kristian said, rubbing his hand on the back of his head, his haircut so much neater than Abbot's.

Sam bounced a shoulder. "He's a good bloke. He'd do absolutely anything for Jazz, *anything* for Ronnie, who he loves like a daughter. He and his club got us out of a pretty sticky situation—"

"And dropped us right back in another," Nate pointed out, brows raised as he sipped his coffee.

"I heard about that," I put in. "Sounds like you're about to be free though."

"And to be fair, we were gonna do this job anyway," Kristian said.

"Yes," Toby said. "But it was for someone else." *Wait, what?* This was information I didn't have yet.

"Someone else?"

Nate nodded. "Someone who'll be real pissed if they find out we did it without them." *That so didn't answer my question.*

"And they will find out," Abbot said. "No way this isn't hitting the papers."

Who?

There were nods and murmurs of agreement before Kris held up his hand and called for quiet. "You know Ronnie sorted that shit out. We never promised anything to Grey himself. It was only a maybe to a couple low-level employees. We gave them some cash and a tip on a luxury car rig and they were happy as Larry."

Grey? I am so lost.

"It still sits a little uneasy with me," Alesha admitted. "They're loose ends that I think maybe we should tie up." She held her hands out in a *sorry, not sorry* gesture.

"*No,*" both Kris and Toby said in unison.

"Just because you're cool around dead bodies, doesn't mean the rest of us are," Kristian continued. "And I promised Ronnie we wouldn't hurt her friend."

Dead bodies?

My eyes widened and I looked to Abbot silently begging for clarification. He leaned close, a slightly amused smile teasing his lips. "Her family runs a funeral home. She used to do the make-up for the viewings. She doesn't go around killing people for fun."

I breathed out a sigh of relief...*that made better sense.* I was still lost on the rest, though.

"Definitely not for fun," she said, obviously having heard. "But I don't mind getting rid of scumbags who pose a threat. The man has greedy eyes."

"*Who are we talking about?*" I stressed, exasperated.

Abbot filled me in. "Ronnie used to run with a crew stealing cars. When they disbanded, one of the guys went to this smuggler for work. He's a skeez and tried to get Ronnie to turn on us, and Kris went all protective boyfriend and made things ten times worse. But Ronnie is a gun and cooked up this drug transport job."

I nodded, following. Kind of.

"Originally, its purpose was to get the Cartel of our backs. We were going to get Ronnie's old crew to broker a deal with the smuggler to get rid of the Cartel—all in exchange for the contents of this drug transport." Abbot paused to make sure I was following.

"But the Grim Order stepped in before the deal was set?" I stated, checking I had this straight in my head. "And now they want the drugs for themselves."

"The way Breaker tells it," Toby explained. "His MC brokered a deal with the Cartel. They provide heroine distribution on the east coast in exchange for releasing Nate from his debt. The contents of this transport is like a golden handshake from us to the Grim Order."

"So, you make no money from this job?" I asked.

"Nope," Kris added. "Freedom is the reward."

"And that's pretty much it in a nutshell," Abbot said.

"We do this job, Nate is free, and we're done with all this high-risk bullshit."

"What will you all do after?" I knew what we were doing, but if we couldn't get out, I wanted to know the kind of work we'd be doing.

Nate let out his breath. "Take a fucking break. I wanna be there for Holland and the baby." A break? Interesting.

Kristian nodded. "Me too, for Ronnie."

I looked around the room, spotting Sam rest his hand at the base of Alesha's neck and give her a reassuring squeeze. She reached up and touched his hand. The gesture was small yet intimate, and I took it to say that that was going to be them too, that if the IVF worked they'd also take a break. I didn't fully know their struggles, but I did hope that for them, understanding the craving that came with the desire for a child.

"So you're quitting this thug life a while. For how long?" I asked, my heart feeling a little lighter because if we were all on the same page, Jasmine couldn't possibly stop us. That did still leave the Grim Order to contend with if they didn't live up to their word.

"I'm quitting for good," Toby piped up, lifting heads like it was the first time those words had left his lips. With a frown, he nodded like he was even more certain now that he'd said it to the room. "If we're lucky enough to come out the other side of this without getting caught or killed, I'm done with this life." He kept nodding, not really focusing on any single person. "I'm fucking done."

"Tobes," Sam said. "*For good*?"

Toby shook his head. "I need this, OK? I *need* to get out." My heart hurt for him. *I tried...* He'd always wanted his freedom. But loyalty had kept him close. Selfless, rarely asking anything for himself and always making sure everyone else was okay, he'd given the best years of his life to the cause. With the rest of the Cartwright brothers finding happiness of their own, it was time for Toby to find his. *Run away and don't stop, Toby.*

Seemed we were all done with this life to different degrees.

I glanced at Abbot, noting how he didn't volunteer any information of our own. *He doesn't trust them.* Or perhaps he wanted to see how everyone reacted to Toby's plans before announcing ours.

"OK, Tobes." Swallowing hard, Abbot nodded in support of his big brother, clapping him on the back. The entire room was eerily still after his revelation. It was as though somebody died. People were staring into their cups or bowls. I suppose it was a lot like a death, an era ending, and their fearless leader turning away. *Jasmine is going to lose her shit.*

"Well," I said after a while. "I've got a bag of locks and picking tools in the car if we want to get to work."

Toby sniffed then nodded, meeting my eyes. "Yeah. Let's get to work."

"WHY DIDN'T you say we were leaving when everyone was talking today?" I asked Abbot in bed later that night, my fingers brushing through the light smattering of hair on his chest.

He drew circles on my back with his thumb. "Didn't you see the way they reacted to Toby?"

"They seemed surprised, but understanding."

"Not understanding. Not surprised. Quiet."

"What does quiet mean?"

"It means they'll talk him out of it. No way they'll let him go willingly. He's a huge part of the whole operation. No one can do what he does."

"But they all want to stop."

"We've had that conversation before. They want a break, which means they'll be back to it within the year, maybe less. It never stops, blue."

"OK," I whispered, understanding that he was desperate to get out and refused to trust anybody with that plan. "Do you really think your life is at risk on this job?"

He nodded. "I've made arrangements for you if I don't come back."

My heart clenched inside my chest, an aching sense of loss flowing through my body and seeping into my bones. I closed my eyes against the sensation.

"You'll come back," I whispered faintly, telling myself that just as much as I was telling him. "You have to. This can't be all we get."

He swallowed audibly then let out his breath. "Blue," he murmured, kissing the top of my head. "It might just be. We have to face that fact."

"No." I sat up, every fibre of my being rejecting that notion. "My God, Abbot. I have waited my whole life to feel what I feel when I'm around you. Don't tell me you gave me the world on a lease."

He took hold of my face, bringing my forehead to his, our noses side by side as he whispered no. *No.*

"I want you, Sloane. Now and always. I know what you're probably thinking, and I assure that I didn't suggest marriage because I thought that maybe I wouldn't have to follow through. *You* and the chance of creating a life with you, *a family* with you—away from all this bullshit—is what will get me through this job. Do you understand that?"

I nodded, hating the lone tear falling down my cheek. I couldn't stand the idea of losing the only thing that was perfect about my life.

"OK." I sniffed. "But what happens if this goes wrong?"

He brushed my hair behind my ear. "Then you bail. I've already organised for you to have access to everything I've stashed away. I want you to take it all and go somewhere no one will ever find you. Raise our child there and never come back." He pressed a hand against my belly.

"Our child?"

"If I don't make it back for a wedding, I want to at least give you a baby before I go."

Another tear fell. "Jesus, Abbot."

"I know I'm putting a lot on you. But let's face it, this three months might be it for us."

I didn't want to think about that at all.

"We can try. But I might not get pregnant in time. I'm not young anymore. It may not happen right away, or it might be too late for me—"

"But we can *try*. And you can promise me, baby or not, you'll go the moment things go wrong."

"You're talking like things *will* go wrong," I whispered, crying openly now.

"All I want is to get this job over with then focus on making a life with you—that's the goal. But this is my contingency plan. And I need you to agree to it."

"OK." My agreement came out as a mere breath. "If you don't come back, I'll disappear."

"Promise."

"I promise."

Closing his eyes, he let out a relieved breath before pulling me against him and crushing his lips against mine, our bodies reaching for comfort in the storm of our minds.

I focused on the way he tasted and the feel of his touch on my skin, losing myself in his arms, finding myself in his body, and most definitely, chasing away torturous thoughts of loss. *If I lost him I would disappear.* He'd become my breath, my heartbeat. He was where I belonged and where I wanted to stay.

I would never let him go.

Never.

He *had* to succeed.

We all did.

"REMEMBER that these locks have false gates as well as true gates," I said, pointing to the whiteboard where I'd drawn all of the locking mechanism components so the Cartwright brothers could better understand what they were working with. "The best way to tell if you've hit a false or true is to tap it gently with your pick. If it wiggles, you've hit a false gate. If it's solid, it's true."

Sam raised his hand like we were sitting in a classroom instead of the office space at their storage facility. "What about drilling them? Could we just destroy the whole fucking thing to get the cases open faster?"

"You drill a lock for the same reason you drill a safe—to get access to the pins so you can turn the barrel and unlock whatever you're breaking into. Even if BiLocks weren't drill resistant, it wouldn't be a faster option. They have two rows of pins—twelve all up—so we'd have to drill each lock twice, line all those pins up perfectly, then turn the barrel to get inside. Picking them is fiddly, but once you learn what you're feeling for, you can work on your speed." I picked up a whiteboard marker and wrote as I spoke. "The intel is forty locks. With the five of you picking during the ten minutes to drop off, you have a maximum of seventy-five seconds per lock." I circled the number and turned back to my overwhelmed trainees. "That's the benchmark, but faster is better. I'm under thirty seconds, and I believe I can get faster than that, which means you can too."

"You pick locks as a career choice," Kristian pointed out.

"That's really not all I do. But yes, I have a lot of experience, but you have picking experience too. If I recall, I taught you all to pick locks when we were kids."

"Basic door or window locks," Sam said.

"Still, you know what it feels like to line a pin in the gate. You guys can do this." I pulled out my own lock and a picking set. "Show me what you've got."

I WALKED them through the picking process daily, over and over—individually and as a group. Teaching these men something so tricky was strangely exhilarating. It felt good to be needed for my expertise. Like a pat on the back for twenty years of skill building. It was frustrating work that paid off just over a week later then Nate was the first to open his lock. His fist-pumped into the air as he yelled, "Motherfucking *yes!*"

The tension that had lived in my body since I understood the importance of this job lifted just a little as an obstacle became just a touch smaller.

"Good," I breathed, moving in front of him and inspecting the lock for damage. He'd scratched it up a bit, but it was in pretty good nick. He'd used a light hand. "Now you can unlock this one." I placed the lock I'd been demonstrating on in front of him and watched the light dim a little in his eyes. "No point in only knowing how to line up one lock. You have to be ready for any configuration."

He nodded in understanding, placing the new lock in his vice and picking up his tools again.

I patted him on the back. "Step one done," I said, my voice gentle. "Do it a few more times, then we'll start timing you."

He nodded again then got back to work.

THE NEXT LOCK wasn't opened until a day later. Sam and Toby got theirs undone within minutes of each other then immediately started rotating locks with Nate. Kristian and Abbot were pissed, not at their brothers, but at themselves. They wanted to move forwards, but they weren't able to get past that first hurdle. Kristian even threw his lock across the room in frustration, embedding it in the gyprock wall from the force of his throw.

"I think maybe we could all do with a break," I suggested. "How about you guys check conditions and go for a surf? Clear your heads." I'd never seen grown men file out of a room so fast.

"You coming with?" Abbot asked when we were back home, standing in the doorway of our bedroom, his wetsuit pulled on his legs but hanging half off around his waist.

"Surfing isn't my thing. You know that." I was relaxed

on the couch, my feet up on the coffee table and a book in my hands providing a little escape.

"Yeah. But you can run, or just watch—soak up some vitamin D. *Or,* you can come out with me."

I smiled. He obviously really wanted me to come. "I don't have a wetsuit. And how would that even work?"

He moved closer and pulled me to standing, sliding his hands around my waist and not stopping until he was cupping my arse. "You can borrow one from Leesh, and then you kneel on the front of the board while I ride the back. It'll be fun. And very coupley."

"I see. You do this with all your girls?"

"You offend me, blue. I've never shared my board with anyone. You are literally my first and last girlfriend."

Girlfriend. I smiled on the inside. After only a couple of weeks, this was still so new and every endearment meant everything. *Pinch me so I know I'm not dreaming.*

"You've never done this board sharing thing before?" I leaned into him. "This isn't convincing me, babe."

He laughed and started walking backwards, pulling me with him. "Well, I'm not gonna stop until you agree so it's easier to just get your arse in a swim suit while I organise a wetsuit for you."

"But the water will be freezing."

"What kind of a triathlete are you?"

"It's a summer sport."

"Please come." He pouted. "I'll miss you something chronic if you don't come, and I'll pay you in orgasms if you do."

"You are such a big kid," I said with a laugh, *not* objecting to his payment offer.

He kissed my mouth quickly and grinned. "I'll take that as a yes. Let's go."

"READY?" Abbot grinned as he looked over his shoulder at an approaching wave.

"No," I yelled. Although, I was laughing. We'd tried this couple surfing thing a few times already and fallen off each time. I'd spent more time hugging sandbanks underwater than I'd spent on the board with him.

"I can't believe you have no skills from when we were kids. Just try to stay in the centre of the board. No leaning."

"I promise you *nothing*." I flicked my arms out the side to dramatically prove my point and rocked the board. "Oh no." I cackled as I overcompensated and wobbled us some more.

He clapped his hands onto my thighs. "I don't even know how you manage to walk in a straight line. You have the worst balance I've ever seen," he teased, laughing as the waves bobbed beneath us and we needed to wait for the next set.

"This is why I couldn't pick it up years ago. The waves throw off my equilibrium and I can't find my centre."

He clapped a hand on my arse. "Lucky I'm enjoying the view."

I glanced at him over my shoulder. "Cheeky."

"OK. Here's another one. We're both gonna stay down this time, got it?"

"Got it."

"Here we go." Lying with his face pretty much up my arse, he powered those amazing arms of his through the water and propelled us both forward.

The wave hit, lifting the board, and I squealed and shut my eyes, holding on tight and trying my damndest not to rock while he laughed and said, "We're doing it, blue. You're surfing."

I opened my eyes, one at a time, and sure enough, we were in a fucking wave.

"Woo," Abbot shouted, stretching out his arm and touching his fingers to the roaring water.

"Holy fuck, I'm surfing."

It didn't last long, but it felt like flying, and I loved every second of it. Even the part where we dropped off the back of the wave and both rolled into the water.

"Happy?" Abbot asked after we surfaced beside the board.

I nodded. "Always with you."

He grinned and moved so he was holding the board either side of me. "Who's the sweet one now?"

"There's nothing sweet about me, Abbot."

"Hmm." He leaned in and sucked gently on my lips. "You're right. Salty."

"So corny." I laughed. "Should we head in?" The

others were already on the beach.

"Yeah. They're doing a bonfire at the beach shack. A few beers then we call it a day."

"OK. But no drinking for me. Just in case."

He grinned. "You think it could have worked this soon?"

I shrugged. "Who knows? I'm not due for my period for another week yet. But I want to be safe just in case."

"OK. I'll stick to ginger beer with you then."

MY PERIOD ARRIVED RIGHT on time, the pink stain on the toilet paper when I peed that morning the most disappointing moment in my life. It started off an irrational thought sequence that had me questioning my abilities as a woman. So stupid. I don't know what I was expecting. It was the first time I'd tried to get pregnant. But, I guess I just wanted to be good at it. I wanted it to be easy. Unlike everything else in my life.

We were still working on the locks. Nate and Toby were working on their speed, and Sam was still a little hit and miss, struggling whenever he had to start again. Kristian had opened one lock. And Abbot was still at a big fat zero.

I wasn't pregnant.

"Come on, come on," Abbot said between his teeth, diligently focused. I knew he was close, but still...*I'm not pregnant.*

"For fuck's sake, Abbot," I snapped. "You have to figure this out."

He took a breath before he lifted his head, something I

had to give him credit for. And even though his voice came out tense, he kept his cool. More than I could say for myself. "I'll get it, blue. Relax. I'm doing my best."

"That's not good enough. There's eight weeks left. *Eight.* How are you going to get below seventy-five seconds if you can't open even one in three weeks?" Granted, our lessons had been interspersed with various other preparation activities, but we'd all put hours into this. They needed to be faster.

Needed. Because our time was running out, and if he isn't ready...*he might not come back*. Then there'll be no us, no family, just my many regrets...and me. Alone again, and *not pregnant*.

Alone forever.

"I'll do it," he assured me.

"What if you can't?"

His jaw ticked. "Then I'll be the fucking getaway driver and these guys'll pick the locks without me."

We locked eyes, the other brothers staying silent, sensing the obvious personal reasons behind my worry.

My heart started hammering.

My head ached.

"I need air."

Rushing from the room, I headed straight for the car park, half thinking I could break into a run and not stop until I was standing on the beach in front of our apartment.

I stopped when my feet hit the gravel, hugging my arms to myself as I caught my runaway thoughts in a deep breath.

Shit. I'm a jerk. Closing my eyes, I lifted my head to the sky and inhaled, calming myself as the sun warmed my skin.

"You know, it's been a good two months since I quit smoking, but every time I walk outside, I still tap my pocket looking for smokes." Abbot stood beside me, hands in his pockets.

"Why don't you just have one then?" I looked into the distance, my hands still wrapped around my middle.

"Well," he started, glancing at me. "I hear that those things can kill you. And I kind of have something worth living for." *I'm melting.* When was this man not the sweetest most understanding person in the face of my fiery attitude? He always knew how to get through to me, whether it was waiting me out or coming at me head-on, he always knew, always stayed calm, and always got through to me.

How did I become so blessed?

"I'm sorry, Abbot. I was a mega bitch to you in there and you didn't deserve it."

He bounced a shoulder. "Eh, maybe I needed it," he said, pulling his hand from his pocket and handing me his padlock.

"You opened it."

"About two seconds after you stormed out of the room."

I ran my finger over the dents and scratches at the keyhole where he'd pushed a little too hard with the tension rod. I could literally see the effort he'd put into doing this. "I'm not pregnant, Abbot," I said, letting a disappointed tear slide from my eye.

"Blue." He pulled me into his arms, wrapping me tight against chest. "It's all right. We'll just keep trying. That's the fun part, right?"

Nodding against his chest, I cried a little harder. "I

don't know why I'm so disappointed. I knew it could take a while. I just couldn't help but hope, you know?"

"Yeah, babe. I know." He squeezed me a little tighter. "I'm sorry."

"It's not your fault."

"I know. But I love you enough that I don't mind if you blame me."

I laughed a little, the sound getting muffled against his chest. "You're ridiculous."

"No. You are," he said with a smile as I lifted my head.

I nudged him. "You are."

He grinned. "You know what's really ridiculous?"

"What is?"

"I haven't let you drive the Jag yet."

My eyes went wide with excitement. "Are you for real?"

He held the keys out and grinned.

"I love you!" I squealed, jumping at him and wrapping myself around him as I peppered kisses all over his face.

He laughed and walked me over to his precious Jag, opening the driver's side, depositing me in the seat.

"For how long?" I asked, gripping the wheel while imagining how cool I looked right now.

"Rest of the day. Me and the guys have some drills to run, so you can knock yourself out."

"You aren't coming?" I was a little disappointed but it was probably for the best. I didn't need him fretting when I smoked up his back wheels.

"Don't even pretend like you want me in there," he teased. "You're happy as Larry right now."

"I am happy," I said, relaxing against the leather seat. "But it's you making me happy. Not the Jag."

"It's a little bit the Jag."

I giggled. "Just a little." Then I reached out for his hand. "I really am sorry about before."

"Hey, I'd be worried if you weren't stressed right now."

"I *really* wanted to be pregnant," I admitted.

"It's OK, blue. When this is over, we have the rest of our lives together. There's plenty of time for us. You're only thirty-eight. You're not fifty."

Plenty of time. Was he purposely forgetting our situation?

"But, *this job*, Abbot. I feel like we're on a clock and even if everything goes perfectly, it still might be too late for me." *And there it was. I'd finally voiced my greatest fear—what if I'm too old?* It had been a few weeks since Abbot had told me to flee if he didn't come back, but as much as I hadn't mentioned it, I hated that the thought had hung around my shoulders every moment since. I wasn't a negative person by any stretch of the imagination, but this terrified me. I wanted forever with this man, not moments. *Tick, tick, tick.*

"Hey, we'll cross that bridge when we come to it, OK? Until then, we just keep fucking each other's brains out and enjoying every moment we can." He brought my hand to his lips.

"I have my period."

"Babe, that's what shower sex and red towels are for."

I laughed as I tugged his arm to bring him closer and kiss his wonderful mouth. "I really do love you a ridiculous amount, Abbot Cartwright."

"Me too, beautiful blue. Me too."

TIME SEEMED to fly when you were preparing for a drug heist. With only a couple of weeks to go, all five brothers had managed to get their picking speeds down to less than forty seconds a lock. Pretty impressive stuff and well with the time constraints of the job. I'd never seen a group of people more focused and dedicated on perfecting a plan. Whoever said that criminals were lazy and only after easy money had obviously never met the Cartwrights.

From the intel they'd received, each case was bullet-proof *and* fireproof and also had a GPS tracker inside it that they'd need to deactivate. The idea was that they'd hit the armoured trucks and load the cases into a bigger refrigerated truck that they'd had modified so the GPS signals couldn't be detected with the doors closed. They needed to get each case opened, unloaded and offline during the time it took to travel from the pickup site to the drop-off site. Meaning they *also* need to pick locks while being jostled.

Two weeks before the job, that was our final lesson.

"I'm so sorry, Lizzie," I said to my panel van as we

pulled everything out of her to make room for the brothers to sit inside. She was up on wheel ramps with Toby underneath her—another rare moment seeing him out of a pants and dress shirt combo—messing with the shock absorbers so she'd rock more. He was making it as difficult as possible.

"We'll put it all back the way it was," Sam said, chuckling at me as I patted her near the fuel cap. "She'll be good as new."

"I think you could actually do with new shock absorbers all together," Toby called out.

"Really?" I turned my mouth downward. "She's losing all her original parts."

"Original parts aren't necessarily a good thing when it comes to cars," Nate pointed out. "This car was released in the nineties. It's a relic."

"Don't listen to them, Lizzie," I said.

Nate laughed.

"How's it going out here?" Jasmine asked, walking outside and sliding on a pair of sunglasses. She was dressed in jeans and an emerald-green sweater. It was winter, but the sun still felt good on the skin.

Toby slid out from under the car, placing tools in the ground with a clank. "I'm done. We'll be on the road soon."

"You're driving?"

"I am," Toby said, standing while wiping his hands on a rag.

Jasmine nodded. "Be safe."

"Always."

She sucked in a lungful of air, like she was trying to let go of tension but couldn't really relax. I understood how she felt because the closer we got to the job, the more anxious I felt too. And it was obvious that the rest of the family was the same. Long hours meant we barely saw each other and spent most nights sleeping at Jasmine's to make life easier. But we were 'on' all the time, the job dominating the vast majority of all our interactions, all of our thoughts. Our time was running out, and I was spending less and less time with Abbot as he ran drills with his brothers and the bikers. I missed him, and I considered asking him daily if we could run early.

"I'll see you some time tonight?" Abbot asked after he walked out of the house with the bag of locks and tools they needed for their drill. He stopped right in front of me —toe to toe, nose to nose.

"I'll be waiting," I told him, wrapping my arms around his waist and pressing against him, wishing I could keep him right here. I was already tired of saying goodbye and not knowing how long until I saw him again.

"Try to have fun with the girls?" He slid his eyes to the side were Holland, Alesha, and Ronnie were saying goodbye to their other halves.

"I have been trying. They just keep doing spa days and shopping trips and I'm not about that life."

He grinned. "I get it. I'll be thinking of you," he said, kissing me softly before moving over to Toby who had just finished reversing Lizzie off the wheel ramps.

"Thanks again for the loan," Toby said, holding up my keys just as all the Cartwright brothers piled in the car.

"I wish we could do some of this with them," Alesha said as they drove off, leaving us, the group of dedicated women behind. "Every time they go it feels like goodbye, you know?"

I nodded. "Yeah. Like we're all on borrowed time."

She met my eyes and pressed her lips together, her gaze shone emotionally. "Exactly," she whispered.

"Want to go shopping?" Holland suggested to the group, her hand rubbing on her growing stomach. She was thirty weeks pregnant now and had a serious shopping for baby items addiction. I figured it was her distraction of choice, but not something I could handle at the moment. The stress of this job had thrown my usually clockwork-like cycle out of whack. I'd gotten excited when it was late, but the tests had come up negative, so I was trying my best not to even think about babies right now. The timing was all totally fucked up, and I couldn't face any sort of hard reality right now.

"I might sit this one out," I said, squinting against the sun when I looked at her. "You guys go and have fun though. I might just go for a swim or something."

"At the aquatic centre?" Alesha asked.

"Yeah," I said. "You're welcome to come." See, I could get along with other girls. Abbot would be proud.

"Do you guys mind?" Alesha directed at Jasmine, Holland, and Ronnie. "You go do some fun baby stuff and we'll do laps." She smiled, looking excited.

"That sounds like the most unfun compromise I've ever heard," Holland said with a laugh.

"It's fine," Ronnie answered for everyone. "It's insensitive for us to drag you around talking about all that stuff anyway."

Alesha waved her comment away. "I really don't mind. It gives me something to look forward to. I just want to go swimming. I haven't been in ages."

"OK," Jasmine said. "Go, have fun exercising. We'll meet you back here for dinner prep?"

Alesha nodded, and I shrugged. Sometimes the traditional roles going on with this family really got to me. We were often separated into 'boys' and 'girls' for domestic activities. I understood the reasoning, and that everyone had different roles to play, but I'd never been the most traditional woman and wasn't much of a cook either.

"Mind if we take your van?" I asked Alesha once they'd left. "Mine's kind of not here."

Alesha laughed. "Of course. I'll meet you out here in twenty?"

"Sure."

It took me less than five minutes to get my swimming gear together, so I spent a few minutes staring at myself in the bathroom mirror, brushing my teeth unnecessarily then putting my hair in a braid.

That still gave me five minutes to spare.

I opened the medicine cabinet and my eyes immediately went to the blue and pink box containing my last pregnancy test. I'd bought it the very first day my period was overdue and had already used up four out of the five, ever hopeful.

Pulling the foil-covered stick out of the box, I held it between my fingers, twisting my lips in thought as I looked at my watch. *What the hell? I've got time.*

Four tests had said no. So the odds were that this one would too. But it wasn't as if I couldn't just buy more later. And I refused to think of it as wasteful, because it would give me peace of mind for one more day, quieting that little question inside my head that kept saying, "*What if?*"

Mind made, I tore into the packet and readied myself over the toilet, peeing on the stick then capping it.

I'd just finished washing my hands when an almighty scream came from one of the other bedrooms.

Oh God. Alesha.

Rushing into the hallway, I raced straight to the room she and Sam had been sharing, my hands up like I was a ninja of some kind as I busted through the door, ready to take on whatever had caused the scream.

"Oh my God!" She inhaled noisily, the sound coming from the bathroom.

"Alesha!"

I burst through the door, expecting something terrible to be happening but found her standing at the basin, fully dressed and crying at her reflection.

"What happened?" *Is she having a nervous breakdown?*

She shook her head, turning towards me, her mouth open and moving but no sound coming out.

"What is it?" Softening my tone, I placed a hand on her upper arm and rubbed up and down, not knowing if it was too familiar, or exactly the right thing to do.

"I…"

"Is it this job? I'm freaking out too. I just got together with Abbot and if this goes wrong I might lose him for good. I feel sick thinking about it."

She cried harder, so it seemed I was on the right track by sharing my worries and continued.

"I've watched a stack of movies with armoured van robberies, trying to compile a list of everything that could go wrong. I think being shot is my biggest worry. They'll be armed and wearing Kevlar, but so will the cops. I don't know how I feel about them killing cops either. A lot of those guys have families, you know?"

Alesha sniffed, seeming to calm down. "They're using those gas grenades first. You know the ones that knock people out?"

"I know. They're actually called knockout grenades. They're using flash bangs too to blind them, but there's a lot of people involved and a lot of things that can go wrong. Nothing is straightforward. I keep wanting to question Abbot and make him tell me every contingency plan they have. But I'm trying not to be needy or put anything in his head that could take his mind off the job. They need laser-like focus if they're going to pull this off."

"Oh my God," Alesha gasped. "You're right."

"I know."

"I can't tell him."

"I know." Then I blinked. "Wait. Tell him what?"

She took a breath then met my eyes. "I'm pregnant." Her voice was such a whisper that I wasn't sure I heard right.

"Come again?"

She smiled. "I'm pregnant."

"Holy fuck! Wow, Alesha. That's...wow. *Amazing*." So many high-pitched words flew out of my mouth at once, and I meant every one of them. I hadn't spent as much time with Alesha as I had with Ronnie and Holland, but Ronnie had explained how hard it had been for Alesha, having wanted a child for so many years. And having only just recently had that time bomb go off in my own heart, I could imagine the anguish she'd felt over the years. This news far outshone my grief. *She deserved this.* God, I was so happy for her.

"Thank you. I didn't want to hope, but I couldn't resist testing."

I know the feeling.

"So, that's what you were yelling about?"

She nodded. "I was so excited, I just started screaming." A sheepish grin took over her features. "Did I scare you?"

"You scared the living shit out of me. I thought you were being murdered."

"Nope. Just growing a baby." She grinned and let out a sigh. "A baby."

"There will be three cousins so close in age." God, I hoped we could make it a forth, my test was sitting unchecked in Abbot's and my bathroom. I desperately wanted to rush in and look at it, but I couldn't face the disappointment of another negative test in the face of Alesha's positive one. I wanted to be completely happy for her news without making it about me.

"We'll be able to help each other out. We don't have a lot of family outside this house, so we can be the village for each other." *It takes a village to raise a family.* No matter the outcome of the job, if Abbot and I managed to conceive a child, that child would be raised on its own away from this family. I knew it was for the best, but I couldn't help feeling a little guilty and selfish for wanting to leave them all behind. *Toby is leaving too. We aren't alone.*

"I thought you had family. They run a funeral home?"

"They do. But they're...difficult, and while we're on speaking terms, things aren't all shiny rosy."

"I just have my mum. But she's never been reliable.

Too busy chasing men. And living the cat burglar life, it turns out."

"Like in the movies?"

I shrugged. "I guess. I only found out a few months ago. Abbot helped me track down my pop's money and it led to her."

"Did she steal it?"

"No. Just moved it." I sighed. "It's a long story. Pop left me his shop, which didn't have any cash flow because he was laundering his money through it. My mum got all the cash, some of which was clean and earmarked for me. But she claimed wouldn't be released to me until I got married." I rolled my eyes, thinking about the ridiculous rouse.

"Oh," she said. "So *that's* why he changed his mind so suddenly."

My spine went rigid. Even though I would have thought the same in her shoes, it didn't sit well coming from Alesha who had an airy voice and big doe-like eyes. The kind of girl guys loved rescuing. She was tall and slim and feminine with a beach boho style that was night and day against my basic jeans and T-shirts look.

I opened my mouth to form some snappy retort, but stopped myself before it came out. She just found out that she was going to be a mum. I didn't need to mar that moment with my own insecurities. I simply said, "He's with me because he loves me."

"I know he does. He was just so anti-relationships, going to great lengths to hide his interest in you from the family. I thought there might be more to his change of heart."

I smiled, remembering how much I wanted him in the

beginning and how quickly I realised I couldn't just be his friend. "There is. He wanted something casual and I wanted more. I wasn't willing to hand over the benefits part of our friendship if that's all it would ever be."

"So it was all or nothing for you?"

I nodded.

"Wow. I think you just became my hero. You beat the Cartwrights at their own game."

"What do you mean?"

"You're the one in control this time. They've always called the shots, but not with you. You're the kind of woman we all hope we grow up to be."

I scoffed, not so sure I was deserving of such praise. Jasmine and my mother did more than a little manipulating to get Abbot and me together. I simply held out until we couldn't stand it any more. I didn't know if that was being in control or just plain stubbornness on my part.

"I don't know that I was ever in control. We were just upfront with each other from the beginning. We thought we could be friends, maybe casual lovers. But when our feelings became real, I took a step back because I knew Abbot wasn't in the same headspace as me."

"Was this when you left after the wedding? You seemed so close that night, I thought you were together."

"No. We were letting each other go there. We figured we'd end it before we went too far but—"

"It was already too late."

I nodded.

"Those Cartwright men can't seem to walk down the aisle without a fight of some sort."

"It wasn't smooth sailing for you either?"

"Far from it. Do you know the story of how Sam and I met?"

I shook my head. "Only that you were forced to marry alongside Nate and Holland."

"Wow, we could probably write a few books on the crazy shit that went down before now, but the CliffsNotes version is that the Cartwrights had targeted *me* as a person of interest. They used to talk their way into women's beds then rob them while they slept. Except they didn't rob me. Nate fell head over heels for Holland and they robbed her instead."

"That's what she was talking about a few weeks back —he robbed her twice?"

With a giggle, she nodded. "It was totally messed up in the beginning, but just like she and Nate clicked, so did Sam and I. We all ended up getting our happily ever afters. And you will too. They'll get through this job. Abbot will propose and you'll have a beautiful wedding. Then we can focus on growing this family and going back to the way things were before the drugs and the bikers and the smugglers."

"Do you think that's possible?" I simply couldn't believe the Grim Order would release a group capable of robbing a government drug transport and getting away with it. *If they get away with it.* Those kind of skills were criminal gold.

"We'll lie low for a while, but when they're ready to work again, I really hope it's going back to their roots," she said, placing her hand on her stomach. "There are three very important reasons to step back once this mess is all cleaned up."

She was right. With babies coming, stepping away

from these high-risk jobs was the best thing for everyone. *Getting out entirely is best for everyone.* But that was never going to happen.

"Do you think Toby will really leave at the end of this?"

"Well, he wants to. And Jasmine believes in letting everyone leave at least once to find their path…"

"She does?" That surprised me, because she'd always seemed intent on keeping her sons near.

"Yeah, But it always leads back here."

"Because she makes it lead here or because they come back in their own."

She met my eyes and smiled. "Whichever gets the job done." That's when I saw something in Alesha I hadn't noticed before—confidence. She knew who she was in this family and she believed in its cause. *A mini Jasmine?*

Suddenly, I didn't want to know the result of my test. I wanted to wait, focus on doing everything in my power to help this job go down without a hitch while helping Abbot plan our escape. Everything had to be perfect or we'd be dragged back into this life. *They can never find us.*

From now on, every spare moment would be spent in planning. I was going to get my happily ever after *goddammit.* After all these years, I deserved my happiness and Abbot deserved to be free.

"WALK ME THROUGH EVERY DETAIL," I said to Abbot and Toby later that night after Lizzie was put back to rights again. We were out by the pool having a beer. Although, mine was my usual non-alcoholic ginger one because anxiety over this whole thing was really starting to get the best of me and it helped to settle my stomach.

"What do you want to know?" Toby asked, his feet stretched out on a lounger and his dog by his side.

Abbot sat behind me, his legs bent to either side while I leaned against his chest. The outdoor heater kept us warm as the sun rapidly disappeared.

"I want to know everything. Every detail."

Abbot and Toby locked eyes, seeming to quietly decide if they were willing to share. When Toby gave a nod, I felt a touch of relief.

"The transport is leaving the courthouse at five in the morning to avoid sitting in traffic," Abbot started, his voice rumbling against my back.

"They're sticking to major roads as much as possible

because it's the fastest route with the least chance of obstructions," Toby continued. "But there are off-ramps."

"Which is where we'll hit them," Abbot said. "We'll block them in on either side then move in."

"What if they shoot while you're moving in?" I asked.

"They won't be able to see us. We have smoke grenades, flash bangs, and knockout gas. If they get a shot off, it'll be pure luck," Toby said.

"What if they have gas masks?"

"It's not on their equipment list, but if they do, the flash bangs and smoke will obscure their vision," Toby explained.

"And yours."

He smiled, looking serious but also amused. "Yes. But we're the ones setting them off so it won't be as disorienting."

"OK. Well, let's say none of that works and they come out shooting?"

"We have Kevlar and riot helmets," Abbot said.

"We'll also have guns of our own. And cops don't get paid enough to risk getting shot over some drugs," Toby added.

"Are you really counting on that?"

Abbot squeezed my shoulder. "No, blue. We're not counting on that. It was a joke. But we assure you, we've run drills for every fucking scenario we can think of."

"Including getting caught or killed?"

Toby stood and clicked his fingers at Rogue. "I'll leave you with this one, brother," he said, his voice soft as he tapped Abbot on the shoulder and gave me an affectionate touch on top of my head. "I'll take care of him for you, Sloane."

I nodded and watched him walk back inside before I turned to face Abbot. "Come here," he said, holding out his arms. I fell into them, tucking my face into his neck, curling up for comfort. He ran his fingers up and down my back in a slow, soothing motion as he spoke. "We've done so many drills for this, blue. Breaker's guys have been great. They've come at us hard and in many different ways, some we hadn't even imagined. They've done stuff like this before, so we're not going in totally green."

"Who's driving the getaway vehicle?"

"Breaker," he said.

"So, all five of you will be in the back of the truck picking locks?"

He nodded. "There'll be way more of us than there will be cops. They're trying to be low-key and aren't publicising anything about the transport."

"But you have someone on the inside?"

"There's always someone willing to talk with the right amount of persuasion."

"Let's say this thing goes off without a hitch and you get away. What happens then?"

"We give the drugs to the Grim Order and they take it wherever the fuck they want. It's out of our hands after that. We're there to steal the drugs and open the cases. That's it."

"There'll be an investigation."

"Yes."

"Do you think there's a chance they could link any of it back to you?"

"We aren't people of interest."

"You don't think they know who you are? Your dad is in jail for killing a guy, and your mum is dating a Grim

Order biker. You have to consider that they'll look this way, even if it's just at Jasmine and Breaker. And with Toby and us taking off, we could make the family look guilty. We could have cops looking for us."

He let out a slow breath. "You're right. I'll talk to Toby about a contingency plan for the rest of them." He looked around before he lowered his voice even more. "But you and I are vanishing, blue. We'll be off the grid. New identities and everything. No one's gonna find us." *God, I hope he's right.*

"I trust you. But I'm still gonna question you about our plan."

He smiled. "Of course you are." Giving me a gentle tap on the side, he got up and kissed me briefly. "How about you meet me upstairs? I'll be up after I talk to Toby."

"Of course," I said, taking a moment to collect my thoughts before switching off the outdoor heater and heading back inside.

"How you doing, sweetheart?" Jasmine's voice floated out of the kitchen, and I turned to find her in there with Breaker. She was wearing a burgundy satin robe and he was just wearing some pyjama bottoms, showing a decent-looking chest that was inked to the hilt. Lots of skulls and boobs were drawn on that body.

"I'm OK. Just heading up to bed." I pointed to the stairs.

"You and Abbot seem real happy."

I smiled, always careful and wary around her. "As do you and Breaker."

Breaker lifted his coffee mug to me in acknowledgement.

Moving a couple of steps in my direction, she beckoned me closer. "How does Toby seem to you?" she asked, voice low once I was within whispering distance. *Toby*? Why?

"Strong, dependable, quiet…" I said, trying to assess what her line of questioning was about.

"Quiet," she repeated. "He's always quiet but he's more quiet than usual I think." I had a strong feeling about this.

"They're all under a lot of stress. Perhaps he's just focused."

"He hasn't…" She paused and took a breath, her pink tongue poking out to wet her lips thoughtfully before she spoke again. "He hasn't mentioned anything about leaving to you has he?" And there it was. She either had an all-seeing eye or someone had filled her in. The latter the more likely of the two.

Since I wasn't a snitch, I shook my head. "Nothing to me. Is he making plans? Are you worried about him?"

She shook her head then shrugged. "I'm the mother to five boys, I always worry."

"Men," I said before I realised I was correcting her.

Her eyes seemed a little sad, or perhaps wistful as she moved her gaze between mine. "Yes." She nodded. "They're all men now. But in here," she said, placing her hand on her chest, "they'll always be my boys. Just like you'll always be the little spitfire I knew as a girl. Just because you're all grown, doesn't mean I stop caring." *Way to make me feel guilty for lying and hiding my own plans.*

"I understand," I whispered. "I didn't mean to imply that you didn't."

"It's all right, Sloane. Just…let me know if you notice

anything different about any of them. This family is everything to me, and you're a part of that now. It's important that we maintain the status quo and don't make any big changes. Especially when the boys all get home. We want to appear as normal as possible."

I nodded. Sometimes I wasn't sure if she was threatening me or just stating a fact. "No big changes. Got it."

She placed the back of her hand on my cheek in a weird kind of motherly way that reminded me of my time in her care as a child. "You were always a good girl, Sloane. I'm overjoyed you're back here with us."

"So am I," I said with a tight-mouthed smile, stepping back to make my excuses to leave. But then I stopped and blurted, "How well do you know my mother, Jasmine?"

Her brow lifted and fell gracefully. "We practically grew up together. Well, in this life we did anyway." She gestured at the air around her, so I took that to mean that she'd known my mother for her entire criminal life. How I hadn't known until recently both baffled and annoyed me. *There were too many secrets in these walls.*

"So, you worked together?"

"We did. Learned the ropes together. Her strengths were in fieldwork, and I specialised in organisation, negotiation and numbers."

"She stole things, and you offloaded them and laundered the profits through front businesses?" *In a nutshell.*

Jasmine smiled and glanced back at Breaker. "You'd think she'd been doing this all her life."

Breaker nodded in agreement.

"Well, I have. Inadvertently. Pop might have hidden most of what he was doing from me, same as Mum, but I was still running a front, wasn't I?"

"Yes, I suppose you were," she said with a Mona Lisa-like smile. "Trevor would have left a comfortable nest egg behind for you and your mother though."

"I don't know what he left. After you two used the inheritance to try and force me and Abbot together, my pride kicked in and I don't want it anymore."

"Pride is an awful thing, Sloane. You could really use that money in the coming months." *Coming months? What does she mean?*

I looked around the room, wondering if listening devices picked up all our conversations. It seemed like a paranoid thought, but why would she say that if she hadn't discovered our plans?

"I don't think I know what you mean?" I glanced towards Breaker who was quietly drinking his coffee and listening.

"It's rubbish night, Sloane. I saw the test in your bathroom when I was emptying the bins."

What test?

Wait.

What? "You were in our room?"

"I promise I wasn't snooping. We were just collecting rubbish from around the house—normal cleaning stuff. It was right there. I wasn't aware you and Abbot were trying." Wow. Something she *didn't* know.

"We've only been trying a couple of months," I said, getting defensive. What was wrong with her? It was embarrassing enough to have gone through an entire pack of tests without *anyone* knowing. Quite another to have it pointed out by the person I probably trusted least in this world. "It takes a lot of people months, sometimes years before they conceive."

Her brow drew together and she shook her head. "What are you talking about?"

"The test, obviously."

"Yes. But you're talking like it's negative when it's—"

"Whoooooo!" The crow call came from upstairs, followed by laughter, hooting and a lot of swearing. Thumping footfalls came running down the stairs. "Blue," Abbot called out.

"In the kitchen," Breaker yelled.

Abbot appeared in a flash and came skidding to a stop in front me, a massive grin on his face. "Why didn't you tell me? Holy shit, blue. *Holy shit.*"

"Tell you what?"

"I think he saw the test too," Jasmine said with a smile.

"You know?" Abbot said, frowning. "What the fuck, Sloane?"

Jasmine laughed. "Wait, Abbot, I don't think *she* knows yet."

I thought I knew, but I was really struggling to believe this right now. "Tell me what you saw," I whispered. "Please. Just tell me."

"I can do better than that, beautiful blue," he said with a smile lifting his hand.

When he held the test at my eye level, all I could do is stare and squeak. It was positive. The test was positive. "I'm pregnant?" I whispered, and Abbot nodded.

"I have super sperm and you"—he pulled me against his chest and hugged me fiercely, grabbing either side of my face and touching our foreheads together—"you're pregnant," he whispered. Then he kissed me.

"Whoooooo!" Another crow call came from upstairs,

followed by a female squeal, joint laughter, hooting and a lot of happy swearing.

"What in the world is going on tonight?" Jasmine asked looking up as if she could see through the floor.

I knew. But I just smiled and waited.

"What's with all the screaming?" Nate asked as he came out of the office.

Sam came down the stairs with Alesha piggybacking on him and laughing. "Put me down," she said. "I can walk, you know."

Moving aside as a curious-looking Toby entered the room, Sam set his wife on her feet. "I don't want to take any chances with you straining yourself."

"I can *walk*." She laughed.

Kristian, Ronnie and Holland came in from the front room. "What's happening?" Ronnie asked, her curly blonde hair a messy bun on the top of her head.

"We're pregnant," Alesha said with a small curtsy.

"Holy shit!" The room erupted in congratulatory cheers and squeals.

"So are we," Abbot yelled at the same time, his eyes so wide with amazement. He filled my heart with joy. I wasn't surprised when my eyes started leaking.

"Oh shit. Didn't you want anyone to know?" he asked, pulling me a little closer.

I shook my head. "I'm just happy. This is a wonderful day."

"And it calls for a celebration," Jasmine said. "Everyone order your favourite food. We're going to feast."

Taking a moment to focus only on me, Abbot looked into my eyes. "This is the happiest I've been since I was ten years old and got my first hard-on watching you change."

Laughter bubbled up my chest. "That must have been a big moment for you."

"Well, it wasn't big at that point, but it certainly had potential."

I placed my hands on either side of his face. "We're having a baby," I whispered. "No backing out now."

He kissed me softly. "Never. You're stuck with me, blue. Til death do we part."

"WHAT ARE YOU DOING WITH THAT?" I asked as Abbot took the positive pregnancy test out of the drawer. We'd kept it as a keepsake, because, well, we were both incredibly excited to have made a baby together.

"It's my good luck charm," he said, opening his vest pocket, the Velcro too loud for the early hour. "Right next to my heart. Along with this." He slid the ring he wanted to propose with in there too.

I smiled, even though I'd rather cry. "You'll be carrying my pee around with you for good luck?" I teased, trying to make light of the situation just a little. Three months ago, this day had seemed so far away. Now it was here and I was so scared. So, so scared.

What if, what if, what if?

"Luckiest pee in the world," he said with a smile, tapping his pocket.

"It better be, because we have to use that stick to gross our kid out on his eighteenth birthday."

"You think it'll be a he?" He grinned while finishing

strapping on his body armour. I struggled to keep the smile on my face as I watched his movements.

"Makes sense," I said, my voice too small. "You're one of five brothers. I imagine you'll all make boys."

"But you're a girl."

"Yeah. But the eggs are all X chromosomes. It's the sperm that decides whether it's a boy or a girl."

He slipped his jacket over the top of the Kevlar. "Huh, you learn something new every day."

"That you do."

He met my eyes as he did his zipper up. "Go over the plan with me."

"I wait here with the other wives until you return. We take part in the traditional celebration with the family and wait for everyone to be happy and drunk before leaving. When we go home, we switch out the beautiful Jag with a Corolla." I grimaced. It was the most popular car in the country and therefore the most inconspicuous. But I loved the Jag and I loved Lizzie, and we had to say goodbye to both. "It's already packed with our bags and new paperwork. Then we take turns driving in four-hour shifts, switch out the car in Sydney, keep driving until we hit the Whitsundays, dump the car again and boat to Hamilton Island where we'll go blond and live the island life." I took a breath. "Did I miss anything?"

"What happens if I *don't* come back?"

My breath hitched and I shook my head, unwilling to voice what I'd already committed to memory.

"Please, blue. I need to hear it. Let me leave here knowing you're ready for anything."

"I take the paperwork stuck to the top of the glove compartment in Lizzie, set fire to the Corolla and drive straight to airport. Then I fly to Auckland, lie low while I get my new identity and make my way to Switzerland where I'll live out my days with our child." My voice wobbled and I needed to wipe at my eyes once or twice. I didn't want to talk about this at all. I just wanted him to come back.

"Come here." I climbed over the bed and met him where he stood at the foot of it. "I love you more than anything else in this world. You know that, right?"

"Abbot, don't," I started, not wanting to hear him say goodbye. "Just say see you later, OK?"

"Blue."

"Please, Abbot. Say see you later."

He pressed a long, slow kiss to my mouth. It held desperation, sorrow and regret. "See you later," he whispered. It felt like goodbye.

"Tell me what will happen when we're gone." I refused to let him leave with a heavy heart. *He is coming back.*

"When they realise we're gone and start searching for clues, all they'll find is the stuff I hid in Lizzie pointing to New Zealand."

"We'll be sunbathing and they'll be hunting for us in Auckland. It's foolproof," I said. "And you're going to be wonderful today. You trained so hard for it. I have no doubt you'll succeed."

With a nod, he let out his breath and took a step back. "Just promise you won't hesitate if you need to bail."

"I'll promise, but I'll *will* see you soon," I insisted.

His face creased as he swallowed and nodded again. "See you soon, beautiful blue."

"TEA?" Jasmine held up a box of Twinings Lemon & Ginger.

I nodded. I didn't know if I was nauseous from the pregnancy or the job.

"They're all gone now?"

"A few minutes ago." Setting a second floral teacup in front of her, she dropped in the teabag and poured the water.

"How did they seem?"

"Focused." She jiggled the tea bag in the water, eyes down.

"Are you afraid?"

"Afraid? No." She pushed the tea across the bench towards me. "Worried, nervous—that fits a little better. But I'm confident in their abilities. No one plans a job like my boys do. They're more than ready." She opened a tin of biscuits and offered them to me. "These always helped when I was pregnant."

I took one and nibbled the corner, the sweet crumble touching my roiling stomach without threatening to come back up. Thankful, I sipped the tea. "Thank you," I said.

Reaching across the bench, she patted my forearm. "He'll be OK. They always come back."

"I guess I'm just not used to this…waiting. I'm normally the proactive one in most situations. I don't sit still very well."

"You get better at it as time goes by," she said with a smile. "The nerves don't really lessen, but I figure it's no different to the feeling wives and mothers of those cops are experiencing sending their men out into the field. We're on the opposite side to them, but the danger is present for all of us. We all want our boys to come home safe."

"That's an interesting way to look at it."

"Without crime, there's no need for police or security. We're two sides of the same coin and feed off each other. You look at this as a job—work. Nothing more."

"I can do that," I said, taking another sip of tea. "He's just at work."

She smiled. "And he'll be home by lunchtime. Try to rest until then."

That was easier said than done. There were only so many ways you could distract your mind from focusing on the ticking clock. With five women in the house, we filled the time talking about nothing, complaining about pregnancy symptoms, and baking enough muffins to feed us all for a month. Midday came and went. Suddenly, the distractions were impossible tasks. *They should have called by now.*

Blackberry phones weren't the most interesting things when they were released back in the nineties. And they certainly weren't interesting now, especially when one was dormant in the middle the table while four women sat around it, staring and chewing our nails while a fifth paced back and forth, raking her fingers through her greying hair. *This is not a good sign.*

"Are we certain it's working?" Jasmine asked, checking her watch for the billionth time in fifteen minutes. *They should have called.*

"It is," Ronnie said, touching the centre button to light the screen. "They haven't sent a burn message so we have to assume that everything is OK." *Do I wait? Or do I run?* My chest hurt from nerves. Abbot wanted me to leave the moment it looked like they might not make it back. But without confirmation that things had gone wrong, I couldn't bring myself to go. I had to stay put.

"Maybe we should turn on the TV," Holland suggested. "If something happened, the media would be all over it, right?"

And they were. *Fuck.*

News stations were showing footage of an overturned armoured van from inside the smoky scene.

"This was a precision attack in which no parties were harmed," a spokesman for the police said in an interview. "The assailants are at large, heavily armed and considered highly dangerous. Police are doing everything in our power to track them down before these drugs can make it onto the streets."

"At least we know the cops don't have them," Alesha said, letting out her breath as she sat back on the couch, still staring at the TV as they detailed the current manhunt.

"But it's been two hours since the hit," Ronnie said. "If the cops don't have them pinned down, where are they?"

I shook my head slowly, not knowing what to say to make her feel any better. To make any of us feel better. We were a group of pregnant women waiting for our men to get home from a drug heist. What could possibly be said to make that better?

I want you to get out of there the moment things go wrong.

I could hear Abbot's voice as I sat rooted to the chair, refusing to leave until I was certain of his whereabouts.

I'm not leaving without you.

"Maybe we should call them," Alesha suggested.

Jasmine shook her head. "We can't risk that. We just need to be—" The Blackberry chirped and vibrated on the table. "Thank God." She rushed towards it, grabbing and jabbing a finger at the accept call button. "Where are you?"

The rest of us held our breath as she listened, her eyes increasing in size and she nodded and said, "Stay put. I'll get someone." Her hand shook as she ended the call.

"What happened?" I asked, a lump in my throat.

"Your ex is a doctor?"

"How did—" Why? *W*hy was this relevant? I blinked. "He is. Yes."

"Will he come if you call him? Can we trust him if we need to?"

"I…uh, I suppose."

"Yes or no, Sloane. This is very important."

I nodded. "Yes. I trust him."

She thrust the Blackberry in my hand. "Call him. We need him."

"But, he is three hours away."

"So are they," Jasmine said. "And they're hurt."

"Who is hurt? *All* of them?" *Oh God.*

"Call," Jasmine ordered.

I punched Mark's number into the Blackberry.

"What happened?" Holland cried.

"An ambush," Jasmine said, looking at Ronnie, her expression set into hard lines.

Ronnie's face fell. "No. They *didn't*," she gasped, covering her mouth with her hand.

"They did." Jasmine looked away, worry creasing the corner of her eyes, tension radiating from her body.

"Fuck," Ronnie sobbed.

"Will somebody please tell me what's going on?" Holland yelled.

"The smugglers found out about the job," Alesha said, piecing it together impressively. "They ambushed the guys on the way to the drop off."

Jasmine nodded. "Get your shit together, ladies. We're going on a road trip."

Still trying to get a hold of Mark, I rushed to get a bag of things for both Abbot and me, trying not to let my emotions overwhelm me. This was not a part of the plan. We had thought of everything except an ambush from a third party. *Fuck.*

The call finally connected.

"Hello?"

"Mark! It's Sloane."

"Sloane. Are you OK? You sound…not OK."

"Remember you said to call you if I needed anything?"

"Of course."

"Well, I need you. And you need your med kit."

"WANT to explain what the fuck I just did in there?" Mark demanded the moment we arrived at the safe house I'd directed him to not far from Bendigo where he worked.

"I promise I will. Just tell me he's OK." My voice came out harsh, edged with panic and worry.

He threw his hands up in the air, this whole experience obviously existing at the edge of his ability to cope. "Your oaf will live, Sloane. They all will. I just cannot believe you put me in this situation."

I gasped with relief, one hand on my chest the other on his arm. "Thank you, Mark. Thank you from the bottom of my heart."

I rushed into the house, desperate to see Abbot and make sure he was okay.

"He's in there," Breaker said when I burst through the front door, my eyes sweeping the room of injured men. *Holy fuck.*

Racing for the door he pointed to, I left the relived reunions between the other brothers and their wives behind me. Nate had suffered a bullet graze to his shoulder. Kristian had a slight concussion, but Breaker and Sam seemed to be no worse for wear. *What about Abbot? What about Toby?*

I pushed through the door startling Toby, who was sitting beside the bed, his skin grimy with what looked like blood and probably dirt and sweat.

"It's not my blood," Toby stated, his voice flat. I covered my mouth as tears sprang to my eyes. In the bed, lying prone, an IV line held up by an old broom was Abbot. *This wasn't part of the plan.*

"Toby," I gasped, my eyes flicking between him and Abbot. "How? What?"

His eyes saw me but he looked right through me, and as he fought for the ability to speak, his brow creased. *I've never seen him look so...shattered.*

"Grey," he said, his voice so rough it sounded forced through gravel. *How did we not account for this?* There had been concern about them finding out. Why weren't they watched more closely?

"The smuggler Ronnie is connected to?"

He nodded then looked at his hands. Palms up. Fingers shaking. "We paid them off. It shouldn't have..." He shook his head. "I should have seen this coming." He forced his breath. "I will make them pay. That man, Dazza is going to be sorry he opened that slimy mouth. He's responsible for this." His gaze moved to Abbot and he swallowed hard. "Everything was fucking perfect. No injuries, locks picked, GPS trackers deactivated, drugs transferred to duffle bags." He swallowed, angry. "We were ambushed the moment we made it to the drop off, attacked before we could get out of the back of the fucking truck, like fish in a goddamn barrel." His hands rubbed together, palms grating. "They got Kris in chest and he went down, Nate got clipped in the arm and Sam was trying to get them behind the cases while Abbot and me were fighting them off at the door…" He hissed in his breath between his teeth. "It happened so fast. We were being overwhelmed then he pushed me out the way and"— he swallowed and took another shaky breath—"they shot him through the side of the vest." *Oh God.* "It was so stupid. They would have shot me in the back, hitting Kevlar like Kris…I would have been bruised but fine. And now…*God.*" *The beautiful idiot tried to save his brother.* I loved him even more for that.

Tears running down my face, I sat on the edge of the bed, taking Abbot's hand in my own, noting his grazed knuckles from a fight I wished I could have stopped.

"His, um, his lung collapsed. Your friend is a great doctor, so he's gonna be all right, Sloane. I…"

Abbot was breathing steadily, his chest rising and falling peacefully. He was shot. *Shot.* It seemed too surreal. This wasn't really happening. He wasn't…

Get your shit together, Sloane. He's alive. He's breathing. He's fighting.

He's going to be OK.

I closed my mind against all the what-ifs and focused on what was.

Brushing Abbot's hair back from his forehead, I ran my fingers down the side of his face, grazing lightly over the line where his dimple lived. *I almost lost him today.* My heart squeezed painfully at the thought.

"I'm just so fucking sorry, Sloane. I should have seen it coming. I should have had the balls to get rid of the threat before it became a fucking issue." Toby dropped his face into his hands, his shoulders shaking. "I just didn't want anymore killing. I didn't want to become..." My heart leapt into my throat as I turned to him and placed my hand on his shoulder.

"Toby," I whispered, just as he lifted his head, his face streaked with tears through the grime, his eyes red and tortured.

"I killed them, Sloane," he whispered. "Every fucking last one of them." He clenched his jaw. Three of his fingers curled in as he pointed two out and relived the moment. His fingers quivered as he curled them back into a fist then spoke through his teeth. "I saw the blood, and I thought they killed him—*my little brother*. I lost it. Shot them all dead like I was a god and had a right to snuff them out."

"Oh, Toby," I said, wrapping my hands around his tight fists.

"I saved the drugs, and *they* all think I'm a fucking hero, Sloane." He nodded his head towards the door. "I'm not. This is never who I wanted to be. *What* I wanted to be. I never really wanted to be a thief, now I'm a killer too."

"Toby," I whispered, touching the side of his face, remembering the boy from twenty-one years ago. He was so much more grown-up than the rest of us, and he'd always had good in his heart. Just like he did now. "You are not a *killer*. They're all alive right now because of you. My *child* has a father because of *you*. You saved everyone. Do you think that smuggler's people were going to leave you alive? You did what you needed to do to survive and you *are* a hero because of it. There's no doubt in my mind."

He turned his gaze away, not wanting to hear what I was saying. So I put both of my hands on his face and made him look into my eyes. "People do things in the heat of the moment because they *need* to be done. That's why they think you're a hero, Toby. Not because you killed. But because you saved them, and you saved the job. You, Toby Cartwright, *are* a fucking god. We owe you our lives and our hearts."

He frowned and nodded, so I just hugged him really tight because we *both* needed it. And I needed him to understand how much I appreciated the man he was. We all knew he was the glue that held this family together. He was always there, always making sure everyone was OK, even Jasmine. Toby was the heart of us all. When he hurt, we all did. Yet he was here alone. Watching over his baby brother, just like he's always done. *God, this man was incredible.*

"You are a strong and amazing man, Toby. Thank you," I said into his shoulder as he held me as hard as I was holding him.

"Fuck, Tobes, I'm not even dead yet and you're moving in on my woman," Abbot croaked.

We broke our embrace to find Abbot awake and watching us. Toby wiped at his face and laughed. "I'm disappointed you made it, brother. Would have had one less pain the arse to deal with if that guy had been a better shot."

Despite their words, they smiled at each other fondly. "Thank you, big bro," Abbot said, lifting his arm. "I know I'm only here because you got me out."

Toby shook his head as he stood, clapping his hand against Abbott's outstretched hand. "Couldn't leave that baby of yours without a father to teach them how to surf. Sloane's never been any good at it." I smiled at how light yet full of meaning their conversation was.

"Thank you," Abbot said again. They acknowledged each other for a moment then Toby stepped back and Abbot reached for my hand. "Beautiful blue."

"Hey baby," I whispered, sitting next to him again and kissing his hand. "You were supposed to meet me back home."

He grinned. "Had a meeting with a bullet. Took longer than I expected." He tried to laugh but only ended up coughing. "You were supposed to leave."

"How could I leave without knowing where you were?" I ran my thumb over the back of his hand, wishing I could hug him but knowing he was in so much pain.

"This is yours now," he said, lifting his other hand to show me the diamond ring around his pinky.

With a small smile, I wriggled it from his finger and held it up, grimy from his fight, a representation of our struggle. "Are you trying to ask me something, Cartwright?"

"Rinse it in the water there, first," he said, pointing to the glass and jug on the bedside table.

"That's your drinking water. I'll wash it after." I wasn't afraid of a little bad-guy dirt.

He took it from between my fingers. "I can't get down on one knee, so just pretend that part, OK?"

"OK." I smiled, lightly touching the side of his face.

"Will you marry me, Sloane Slater?"

"Yes," I said immediately.

"I'm not finished. We can't leave yet. There'll be retaliation, and until the smugglers are no longer a problem, I can't leave my brothers."

"I understand," I whispered, leaning down and kissing his damaged knuckles. "You're a wonderful, sweet man with a huge heart. Of course I'll marry you, stay with you, fight with you. As long as I'm with you, nothing else matters."

"So, that's a yes." He grinned.

"It's a yes."

Sliding the diamond band onto my left hand, he released a happy sigh then met my eyes. "This is the part where I'm supposed to kiss you, but you're gonna have to help me out."

With a slight giggle, I leaned closer and pressed my mouth to his, kissing him softly yet intensely because he was here and I was here, and we were going to make a life together. It was going to be different to what we planned, but as long as we had each other, we'd survive anything.

"We can talk more later. You should rest."

Touching the side of my face, he nodded. "I'm glad you're here, blue."

"Me too," I whispered, holding on to his hand and sitting quietly while he closed his eyes again. I knew that Mark had said he'd be OK, but I was scared. This whole ordeal had been more than sobering. It seemed that little voice inside me had been right all along. There was no real escape from this life. Something would always happen to pull us back. I was living proof of that.

"Everything OK in here?" Jasmine asked, cracking the door and poking her head in.

I nodded. "He's resting."

She moved over to the side of the bed, her eyes shining

emotionally as she looked over her son. "My boy," she whispered, whisper touching the hair that kept falling over his forehead. "Your doctor friend seems to think he'll recover fine."

"Mark's always been good at his job," I replied. "I'm grateful to him."

She nodded. "Why don't you go talk to him for a bit? I think he needs a little reassurance. I'll stay with Abbot."

Pressing a kiss to Abbot's cheek, I stood and let go of his fingers, giving him one last longing look before I went through the door. The last thing I wanted to do was let him out of my sight, but I owed Mark a great debt. I needed to talk to him.

The living area had mostly cleared out, the injured bikers heading out after Mark had finished patching them all up. It was only Cartwrights and a handful of bikers recovering from wounds that prevented travel remaining.

It looked like a battlefield hospital.

"Haven't seen you with a cigarette in a long time," I said when I found Mark out on the porch blowing smoke.

"My babysitter was kind enough to give one to me," he said, indicating the long-haired biker who was sitting on the steps.

"I'm sorry I dragged you into this," I said, leaning on the railing next to him.

He shook his head. "I've gotta tell you, Sloane. I don't even know what this is. I mean, I get that it's some serious shit that could cost me and my family and my job. But what the fuck do you have to do with bikers from the Grim Order? And why did you get me mixed up in this?"

"Because I needed you, and because I trusted you to save the life of the man I love."

He met my eyes and sighed. "The collapsed lung."

I nodded.

"Jesus, Sloane. I knew you were going through something. But this—"

"Is my roots. These people. They helped raise me."

"Bikers helped raise you?"

"No." I closed my eyes, trying to explain without giving too many details. "The ones without the beards. Remember the brothers I used to talk about?"

"The ones you spent your summer school holidays with?"

"Yes. We reconnected, and now—"

"The shit has hit the fan."

"A little. But it was a means to an end and it's because of your help that my child will grow up knowing his father."

"You're *pregnant* to that guy in there?"

"Engaged to him too." I held up my hand, showing him the ring.

He pinched the bridge of his nose, the way he always did whenever I frustrated him. "Jesus, Sloane."

I smiled. "I never did do things by halves."

"That's true." He took the last drag of his cigarette then flicked the butt somewhere into the damp grass. "Are you happy at least in this…this chaos?"

"Yes," I said, biting my lip to stop the smile from taking over. "Very."

"OK. I guess…" He leaned his elbows on the railing and ran his hands over his face. "I never wanted to hurt you," he said suddenly. "You know, over the whole marriage and kids thing. I…I never thought I wanted it."

"Then you met her and you did."

He pressed his lips together and nodded.

"I get it," I said with a deep breath. "At the time, I really didn't understand at all. But, now I do. It wasn't right with us. We weren't right for each other."

"Probably should have stayed just friends."

I nodded. "Yes. We were only ever friends with blurry lines."

"You really think this is the right guy for you though?"

"I don't think it, Mark, I *know*. And if there's any part of you who still cares about me, I need you to never breathe a word of what happened here tonight. Not even to Terry."

"I get it, Sloane. Your secret life is safe with me, I promise. One last secret for the best-friend vault." He held out his hand and I took it.

"One more for the vault." We shook twice then hugged, a final goodbye to a lifelong friendship. I wasn't sad. I was only grateful. *This was a better way to say goodbye,* knowing that everything that had happened between Mark and me had led me to Abbot. *Back to Abbot.* There was only happiness in that.

THE NEXT MORNING, Mark left the safe house giving strict instructions on Abbot's care to ensure he recovered properly. "Call me if he has any difficulty breathing."

"I will. Thanks again, Mark. You are truly an amazing friend."

"Yeah, remind me of that while I'm in the doghouse with Terry."

"Tell her you were called to the scene of an accident. Then you aren't lying."

He gave me a half-smile before he enveloped me in a hug. "Good luck with the baby. You'll make a great mum."

"You think?"

"I know." When he let go, he looked at the farmhouse and frowned. "Goodbye, Sloane."

When he drove off, I waited until he was off the property before I went inside to the rest of the family, the last few bikers all being transported back to their world before the sun came up. Breaker was still here, but there were whispers about him leaving too. The drug heist and the resulting shootout was all over the news. Both the smugglers and the Grim Order had suffered casualties and the heat was on, so all involved would need to lie low.

"What about us?" Holland asked, her primary concern of course being the baby, who was only a couple of months away from being born.

"We need to lie low too," Jasmine said. "Grey is still a problem and my guess is we'll be questioned at some point. But if we keep our heads down and deny any involvement, there'll be no reason to link us."

"What about blood at the scene?" I asked, worried about Abbot.

"The truck was torched," Breaker assured us. "The rest of the place was a blood bath of my boys and Grey's boys. But, war's comin'. I promise you that."

Jasmine set her jaw. "*No one* crosses us and gets away with it."

I imagined tough times ahead, especially for the Grim Order guys. They were rarely out of the papers normally and today were splashed all over it. *Drug Related Massacre: Smugglers vs Grim Order,* the most prominent headline.

"You know, I don't think they did get away with it," Alesha said, holding the folded broadsheet in her hand. When she turned it to show the rest of the room, a different headline jumped out, *Related: Couple Found Dead in Torquay Home.*

Ronnie rushed Alesha and took the paper from her hands, scanning the article with desperate eyes. "Oh no," she gasped, her hand over her mouth. "Maree."

"I'm sorry, doll," Kristian said, sliding his arms around

his wife. She turned and dropped the paper on the floor, sobbing against his chest.

I wasn't fully aware with her involvement with these people, but I knew enough to know she felt responsible for the job going sour. I felt terrible for her, from what I'd gathered, she'd done what she could to save these people. It was their greed that had gotten the best of them.

War is coming...

Touching my hand to my stomach, I pushed my fear down, hoping we'd all survive this period of retaliation. It was a scary time to be bringing a baby into this world.

"I should get back to Abbot," I said, turning away from the living room scene.

"Mark get off OK?" Jasmine asked before I made it to the door.

"Yeah. He's trustworthy, won't say a thing to jeopardise his career or his marriage. So..." I shrugged, feeling the emotion in the room pushing in around me.

"We're going to be fine," she assured me, guiding me to the kitchen by the elbow. "Breaker's men won't allow anything to happen to us or your babies." I bloody hoped so.

"What about your sons?"

"This is their fight, too. But I have the utmost confidence they'll teach those smugglers a lesson they'll never forget."

"Because they're dead?"

"A dead smuggler is a good smuggler." She grinned and placed some food on a tray before holding it out to me. "I was in there while you spoke to Mark. I gave him his meds."

"He's awake?"

"Hasn't been for long."

I felt bad that I wasn't in the room with him when he woke, but the drunken smile he gave me when I entered told me I needn't have worried. "Those painkillers are good, huh?" I asked, bumping the door shut with my hip.

"Want some? I got a bunch."

"Not sure that'd be good for the baby."

"Oh my God. Yeah! Oh, blue, I'm so spun out that *we* made a *baby*. Did you know that it's only the size of a pea right now? I read all about it before the job, and that really weirds me out. It started out as a tiny dot and one day it'll grow to be as big as you and me. That's fucking wild." He held his fingers to his head then motioned away, opening his hand and making an explosive noise with his mouth. "Magic."

"It is magic. The magic of creation." I chuckled as I took his tray to the bed. "I think we'd better get some food into you. How are you feeling today?"

"Better now that you're here, beautiful blue. I love you." He sing-songed the last part.

"I love you too. Even though you're high as a kite right now and scared the shit out of me doing this job."

"Fucking job. I thought I was a goner, Slater. I got hit and all I could think was no, it's too soon. I only just found you and we have a baby coming who I want to teach to surf and how to pull chicks. I wouldn't get to do that. I was cryin', blue. Then Tobes, he went mad like those guys in the movies, walking through the middle of everything like nothin' could touch him. Amazing. Wait. Where is he? *Toby!* I need to tell him he's the wind beneath my wings."

"Why don't you eat some of this toast and I'll go find

him, OK?" I put a piece of toast in his hand while he hummed the Bette Midler tune.

"This toast. Is the best toast." He took a bite and closed his eyes chewing. I kissed his forehead and chuckled as I stepped out the door.

"His Royal *High*ness would like to see Toby."

"He being a pussy in there?" Kristian asked, sitting on the sofa with his arm around Ronnie, who seemed to have calmed.

I smiled and shook my head. "No, he's just off his face on pain meds."

"Oh, I get it." Holland giggled. "Royal *high*ness. Well done."

I smiled in her direction while Nate frowned and said, "Sam, you see Tobes this morning?"

"Not since late last night. Said he was getting some air."

"Did you see him come back?" Alesha asked, standing to look out the window.

Sam shrugged. "I don't think so."

"Jasmine?" Alesha called out, walking through the kitchen to the laundry where Jasmine and Breaker were in quiet conference. "Did Toby say he was going somewhere?"

Jasmine stepped out into the open, her brow dipped in concern. "He's not here?"

I shook my head. A sense of loss creeping over me. *I'll make them pay.* "I think he's gone."

"What do you mean, you think he's gone?" Jasmine demanded, sounding a little panicked. "He can't be gone. Cartwrights don't leave."

I picked up the paper and showed her the article. "He mentioned cleaning this up."

"Oh." She lifted her chin, understanding what he'd done. "We should find him."

Part of me wanted to agree and the other part was hoping he'd tied up what he considered a loose string and left. He'd done more than his fair share already. I didn't think his soul could take any more battles for a cause he didn't believe in. "Maybe he just needs some time to clear his head. I think he's a bit traumatised over everything that happened yesterday," I pointed out.

"The boat," she blurted, her eyes sparking as she looked at Breaker.

"I'll go," he said, but Jasmine placed her hands against his chest.

"You can't. You need to get out of here yourself."

"I'll go," Nate said, standing up. "I'm the reason all this shit happened, so it should be me."

"But—" Holland started, grabbing for Nate as he stood and picked up his jacket.

"Duchess," he said, turning to face her.

"What if the cops are looking for you?"

"Then they're looking for him, too, and I owe him. You know I do."

She frowned but nodded, obviously warring with her emotions and understanding Nate's need to find Toby. *I hope he's long gone.* As much as I'd wanted to run away to an island paradise with Abbot, I wanted that for Toby even more. We could stay and fix this. He could be free.

"When you find him, take him back to my house," Jasmine said, nodding as she pressed her hands to the side of her jeans. "We should all go back there. Business as usual, understood?"

Everyone in the room nodded. Except me. "What about Abbot? We aren't supposed to move him for a few days."

"We have to, Sloane. He was shot at the scene they're processing right now. We need to get him home and out of sight before they even think to question us."

Fuck.

"Wait. Why will they question us again?" Holland asked.

Sam scrubbed a hand over his stubble jaw. "Even though the truck was torched, there's a slight chance they could find some blood or DNA. Not to mention the fact we've been consorting with the Grim Order for a few months now. We might already be on their radar," he pointed out.

"Then shouldn't we be fucking off?" Holland asked, eyes wide.

"Running looks guilty," Jasmine stated. "We stay put unless we don't have an option."

I closed my eyes, releasing my breath and telling myself that everything was just fine. There'd be no DNA pointing our way, Abbot would heal, the Grim Order will get rid of Grey, and we'd get married and have our baby, and we would *never* do another job again. *Happily ever after.* Just like that.

It was a crazy dream, but it would keep me sane.

"OK," I said. "Let's get him home. But not to your home, Jasmine. To ours. I'll take care of him myself."

Jasmine immediately shook her head. "I don't think—"

"That's fine," Nate said over the top of her. "I actually

think everyone should go back to their own houses. As you said, Jazz, business as usual, and we don't live with you."

"But Grey—"

"We'll get people watching Grey," Breaker said. "I don't want you girls stressing about safety. Especially you, Ronnie. I promise to keep you safe, OK?"

Ronnie nodded and thanked him.

Then Jasmine pressed her lips together. "Fine. Go to your own homes. Rest up and we'll discuss the next steps when the heat dies down."

A low murmur of agreement went around the room, and I took that opportunity to slip back into Abbot's room to let him know he needed to be moved. He was sleeping and woke up with a start when I closed the door.

"Blue," he said, voice a little slurred. "Did you find him?"

"Toby left," I told him, moving closer to we could talk without anyone listening in.

"For good?"

"I hope so," I said with a small smile.

"Me too. He deserves the chance to be happy. It was never gonna happen for him here." Even though he was still high on morphine, he made sense.

"You think we can be happy here—in this life?"

"We'll be happy anywhere, blue. But this is only a temporary setback. We'll leave once we know everyone is gonna be OK. Then we can be happy without feeling guilty about it."

"You're very wise on drugs." He moved his mouth like he was thirsty, so I offered him water.

"I'm wise all the time. You're just too busy talking over the top of me most times."

I smiled. "You're probably right. Listen, you can't go back to sleep just yet. We have to get you home and hidden away in bed before the cops come to question us."

"Why are they gonna question us? They torched the scene."

"Grim Order affiliations." I left out any other concerns, because he didn't need those on his mind right now.

"Fair enough. Help me up then."

"Not so fast, big guy. We'll get everyone packed up then Sam and Kris will help you out, OK?"

"Sure, blue."

We reclined the seats as much as we could in Alesha's people mover and settled Abbot inside, his bag of IV antibiotics hanging on the coat hook.

"I wish you'd reconsider coming to stay at my place," Jasmine said, worry setting her expression as she tried to stand back and let me fuss over her son. "I could help you with him when you need a break."

"You're welcome to come and help at our place during the day, Jasmine. But I think sleeping in his own bed is best, don't you?"

"He has a bed at—"

"Mother," Nate cut in, warning in his tone. I understood Jasmine's desire to keep her boys close, but she needed to understand that her boys were men now, and they had lives of their own. There seemed to always be dangers out there, it was a consequence of the life they led. And she couldn't control those things no matter how much she wanted to. My mother had told me that Jasmine was looking to retire from the life herself. So, there had to be a time when she let go and handed the reins to her sons. After this shitshow, now just might be that time. Revenge against Grey and his men was inevitably going to happen, and I imagined it would link us to the Grim Order forever. And as much as I kept running from this life, even I understood that there would always be 'one more job'.

This life was in our blood after all. Whether we were lying low or fighting hard, we needed to live it. No regrets.

"MUM," I said, half-asleep as I sat up in bed, achy all over.

"I came as soon as I heard," she whispered, glancing at me before her gaze was drawn elsewhere.

"Hi, Emma," Abbot said, standing from the chair he was reclining in, my beautiful giant man. Mum leaned in and kissed him on the cheek.

"May I?" she asked, indicating the bundle of soft skin and long lashes in my husband's arms. After all, the birth of our baby girl was the entire reason she was here. Nine pounds and seven screaming ounces of pink skin and dark hair came into the world in the early hours of the morning. We named her Willow for no other reason than the fact that we both liked the name. We'd been calling her that ever since we had found out she was a girl at our twenty-week ultrasound. Abbot spent months talking to my belly and singing to his little girl—it had been incredibly adorable. He was going be the best father a girl could ever have whether she turned out to be a tomboy like her mum, or the princess her dad was already calling her.

"Watch her head," Abbot murmured, handing his precious daughter over to my mother, who cooed and tickled her chin. Then he sat next to me on the bed and held my hand as we chatted to my mum about the birth and life in general. While we spoke, he lifted my hand and kissed my knuckles while I leaned into the warmth of his body. I loved that man even more than I did the day before.

Each day I thought that. And each day I thought I couldn't possibly have more love to give, but then it would grow, and I realised there was no limit to the amount of love I had to offer. Abbot was the man of my dreams.

Ever since the drug job, the entire Cartwright clan had put a hold on the thieving side of their criminal enterprise in favour of focusing on our growing families. Nate and Holland had a boy six months before, who they named Daniel. He was dark haired like all the Cartwright boys and had honey-coloured eyes like his mother. He was always happy and loved to sing in a high-pitched baby squeal whenever there was music on. Three months after that, Ronnie gave birth to a boy she and Kristian named Oscar. He had the trademark dark hair and blue eyes, but he had his mother's curls. Now, we were adding a girl to the mix. Fitting, because I was that original girl, running around with a bunch of Cartwright boys. I wondered what life would bring for this new generation of Cartwrights that was due to grow again in only a matter of days. Alesha was still pregnant, the sex of their child a planned surprise. Sam was so ready for her to go into labour that he kept running drills to make sure he had chosen the fastest possible way to the hospital. Some habits never changed, and planning things meticulously was always one of the Cartwright's fortes.

Jasmine was on cloud nine. Grandchildren were her greatest desire second to seeing all of her sons married and happy. Still, there had been a gaping hole in her heart for the six months following the Nagambie Massacre (as the papers had dubbed it). Breaker was gone, only contactable via his Blackberry while the MC worked on keeping their members out of prison. We'd all been questioned and denied knowing anything about his MC dealings—"*He's just a family friend*," we'd said. The cops got the same story out of all of us, and despite keeping a watch on Jasmine's place for a few weeks, they seemed to drop off our tails entirely. It seemed the Cartwrights were free and clear with no DNA or any other ties to the drug heist— thank God something finally went our way. We needed a win to keep our spirits up and our stress low.

The next win came when Breaker turned up at the end of a Sunday dinner carrying an early edition of the next morning's paper. *Smuggler's Racket Uncovered. Drugs Recovered,* read the headline. Basically, the Grim Order had tracked down Grey's storage facility, planted some of the stolen cocaine there, and anonymously tipped the cops. Grey had been arrested and his business was in pieces.

Breaker's grin was huge as he held the paper up and Jasmine squealed, rushing into his arms and jumping at him like she was a much younger woman than she was. It was beautiful to see. Although the sounds coming from upstairs not long after that sent us all rushing for our cars. No one needed to listen to that.

Unfortunately, Grey in prison didn't mean it was all over. There were still people loyal enough to him to keep the fires burning. Our plan was to systematically take down each of those smaller operations and break the whole thing apart, one puzzle piece at a time. It would mean that the Grim Order ran everything at the end of it. But, better the devil you know, I supposed. It was better than the alternative, and the Cartwrights were all in agreement that smuggling wasn't a business we wanted to get into. We were the Robin Hoods of this world. Not the pirates.

Speaking of pirates, Toby had taken his dog and his boat after Nagambie, and no one had heard from him since. The brothers understood that he didn't want this life anymore. Jasmine, on the other hand...

"When Toby comes back, we'll work together on our own jobs again," she kept insisting.

"I don't think he's coming back, Ma," Abbot had told her the last time, keeping his voice soft while trying to get her to understand that it was OK to let him go. Her youngest sons were all happily married and raising children of their own. Toby was in his forties now and didn't have what the rest of us did. He had given his youth to the Cartwright cause. He needed a chance to find a cause of his own. I just hoped that wherever he was, he was OK.

"I think she has your eyes, Sloane," Mum said as she peered into Willow's face. Then she touched her nose to her little head and inhaled. "Mmm, there's just something so wonderful about the smell of a new baby."

I nodded and smiled, thinking it was strange how everyone kept doing that. She'd literally just came out of my vagina and they were basically inhaling my bodily fluids. It was really gross when you thought about it. But, she did smell good. I wouldn't deny that.

Willow began to get fussy, so Abbot hopped up and took her from Mum's arms then handed her to me to breastfeed. It really wasn't the easiest thing to do, but Willow seemed pretty eager to latch on, so I'd been told I was lucky that she was a natural at it. I was feeling lucky anyway, because pregnancy had made my boobs grow. I had cleavage now. I was chuffed.

"I have a gift for you," Mum said as she smiled over my little family.

"You didn't have to bring anything, Mum," I said, meaning it. We'd gone a bit crazy with the whole baby preparedness thing—Abbot more so than me. That man had made baby shopping his hobby. The second bedroom in our apartment had been turned into Willow's nursery. She had an entire room packed full of things she may never even need. It was adorable how much he'd looked forward to being a daddy.

"Technically, it's not a gift," she said holding out an envelope that Abbot took for me. "It's the money from your grandfather. Take it, use it in good health."

"Thank you, Mum," I said, giving her a small nod. I appreciated that even though I'd torn up the paperwork to this once before and thrown it at her screaming, she'd kept the money safe to give back at the right time. She could be thoughtful at times. Sometimes.

She bounced a shoulder. "It was always yours. I was just holding on to it for you. And I do apologise, Abbot, for using it to try and make you marry my daughter." The apology was one of those ones said with blinking eyes that indicated she wasn't in the least bit sorry but was saying so because she was trying to be decent.

"It's all good, Emma. As long as you keep your nose out of our relationship in future, we're sweet." He winked at her. I loved a man who wasn't afraid to say with he thought.

"Oh, I've learned my lesson. I hope Jasmine has too."

"Jazz may never be through meddling, but she keeps out of our business just fine," he said.

"How is she? I hear things are different with Toby gone."

"Heard from who?" Abbot narrowed his eyes.

"Little birds are everything, darling. And things have been quiet on the Cartwright front."

"We've been focusing our efforts elsewhere," Abbot said, nodding towards Willow as she snuffled at my breast, her tiny hand curled in a ball.

"Family is important," she said. "But so is strength. Don't leave things too long. You don't want the vultures swooping in to pick at your bones."

"What have you heard?" I asked, glancing at Abbot.

"Just that. Toby is gone and your network is falling apart."

"Thanks for letting us know," Abbot said, his voice steady but his mind obviously working.

"I'll keep my ear to the ground and let you know if I hear anything. But, you might want to talk to Nate since he's next in line. He needs to reach out and calm the whispers."

"Will do."

"OK. Well, I'll leave you to rest for now. I'll come back and visit this little bundle soon. I can't possibly screw up being a grandmother anywhere near as badly as I messed up motherhood."

I actually managed a laugh at that, my understanding

towards my mother a lot better since she helped me fill in some gaps about my role in this family and their criminal organisation. "Goodbye, Mum. And thank you for this." I nodded towards the envelope. "It'll go a long way to taking care of our little family."

"Oh, sweetheart, it'll do a lot more than that. Your grandfather and I have been growing that little pot of gold for you since you turned seventeen and we realised you didn't have the stomach for the family business—not that that part turned out, thank God. But still, we put a substantial amount of each year's *clean* money into investment accounts for you, one to inherit from your pop, and one to inherit when I die. Although, don't get any ideas."

"Never, Mother," I said with a smile. "And thank you for doing this to take care of me. I appreciate the thought, especially the timing."

She gasped. "Wow. This is the first moment I don't feel like a total screw-up of a mum. If I'd realised praise would be this good, I'd have started throwing money at you years ago." I rolled my eyes at her attempt at humour. "In all seriousness, though, I'm glad I didn't. If you'd had money, you may not have said yes to that job and you may have never reconnected with Abbot. It makes me so happy to see you like this, sweetheart. It really does." *Are those tears in her eyes?* I'd never seen my mother get so sentimental. Who knew?

"OK," she said after a moment, wiping at her eyes. "I'm going this time." She blew kisses on her hands and backed away. "I love you guys. I'll see you really soon."

Then she was gone, the gentle scent of her perfume lingering behind.

"How long until you think we see her again?" Abbot asked, taking a sleeping Willow from my arms and placing her gently in the hospital crib.

"A year. Maybe two. She breezes in and out without any thought to time."

"That's what I thought. What do you reckon about what she said?"

"I think you should call Nate and tell him."

"Agreed." He leaned down and kissed me on the forehead. "I'll call him outside."

Despite the fact my body had just gone through the rigours of childbirth, I happily perved at his arse while he walked away. I would always be attracted to that man. He was a fine specimen. And he was mine.

We hadn't run away to live on an island paradise like we'd planned, but we did find our own paradise in each other. From the time that we were kids until the time we met again, our hearts had kept a place waiting for the other. We may not have known that at the time, but it became quickly apparent in the days we spent together, playing our games and teasing our attraction that there was something amazing happening between us. Abbot was a man who made me laugh, who treated me like a woman in all the best ways, and also saw my value as a friend. He was my equal, and there wasn't a moment where I wasn't giddily happy that I'd spend the rest of my life with him.

"OK," Abbot said, walking back into my private hospital room and slipping his phone into his back pocket. "Nate said he's on it. He'll make some calls and set up meetings to keep things running smoothly."

"Do you get a feeling that our dream of running away to life crime free is a bit of a pipe dream?"

He sat back on the bed and slid his arm around me. "Yeah, blue. I do. But it's a good dream to have. I think if we let it go and decided that this was the forever life for us, we'd lose our souls a little. There always has to be an endgame. We'll find ours. Eventually."

"I hope so," I said, leaning my head against his shoulder and sighing, content to just be near him.

"Hey. Wanna see what this is?" Abbot lifted the envelope then waved it up and down, fanning me with it so my hair shifted a little.

"Open it up. Maybe we can buy a nice house with a big yard or something."

He pulled out the sheet of paper and let out a slow whistle.

"What?" I asked, leaning in to scan the page. "Holy fucking hell." I winced when I realised little ears could hear my bad language. "I mean, holy moly, look at all those numbers. Do you know how many Jags we could buy with that?"

"Or how many houses with big yards?"

"Or yachts. We could buy a yacht and live on it with staff and everything."

"We could literally *buy* an island." Abbot and I looked at each other. The dream was so tempting, and this amount of money would make it so much easier to achieve.

I stared at the numbers, pulling at my bottom lip with my teeth. It was so tempting to take this money and forget everything else. But we had our loyalties. With Toby gone and Grey's minions still a threat, we had to stay. We couldn't leave them another man down. Not yet. But, one day...

"It's good to dream, blue," Abbot whispered, kissing

my head as he folded the paper and set it aside. "And one day, we'll have that dream, and it'll be perfect."

I slid my arm around his waist and breathed him in. "You know, this is pretty perfect right now."

"Oh yeah?" He grinned.

"Yeah. You and Willow. It's all I need, really."

"Who's the sweet one now?"

"You are," I whispered, turning my chin up to meet his lips, kissing him softly the way I had hundreds of times before and will hundreds of time more. Abbot Cartwright was my heart, and I was his soul. Wherever we were, whatever was happening in the world around us. As long as we were together, laughing, teasing, playing and loving each other, then we were living our perfect life. After all, it was in our blood.

The end.

Sign up to the Lilliverse Newsletter to discover more titles, limited offers, and upcoming releases by Lilliana Anderson
https://www.lillianaanderson.com/newsletter

Next in the series, *Fool's Paradise*, the fifth and final Cartwright Brothers novel

MY JOB HAD A VERY specific goal: I found people who didn't want to be found and delivered them to whoever employed me. After that, well, I tried not to think about what happened while I spent my money on things that made me happy. Resorts, men...I lived life by the seat of my pants because I never knew where I'd be the next week, or who I'd be looking for.

When the head of a lesser-known criminal family hired me to find her son, I wasn't sure what I was walking into. I had his photo, so I knew the man was hot with a capital H. But I expected the usual agitated scumbag I normally went after. Not some guy running a fishing charter and looking like he didn't have a care in the world.

I might have been curious.

I might have gotten a little too close.

I might have done a lot of things I shouldn't have.

Things that could get *me* killed this time.

But hey, life wasn't always about making the right

choices. It was about making good ones. And Toby Cartwright was a *great* choice.

books2read.com/u/47Zq6N

ALSO BY LILLIANA ANDERSON

Zac & Evie

Hugo & Meg

Beautiful Series

Too Close

A Beautiful Struggle

Phoenix

A Beautiful Forever

Commitment

A Beautiful Melody

A Beautiful Rock

Devotion

A Beautiful Star

A Beautiful Taste

A Beautiful Danger

Entwined Series

Our Hearts Entwined

Our Lives Entwined

The Confidante Trilogy

Confidante: The Brothel

Confidante: The Escort

Confidante: The Madame

For more information on upcoming releases visit

www.lillianaanderson.com/preorders

Bestselling Author of the Beautiful Series, Drawn and 47 Things, Lilliana has always loved to read and write, considering it the best form of escapism that the world has to offer.

Australian born and bred, she writes New Adult Romance revolving around her authentically Aussie characters with all the quirks you'd expect from those born Down Under.

Lilliana feels that the world should see Australia for more than just it's outback and tries to show characters in a city and suburban setting.

When she isn't writing, she wears the hat of 'wife and mother' to her husband and five children.

Before Lilliana turned to writing, she worked in a variety of industries and studied humanities and communications before transferring to commerce/law at university.

Originally from Sydney's Western suburbs, she currently lives a fairly quiet life in suburban Melbourne.

For more information on Lilliana and her work:
www.lillianaanderson.com
info@lillianaanderson.com

To join her Facebook reader group and talk books
https://www.facebook.com/groups/438800699591852

facebook.com/LillianaAndersonAuthor

twitter.com/confidante_lili

instagram.com/lilliana_anderson

ACKNOWLEDGMENTS

AS ALWAYS, there are people to be thanked! Many sets of eyes go in to the creation of each of my books and I am very grateful to every person who takes time out of their lives to help me.

To my editor, **Marion Archer**, I thank you all for your keen editing eyes and funny comments. **Margaret Neal**, thank you for helping to proof the final copy—hopefully we got them all!

To my team of sharers, you're all so wonderful. I don't ask you to do what you do, but you see something I post and share it far and wide. I'm eternally grateful. Thank you all so much. I love you all!

To every blogger and reviewer who has an ARC or has signed up to post about my book – I thank you too. You are the first step to announcing my work to the world. No author can do this without you xoxox

Also, a big thank you to my husband for putting up with my bitching and moaning and his unending support and encouragement.

Thank you to my kids for being so patient while I stare at a computer screen and finish typing out a thought. I love that you all come and sit with me while I work just to spend a bit of extra time with mummy!

And of course – thank you to all of my readers. You are the most important of all. Without you, I would be writing to the crickets.

Mwah! xoxox